Amanda Kyle Williams has w   e
Atlanta Journal-Constitution a   a

Avondale Estates, Georgia, a nonprofit animal welfare organization.

In order to lend authenticity to her Keye Street series, she took courses geared to law enforcement in criminal profiling and serial homicide investigation under the tutelage of a well known criminologist and profiler and worked with a PI firm in Atlanta on surveillance operations. Amanda regularly consults with experts in bond and law enforcement from the Georgia Bureau of Investigation and the Atlanta Police Department.

Amanda Kyle Williams lives near Atlanta, Georgia in the American South, which provides unending fodder for fiction. She is currently at work on her third Keye Street thriller.

Praise for Amanda Kyle Williams

'This is one Street worth acquainting yourself with' *Sun*

'Smart, ironic and compelling, this 21st century heroine is certain to gather ever more fans as the series unfolds. She is too great a character not to last. Catch her before she becomes a household name' *Daily Mail*

'Keye Street immediately puts herself in the top echelon of suspense heroes. She's a mess of fascinating contradictions – effortlessly brilliant on a case, totally inept in managing her own life. She is brutally funny and powerfully human. Williams has created one of the most realistic protagonists in crime fiction that I've had the thrill to read' TESS GERRITSEN

'An explosive, unpredictable, and psychologically complex thriller that turns crime fiction clichés inside out' *Publishers Weekly*

'An exceptionally smart, funny and character-driven debut' KARIN SLAUG

Also by Amanda Kyle Williams and available from Headline

The Stranger You Seek

Amanda Kyle Williams

STRANGER IN THE ROOM

headline

First published in 2012 by
HEADLINE PUBLISHING GROUP

First published in paperback in 2013 by
HEADLINE PUBLISHING GROUP

1

Cataloguing in Publication Data is available
from the British Library

ISBN 978 0 7553 8422 8

Typeset in Century Schoolbook by Avon DataSet Ltd,
Bidford-on-Avon, Warwickshire

Printed and bound in Great Britain by Clays Ltd, St Ives plc

Headline's policy is to use papers that are natural, renewable and
recyclable products and made from wood grown in sustainable
forests. The logging and manufacturing processes are expected to
conform to the environmental regulations of the country of origin.

HEADLINE PUBLISHING GROUP
An Hachette UK Company
338 Euston Road
London NW1 3BH

www.headline.co.uk
www.hachette.co.uk

To my friend Kari Bolin, whose diabolical imagination inspired me even on dry days.

Acknowledgements

To everyone at Headline Publishing Group, thank you for your amazing efforts and dedication. I'm so honored to have the opportunity to work with you. Special thanks to Imogen Taylor, Jane Morpeth, Ben Willis, Frankie Gray, Holly McCulloch, Anna Bowen, Aslan Byrne and the rest of the brilliant Sales team, Laura Esslemont and Craig Fraser. Thank you also to Judy Jamieson-Green and everyone at Hachette Australia.

A great big thanks also goes to the following professionals who so generously shared their time and put up with all those emails and phone calls: Georgia Bureau of Investigation Special Agent Dawn Diedrich; Dr Jamie Downs, Coastal Regional Medical Examiner for the Georgia Bureau of Investigation; GBI Special Agent Lanny Cox; Brent Turvey, MS, forensic science; Atlanta Police Department Homicide Unit Sergeant Liane Lacoss; Lesley Slone, forensic psychologist; Mitch Holland, director, forensic science, Penn State University, and founder of Forensic DNA Consultants; Gabriel Gates; Angie Griffin and

Dragonfly Copters; and Betsy Kidd of Blue For You, Inc.

And finally, to my friends who graciously offer up the names I love and allow me to have my way with them, thank you for being good sports.

Prologue

eadlights arced up over a giant magnolia as she topped the Elizabeth Street hill. The fat white flowers looked lit up against the night, like white teeth under a black light. The Inman Park section of Atlanta was rolled up tight at almost eleven o'clock on a drizzly Thursday. A family neighborhood, renovated, the high side of middle income, quiet.

Two vodka martinis had landed squarely, and Miki Ashton yawned between the slow passes of windshield wipers. Yes, she was fine to drive, she had assured friends. What she hadn't said was how she dreaded going home to that empty old Victorian. What is it about driving away alone from a place of laughter after a few drinks that can make one feel so utterly abandoned? She missed having animals, a dog to greet her. She'd grown up with them. But her career, the travel – it wouldn't be fair. She parked the '76 Spitfire in the cobbled drive. Grass shot up between the stones. How was it her neighbors seemed to have no problem at all keeping manicured lawns?

She pushed open a waist-high wooden gate, painted in the years before she owned it and needing a fresh white coat. The neighborhood association resented her inattention. More than one polite notice delivered to her mailbox had reminded her of her responsibilities. Didn't they have lives?

Bag over one shoulder, she took long strides in knee-high boots down the wet walkway to the front steps. Her heels sounded hollow against the painted planks on the wraparound porch. An eerie, ghostlike sensation got her attention – that feeling of being watched. No. That wasn't it exactly. Being watched she could deal with. Being watched she was accustomed to. Miki Ashton had been told she was pretty for as long as she could remember. This was different. This had teeth and nails. It set the back of her neck on edge. The urge to run hit her like she was six years old – like there was a monster under the bed and she couldn't get her feet off the floor fast enough. And there had been a lot of monsters over the years – institutions, prescriptions, attempts, razor blades, overdoses. The armed conflict against her own flesh began at fourteen, when she first pushed a razor blade into the paper-thin skin inside her wrists.

She fumbled with her keys under a single globe-covered bulb. She needed better lighting. She'd been putting it off. That feeling again. Alarm. Like someone was going to leap out in a hockey mask with a chain saw. Too many movies. Too many airport paperbacks.

Get the goddamn key in the door.

And then she heard it. Miki had memorized every complaint and shudder the old house could dish out. Maybe she shouldn't have stopped the meds. Maybe her imagination –

There it was again – the floorboards.

Inside.

She inched her way down the porch to the picture window, the tiny penlight from her keychain locked in her hand. She pressed the button and a weak shaft of watch-battery light skipped over her tasseled fainting couch, the wood floors, the antique rocker she'd bought and had shipped home during a road trip, the book she'd left facedown on the coffee table just today.

Then it was gone, the light blocked out. It took a second to understand what she was looking at – the dark outline of a man standing on the other side of the window. He faced her – black clothing, a ski mask – motionless. Then his arm lifted smoothly. He made a gun with his thumb and forefinger, squeezed the trigger.

The shock jolted her back. Dizziness swirled through her head, then hit her soft palate. She lost her martini dinner.

An engine started somewhere on the street.

Miki's hand was trembling when she dialed 911.

1

I t was ten-thirty when I answered the phone, the Thursday night before Independence Day. Atlanta's tree-lined neighborhoods flew flags in anticipation from front porches and garden stakes. Red, white, and blue ribbons decorated mailboxes. In town, the city's diverse population celebrated July's holiday weekend with food and art and music festivals, rooftop bars and ground-shaking fireworks displays.

'I need to see you,' my cousin, Miki, told me.

Oh boy. Miki, the daughter of my adoptive mother's troubled sister, Florence. She'd lived on a houseboat in her own backyard when Jimmy and I were kids. I hadn't seen Miki in a couple of months. She was probably embroiled in some drama. She might also be in real trouble. Miki had a flair for trouble.

I was in my office late, catching up on the work I'd put off all week, a last-ditch effort to take a long weekend off. The air-conditioning was working overtime. Atlanta's smoldering summer had dropped down around us like a burning building.

My name is Keye Street. I run a little detective agency in Atlanta called Corporate Intelligence & Investigations. And when I say 'little', I mean it's just me and my red-eyed computer guy, Neil Donovan. And when I say 'red-eyed', I mean he probably smoked a joint with his scrambled eggs this morning. My background is in law enforcement, criminology, psychology, and, well, drinking. I was once a criminal investigative analyst in the Behavioral Analysis Unit (BAU) at the Bureau. But I set fire to that and to nearly everything else in my life back then. So this is what I do now. Detective work suits me.

'What's up, Miki?' I asked. 'You okay?'

'*No,*' said my lovely sandy-haired cousin. Put us side by side and we looked like the photograph and the negative. I'm a Chinese American recovering alcoholic with a southern accent, white parents, and a gay African American brother. Neil is convinced there's a way to cash in on this – reaching minority status on so many levels. A government program, perhaps. But that's what happens when you combine Neil's Generation-Y sense of entitlement with his subversive stoner's brain.

Neil handles most of the computer searches and I collect the human intelligence, which means I trail around behind certain folks, search their trash, take unwanted pictures of them, listen in on their conversations when I have the opportunity, and generally intrude on their private affairs. It's all very glamorous. There's a pile of Little Debbie wrappers and Starbucks cups in my car to prove it. Our client roster is mostly law firms and headhunting agencies, but we'll work for anyone who wants the secrets swept out from under the rugs. Missing persons, surveillance, bond enforcement, and process serving keep the cash flowing when business slows to a crawl over the winter holidays. But when Atlanta starts to heat up and the glaring southern sun sets our bloodstreams ablaze, when the clothes get skimpy and overworked servers stagger out with trays of frosty pitchers at packed pavement cafés, my phone gets busy. The badly behaved fill my coffers. I'm fine with that. It buys the Krispy Kremes. Original glazed, warm – the current monkey on my back.

'Keye, I need to see you right away,' Miki insisted. 'It's serious.'

I rolled my neck a couple of times. Everything was always massively serious with Miki. I was tired. I'd served two subpoenas today; one of them meant following someone to work, bullying my way into her workplace, and tossing it at her before she could put her coffee down. I then dealt with the cluster-fuck they call a parking system near Fulton County's courthouse, filed the paperwork for the attorney, left there, and picked up a bail jumper for Tyrone's Quikbail in East Atlanta and delivered him to the police station. Also, my bitchy cat hadn't had a shot of half-and-half in hours.

'Someone broke into my house, Keye. I don't even want to be there right now.'

I grabbed my keys. 'I'll pick you up.' Miki's Inman Park home was just a few blocks from my North Highland office.

'No. Meet me at Gabe's. I need to be around people. And I need a drink.'

I picked up my ink pen and bit into it. I needed a friggin' drink too.

'Keye, please,' Miki said, and I heard it for the first time – genuine fear in my cousin's voice.

Nine minutes later I pulled into the small parking lot across the street from Gabe's on Juniper. It was a fireplace bar and restaurant with plush seating and room to lounge, a cigar room, the kind of place that served single malt at exactly the right temperature. In spring and summer, the big deck that edged right up to the street with a view of Midtown's crowded skyline cranked out gourmet tapas and stayed packed late into the evening. Runoff from the 14th Street Playhouse, the Alliance Theatre, Symphony Hall, and The Fox Theatre, all kept it brimming with hip clientele, multitaskers who can chat with you while conducting text conversations, updating their Facebook status, and Tweeting the wine list.

I saw a crowd in the parking lot as I searched for an empty spot for the Impala. Instinct told me Miki was at the heart of it. Miki always seemed to be putting on some kind of show. I'd never been out with her when she didn't have an entourage, faithful followers to bask in her brilliant light. It was how she kept everyone at arm's length while soaking up the adoration she craved.

I parked, took a ticket stub from the attendant, and headed that way. The knot of nicely clad humans loosened just enough for me to glimpse my cousin's wispy figure at its center. As I moved closer, I smelled something burning and saw a small fire of twigs and leaves and something made of fabric. I stopped on the fringe.

'It's her black gloves,' the woman next to me whispered

reverently. Ah, the black gloves. No need to explain. Everyone in Miki's life knew about the gloves. They had become a part of Miki's depression rituals. I think we had all hoped at some point that wearing them would be expression enough of her misery to prevent her from hurting herself again. But the gloves had merely acted as a warning. Someone would find her in the bathtub, on the floor, in the bed, with her veins open and enough barbs in her system to give Keith Richards a run for his money.

I moved through the group and saw Miki standing over the smoldering pile. Someone handed her a champagne flute. She held up the glass dramatically as the last bit of fabric curled into the fire. A cheer went up as she drained her glass.

She spotted me and smiled, raised her voice. 'I've turned the corner, Keye. The curtain has lifted.' And then she stepped out of the circle and walked away from her fans without so much as a word. She hugged me and whispered: 'Be my date tonight. Protect me from the wolves.'

I laced my arm in hers, and we crossed Juniper to Gabe's, maneuvered our way across the busy patio and went inside. The first whiff of tequila and lime wrapped its arms around me like an old friend. Most of the time now, I don't even really want a drink. Not when I'm thinking. But when I'm reacting to some trigger – a smell, a certain glass, a social situation – my addict's brain gets busy romancing the memories – the way that first drink of the day settles in on your stress, the way a good tawny port feels in your mouth and lingers on your lips after a meal. That's when my sobriety feels fleeting. I felt prickly heat on the back of my neck. I needed to get back to AA. Not surprisingly, I'd made a mess out of that as well.

Miki was wearing a black dress that flared out above her knees, more Judy Jetson than Audrey Hepburn, and over-the-knee boots. She stood near me at the bar, searching my face. We must have looked like lovers, something Miki had already calculated, I was sure. And another way of keeping her flock at bay.

'Are you all right?' she asked, then went on without giving me time to answer. 'Oh, right. The alcohol thing. What's the big deal, anyway? I won't let you get wasted. Just order a fucking drink.'

'That's the worst idea I've heard all day.'

She reached into her bag and withdrew a tiny glass vial with a black cap. 'I've got some coke. Would a line help?'

That's my Miki, always thinking of others. 'Probably not,' I answered, with more revulsion than I wanted to show her. We'd all been watching Miki's self-medicated self-destruction for years. I felt really over it at the moment. I'd been down that road. We are always less tolerant of our own reflections, aren't we?

I ordered grape juice and got the same smirk I'm usually subjected to when I order grape juice in a bar. They didn't have it, of course. 'Okay, how about a Diet Pepsi?' A couple of heads turned. Ordering Pepsi in a Coca-Cola town was an act of treason.

'We have Diet Coke,' the bartender told me.

I settled on club soda with a twist and Miki ordered an Absolut martini, extra-dirty. We found an empty couch with a coffee table in a back section off the main bar. The room was set up with lacquered cherrywood tables and chess-boards. And though our long, hot summer was in full swing, the bar was air-conditioned to frosty cold so the gas fireplaces could warm it back up. I could see the bar from where we sat, mirrored and glimmering in the soft light. I looked at Miki and tried not to notice the marks on both her arms. The thick horizontal streaks of white scar tissue were a reminder of how desperate she'd been, and how utterly incapable she was of loving herself. There must have been eight or ten slashes on each arm. They seemed especially out of place on my porcelain-doll cousin. She'd just burned the long, black gloves that had covered those scars. Perhaps she was ready to look at them. It wasn't the first time I'd been grateful the DNA that had poisoned Miki's mental health and her mother's, and perhaps even flirted with my adoptive mother's happiness from time to time, was not surging through my own veins. Mother's family had a history of quiet and hidden gloominess. Depression isn't something one freely admits to down South. But Florence and Miki had blown the lid off the family secrets vault with their overt and sometimes public illness. Fortunately, someone had always managed to find Miki after she'd sliced herself up or swallowed a mountain of pills – a self-appointed watcher, a groupie, one of the countless men or women who flocked to her like hungry gulls. They couldn't help themselves. A radiant, brilliant, dark, and emotionally unavailable woman is irresistible to the demons and obsessions of codependent fixers and masochists. Miki's illness only sparked theirs.

'So what's up with the gloves?' I wanted to know. We had leaned back, drinks in hand, legs crossed, facing each other.

'That part of my life is over.'

'You taking your meds?'

Miki shook her head. 'I can't live like that. I can't do my life numb. I just can't.'

Yeah sure. Coke and alcohol wasn't numbing at all. She was probably on some manic tear with stimulants and booze and no meds. I wondered if the break-in was real, imagined, or outright fabrication. She must have read the concern on my face.

She leaned in close and whispered, 'I think I'm following someone. I'm just not sure who.'

I stared at her blankly.

'Oh, come on, Keye. Lighten up. It's a joke.'

Stress hormones began to jet-ski through my bloodstream. My eyes dropped to the martini. It was cloudy and cold. My saliva glands were working overtime. I didn't want to be here. *What's the big deal, anyway? . . . Just order a fucking drink.*

A busty brunette with an old-fashioned cigarette tray attached to her by a neck strap passed through and headed for the cigar room, where she'd clip ends and refill cognacs. Someone at the bar was licking salt and lemon and shooting tequila. I squeezed lime into my club soda and blinked up at Miki. *Patience.* Something had frightened her. She wanted to be here right now, and I needed to function in the real world, where people drink and want to talk to me in bars. I'm a PI, for Christ's sake. Half my clients are drunks. The old tapes were playing, telling me this was hard, telling me I wanted a drink. I didn't. Not ever. I reminded myself it wasn't real. Just the mind stalking shadowy old corridors. I reeled myself in, knowing that each time I did that, each time I said no, new pathways were burned into me that might help avert the next crisis.

'I hired this trainer who uses alternative treatments as mood stabilizers to get people off meds,' Miki told me. 'Exercise and supplements, acupuncture and diet. It's working. I exercise my ass off. It releases some kind of chemical that keeps me healthy. You know I've been good for a while, right?'

By 'good' she meant she hadn't been institutionalized for cutting or overdosing in a couple of years. She took the vial out of her bag, filled the cap with white powder, glanced around the room before she lifted it to her nostril and inhaled.

'Cocaine and vodka part of the regimen?'

'So judgmental, Keye.' She swirled the martini glass gently, then sipped it. I smelled the olive juice. Her blue eyes lifted to mine. 'It's really disappointing.'

'You're not the first bipolar patient to argue against meds.'

'I'm not a fucking patient!' Miki exploded. Heads turned. She set her martini down too hard. Liquid sloshed over the rim. 'I'm *family,* Keye. I mean, what the fuck?'

'It was a valid question, Miki,' I shot back.

'I was a finalist last year, Keye, for a Pulitzer for feature photography. A goddamned *Pulitzer.* You ever notice how many World Photography Awards I have on my shelves? Some of us can manage our cravings just fine. How about you?'

I felt that knife twist in my gut. 'I fought for my addiction too, Miki,' I replied evenly. 'For a long time. It didn't pay off.'

'Someone was in my house when I got home tonight. Can we just focus on that?'

'Tell me what happened,' I said calmly. I wanted the heat to dissipate a little.

She told me about fumbling with her keys at the door, then hearing something and knowing someone was inside the house. The combative demeanor began to peel away. Tears spilled out and ran down pale cheeks. She swiped them away and picked up her martini glass with a shaky hand. 'I went to the window off the porch, and I saw him. Inside my house, Keye. He had walked from my front door to the window. And he just stood there looking at me. He made his hand into a pistol like this.' Miki raised her thumb and jutted out her forefinger. 'And he squeezed the trigger.' Another tear trickled.

I reached across the table and put my hand on hers. 'Was anything taken?'

She shook her head. 'Nothing that I could see when I walked through with the police. I didn't hang around. It's too creepy knowing someone was in your house, touching your things. I left and parked down the street and called you.'

'If he'd wanted to hurt you, he wouldn't have let you know he was there.'

Miki signaled one of the waitstaff, held up her glass, and said, 'Absolut, dirty.'

'Any reason someone would want to scare you?' I asked.

'No. I mean, I don't know. My neighbors hate me because I don't spend my time beautifying my yard or having mommy meetings or whatever.'

'Seems a little drastic for the neighborhood association.'

'You don't believe me, do you? I can tell from your tone. You're just like those fucking cops.'

Alcohol had thickened her tongue. I wondered how many drinks she'd had before she got to Gabe's. 'Anyone mad? Any breakups lately?'

'I don't do breakups anymore. It always gets messy. I keep it casual.'

'Tell me about the messy ones,' I said. The server came with Miki's drink, and I borrowed her ink pen.

'Messy? I had one of those. A big one,' Miki said, sliding the drink and the cocktail napkin in front of her. 'I thought I was in love. But he wanted to own me. I don't go there anymore.' Her tone was as icy cold as the martini on the table. 'Soon as they get clingy, I'm gone. It's not worth the hassle.'

'You mind giving me a name?'

Miki hesitated. 'Cash Tilison.'

'What happened?' I jotted his name down on a napkin. I recognized it. Tilison was a Nashville singer and not Miki's first affair with a famous performer. I couldn't remember any of Miki's other boyfriends. But we hadn't hung out since high school.

'He couldn't take no for an answer. Lot of phone calls, name-calling, text messages, emails. Didn't have a clue about how to deal with rejection. He flipped out for a while. He said he'd never had his heart in anything before me. I guess he told himself that gave him some right to talk to me like that.'

'Talk to you how?'

'Called me a bitch a lot. Mean bitch. Cold bitch. Heartless bitch. Really liked the whole bitch theme.' She took a sip of her drink and smiled. 'He used to call me that when we were fucking. He'd hold my hair. But I liked it then. What can I say? I'm a bottom. Know what I mean?'

I wasn't prepared to share with Miki whether I knew the dominant- and submissive-tinged bedroom games people play or how entirely they dissociate from them in life. I thought about my big Homicide lieutenant and how different he was in bed from the tough, real-world cop – so intensely confident in his masculinity that he wasn't afraid to let go of control.

'How long did this go on?' I asked Miki.

'Ten, fifteen minutes, if I was lucky.' She smiled at me.

I laughed, held up my club soda. Our glasses touched, some tension peeled away.

'He started showing up places. Even when I was traveling. Nobody knows how to date anymore. They always get attached.'

Sure, sure, everyone wants Miki. 'Cash fit the body type for the guy you saw in your window tonight?'

Miki thought about it, started to speak, was silent. I was trying to understand the hesitation, why she wanted to protect him. Was it because she was lying? Or was it because she still had feelings for him? 'I guess,' she said, finally. 'He was tall with broad shoulders.'

'Police say how he got in?'

'They told me there was no evidence of a break-in. And I said, what about the guy standing inside my living room? Isn't that considered goddamn evidence?'

'Cash have a key?'

'I don't think so. I think I got it back. I might have even changed the locks since then.' She ate an olive off a plastic pick in her drink. 'I felt like someone was watching me when I got out of the car at the gym today on Ponce. I felt it again on the treadmill.'

'Must be ten sets of eyes on you right now. You're gorgeous.' I glanced at the sparkling wonderland in the other room. A bottle of Grey Goose was making eyes at me. What's not to love about vodka made in Cognac?

Miki looked at me. 'Funny you think so. I always thought that about you. I wanted to *be* you when we were in high school.'

'God, why? I was just the Chinese chick,' I told her, but I am a product of the American South just as surely as if I'd sprung up out of the dark green leaves of the wild, creeping kudzu carpeting our towering pine forests. Georgia's simmering sun turned my shoulders golden as my brother and I played in the thick Saint Augustine grass in my parents' white-fenced backyard. It was my branding iron. You learn this about the South. You don't merely exist here. You make a blood pact with it the moment the soft, moist air fills your nostrils with the sensual scent of Confederate jasmine and floods your DNA like reproductive seed. This is my South, the one that gave me a home and a community of soft-spoken and well-intentioned people who proudly waved their liberal credentials when my brother and I were the first kids in our neighborhood who didn't look like everyone else. Jimmy's South was not as kind. My black-skinned, light-eyed homosexual brother was viewed with suspicion by just about every community within our orbit.

High school handed me a strawberry-blond boy named Bobby Nash who was the best kisser I'd ever known. Propped up in the back of his pickup truck, Bobby played his guitar and sang quietly to me on moon-brushed evenings in the Winnona Park neighborhood, where I grew up among the filigreed leaves of massive pecan trees and fat white oaks in the only blue county in the state on our voting map. Years later, just a few yards from where Bobby's bashful hands helped me to discover myself, the ruthless fluidity of life, as razor-sharp as a machete, brought me to my knees in the cold, red clay. But that's another story.

'You were the *hot* Chinese chick.' Miki laughed. 'Good-looking, track star, honor roll. Me, I was already cutting myself by high school. You know it wasn't always about trying to kill myself, right? It just felt good. To hurt, I mean. To bleed.' Miki ran a finger over scar tissue inside her left arm. 'I think those rude cops had my hospital records. One of them said something to the other about calls from my address. It's been, like, two years since I was that sick, but I guess once they see you as fucked up, you're always fucked up. Can't you say something to your boyfriend about how the police treat people?'

'Did anyone else come out? Did you speak with detectives?'

'No,' Miki said. 'But I'll never forget the way that freak looked at me. Eyes through the slits in that mask. So scary.'

'Could you tell what color eyes?' I glanced back at the bar and the flirty bottle of Grey Goose. I drank some club soda and thought about the way the carbonation hits your nose when it's loaded with good vodka – clean and sharp and just a hint bitter. I needed to get out of the bar.

'No. It was dark.'

'Make me a list later of people you've dated in the last couple of years. We'll also check out your neighbors and poke around a little. I'll apply to APD for increased patrols on your street. It can't hurt. How about coming to my place tonight?'

Jesus, what was I thinking?

2

I woke to Aerosmith's 'Dude (Looks Like a Lady)' coming out of my phone – Homicide Lieutenant Aaron Rauser's ringtone. I fumbled for the clock. Two a.m., just one of the hazards of dating a cop. I'd been asleep for exactly an hour. 'Long day, huh? You get all the bad guys?'

'Uh-huh,' Rauser said in that slow, drawn-out way meant to express his cynicism. 'Be more likely Lisa Ling would wanna make out.'

'You have a thing for Asian girls, don't you?'

'I got a thing for you.' He had said it with no enthusiasm. I knew him. Something was wrong. Then I heard noise in the background, a lot of it, voices, the random blast of police scanners. A siren blared. He yelled, 'Tell them to turn that shit off. Listen, darlin', I got five open cases and we gotta keep moving before they get cold. That long weekend we were planning, it's just not gonna happen.'

I thought about long days on the couch with paperbacks and the Braves on television, making love in the afternoon, dinners out. It was so rare. We'd planned music and a catered picnic basket at Chastain Park, a cookout at my parents' house on Monday, the fireworks on the square in Decatur. *My parents. Yikes.* With Rauser working and my brother in Seattle, there was no one to deflect Mother's attention. She always seemed to behave better when there was a man around. Maybe I could talk Miki into going with me.

'It's a kid,' Rauser said. 'I fucking hate it when it's a kid.'

'Oh no. I'm sorry.'

'He was left in the bushes like he was disposable or something.'

I sat up. Switched on the bedside lamp. 'How old was he?'

'Twelve, thirteen maybe.'

'You have a cause of death?'

'Looks like he was strangled. Ligature marks on his neck.'

I thought about that. 'Disposal site in the boy's neighborhood? Can you tell if it's the primary scene?'

'Still processing the scene, but that's what it looks like. Victim was only two blocks from home. We're talking to people, but we haven't established motive yet.' He was quiet for a minute and I could hear the sirens and police scanners. 'Neighborhoods used to be safe, Keye. We're failing. We can't keep up. Oh shit. News trucks are here. I love ya, Street.'

My bedroom door eased open shortly after four a.m. Rauser's square shoulders in the shadows. He leaned over the bed and kissed me. 'Where's White Trash?' Rauser and my cat were having a thing. Lately, she seemed to prefer him over me. But then, he's hairy and hot. It's like spooning a fuzzy furnace. Cats are all about body heat. I try not to take it personally.

'Miki took her to bed,' I told him.

Rauser unzipped his jeans and let them fall on the floor. Boxers underneath, a gift I'd given him last Christmas, black and white checks. 'Miki's here? That can't be good.'

'She had a break-in at her house. It shook her up. I'll tell you about it tomorrow.'

'It is tomorrow.' He pulled his T-shirt over his head and dropped it on top of his jeans. 'I'll pull the report later.' He went naked to the shower. I lay there looking after him, remembering coming in late from crime scenes and morgues and heartbroken families and standing under a stream of hot water until it turned cold. I could never wash it away, though, and I didn't think Rauser could either.

I drifted off while he showered and woke to his arms around me, lips against my neck, hot breath. He didn't say a word when he pushed into me and we made love. My big Homicide lieutenant is no different from the rest of us. He uses whatever he can to putty up the cracks his job hammers into him. Sometimes I think there's more pain in him than desire. I wondered if my life would have been different if I'd come home to open arms after spending the day reconstructing murder scenes. If my ex-husband had wanted me, pushed his slim fingers through my hair just once, whispered, pretended. Would I have still reached for the cognac that put me to bed? I didn't think so. I wasn't trying to shift blame for my drinking, but it would have been goddamn decent of Dan to give me a soft landing just once in a while.

At seven, when the bed jiggled, I opened one grouchy eye. Rauser was sitting on the edge holding White Trash. He was shirtless, wearing navy slacks, the only clean spares he had at my place. I smelled coffee and turned to see my favorite cup, a mug from Jekyll Island, filled and steaming hot on my bed table.

'I see you found White Trash.' It was the nicest thing I could think of to say. I wanted to sleep about six more hours.

Rauser kissed White Trash's head and put her down, then pulled on dark blue socks. 'Uh-huh. And I saw your cousin in her underwear too. Big morning.'

I sat up. 'I'm sure that was excruciating for you.'

'Horrible. Plus, she was kicking White Trash out of the guest room, said she was staring at her like she was judging.'

I reached for my coffee. 'Yeah, White Trash gets really judgmental when she needs her litter box.'

Rauser chuckled. 'What's your day like?'

'A failure to appear for Tyrone, a bunch of routine assessments to be delivered. The usual.' I took a sip of coffee. It was strong. Rauser didn't have a lot of patience for measurements. 'How 'bout you?'

'The usual,' he said, and kissed my cheek. 'Thanks for letting me pop in last night.' He stood, grinned down at me, raised his eyebrows up and down a couple of times.

'You're so immature.'

'You didn't think so last night,' he said, then ducked the pillow I hurled at him. 'You want some breakfast? I'm going to have some Shredded Wheat.'

'I'd rather eat a bale of pine straw. But I guess you have to think about fiber at your age.'

He grinned at me, pointed his finger. 'You better be nice to me, Street. I'm probably the guy that's going to go through menopause with you. And we all know that ain't gonna be pretty.'

'Get out!' I hurled another pillow.

He stuck his head back in the door a minute later. 'Hey, talk to me for a sec?'

I smiled, looked at him over my coffee cup. He was holding a file folder. 'What?'

'That crime scene last night, something about it is bugging me.'

I set my coffee down and held out a hand for him. 'It was a little boy. Of course it bothers you.'

'It's more than that.'

'You didn't find motive?'

He ran a hand over his face. Bright morning light came through the long windows along Peachtree Street, and the lines around his gray eyes looked dug in like trenches. Snowy dark hair touched the tips of his ears. 'There's no sign of molestation, though the autopsy isn't scheduled until later this morning. We're looking in the usual places.' He looked at his watch. 'Starting with the parents' interview in an hour.'

'That's where the treasure's usually buried,' I reminded him, but this was something he was already well aware of. Motive in child murders is usually found in family and close associates. I glanced at my coffee cup. I couldn't believe we were having this conversation five minutes after I'd opened my eyes and with only half a cup. I thought about Miki and the bar last night. The urge to spike my coffee slapped me awake. Four years of waking up sober and it was still a choice I had to make every day. It felt especially hard this morning.

He sat down next to me, opened his folder, spread it out on the bed between us. 'Wow. Will the fun ever stop?' I said, and looked down at photographs from the crime scene that had kept him away most of the night, at a boy's lifeless body, facedown, shorts, athletic shoes, an arm at shoulder level, another over his head, one knee slightly higher than the other. He looked like he was trying to crawl away. There was a baseball cap on the ground next to his outstretched fingers. I studied the photographs of the scene around the body – cigarette butts, a piece of red plastic, fast-food wrappers, cups and straws. 'What's with all the trash?'

'Construction site a few yards away. People that own the lot where the kid was found said it blows onto their yard all the time. We bagged everything around the body.'

'Who found the body?'

'Jogger,' Rauser said. 'We haven't excluded him yet. Or anyone. Hard to get a lot out of the mother and father last night. Kid was some kind of super-athlete. We know that much. Varsity coaches were waiting for him to get to ninth grade.'

I studied another photograph of the body. 'Another athlete might have motive. And the strength. Looks tall for his age, and sturdy. No other wounds on the body apart from the ligature marks?'

'Nope. We think the perp grabbed the kid from behind, knocked him down, and got the rope round his neck.'

'It was fast,' I told Rauser. 'Ground cover's barely disturbed around the body. And see that?' I pointed at the victim's clenched right fist. 'It happens sometimes with hangings and violent strangulation.'

3

Neil was wearing shorts or swimming trunks, I wasn't sure which. They were cobalt blue with big black flowers that reached his fuzzy blond knees. The shirt was cream and tan, Cuban, with wide vertical panels, partially unbuttoned – Neil's uniform. It varied only slightly from season to season – shorts or long pants with deck shoes, Vans slip-ons in checkerboard or plaid. He liked his shoes loud. The TV was on the morning news. Neil had nearly everything in our office controlled by a voice-activated smart panel with remote-control backups. The big flat-screen, the brainchild of the passionate and perhaps disturbed designer I'd hired, eased down smoothly on a silver pulley system from the rafters in our converted warehouse. It was one of my favorite things about our commercial loft.

'Morning,' I said when I walked into the office early. I'd showered as soon as Rauser left me to go save the city, fed White Trash, and left my cousin still asleep in the guest room. 'I need a list of property owners in Inman Park.

Satellite images with the owners' names on the appropriate lots would be great.' I went to my office, which was really just a desk and chairs and two file cabinets behind a towering fence – part chain link, part barbed wire – another gift from the designer whose vision for our space had not exactly matched mine.

'It's nice to see you too,' Neil grumbled. He seemed even poutier than usual. I get this attitude from him whenever he feels barked at. I first met Neil Donovan when I was working with a digital evidence specialist at the Bureau on a series of cyber-crimes. Neil, being a repeat offender in the piracy and cyber-crime arena, ended up making a deal with the Bureau. Later, a few of the companies whose security he'd breached hired him to design and maintain their security systems. When I was ready to start my private investigating business, I looked him up. A guy like Neil is a real find. He has the perfect attention span for skip traces and absolutely no moral borders when it comes to privacy.

I dumped my things on my desk and looked up at Neil's back through squares in wire fencing. He was in the new black-and-nickel Aeron desk chair he'd just dropped a thousand bucks on. It looked like something out of a futuristic survival movie.

'I'm sorry,' I said. 'Didn't I ask politely enough? Good morning, Neil, you beautiful man. *Please* get me the goddamn Inman Park property owners.'

'Oh yeah. Much better.' He tapped at his keyboard while I explained what happened at Miki's, the break-in. A few minutes later the volume on the morning news faded.

'It's on-screen,' Neil said. 'Want some coffee? I do.'

'Oh, you *are* a beautiful man. I'd love some.' I left my

office to see satellite images of Miki's neighborhood. Property owners' names appeared on each lot with the house number. Neil handed me a hot cup. It smelled amazing. I peered down at something reddish and foamy.

Coffee in all its variety is a sort of subspecialty for Neil. He's as shrewd as an international coffee buyer when he shops for beans. I've seen him grab a handful and bring them to his nose and close his eyes. He studies the color and texture and pops them in his mouth like peanuts. They tell him a story – wet-processed, shade grown or light, single origin or blended. Different beans, then different grinds for different days and different moods.

'Let's start with the three houses on each side of Miki, everyone across the street, and the closest neighbors behind her.'

'That's, like, thirty people.'

'You have something more pressing?' I handed him the cocktail napkin on which I'd scribbled Cash Tilison's name. 'One of Miki's boyfriends. She claims he stalked her.'

' "Claims"?'

'It's Miki.' I shrugged. 'She's making a list of the others.'

Neil returned to his desk and fell into his chair. He then sighed loudly. I watched the back of his head for a few seconds. Something was bugging him. And he obviously wanted me to know.

'So, you have plans for the big Independence Day weekend?' It was awkward, but it was the best I could do.

'I think I'm in love.' He said it flatly, in the disenchanted voice of a man who'd just realized he was going bald. 'With two women.'

I took a sip of coffee. 'Well, then I guess you're twice as

likely to have plans. This coffee is delicious, by the way.'

He looked at me as if I'd just told him Santa was dead. 'What?'

'I guess I was hoping for some advice or something, Keye. I mean, this is kinda huge.'

'Oh. Okay. Just give me a minute to recall my experiences as a heterosexual man. *Hmm*. Nope. Nothing's coming to mind.'

'You're an ass,' he said, but he was fighting off a smile.

'I was just afraid you were going to tell me you're becoming a leather daddy or something. Everyone else in my life seems to have some kind of sexual identity crisis. I swear to God if Rauser ever tells me he's gay, I'm going to drink antifreeze.'

'Wow. This was so not supposed to be about you.' Neil threw up his hands.

'Awww. Do you need to talk about your feelings? Come here, you.'

I made kissing sounds and tried to get my arms around him. Laughing, he held me off. We were close to a full-on wrestling match when the phone rang. Neil told the smart panel to switch the call to speakers. He had made our office his playground for electronics. Audio boomed from every corner of our super-wired office space. He adjusted the volume.

'Keye, it's Larry Quinn. How's my favorite detective? Hey, I got a job for you up north. Nice little resort area. You free?'

'It depends,' I said, and winked at Neil. 'I don't trust you, Larry.'

Quinn chuckled. 'It's nothing like the cow thing, Keye.

There's almost no chance you can get yourself arrested.'

Last year Larry Quinn had hired me to find a family pet in rural North Georgia. Okay, it was a missing cow named Sadie. I'd gained ten pounds on fried pies, which is apparently all they eat up there unless you count gravy, gotten arrested, and taken to jail in the back of the Gilmer County sheriff's car with a cow thief who'd smelled like poo.

'It's up in Creeklaw County,' Quinn said. 'Southern Appalachians. Little town called Big Knob near the North Carolina line. You know it?'

'Um . . . no.'

Neil made a childish reference to the town's name by first grabbing himself, then spreading his arms the length of a yardstick. I did a lot of overt eye rolling to prove I was above this primitive level.

'There's a married couple up there with an interesting story. Fella named Billy Wade drops an urn containing the ashes of his deceased mother. Well, what fell out didn't look like ashes. The Wades had an independent laboratory analyze the contents. Cement mix with some chicken feed.'

'Uh-*huh*.'

'Naturally, they want to know what happened to the real ashes.'

'Naturally.' They probably also wanted to sue the shit out of someone. I didn't say that. 'So why not just ask the crematory operator?'

'That's just it,' Quinn answered. 'They did. Several times. The owner, one Joe Ray Kirkpatrick, dodged their calls for a couple days, then finally offers a big apology, says an employee spilled and contaminated the ashes and filled the urn with cement mix to protect his job and spare the family the pain of lost remains. Kirkpatrick says he dismissed the man at once. He also reimbursed the Wades for *all* their funeral expenses, not just the cremation.'

'So what's the problem?' I found a pen and wrote a note – *Joe Ray Kirkpatrick*. We had access to databases that would give us the skinny on the crematory operator in no time flat, and what our paid-for access wouldn't get us, Neil was perfectly capable of finding on his own.

'They smell a rat, Keye,' Larry Quinn told me. 'And I do too.'

And a big settlement.

'So why not call the cops?' I asked.

'They did. Kirkpatrick reimbursed the Wades for all their funeral expenses. Cops don't see it as a civil matter at this point. The cops may also be in this guy's pocket.'

'So the Wades called you.'

'And here I am,' Quinn said. 'Keye, these poor people are distraught. Billy's mama wanted her ashes sprinkled in the ocean. Now that family doesn't have a pot to piss in. The whole county is in the bottom tier in the state as far as income and education.' Quinn was getting breathy and worked up. I'd seen him like this at depositions, when he sensed deceit. 'Nowhere to work but in service. Golf courses. Big lake. Lot of division between the haves and have-nots. But the Wades were about to take off work, which they can't afford, and drive seven hours from Big Knob to the coast, pay to charter a boat just to toss a bunch of cement mix into the Atlantic.'

'And chicken feed,' I added.

'That's right. And chicken feed, for God's sake.' Larry chuckled. 'How would you feel?'

'Lord knows.'

'See what I mean?'

'And you just want to help,' I said. 'What a guy.'

'That's exactly right,' Quinn agreed, and I could tell he was smiling that big smile that was famous on Atlanta television. *Make one call before the fall,* he'd say in that Old South accent, and point at the camera.

'So, what's up with the chicken feed?'

'According to the owner,' Larry told me, 'this person stored the bag of cement mix he intended to use in the urn with the chicken feed. There was a spill and it ended up getting mixed together somehow.'

'Chickens? At a crematory?'

'Fried chicken,' Neil muttered.

'Look, Keye, the point is the ashes weren't ashes.'

'Yeah, I get it. And I still want to know why there are chickens at a crematory.'

Quinn sighed, as if his detective shouldn't pester him with questions. 'Well, the way I understand it is it's a little farm. Sixteen acres. It's actually a good thing the chicken feed got mixed up in there or nobody would have noticed. Cement mix looks pretty much like cremated human remains. Or so I've been told.'

I thought about the blown weekend planned with Rauser. I thought about the desserts my mother would have on the long picnic table in their Winnona Park backyard – deep-dish blackberry cobbler, sweet-potato cheesecake, banana cream pie. Then I imagined what she'd say when I walked in alone. *Keye, bless your little heart. You have always been attracted to the kind of man who would leave you all alone on a holiday.*

'This weekend might be a great time to catch people at home,' I told Larry. 'I'll do it. Email me contact info on the Wades and the crematory's sneaky employee.'

'That's another thing fishy about this guy. The Wades claim folks up there don't remember any employees since the father died and the son took over the business a couple of years ago. Kirkpatrick says he doesn't have a way to get in touch with the man. Hispanic, no green card. Says he was paying him under the table.'

'Illegals have names too, Larry.'

'Not this one.'

I disconnected and stood leaning against the kitchen counter with my coffee cup in my hand. 'That was totally weird,' Neil said, and switched back to his morning news program.

'Tell me about it.'

'Think you'll have to see dead people?'

I took a last drink of red foamy coffee and left my cup on the counter. 'I hope not.'

'Yeah, that would be creepy.' Neil tossed his head to get the bangs away from his eyes. 'Can I go?'

'Seriously?'

'I need to get away.'

I grinned at him. 'You made plans with *both* of them, didn't you?'

'It was an accident.'

'And now you're just going to stand both women up and run away?'

'Pretty much.'

I grabbed a soft leather file bag with a shoulder strap and stuffed it full. 'I'm going to drop off some background reports and pick up a job from Tyrone. I have my phone.' I glanced down at it and saw a new email had arrived. Miki's list of six men she'd dated in two years. Four in the United States, two in Europe – the complications or benefits of traveling for a living. I forwarded the list to Neil's mailbox.

'Bring some food back, would ya?' Neil asked. He'd cleaned out whatever supplies we had in the refrigerator and cabinets, and resorted to eating one of those sample boxes of cereal that arrived in the mail. We were out of milk too, but he poured the cereal in a bowl anyway and ate it with a spoon.

'You know,' I said, 'this problem is easily solved by grocery shopping. It's way past your turn.'

'You look hot this morning.'

I was wearing a light heather blazer and skirt with a chocolate tank, a simple brown pump. Okay, so a simple pump from Louboutin meant a week's salary. But they were gorgeous. I kind of wanted to lick them. I kissed the top of Neil's head. 'Flattery will not get me to the grocery store.'

'A pox upon you.' He said it with a wave of his arm like a Shakespearean actor. 'And your trashy little cat too.'

His eyes drifted up to the television. Something in the way his expression changed made me follow them. I saw Rauser on the screen in the jeans I'd watched him peel off in my bedroom a few hours ago. Crime scene tape flickered in the foreground. Lights from police cruisers reflected off cars and dark streets. They were replaying a live shot from Rauser's crime scene last night. *News trucks are here. I love ya, Street.* Med techs with a gurney from the ME's office backed awkwardly out of a row of shrubs. Frank Loutz, the Fulton County medical examiner, followed the techs and the gurney out of the shrubbery. Loutz leaned in close to speak to Rauser, covered his mouth with his clipboard like an NFL coach on Sunday hiding his plays from the lip-readers. The reporter informed us grimly that a child had been found dead by a jogger. Cause of death had not been made official, but circumstances were suspicious. We were shown the moment the child's mother stumbled on the scene – her screaming, breaking through scene tape, barreling toward the ME techs, running with a mother's certainty that it was her son on the gurney. I lowered myself onto one of the leather sectionals scattered around the office and stared up at the television as the horror unfolded.

Homicide Detective Linda Bevins leapt in front of the shrieking woman like a professional goalie. I knew Bevins. She was a good cop. The woman was crying, arguing, hands flailing. Bevins held her shoulders, said something. The woman seemed too heartsick to keep standing. She dissolved into the pavement.

I thought about what the next few days would be like for her. This grieving woman, the family, friends, schoolmates, the detectives and techs, the unnamed jogger who stumbled over the lifeless body of a murdered child – they all would be altered in a hundred different ways, large and small, irrevocably.

Raised voices and loud noises had been my trigger. *Where's the money, old man? Give us the fucking money.* Then gunshots. Me shivering behind the counter. As a child, I carried the scars to new parents, who found themselves with a brooding, remote little girl. An intricate kind of dominoing takes place in one's life after murder's big net tangles you up. It goes on for years.

The gurney was pushed into the back of the ME's van. There would be a counselor on the scene soon to help deal with the collateral damage – traumatic stress, the depression and disbelief that would tear apart everyone who loved the boy. The parents would have a blur of questions coming at them, questions that would anger and bewilder them. The detectives would be chomping at the bit to exclude them as suspects as quickly as possible. The grief counselors would show up and do their best. But nothing would ever return to the kind of normal it had once been for that boy's family.

The camera moved to Rauser. I felt Neil's hand on my shoulder. We watched Rauser help Detective Bevins pull the mother up off the ground and get her into a vehicle, away from the pitiless television lights. He tried to move past the cameras, but the reporter intercepted him. 'Lieutenant Rauser, can you tell us anything about the murdered child?'

Microphones stabbed up in his face. His square jaw flexed under a stubbly charcoal shadow, gray eyes passed over the camera. If anyone had seen or heard anything suspicious in the vicinity of Kings Court and Amsterdam, he asked that they call. He gave out the main number at APD, then ducked back under the scene tape.

4

I delivered the weekly reports to Super Nannies On Call, then stopped at Rapid Placement, a headhunting agency at One Atlantic Center on West Peachtree in Midtown to deliver routine background checks. It wasn't the most exciting work, but both these companies, along with a handful of law firms and a couple of insurance agencies that used me for everything from surveillance to process serving, paid my ridiculously high mortgage every month. And then there was Tyrone's Quikbail.

I had been a registered bond enforcement agent since leaving the Bureau. Turns out I have a knack for fugitive recovery. It supplements my income nicely, and it's far more interesting than most of the work I do, which usually consists of sitting on some street somewhere, trying to guess what color the next car will be, listening to audiobooks and drumming my fingers on the steering wheel to stay awake until somebody runs out without their crutches or shows up with a prostitute. Bail recovery is also the part of my job that Rauser hates most. But he is not allowed to go on about this. We have an agreement. I don't whine about him being a cop and he doesn't interfere in my career choices. At some point, both of us had stretched the limits of this agreement. Out of fear, mostly. After we'd both been hurt so badly last year, making peace with him going back to APD took some doing. But I did it. While he was home recovering, he worried when I left the house. He insisted I carry my gun everywhere. I was the only woman in produce with a mango, some asparagus, and a 10mm Glock. We've adjusted because we have to. When it comes to career, neither one of us is willing to give an inch.

Tyrone's Quickbail is in a chipped yellow stucco building near the capitol, Fulton County courthouse, tons of county service offices, block after block of bail bonds companies, and some pretty good soul food. I found a metered spot across the street from Tyrone's office in the three-hundred block. I saw him through his third-floor window at the desk that looks out onto Mitchell Street. I got out of my car and dropped a couple of quarters in the parking meter, then went back for the bag I dared not leave. A block and a half from about a million cops around the government offices and it was still a terrible place to park a classic car. I wished I would have thought to bring the other car, a banged-up Plymouth Neon no one ever seemed to notice. It was like driving around with some kind of cloaking device.

I grabbed my bag and looked at the green-and-white box of doughnuts I'd stopped for on the way. What was left of them. Krispy Kreme had picked up where alcohol left off. Few things sent oxytocin surging through my system like the glowing neon *Hot Doughnuts Now* sign and the promise of an original glazed right off the line. Dr Shetty says replacing one addiction with another is dangerous. She recommends developing better coping skills instead. Apparently, my love of and perhaps obsession with food is symptomatic of the larger problem, which is: I'm insecure, needy, controlling, and stressed out, and I have intimacy issues out the wazoo. Oh, let's not forget the penis-envy thing. I cannot believe I pay a shrink to tell me this stuff. I mean, what's the friggin' problem with a little replacement therapy? I exercise, if you count pacing. And it's not like I'm shut in a closet somewhere with sugar all over my face and my finger down my throat. I often remind my brainy doctor that sometimes things are exactly what they seem. I love food because my mother, Emily Street, is just about the best cook in town and I grew up with her gourmet take on traditional southern. I love doughnuts because, well, they're good. Okay, so maybe my cut-off switch is broken. Thankfully, my metabolism is something like a wood chipper. I thought about that. Would it last? Once I moved past the mid-thirty point, would it slow to a crawl? *Shit.* Okay, so maybe I needed to get the goddamn doughnuts out of my vehicle and into Tyrone's hands.

'What up?'

I heard a deep male voice behind me. I turned and found myself looking into the soft brown eyes of a young man standing too near – skinny, eighteen, nineteen, jeans hanging off his hips exposing white boxers and a flash of brown abs, jacked-up Nikes. He was cute, although I had a bad feeling cute wasn't what he was going for. His eyes dropped to my breasts.

In the background, three guys about the same age leaned against a brick storefront, watching. One of them made a big show of licking his lips. I leaned back against my car, looked him up and down. I didn't want to show him anything. Guys like this feed on fear. 'What can I do for you?'

'What can you do for me?' He turned to his friends. 'She wanna know what she can do for me.' This brought on waves of laughter from the theater section, more lip licking than a supermodel photo shoot. 'I tell you what you can do.' His tone had changed. He was talking tough now. 'How 'bout you be my bitch for the day.'

'Seriously? Has a woman ever once said yes to that?'

'Bitches don't always know what's good for them.' He folded his arms over his scrawny chest. 'They need somebody smart to tell 'em.' His friends applauded his genius, shouted encouragements.

'If you'll excuse me,' I said, and tried to move past him.

He blocked my way.

'Look, I've had almost no sleep. My cousin, who may actually be delusional, is in my house. My boyfriend *the cop* never sleeps. And I just delivered background reports to a fucking nanny agency. One of them had bad credit. That's it. Bad credit. Exciting stuff, right?'

'The bitch' oversharing momentarily stumped him. He was smiling at me, but his eyes couldn't stay still. Bad sign. His nerves were firing. A tranquilizer gun would have been nice. He took a step forward. I looked up into his muddy eyes, smelled beer and cigarettes on his breath.

'I swear to God, if you take one more step, you're going to be *my* bitch.'

He grabbed my arms at the shoulders. The heel of my eight-hundred-dollar pumps sank into his bony shin, and when he let go, my hand came out of my bag with the 10mm and slammed it against the side of his bony head. He yelped, hopped backward, went down on his butt. His buddies had that wide-eyed, excited schoolyard stare kids in packs get when a fight breaks out. I made sure they all got a good look at the Glock.

The lobby door opened across the street and Tyrone came out fast, wearing a white suit and wingtips. He looked like a mocha latte. Not a lot of guys could pull it off, but Tyrone looked cool in anything.

He jerked the street thug up one-handed by the collar with forearms about the size of Virginia hams, held him in front of me like a puppeteer. 'You look at her real good, son. She's one of my people, which means she will flat kill your dumb ass.' He turned to the group. I saw the shoulder holster loaded with his 9mm under his coat. 'Any y'all mess with one of my people again, we gonna hunt you down.'

He let go of the thug. We watched him wobble off to his friends, holding up his droopy pants with one hand and his bloody ear with the other. Not one of them looked back.

'Remind me not to get on your bad side.'

'Don't get on my bad side,' I reminded him.

He pulled an envelope from an inside pocket and handed it to me. 'Steven T. Wriggles. Robbery, grand theft auto, and resisting arrest.'

I scanned the report, looked up at Tyrone. He was grinning at me. 'He robbed a Seven Eleven with dried nasal mucus?'

Dimples cut craters in his handsome face. On a normal day, I might have swooned a little. But not today. 'Clerk gave him three hundred from the register,' Tyrone told me.

'Which just proves nobody wants a booger touching them.'

'Good Lord.' I sighed and looked back at the report. This wasn't exactly a step up from nanny backgrounds. After the robbery, Wriggles had commandeered the convenience store clerk's vehicle when his own car had stalled in the parking lot. He then stopped at the McDonald's on Ponce for a cheeseburger, the very McDonald's that happens to be one block from the cop shop. Just so happened three of Atlanta's Finest came in for lunch. Wriggles didn't get halfway through his Big Mac before he was arrested. Given his weapon of choice and because he had no priors, the judge set bail. Tyrone had guaranteed it. Wriggles didn't show up for court. There was no known address.

'Is this all you've got?'

'Is that all? Oh come on, Keye. I saved this for my best tracker.'

I took the box of Krispy Kremes from the front seat and handed them over.

'Thanks.' He opened the box. 'There's only eight. Dang, girl. You gonna have a huge booty.' He tore one in half and stuffed it in his mouth, licked the sugar off his fingers. 'Your eye is twitching. You know that, right?' He shoved the other half in his mouth with no apparent concern for the size of his own booty. 'It's kind of creeping me out.'

I got in my car and slammed the door.

'What?' he yelled, as I pulled out of the metered space. 'Hey, wait. What'd I say?'

The door slammed behind me when I walked back into my office. I went to my desk, wished yet again I had walls instead of a big wire fence. Neil spun around in his overpriced desk chair and squinted at me. 'Anything I can do?'

Most days, I am at peace with where my life is now. I'm sober. I'm making a living. I'm in love. I own my own business. I've been luckier than most in this economy. But sometimes there's a big hole where meaningful work used to be. I needed to buck up and take it like a man. There are consequences for actions. I torched my career, drank it away. I thought about Miki, about her awards, her soaring success. It never seemed to matter how much she drank or how many drugs she played with or how many times it had interrupted her work. She was so wildly talented, she was always welcomed back. I loved my cousin. I wanted the best for her. I wanted to celebrate her accomplishments . . . deep down. But some days, it was a very bitter pill to swallow.

'Where are you on Miki's boyfriends?' I asked Neil, and logged in to one of the programs we use to assist us in skip traces. I started a search for Steven T. Wriggles, Tyrone's bail jumper, the mucus guy. A dispossessory had been filed a couple of months back and he'd been evicted from an apartment off Briarcliff Road, his last known address. I located his mother, jotted down her address and anything else that might lead to Wriggles, including a first cousin.

'As far as I can tell so far, it would have only worked logistically for one of them. The country singer, Cash Tilison. He has a house up near the lake.'

'The Lake' is what Atlantans call Lake Lanier. Not only is it the main source of water for the metro area and a major recreation area, it's where the well-off build waterfront homes and dock their boats.

'He made an appearance at the children's hospital yesterday. Fund-raiser from six to eight. He would have had plenty of time to get to Miki's before she came home.'

'He also fits the body type for the guy in the window,' I said. 'Hey, I'm sending you info on a guy named Wriggles. See if you can dig up a current address before I have to go knocking on his mother's door.'

I called to check on Miki. Voice mail. I paid a few bills and pulled up the receivables program. Billing. It was mind-numbing. But a necessary evil. I worked for a few minutes, tried Miki again. No answer. Maybe she was still sleeping. Maybe she slept all day and partied all night. I had no idea about her routines. I knew one thing: I was dreading going home to another confrontation.

'Bingo,' Neil said, and spun around, smiling at me. 'He wrote a check for eight hundred and fifty-seven dollars made out to Sunshine Duplexes. The notation says rent plus late fee.' He gave me the date. It was the day after Wriggles held up a store clerk with some, well, DNA. I didn't ask how Neil got access to the information. We have an office 'don't ask, don't tell' policy.

I typed *Sunshine Duplexes* into my search engine. 'I couldn't find current employment information. You see anything?'

Neil said he couldn't find an employer for Wriggles either. Why work when you're okay with taking what you want? I don't have a lot of patience with takers and deadbeats. I'd worked for everything in my life, and what I didn't provide for myself, my parents had worked their butts off to give me. I thought again about Miki and her goddamn awards. A little spurt of anger flushed my cheeks.

I was in exactly the right mood to pay a visit on Steven T. Wriggles. But first I needed to go home, get into the right clothes, and see how – or what – my cousin was doing.

5

The Georgian Terrace was built less than fifty years after Sherman's red-hot March to the Sea torched our architectural history. It's all buttery brick and limestone, a French Renaissance design meant to evoke Paris in a city that was literally rising up out of its own ashes. That I had scored living quarters here at all was still a source of amazement. The first-shift manager and his crabby concierge in the little black blazer would agree with that. They are the only hotel employees who flat-out refuse to warm up to me. Who can blame them? I have the only two thousand square feet in the hotel the manager can't control. I try to be respectful. I'm fully aware that I'm a visitor in every other pocket of the Georgian Terrace. I made the deal with the previous owner to buy and renovate his private living space after I helped him resolve some personal matters. Okay, so I got the goods on his cheating wife before she walked away with a disproportionate slice of his fortune. My contractors jammed the garage with their oversized trucks, set up a construction dumpster, marched in and out with drywall dust on their boots, and were not always sensitive to the new management's daily trials. On those rare occasions when White Trash needs to leave the building, I'm aware of their displeasure at seeing me hauling an awkward carrier through the lobby with a yowling cat. What is it about towering ceilings and crystal and glass and marble that creates something like an echo chamber when an unhappy feline's voice is thrown into the mix? And White Trash doesn't know when to stop. It's not just a little meow; it's a howling torrent of misery. By the time we get from the tenth floor to the lobby, she's just getting warmed up. Anyone who had been unlucky enough to share the elevator ride stumbles out a glassy-eyed cat hater for life.

Having the only privately owned living space in the hotel took some getting used to at first. While the anonymity of a revolving neighborhood is really nice on a bad-hair day, I missed having a sense of community. But over time, a working-class neighborhood came into focus – servers, housekeepers, the baristas, chefs, cabbies and security guards, clerks and valets. Once it was clear I did not have to be treated like a guest, I was allowed to tiptoe my way into this after-hours society where food is shared along with complaints and gossip about guests and supervisors and sometimes fellow employees. A couple of months ago, Rauser and I were invited to a rooftop pool party. All very hush-hush. Management had gone home for the night, uninvited and uninformed. Second- and third-shift employees staggered their hours to relieve one another and showed up in waves. Rauser drank too much and went swimming in his briefs along with Marko, the brilliant chef at the hotel's Livingston Restaurant. When it got very late and there were only a few of us left, we all took a chaise longue next to the pool, Rauser and I sharing one, me leaning back into his arms. With Atlanta's purplish chessboard skyline in front of us, we all took turns saying something about ourselves and our lives. Every story seemed to lead us into another conversation, and I remember the gradual brightening of dawn and Rauser's breathing changing. He'd fallen asleep with his arms around me.

'Hello, my friend.' I heard Marko Pullig's thick Slavic accent and big booming voice. I had nearly reached the gleaming brass elevators. 'I was just taking this upstairs to Miki.' He was balancing a covered tray. He bent and gave me one cheek, then the other.

'Room service isn't one of the perks I'm allowed here, Marko.'

He glanced at the manager, who was having a conversation with a clerk across the sprawling, gleaming lobby. 'The order came directly into the restaurant. Since I was fortunate enough to meet your charming cousin today in the lobby, I volunteered.'

'Marko, you're hitting on my cousin?'

'Keye, please. Find your romantic self. We've talked about this. There is such a thing as being too firmly grounded.'

Oh yeah. That's me. Grounded.

'I prefer to think of it as exploring the possibility of new love,' Marko said.

'Uh-huh. Well, I don't think Miki's here. I tried to call a bunch of times.'

'You look worried. Relax. She was out shopping. That's

how we met. I helped her with groceries. She told me about the break-in at her home.'

The elevator doors opened. 'You want me to take that up, or are you going to make me watch you flirt?'

Marko bowed with his usual flair, handed me the tray. 'Please deliver this with my compliments. And in the event she has further needs, feel free to give her my private number.'

I smiled as the doors closed. I love this hotel and the people.

It's interesting that I would end up living in a hotel. Before my drinking days came to a screeching halt, I had a kind of love affair with hotel rooms. It was where I was free to do what was unacceptable everywhere else – drink until I was out cold. Even now, when room service is at full-blast on weekends and holidays, the smell of tomato juice takes me back to a cold Bloody Mary with a stalk of celery and a lime twist. I'm no different from any other addict. I romance the memories. Tipping my chair over backward in a nice restaurant is never what springs to mind when I want a drink. No, what I remember is the way good cognac coats a glass, meets your nose, then your palate, like liquid calm. Or the cold, hard edge of vodka and soda loaded with ice and lemon on a hot day. My mouth still gets wet when I think about it – the cellular memories of a drunk.

I pushed open the door to my loft and smelled cooking food. Miki was in the kitchen, wearing jeans and a T-shirt that looked very familiar.

'Hey, you're early. I was going to surprise you with dinner.' She was standing over a steaming saucepan, tasting something with a wooden spoon. 'I took a shower and borrowed some clothes to go to the market. Not quite ready to go home alone. I hope that's okay.' She was surprisingly perky. 'What's that? It smells yummy.'

'The food you ordered from downstairs,' I said, setting it on the bar. I headed down the hall to change. 'Marko offered his phone number too, by the way.'

Miki appeared at my bedroom door. 'Why would I order food? I'm making dinner.'

'I wondered the same thing,' I told her, and got out of my skirt, pulled on some Levi's, searched my closet for a blouse.

'Keye, I'm serious. I didn't order anything.'

'Okay,' I said lightly. But what I was thinking was *Ooo-kay, sure.* I pulled out my running shoes. I discovered awhile back that comfortable shoes were necessary equipment for bond enforcement. 'You okay today?'

'Yeah. I mean no. I mean, I didn't order that food.'

I looked at her. She seemed to be fraying. *Oh boy.* Would the fun ever stop? 'Hey, it's no big deal. Maybe Marko just wanted to come upstairs.'

A slight smile. She touched her hair. 'He helped me with groceries earlier. He did everything but dim the lights before I could get him out.'

I slipped into a pullover and followed Miki back to the kitchen with my shoes in my hand. 'He's a charming guy, huh? Any interest?'

Miki lifted the cover on the tray and we eyed Marko's shrimp ravioli with shaved truffle, an arugula salad, his famous homemade leek bread, and a flourless chocolate cake about the size of a hockey puck on a white plate with a sprig of mint.

'They're all charming at first,' Miki said, proving she was just as jaded as I was. She handed me a fork and got one for herself.

I took a stool at the bar that divided my living area and kitchen, speared a pillow-shaped piece of Marko's homemade pasta. 'All I've eaten is doughnuts and coffee,' I confessed. 'I have stress hormones bleeding out my eyeballs.'

We both had a bite and took a minute to enjoy it. Marko was an artist with food and with plating it. He had an incredibly delicate touch. Miki turned around and stirred whatever she had in the pot, adjusted the flame on my gas burner. 'I didn't know you cooked,' I said.

'We don't know one another, Keye. Not really. We haven't since we were kids.'

Miki is a photojournalist, successful and sought after. Her moods had derailed her career a time or two, but she had always been welcomed back to her professional life. I knew some of the details only because my mother is an unapologetic gossip. I'd seen Miki's photographs in magazines for years. And in her house. Huge talent. Walks into war and natural disaster with cameras hanging off her. It seemed the perfect job for someone perpetually suicidal. She'd made the tabloids a few times during a steamy three-year relationship with a famous rocker. And then again with Cash Tilison.

She cut a piece of ravioli with her fork. Shrimp and cream spilled out. 'Ever think about finding your biological parents?'

'Where'd that come from?'

Miki shrugged. 'Just curious.'

'Like I need another crazy mother?' I broke off a piece of leek bread.

Miki chuckled. Crazy mothers were something she was intimately familiar with. 'I mean seriously.'

'Don't get me wrong. I have a narcissist's desire to see if they look like me. But that's all it is. Medical questions, maybe. Oh, and I'd like to know when I was born. And where. There are no hospital records. And my grandparents hadn't enrolled me in school yet when they were killed. No paperwork at all on me until I went to the children's home.'

'So your bio mom just squatted in the woods and squeezed you out or what?'

'More likely she squatted in the back room of some strip joint.'

Miki grinned at me. 'So April Fool's Day isn't your birthday?'

'I think somebody with the State ballparked me and wrote in April first just for fun. Bastards.'

'Sure was fun on your birthday when we were kids,' Miki remarked.

'Yeah. Good times. Huge shocker I'm in therapy.' I stabbed at some arugula. 'You know, what I really want to know is how I ended up with the last name Street. I know my parents had tried to have biological kids for a long time. They always told me that. I know they'd decided to adopt when Mother couldn't get pregnant. But I'm pretty sure adopting a Chinese kid wasn't in the plan.'

Miki frowned. 'But, Keye, they love you so much.'

'Oh I know they do. But something's off. I know it. I've always known. I mean, who adopted minority kids thirty years ago in Georgia? I guess somebody did, but not my mother. You know what kind of shit my parents had to put up with from neighbors and teachers and everyone. Back then, nobody in our lily-white neighborhood looked like me and Jimmy. I overheard them talking when I was little. It was just before Jimmy came. Mother was venting, saying life would have been easier with a white child. She said it was Dad's fault. I always assumed from that conversation that something in his past put them out of the running. Everybody knows the paperwork got a little fuzzy back then on kids with alternate ethnicities. They were practically begging people to take us and make room for white children who were actually considered adoptable.'

'But then they adopted Jimmy,' Miki pointed out.

'Yeah, well, maybe it's like adopting a shelter pet. It changes you. Once you've seen the need, you don't go back to a breeder. My parents are decent people. My father has this huge sense of social responsibility. Plus, they'd always wanted a boy and a girl. I wanted to run the records on my dad when I was at the Bureau, but you can't do that unless it's tied to an investigation. Every request for sealed records has to be explained. It's not something they take lightly. And, to be honest, I've always been a little afraid of finding out the truth.'

Miki used her fork to stab the cake. Gooey dark chocolate ran across the plate. 'Does it really matter?'

'No. Not anymore.'

Miki touched my hand. 'I can't imagine growing up without you and Jimmy.'

I liked my cousin. I always seemed to forget this during the long stretches between our visits. I liked her sober. Not so much last night. I'd had enough drama in my life. I'd avoided hers. Maybe I hadn't been there when she'd needed family. Miki's mother had been institutionalized for years. Her father was dead. Jimmy and I and our parents were what she had left. She was right: We'd been close as kids.

I thought again about Miki going shopping, then ordering food. Or not ordering food. Or not remembering that she'd ordered food. And not answering her phone. I thought about the cuts up and down her arms and the unsettling darkness inside her. I thought about how confrontational and defensive she'd been at the bar last night. Creeklaw County and the counterfeit urn were starting to sound pretty good.

'Thanks for taking care of me last night.' Miki must have seen something in my face. 'I was pretty shaky. And I got a little drunk.'

'Understandable.'

'I'm sorry I'm still here, Keye. I'm sorry I'm wearing your clothes.'

I loaded my fork with chocolate cake. 'You should be. You've got camel toe really bad.'

She laughed. 'I promise I'll go home tomorrow. I've just got the creeps right now. I need a day.'

'It's okay. You're family.' I remembered staying in her house when mine was unlivable because of construction. She had handed her keys over without a second thought.

I felt White Trash weaving around the stool legs. She was as accomplished as any beggar I'd ever met on Peachtree Street. I picked a piece of feta out of the salad and dropped it for her. 'Listen, I have a job up in Big Knob, so if you want the place to yourself for a couple of days, it's all yours.'

'Big Knob?'

'I know, right? I'll have Mom come by and take care of White Trash.'

'Are you kidding? I can take care of White Trash. We're buds.'

'I mean *really* take care of her.'

'I grew up with cats and dogs just like you did, Keye. I know how to take care of them.'

'She has a litterbox and she needs fresh water and food and stuff.'

'Oh really. Well, the deal's off, then,' Miki said. 'I get it. You think I'm a drug addict. And flaky. Anything else?'

'I think you might be an alcoholic,' I said. I didn't feel like pulling the punch. And I sure as shit was not going to leave my cat with someone I couldn't trust. I'd found White Trash having breakfast in a garbage bin on Peachtree Street when I'd first moved into the Georgian, half starved, covered with all forms of parasite, half wild and extremely unappreciative of my efforts. But she'd warmed up very quickly to regular meals and human attention. New people still scare her at first, as do Rauser's big shoes on my hardwood floors. He gives in to her neurosis most of the time and tries not to stomp. Or he removes his size-twelves when he comes in.

'I was hitting it pretty hard last night, Keye. It's not my usual. I swear. I'll take really great care of her. And I appreciate you letting me stay. It means a lot.'

'Where's the coke?'

'It's gone. Look, I was out with friends. We had dinner, drank, did some coke. I had a little left. That's all.'

'Great,' I said, but I'd already decided to call Mother and

have her check up on both Miki and my surly feline. Miki had freely admitted to drinking and drugging before seeing the man in her window. If there had been a man at her window. Most people who use stimulants also use pills to come down. No telling what else was in her system. And then there was the thing with Marko and the food. She'd seemed completely stumped, like she'd really forgotten she'd called the restaurant. None of it was sitting well with me.

I looked at the time display on my phone. 'I have to get moving. Somebody blew a court date.' I went to the couch and put my shoes on. 'I need to pick them up.'

Miki followed me. 'A bail jumper? I want to come. I'll get my camera.'

'I don't think that's a good idea.'

'Oh come on. Don't you want company? I'll turn the stove off and we'll go.'

I was silent.

'Keye, look at me. I'm clear as a bell.'

If that was true we wouldn't have a dinner tray from the restaurant sitting in the kitchen. I looked up into her blue eyes. I fully intended to tell her she absolutely could not come. But she had that caged-animal look. I knew it well. 'Okay, but you have to do what I say. I'm serious. This is my work.'

Miki kissed my forehead. 'I'll behave. I promise.' She skipped off down the hall to get her equipment. 'Is it dangerous?' she called from the guest room.

'Only if you're afraid of boogers.'

6

The hours between five and seven are great for bond enforcement. Southerners never seem to think things can go wrong at suppertime. People are just getting in from work and preparing dinner. They've left the outside world behind and walked into the safety of their homes. It had been a sacred time in our household growing up. No one shows up at your door during those hours unless they want a seat at the table. It's just common decency. No business. No solicitors. No telephone calls. My parents had been fanatical about this. Mother was passionate about cooking, and if she spent all day doing it just to see our faces light up, our faces better be at the table and friggin' lit up on time or she would throw a full-on fit. And Emily Street could really pitch one.

We pulled into the Sunshine Duplexes in Chamblee near I-285 in the scarred-up '97 Neon I use when I don't want to make a big splash. The dented hood was an unrepaired reminder that texting while driving is irretrievably stupid. It was a low-income area, ethnically diverse, with a heavy concentration of Korean, Vietnamese, and Hispanic immigrants who had gathered near Buford Highway, the strip in Atlanta for just about any kind of authentic flavor you're craving, from Japanese to Ethiopian and everything in between. And it was a good place to find honest employment if your English or your green card wouldn't hold up.

'So what did this guy do?' Miki wanted to know. She had her camera hanging around her neck.

I gave her the short version and omitted certain details involving Wriggles's attempted transfer of DNA. 'He robbed a convenience store.'

She was checking her camera. The light was still good and would be for a while. She leaned out the window with the camera to her eye. So much for keeping a low profile. A group of boys with baseball gloves and a bat were playing on the crumbling pavement. There was no green space at all. The entire complex was paved, cracked, forgotten. 'This is fantastic,' she said. 'Let me out.'

I parked at a closed-up duplex. *No trespassing* signs were hung on the boarded windows. The pavement had broken away so badly that the tiny driveway was nearly all weeds. A tin overhang that had once been a carport drooped hopelessly. Miki got out and headed for the boys playing ball. Miki had a way with boys of all ages.

I looked back at Wriggles's file. He was white and six feet tall. The photograph showed a receding hairline and a mousy brown 'fro – a poor man's Steven Wright. That he moved into a community where he'd stick out like a football bat when he was supposed to be on the down-low was cementing the idea that Wriggles wasn't a very talented criminal. Fine with me. Easy money.

The boys had gone back to their game. Miki was talking to them while she snapped pictures. I walked over. 'Anybody want to earn five bucks?'

I was practically mobbed. I showed them Wriggles's photograph. They recognized him at once. They all wanted a slice of the pie. We settled on five bucks each. One would come with me and the others would slow him down if Wriggles made a run for it. After a brief powwow, one boy emerged as the chosen escort.

'What's your name?' I asked.

'Angel.' He didn't look up at me. He was dark-haired, around ten years old, wearing a Braves cap and generic high-tops, the kind you get at discount stores. I thought about the strangled-child case Rauser was working, then about Rauser. He'd slept all of two hours. Rauser had children of his own, grown now but loved no less. The cases with kids always wore deep lines in him.

'Don't be scared, okay, Angel? All I want you to do is knock, yell through the door your mom wants to borrow something. Then you take off. He'll never see you, okay?'

'I'm not scared,' Angel said, and squinted up at me in the late-day sun.

We walked up the cracked drive past little brick duplexes, each with two narrow windows in the front and one in the carport. Miki was taking pictures of asphalt and brick and everything else, moving lightly over potholes and dips like the camera was part of her. Whatever her photographer's eye was seeing, I hadn't seen yet.

'You know if this guy has a job, Angel?'

'Don't think so. He walks to the beer store in the middle of the day.'

Wriggles's carport was covered in the same rusty overhang I'd seen at every unit. It was empty except for a trash can and a recycling bin full of Michelob bottles. His car had broken down at the convenience store he'd robbed, I remembered from his file.

'He was in our house once,' Angel told us quietly, as we stepped in the carport. 'He smelled bad.'

'Good to know,' I said. Vertical blinds were closed – the plastic ones you get for seven bucks at Home Depot, standard issue for apartments around here.

'The guy's a freak. My dad says he's bringing the neighborhood down.'

Miki hung back with her camera. Angel and I went to the door. I could hear a television. I knocked. No answer. I knocked again. An impatient male voice shouted over the television. 'I gave at the office!'

'Hey, man, my mom needs to borrow something.' The volume muted on the television. 'It's José from down the street.' Angel smiled up at me. 'White people think we are all named José.'

'Nice touch,' I whispered. We heard someone approach the door. Angel gave me a thumbs-up and took off. The door opened.

Steven T. Wriggles was shirtless and in his underwear. And we're not talking Calvin Kleins here. I mean just plain underwear, Walmart special, the kind boys wear in school. I'd seen more of them than I wanted to admit. White with a red band. And not attractive. Wriggles was tall, with a pasty beer belly and sparse tufts of curly brown hair on his chest. I stepped up in the door frame. Wriggles frowned.

'Was that your kid? I don't have kitchen stuff, if that's what you want.'

'You forgot to show up for court, Mr Wriggles. Need to get you in and get a new date set.'

He tried to close the door on me. I pushed back with my forearms and squeezed in a little further. I felt for my cuffs. 'So get dressed and let's go.'

He put his hands on his hips, planted himself with feet shoulder width apart, defiant in his dingy underwear. I heard Miki's shutter buzzing. He scowled at her. 'Who the fuck is that?'

I charged the rest of the way in and slapped the cuffs on his right wrist. Wriggles jerked his arm away, and the dangling end of heavy silver handcuffs flew up and smacked him in the face. I think his eyes crossed for a second. Miki was in the house now too, circling us with her shutter humming like she was covering Afghanistan. And then Steven T. Wriggles did the unthinkable. With handcuffs swinging off one wrist, he brought his hand to his nose and jammed his finger inside. Then he jabbed at me with the offending finger.

'*Jesus!*' I leapt out of the way and with delayed empathy understood why the clerk had emptied the cash register that day and handed Wriggles three hundred dollars. I think even Homeland Security would have caved. TSA agents would run screaming at the sheer repulsiveness of the act.

Miki was laughing, moving around us. I whipped the Glock out of the duty holster on the back of my jeans. Wriggles's eyes got wide. If you've never seen a full-size 10mm Glock, it's an imposing weapon. The Bureau had experimented with making them standard for agents, but the size was unmanageable for trainees, and the recoil will make your teeth rattle. I got attached to mine, though. It's a great deterrent. Dr Shetty has some ideas about why I continue to work in fields that require a big-ass gun – something about being short and not having a penis. But even a full-on dimwit like Wriggles appreciates the sinister character of my weapon.

His hands went up. 'Okay, okay. Just don't fucking kill me.'

'We're going to go in back and you're going to get some clothes on,' I told him. 'And just so you know, the safety on this thing is in the trigger. It's not even really a safety. It's really awkward. You do something gross, there's going to be an accident.'

I followed Wriggles to a bedroom piled up with dirty clothes and ashtrays and beer cans. He pulled jeans over his underwear and put on a blue T-shirt that had *K-Y Lubricating Jelly* printed on it in white. Just the thought of that kind of hit my gag reflex. He pushed the hanging handcuffs through the sleeve.

'Get on your stomach on the bed.'

'My *God,*' Wriggles exclaimed.

'Oh right. As if.' I waved my Glock at him and he got on his stomach. I pushed my knee into his back, pulled his arms up behind him, and got his other wrist cuffed. I used a plastic zip tie to attach them to his belt loop. Then I pulled a shirt out of a pile on the floor, rolled it up, and tied it around his head like a bandanna, pushed it down under his nose.

Wriggles started flopping around like a seal. 'I can't breathe,' he protested. 'It smells bad.'

'Sorry, pal. I'm not letting that nose of yours in my car.'

Miki helped me get him turned over and up on his feet. We put him in the passenger's seat. Miki got behind him.

Wriggles was processed while I waited for the paperwork I would need for Tyrone's Quikbail. My cousin was surrounded by cops and, I suspected, flirting her way into some seriously great photographs of Atlanta's Finest. There was a lot of laughing.

'I woulda put on my mascara if I'd known it was picture day,' Rauser said. He slipped his arms around my waist and bent to rub his rough cheek against mine. 'Commercial Robbery says you brought in the snot guy.'

'Don't you have enough to keep you busy in Homicide?'

He pulled out his phone, moved some things around with one of his knobby fingers, then showed me the screen. 'Miki sent it to me. I'm thinking it should be my wallpaper.' It was a still shot of Wriggles in his underwear lunging at me with his nasty finger. 'Can't wait to see it on YouTube.'

'She uploaded a video?' I shot a look in Miki's direction, and realized now why she and the cops were doing so much laughing. 'I'm going to kill her,' I growled, and Rauser laughed. 'As soon as I get back. Right now I need a backup pet sitter.'

'You're going somewhere?'

'Larry Quinn called today with a job. It sounds interesting.'

'The cow lawyer? Uh-oh.'

I walked with Rauser to the breakroom and watched him pour burnt coffee into a cup. I could see the muck inside the pot. He offered me some, but texture is not really what I look for in a cup of coffee. 'Somebody up near Lake Chatuge says the crematory put chicken feed and cement mix in their mother's urn instead of ashes.'

'You're shittin' me. Why?' He took a sip and made a face, then added a ton of powdered non-dairy creamer, which he poured out of a sugar jar.

'I haven't come up with an answer to that,' I told him.

'Motive is usually money,' he reminded me.

'Where's the value in cement mix when you've got cremains on hand?'

'What was the explanation?'

'An employee spilled the real ashes and tried to cover.'

'Sounds plausible.'

'Larry doesn't think so.'

Rauser made a *humph* sound. 'Larry Quinn smells green. You know how he is.'

'Well, I could use a little green myself, and it means I won't have to spend the Fourth of July with Mother *alone.*'

'Ouch. Guilt. Won't Papa Bear be there to protect you?'

'Dad can't help me. I think she beats him.'

'I hope that runs in the family,' he said, and did that up-and-down thing with his eyebrows.

'You're a freak.' I smiled.

'Can I sleep with you tonight?'

I touched his rough cheek. 'You better.'

Loud voices from the outer room drew our attention. Through the glass walls we saw Miki with Balaki, Williams, Velazquez, Bevins, and Angotti from Homicide and a handful of other detectives, some I recognized vaguely from Robbery. Some I didn't know at all. A few uniformed cops had joined the mix, all of them looking up at the wall-mounted screen at the head of the detective cubes. I followed their eyes and saw Steven T. Wriggles slapping himself in the face with the handcuffs, then my own image leaping out of the way of his filthy finger. My Glock came out. It ended with me telling Wriggles, 'I'm not letting that nose of yours in my car.' Text shimmied across the screen: *Booger Bandit Bounty Hunter.* The room came apart.

'She is *so* kicked out,' I murmured.

Rauser's phone rang. He pulled it from a back pocket, listened for a minute. 'What kind?' he asked. 'Frank, give me the short version.' He waited. 'Well, can we get a profile?' He waited some more, let go of a half growl, half sigh, returned the phone to his pocket. 'Loutz,' he said, meaning Fulton County's medical examiner. 'Forensic light source picked up some kind of fluid on the Delgado boy's skin. ME's gotta send it to the lab.'

'Where was it?'

'Left shoulder and the side of his neck.'

'The boy was on his stomach,' I said. 'So this happened while the offender was behind him, probably on top of him during the murder.'

'Or after,' Rauser said.

'Was Frank able to exclude anything?'

'He knows it's not blood.'

'In this heat and from that position, sweat would be a good bet. Saliva.'

'Semen or urine,' Rauser added. 'They found it by accident. Some kind of fluorescently labeled dye one of the techs had, something they don't use on skin, ended up on the body. It's for eyes or something. UV picked up drops and spatter from the fluid under the dye. Frank said it lit up like a Christmas tree.'

'When will you know?'

Rauser chewed his lip. 'We send everything out now. GBI is backlogged, even on priority cases. Budget cuts have been unreal. Everybody wants smaller government. Well, this is what you get.' He blew out air and tension. 'Jesus, I want a cigarette.'

Rauser had quit smoking last Thanksgiving, but he had not stopped wanting one. He pulled a packet of nicotine gum from his pocket. 'Can you believe I'm eating this pansy shit?'

7

I picked Neil up at his house in Cabbagetown, an old mill workers' district turned hip. I hoped we'd be able to function without drawing too much attention to ourselves up in Creeklaw County. Okay, so it's rural North Georgia, I'm Chinese, and Neil's a '60s beach movie on downs. But, hey, it could happen. It was our first road trip together. In the past, Neil had shown only sporadic interest in anything beyond his job description, whatever that was. He seemed to always be tweaking it. I'm never quite sure what will pique his curiosity. Apparently cement mix, chicken feed, and dead people do it for him. That and too many girlfriends.

I glanced over at him in the passenger's seat looking down at the phone in his hands. This was normal – busy thumbs on tiny keys, a downy coating on slender knuckles that looked like corn silk in the bright sunlight. He might have been Tweeting or stealing the formula for Coca-Cola or making the garage doors in his neighborhood go up and down. One can never be sure where Neil's perpetual boredom and freakishly overdeveloped technological skills will lead him.

We took I-85 North out of the city with the top down in my old Impala, sped past exit ramps with office parks, chain restaurants, furniture outlets, and shopping malls that became sparse as we moved farther north toward rolling farmland and orchards and long stretches of forests.

We split off on 985 and crossed Lake Lanier on 129. I pulled into a filling station. I needed to suck it up and call my mother, and I knew she would not appreciate the background noise of my convertible. Neil lifted his head, took in our surroundings briefly – gas pumps, convenience store, racks of propane tanks for rent – and went back to his phone.

'Hi, Mom.'

'Keye? What's wrong?'

I floundered. 'I just thought I'd say hi.' Neil looked at me.

I heard the screen door open at my parents' house. I'd heard it a million times, same door, the one going to the back deck. My father had cans of WD-40 in strategic locations, one just outside the door my mother had pushed open, and he could quiet creaky hardware in the wink of an eye – a quick-draw Clint Eastwood with an oil can and a flathead screwdriver.

'Howard, it's your daughter calling to say hi. Do you remember the last time she called *just* to say hi?' An indecipherable grunt from my father. 'No you don't, because your daughter *never* calls *just* to say hi.' The hinges squeaked again. Mother was back inside. 'I swear I don't know why I even bother to speak to him. He's so full of himself lately. Ever since he sold another one of those metal sculptures. And to an art gallery, Keye. Can you imagine? For thousands of dollars! Now all he says are things like *target audience* and *the World Wide Web*. Lord help us.' Mother's buttery southern accent was heating up. Emily Street always became more southern when she was in the middle of transforming herself – outrage, courage, martyrdom, offense – Mother deftly seized any opportunity. She was a born actress. 'I've got your father out on the deck right now blistering some poblanos. Might as well put that torch to good use.'

'Mother, he's getting thousands a pop for his sculptures. It sounds like he's putting it to work just fine.'

'Thousands a pop? I swear, Keye. Where did you learn to talk like that?' She paused. 'You're going somewhere dangerous, aren't you? That's why you're calling. No, don't tell me.'

'It's not dangerous.'

'You always say that. What kind of riffraff are you chasing after this time?'

'I don't know yet.'

'We've told everyone you'll be here with Aaron for the big neighborhood barbeque.'

'I'm sorry, Mom. Rauser has an impossible caseload right now. And I really needed to take this job up north.'

'Well, at least his work is important.'

'There goes another year of therapy.'

Mother fake laughed. 'Oh please! You are not that fragile, Keye. And why do you have to call him Rauser? Why can't you call him by his name? I'll tell you why. Because *Rauser* is impersonal. It's exactly like Dan said. You have a problem with intimacy.' *Zing*. Score one – Dan, ex-husband, sensitive area. Intimacy – a slam dunk.

'I learned it from the best,' I said, and the bitterness in my voice surprised even me.

'What is that supposed to mean?' Mother pounced. 'And you wonder why relationships are difficult! Maybe that's what you should be talking about in therapy instead of your parents, who worked hard their whole lives to take care of you and your brother.'

'Okay, well, this has been really fun. Listen, Mother, I need you to check on Miki and White Trash at my house, okay? I'll only be gone a couple of days. Will you just call and make sure she's taking care of my cat? And if she's not, will you?'

'What's wrong with Miki? I just spoke to her the day before yesterday.'

'There was a break-in at her house. She seems, well, jumpy. She's staying at my place while I'm gone.'

'Oh my Lord. Was she hurt? What happened?'

'She's fine. She wasn't hurt. Maybe you should call her,' I suggested.

'I'll invite her over for our cookout. I'm making black-eyed pea and roasted poblano salsa, butterbean humus, tomato-and-eggplant bruschetta with artichoke pesto, and we're going to grill some pizzas and pile them up with arugula and feta.' Emily Street was self-taught, but she could flat-out cook her ass off. A line formed at her door when she was testing new recipes.

Her voice turned sugary and singsongy. 'I just can't decide which of your favorites I should make. Peach empanadas with homemade crème fraiche ice cream or red velvet whoopie pies.'

My mouth watered. First of all, we know how to grow peaches down South. They are meaty and sweet, and when they're lightly cooked, all that juice runs out and seeps into the pastry, and it will damn near take your head off. And red velvet cake, well, when it's done just right, it's a southern delicacy. No picnic or family gathering I could remember came without it. Of course my mother had to put her own spin on everything. Over the years that peach pie on the checkered tablecloth evolved into a plate of gorgeous empanadas. The red velvet cake now comes in personal handheld sizes, with vanilla cream that squeezes out between the layers.

'Jesus. That sounds amazing.'

The door squeaked again. 'Howard, do you know your daughter just used the name of the Lord in vain?'

'Bye, Mom. Love you.'

'Keye, wait.' The screen door again. 'I have some news, and I want you to hear it from me.'

I braced myself.

'There was this video recipe contest on that cooking network, and mine won.'

'That's fantastic. What did you win?'

'The opportunity to submit an audition tape for my own cooking show. Miki knows TV people who will help me make it. My own cooking show, honey!'

'You're auditioning for a television show?'

'Isn't it wonderful? I may have to go to Hollywood.'

'Is that where they make cooking shows?'

'Okay, well, maybe New York. Or someplace.' Her voice lowered to just above a whisper. 'But you know your father won't support me. Frankly, Keye, we're moving in different directions.'

'What? It sounds like you're going in exactly the same direction. You're both beginning second careers and finding things that make you happy. Lots of couples do it, Mom. Dad always liked you doing your own thing.' He liked it when she stayed busy and left him alone, but I decided not to say that.

'Maybe you're right, honey. But I tell you one thing, nobody's going to get in my way. I'm going to be the next Paula Deen.' She paused. 'Only prettier.'

I laughed. 'What does the current Paula Deen think about that?'

'Oh come on, Keye. She's in so much hot water. You know that slot is going to open up.'

'Bye, Mom. I love you.' I disconnected and leaned my head back on the seat. '*God.*'

'So how's Emily?' Neil was smiling at me.

'Brutal. She's a hammer. A friggin' ice pick in the eye.'

Neil and my mother had terrible chemistry when they first met. They had each later complained privately to me about the other's rudeness. But last year when all hell broke loose, Neil stepped up and ran the business and Mother came onboard to handle the phones and filing and billing. Miraculously, they ended up liking each other.

'She's . . . the . . . pick . . .' Neil was speaking in that strange, choppy way that let me know he was typing the words as he said them. 'And I'm the ice.'

'You're Tweeting that?'

'New Facebook status,' he said. 'Forty-five people "like" it already.'

I pulled back out on the road and followed a shady, muscadine-laced two-lane past split-rail fences, fescue pastures, and grazing horses. The magnolias were blooming, and that citrusy scent drifted into the open car, bringing with it the particulars of my southern childhood. I remember sitting under the enormous magnolia tree in our Winnona Park backyard with Jimmy, smelling that delicious scent – like lemon cream and butter. We tried picking them for Mother's table, pulling flowers off the tree by their short, fat stems without touching them. She had warned us that magnolia blossoms weep when touched by humans. And sure enough, everywhere our tiny fingers accidentally grasped a lush white petal, a brown spot appeared to betray us. And something else – that tree and those big, fragrant blossoms are my earliest memories of coming home with my new parents after losing my grandparents, after the terror of seeing them murdered, and the terror of living with strangers – a temporary foster home, a children's home. I thought about the wailing woman whose child had been strangled last night and the way the grief webs out through your life.

'It's the next right,' Neil said, looking down at the map on one of his devices.

White fences surrounded the property. A guard shack sat square in the middle of a two-way entry/exit, painted white with its own little fence to match the others, a miniature Cape Cod design. A uniformed guard came through the door when we stopped, waddled down the steps with a clipboard in his hand. No weapon, I noticed.

'How can I help you?' He was in his forties, thinning hair, his eyes looked puffy. A second job, I thought. This one couldn't pay much.

'Hi.' I smiled. 'We're going to eight-twenty-eight Murdock.'

'Mr Tilison's residence?' He glanced down at his clipboard. 'Name, please.'

'Keye Street.'

He glanced up at me. 'I'm sorry, ma'am. I don't see you on the guest list. Was Mr Tilison expecting you?'

'It's a surprise,' I said, truthfully.

The guard smiled indulgently. 'Yes, ma'am. Mr Tilison gets a lot of surprise visitors. I'm real sorry. But I can't let y'all in unless you're on the list.' He glanced at Neil.

I showed him my identification, which had the state seal, the secretary of state's printed signature, my business name, and my name and address. I had a badge too, but decided not to break it out.

He handed it back. 'Same agency gave you that licenses security personnel. I got one almost just like it.'

'This concerns a friend of Mr Tilison's,' I said. 'It really is important I speak with him.'

'I am sorry, Ms Street, but I'm going to have to ask you to leave.'

'Neil, would you mind getting Cash on the phone, please?' I wasn't thrilled about tipping Tilison off. I wanted to surprise him, judge his steadiness with an unscheduled visit. But unless I ran the barricade and dinged up my currently unblemished Impala, it didn't look like I was going to get inside.

Neil punched in the number Miki had given us. The sun was heating up, beating down on us. He handed me the phone. 'Mr Tilison, my name is Keye Street. I'd like to speak to you about Miki Ashton.'

'About Miki? What about Miki?'

I recognized his howdy-ma'am country-singer voice. I'd

heard it in television interviews. 'I'm at the guard shack. Would you mind instructing security to open the gate?'

The call came half a minute later, the arm lifted, and we pulled in to Cash's multimillion-dollar neighborhood – a honeymoon of Old South and new money, with three-acre lots, weeping willows bending over garden bridges and koi ponds, gigantic shoreline homes overlooking Lake Lanier. And so far out of my price range I couldn't have hit it with a high-powered scope.

We found the address and pulled into a long driveway. The antenna on my old ragtop teased a row of twilight crepe myrtles and the blossoms drifted into my open convertible like lavender snowflakes. Tilison's limestone mansion shimmered with the water behind it like it was the end of the rainbow.

I parked in a circular drive in front of the house. We both got out. I looked back at my car and decided it looked good in this neighborhood. My sixty-nine Impala was in perfect condition, thanks to my dad, who'd pieced it back together after some bad luck last year – a serial killer with a tire tool and an angry subpoena recipient with a thirty-eight. Just so happens, as my dad loves to point out, I'm just as tough on cars sober as I was as a practicing drunk. *Thanks, Dad.* Why do people enjoy reminding you of the past? And when I say 'people', I mean parents. They hold on to *everything*. Doesn't matter if you've recovered from alcohol, Jehovah witnessing, an attraction to guys in ball-gags, or once had a bout with gender dysphoria, your parents will clobber you with it eventually. And given the tiniest opening, they will share it with whomever you've decided to bring home for dinner.

Cash Tilison came out his front door in western boots, a short-sleeve T-shirt that hugged his biceps and pumped-up pecs and was tucked into blue jeans. Thick crop of reddish-brown hair, brown eyes, wide-shouldered and tall. *Yum.* Just my type. Well, except for the stalker thing. And the Miki thing. Oh, and the Rauser thing. But, hey, it does not hurt to look, right? Neil elbowed me. I think my jaw had dropped a little.

'Cash Tilison.' He extended his hand to me, then to Neil. I introduced them. 'So tell me Miki's all right.'

'There was a break-in at her house Thursday night,' I said.

He stopped. 'Oh God. Was she hurt?' He was leading us down a sidewalk that twisted around the house. I saw a terraced rock garden, a pond, a bridge, a limestone patio with stone bar that matched the house. An elaborate outdoor kitchen.

'No.'

'Thank the Lord for that.' We walked up stone steps to the patio. He gestured toward the chairs. 'So how can I help? Why didn't Miki call me herself? How do you know her?'

'Where were you Thursday night, Mr Tilison?'

'Where was I?' He looked confused. 'Who are you again?'

'My name is Keye Street. I'm a private investigator.' I didn't want to tell him Miki was my cousin. I wasn't ready to give up anything that a stalker could use later.

'Miki hired a PI to find out who broke into her house?'

'Where did you say you were Thursday night?'

'You think *I* broke into her house?' He started to laugh. 'Oh that's sweet! Why on earth would I do that? First of all,

I don't need to rob houses for a living. I'm doing pretty good, as you can see.' He gestured to the excessive mansion we'd seen only from outside. 'Secondly, I have a key.'

He leaned back, crossed an ankle over a knee, and grinned at me. 'I don't mean to be rude, but I hope you know how ridiculous this is, Ms Street. Does Miki know you're here?'

'No.'

'I didn't think so.' He laughed again, shook his head. 'Why aren't the cops asking the questions?'

'Nothing was stolen,' Neil said.

'So what was the point of the break-in?' Tilison wanted to know.

'Miki mentioned that after the two of you discontinued your relationship, you had some trouble adjusting,' I said, ignoring his question.

He looked at me, looked at Neil. 'We didn't discontinue our relationship. We're still in a relationship. We're friends.'

'So when you were calling her even after she asked you to stop,' I said, 'and stalking her while she was working and leaving messages saying she was a cold bitch, that was because of your friendship?'

Tilison uncrossed long legs and sat forward. Color hit his face and neck, but he stayed cool. 'Look, I fell in love with Miki.' He clasped big hands. 'It was hard to accept at first that she didn't return my feelings. I made a whole lot of mistakes. I admit that. I acted like an arrogant ass. But we moved past it. I've apologized for the way I behaved.'

'Did you come back here after your fund-raiser Thursday night? I believe it ended at nine.' I looked at Neil for confirmation. He nodded.

'As a matter of fact, I stayed in Atlanta. I drove back yesterday morning.' The singer's tone had grown icy.

'Were you alone?'

'I don't have to answer that.'

'Miki came in late,' I said. 'There was a guy about your size, Mr Tilison, standing inside her house.'

'I resent the hell out of the implication.'

'And no evidence of a break-in. It's almost like he had a key.'

Cash Tilison came out of his chair, an impressive sight. He was about a foot taller than I was, and his nostrils had started to flare. I didn't mind. Sometimes you have to punch a few holes in the bag and see what falls out. 'You're on the wrong scent, Ms Street. Just so you know. And this is a waste of my time.' He walked to a set of French doors off the patio, turned the handle, and went inside. We watched him cross over marble floors.

'So what do you think?' Neil asked.

'Gorgeous,' I said. 'Makes me want to listen to country music.'

'Wow. Why don't you just totally objectify the guy.'

We headed back down granite slab steps, through the rock garden, and back to the Impala. 'He still has a fierce attachment. You see how he reacted when I mentioned discontinuing the relationship? It doesn't mean he's stalking her, though. Not sure I bought the contrition act. Embarrassment, maybe. But after so many months of calm with Miki, it doesn't make sense. How 'bout you? Any thoughts?'

'Yeah,' Neil said. 'I think you should skip applying for diplomatic service.'

8

We drove another hour through gently rising landscape into the foothills, then twisting mountain roads took us into Creeklaw County and Big Knob, a battle site during the Civil War, according to the historic markers. A sign pointed the way to a Confederate cemetery. A mountain wall rose up on one side of the narrow main street. Gift shops advertised authentic Native American jewelry, and property rental offices built to look like log cabins dotted the stretch of land between the mountain and the road. On our right, Lake Chatuge cut a deep blue gash into the lush mountains. Boat docks and gear rentals, walking piers and fish houses lined the banks in downtown Big Knob. Vendors sold funnel cakes off carts, and a pontoon with a *Rent Me* sign was anchored next to a restaurant with a full patio. The air was spicy with lake fish and fried dough. Jet Skis and sailboats skirted the lake. Lake Chatuge's advertised one hundred thirty miles of stunning shoreline went on far beyond our line of sight. Traffic was heavy and slow, lots of stoplights. We'd go like hell for fifty feet, then sit for a couple of minutes. The town looked like it was about to burst its seams. It had never crossed my mind that Big Knob was a big deal on a holiday weekend. This might have been good news. For once everyone seemed to be dressed like Neil.

'So how does it work, exactly?' Neil's first words in nearly thirty minutes startled me. 'The crematory, I mean.'

I looked at him. 'That's what you've been thinking about all this time?'

'Is it just, like, a big, long oven?'

'Kind of.'

Neil thought about that. 'With rollers to slide a casket in?'

'I think a lot of the time it's just some big cardboard coffin. I'm not sure how they load them.'

I focused on a Confederate flag in the back window of the pickup truck in front of us and felt my anger spike. There has been a good, long debate down South about this flag and its current appropriateness. People who fly it claim it's about Georgia's rich history, about state's rights and southern identity. *Bullshit*. Everyone knows what it's really about. Whatever the flag meant once to the Confederate States, the Civil War South, for people of color it came to represent prejudice and terror, pure and simple. It has been marched down the street on the shoulders of hooded Klansmen. It was used as a symbol of white supremacy by Strom Thurmond supporters during his segregationist presidential bid in '48. After that, everyone knew what the Confederate flag had been turned into. If I could, I'd set fire to every one of them. Screw free speech.

'So there's just a pile of ashes left?' Neil said again, obsessing. It was wearing a little thin.

'Okay, so what's the fascination with the crematory?'

He shrugged and didn't answer for a while. My car moved a full twenty-five feet in traffic. There was a nice breeze coming off the lake. 'I guess I'm just wondering about the person whose job it is to do all that,' he finally admitted. 'I mean, here's a man who knows how hot a fire has to be to burn flesh and bone. What do you think he talks about after work? He probably has, like, trade publications about cooking people and catalogs for creepy instruments. He knows all about disposing of the dead, this guy. You think he just sees bodies now? Like maybe in the beginning he saw people who had lives and stuff but now he just sees some dead flesh to be disposed of.'

'*God,*' I said, and looked at him. 'I'm so glad I asked.'

The truck in front of me with the Confederate flag stopped suddenly, even though there was plenty of space in front of it. I jammed my foot on the brake pedal. Neil's phone and a couple of other devices flew out of his hands and landed on the floorboard. He cursed.

In the pickup, a teenage boy was leaning out his window, talking to a group of girls on the sidewalk. He had thick biceps, a crew cut, a dangling earring that picked up the sun. The driver got involved. Everyone was chatting and laughing. The light ahead changed to green and more space opened up in front of the truck. My heart was still doing a hundred and fifty after nearly driving up his tailpipe, so I didn't find any of it particularly endearing. I laid on my horn.

The passenger door opened. *Oh boy.* A big number seven sat squarely in the center of the boy's chest on a sky-blue football jersey. 'What's your problem, lady?' he yelled back at us. He was wide-shouldered and thick-necked.

'Oh great, get our ass kicked by rednecks. Good thinking,' Neil mumbled.

The young man shaded his eyes with one hand and squinted, then leaned into the truck and said something to the driver. The driver's door opened, and he got out too. Same color jersey, thicker neck and shoulders, a double-digit number. There was a lot of conversation, looking back at us, nodding. Neil and I exchanged an uncertain look.

Number Seven yelled to the girls on the sidewalk he'd been flirting with, 'Hey, it's the Booger Bandit Bounty Hunter!'

'Oh shit.' I sank down low in the driver's seat. Heads turned our way from traffic, from pavement cafés, from the sidewalk.

'What the hell?' Neil wanted to know.

'Miki YouTubed a bond-enforcement job,' I grouched. 'I'm never taking her with me again.'

Neil typed something into his tablet. Chipmunk-like sounds came from tiny speakers. His shoulders began to shake. 'This is hilarious. *Ooohh*. Look at that. This thing has gone totally viral. *Awesome.*'

So much for blending in. The car behind us honked and the guys in the truck finally got back in, but Number Seven pressed his face up against the back window and pressed a knuckle into his nostril so it looked like his finger was jammed up there. Neil laughed. We inched forward another few yards. I found a crack in traffic and turned off the main drag. We went about three blocks, then turned right on Chatuge Drive. This is where Big Knob lifted its tourist mask. Here, all the makeup came off and the town's support staff came home to squat frame houses in need of paint jobs, broken-down cars, and oil-stained driveways.

'So back to the ovens.' Neil was still on the crematory thing. 'A body goes in and a little pile of ashes rolls out?'

'It's not ashes, Neil. Basic elements like calcium don't burn. It's bone fragments, mostly. Pulverized.'

This seemed to shut him up. He looked away. We found the suspension bridge that would get us to Highway 75, which twisted through the mountains toward the North Carolina line. There was a distinct change in real estate after we crossed the bridge. No more glitzy tourist town. No cement-block foundations and beat-up cars either. This was the resort community Quinn had talked about – gated communities with huge homes, lake views, and immaculate lawns, surrounded by mountains and golf courses. A discreet sign in muted colors at the entrance of one of the lakeside communities went almost unseen until we passed: *Water's Edge, from the Low 3.5s.*

Neil had pulled up satellite imagery of the area. 'Crematory's about three miles north. The hotel's coming up on our left. I'm starving. Can we get some lunch and get checked in?'

It had been awhile since I'd had a partner. I'm fine with teamwork. You have to learn how to function as a unit in the field. The Bureau had drilled this into me. But I wasn't happy about my current partner's nutritional requirements. I would have been just fine scoping out the crematory grounds, maybe finding a few neighbors at home, poking around a little, and locating Billy and Brenda Wade and their urn full of fake ashes. I glanced at Neil. He looked pouty.

We rounded a turn and saw rising up over flowering gardens and a rolling green golf course the Big Knob Resort and Spa – an enormous granite slab lodge, part railway hotel, part castle, nestled in the southern Appalachians and staring at the vast blue waters of Lake Chatuge. I slowed the car. We gazed at it.

Neil brightened. 'Larry booked this?'

'He did. Said everything else was full.'

'Least he could do after he sent you to find that cow at some lesbian colony last year.'

'It wasn't a colony. It was a *couple* that owned the cabin where I stayed.'

He grinned at me. 'Fun to think about, though.'

I pulled onto the long drive that led to the Big Knob Resort and Spa. Golfers, two to a cart, cruised over the paved paths next to the green. 'What's the appeal, anyway? I don't get the obsession men have with lesbians.'

'It's about challenge, Keye. We'll pretty much do anything that moves. The cat stops purring when I walk in.'

The lobby was furnished with heavy wood, claret rugs, a high beamed ceiling. A couple of huge granite fireplaces that probably burned all winter were unlit now. We were told our adjoining rooms were ready even though we were here way in advance of the official three-o'clock check-in time. My room was small but nice, more lodge than hotel, crowded with heavy furniture. A mahogany four-poster bed was angled in one corner with a view of the lake. I pulled the covers back and checked the sheets and the mattress. Don't judge. The bedbug thing really gives me the creeps.

My feet didn't reach the woven rug on the floor when I sat on the edge of the high bed. I sat there for a minute, glanced at the wrist that had been sliced open the night a killer broke into my bedroom with a knife. I remembered letting my 10mm loose, blood spatter and tissue flying at me, filling my nose and mouth, the killer's carotid artery gushing wide open like black oil spilling out into the dark night. And the taste – unlike anything I'd ever known.

Why was it taking so long to get past the memories? I'd spent most of my adult life learning about sadists and psychopaths, profiling their crimes, their victims' seemingly unendurable pain. So many people had been through so much worse than I had ever suffered. They'd grown and become healthy and whole again. On most days, it's like the scar on my wrist; it's healed over, unthought-of. But when it hits, it's as blunt and ruthless and unexpected as the killer who shook my trust and almost took my life that night. And just for those few moments, I'm in it. I'd studied psychology and criminology. I am a PhD, for Christ's sake. I didn't need Dr Shetty to tell me that something as simple as noticing that scar could act as an external cue and spark me to reexperience the trauma. The mind has a terrible time processing an act of violence perpetrated by another human. I'd noticed the changes in me, observed myself swinging from heightened anxiety and hypervigilance to a kind of psychic numbness. I recognized the symptoms of post-traumatic stress. Seeing them for what they were – memories, flashbacks, reactivity, psychological distress – was what kept me mentally sound. My professional self understood it was happening *inside* me. I wanted to move past it. But my obsessive addict's brain had found something new to latch hold of. 'No, no. Don't blame yourself,' Dr Shetty would have said. 'That's part of the problem.'

I was mentally addressing invitations to my pity party when I heard a tap at the door that joined my room to Neil's. I opened it and saw blond eyelashes peeking out behind a smooth coating of dark grayish-green facial mask. To keep his hair off his forehead, he had twisted it up with one of those fuzzy rubber bands. It stuck straight up on top of his head Pebbles Flintstone–style. I was reminded of how much I loved the men in my life – my dad, Rauser, Neil, Jimmy – and how silly they were.

I stood there staring. I was utterly speechless. His skin was drawn so tight he had that weird wide-mouth post-plastic surgery look. He was wearing a white hotel robe with *Big Knob Resort and Spa* embroidered over crossed golf clubs. Behind him, his espresso maker was on the dresser next to a yellow-and-red Café Bustelo can. His socks were folded and lined up on the bed with his other clothes, an impressive collection of hair- and skin-care products, and a snakeskin shaving kit. I don't unpack when I travel anymore. The bedbug thing. Until they bring back DDT, my shit stays in my suitcase.

Neil spoke through clenched teeth without moving his mouth. 'I knee ten ninits.'

'Ninits?' I laughed.

He asked again for ten minutes and heard himself this time. He tried to squash the smile that was causing creases in the plaster at the corners of his mouth. A section of mask flaked off his right cheek. We watched it float to the pine floors.

'Can I borrow a tampon?' I asked, and Neil swung the door closed in my face.

9

We crossed over the suspension bridge and drove back into another one of the neighborhoods skirting Big Knob's touristy downtown, a hidden community visitors would probably never see. The pavement stopped, and we went for a hundred yards over a sandy one-lane that ended at a gate with a wooden sign. *Lakeshore Gardens,* it said, in pastel green and pink. We peered past the entrance at a trailer park with neither a lake nor garden. Children were out playing. I saw a couple of bright plastic Big Wheels, bikes lying on their side or propped against trailers, more sand and dirt, a few small tomato gardens, some folding chairs.

'They know we're coming, right?' Neil asked. He'd been fully coffeed, facialed, and stuffed with catfish and jalapeño hush puppies at the resort restaurant. 'That whole thing with the cowboy was really stressful.'

'*Aww.* Didn't the facial help you relax?' I reached across and touched his check. '*Nice.* Baby soft too.'

He slapped my hand away as we pulled up to a white

mobile home with burgundy trim bottom and top. A small built-on deck made from the same raw wood that had been used for the three steps led to the front door.

We got out. 'Mr Wade?' I said to the man on the deck scrubbing a grill with a wire brush.

'My daddy is Mr Wade. I'm Billy.' He smiled and brushed his hands off on well-worn jeans. He was thin, had a mustache, hair below the collar, and an accent so thick Wade sounded like *Waa-aid*. He came down the steps and extended his hand. 'You must be Mr Quinn's investigators.'

'Thank you for seeing us today.' I shook his hand. 'I'm Keye Street and this is Neil Donovan.'

Billy Wade invited us inside the double-wide. The metal door opened into the living room. Billy veered off to the refrigerator. 'Brenda's in the back somewhere. Can I get you something? I got beer and water.'

'I'm good. Thanks.'

'I'll take a beer,' Neil said.

Billy Wade delivered a Bud Light in a can to Neil and kept one for himself. Two pop-tops went off almost simultaneously. 'Come sit down,' Billy said. 'Honey,' he called out. 'They're here.'

'Nice place,' Neil said, as we sat down on a tweedy Rooms To Go couch. Two chairs matched it. The heavy coffee table with a place for magazines matched the entertainment center. The trailer was spotless. Photographs of Billy and Brenda's wedding, the two of them on the beach in bathing suits, Brenda with curves and wavy dark hair – L'Oréal black #3 – were lined up on a shelf braced by metal brackets. There was Billy with spindly white legs sticking out of baggy trunks and hair halfway down his back on a beach.

Another with Billy and Brenda, arms around the other's waist, NASCAR caps, smiling at the camera, with a race track behind them, Brenda's shirt tail tied up, showing cleavage.

'That's my wife,' Billy said, following my eyes. He raised his voice. 'Honey, we got company.'

I smiled. 'She's really lovely.'

'She sure is.' He took a sip of beer.

'Mr Wade . . . Billy, we need to talk about your mother's ashes. I'm so sorry for your loss. Can you tell me how you discovered the mistake and what happened then?' Quinn had given me the skeleton version. I wanted to make sure I understood the facts as the Wades interpreted them.

'I'll tell you what happened.' I felt the trailer rock in the same way an overpass sways a little in heavy traffic. I heard Brenda's voice coming down the narrow hallway. And then she appeared. Same face as in the photographs, but let's just say Brenda's weight had gotten away from her since the wedding. Hey, I don't judge. I glanced at the end-table picture of them at the racetrack. Admittedly, North Georgia skinny and city skinny is not the same thing, but in this small, honeysuckle-kissed pocket of the Georgia mountains where a Ford F-150 means you're knocking 'em dead and church and line dancing are the main activities, Brenda had been a compact little hottie. She took one of the chairs, knees popping like rice cereal when she bent them to sit. 'I heard a loud crash,' she said, without bothering with introductions. 'And I ran out here and found him standing in the kitchen, looking down at the floor.'

'Brenda doesn't like a lot of noise inside,' Billy interjected.

She didn't skip a beat. 'And I said, "Billy, did you spill your *own* mama's ashes?" And then we started looking close and realized something was really *wrong.*'

Billy scooted his chair close to hers and put his hand on her arm in that perfectly easy way couples reach for each other. 'We scooped it all up and sent it to the lab when the funeral director said he couldn't help and that crematory operator wouldn't take our calls,' he told us.

'You mind giving me the name of the funeral home?' I asked.

Brenda got up and went to the kitchen, pulled open a kitchen drawer, and brought me a business card. 'We just wanna know what happened to Shelia Marlene's remains. We're old-fashioned about these things. We feel like we have to put our dead to rest.'

Neil shifted in his seat, tilted back the beer.

'It's my understanding you did eventually get hold of the crematory operator,' I told them. 'Is that right?'

Brenda nodded. 'He said he hired some help and this so-called employee somehow destroyed the remains.' Her tone made it abundantly clear she wasn't buying the story.

'You have questions about the employee.'

Brenda shook her wavy L'Oréal allover color. 'There's never been any employees up there. It's been a family business as long as I can remember. The Kirkpatricks been here a long time. Our kids go to the same school. Everybody knows everybody's business. But Joe Ray's not like his daddy. Everybody in town loved Mr Kirkpatrick.'

'And Joe Ray Kirkpatrick reimbursed you for your expenses?' I asked, and Brenda nodded. 'Did he ask you to agree to drop it?'

'We didn't sign anything,' Billy said. 'He didn't ask outright, but it was kind of implied. We said we understood. I guess that sounds like an agreement. But we weren't thinking straight. Once we thought about it, it sounded suspicious. It's not about money now. We need peace, and so does my mama.'

'Do you know anyone else that used the same funeral home and crematory?'

'Just about everybody in Big Knob uses the same funeral home. And Northeast Georgia Crematorium serves people in two or three states. Unless they bury their dead,' Brenda told us.

Neil took another long pull from his beer.

'Are you thinking of asking people for their urns to test what they got too? Oh my Lord. I wouldn't want to put anyone else through this,' Brenda told us.

'And you received a written report from an independent laboratory analyzing the contents of the urn, is that right?' I asked.

'Yes we did,' Brenda answered. 'We have it in a fireproof safe.'

'Would you mind jotting down the name of the lab? Was it close by?'

'Pretty close,' Billy said. 'Only took two days.'

'And it was cement mix and chicken feed,' I said.

Billy and Brenda exchanged a glance. Billy squeezed her hand. 'We couldn't believe it,' she said. 'None of it made sense.'

'Larry Quinn said the employee spilled the ashes, replaced them with cement mix to cover, and accidentally got them mixed in with the chicken feed,' I said.

'We could forgive that. As horrible as it is, accidents happen.' Brenda shook her head. 'When you see the layout of the place you'll understand. The crematorium is on the other side of the property from the barns and the residence. If Joe Ray Kirkpatrick ever did have an employee, there's no reason he'd be up at the house.'

'Maybe he doubled as a farm hand,' Neil suggested.

Brenda pointed a short, thick finger at him. 'Joe Ray Kirkpatrick did something to Miss Shelia's remains. I feel it in my bones and so does Billy. It's not enough to lose somebody, but then . . .' She trailed off, her wide eyes filled with tears.

'I'm sorry. It must have been quite a shock—'

'More than a shock, Ms Street. It's a downright outrage. All that chicken feed in Mama's urn. I mean, holy shit.' Billy made the sign of the cross. 'Mama *hated* chickens.'

10

Walking out of the trailer where there had been almost no natural light and into the bright blue day was a welcome change. Billy and Brenda kept their space neat and clean, but it was closing in on me.

We eased the car back over the sandy drive past mobile homes in varying condition, some spanking new and some dappled with age spots and mold along the bottom edges.

'That was totally weird,' Neil remarked, as we pulled back onto the pavement.

'Tell me about it.' I looked across the car at him. He had his arms folded over his chest like he was cold. It was at least ninety degrees. 'Brenda and Billy have a hunch, and we have a reputable local businessman who explained, apologized, and reimbursed them. Be interesting to find out if there's really anything here.'

'If she said something about *the dead* one more time, I was going to hurl. Creepy.'

'It's obviously emotional. It must dredge up all kinds of feelings.' I handed him the business card Brenda Wade had given me for Reuters Funeral Care and Chapel. 'You think you can get their client list? I need to find an urn that came out of that crematory around the same time Shelia Wade was cremated. I'm thinking we need a feel for what was coming out of Northeast Georgia Crematorium that week. It's a place to start.'

We headed back to the hotel. I needed to change into something slightly more official. Neil got busy as soon as we arrived, trying to figure out if the funeral home the Wades had used was automated. There were three funeral homes in Creeklaw County. Two of them had websites. One of them was Reuters Funeral Care and Chapel in Big Knob. They had a slick website that advertised a 'beautifully landscaped and peaceful memorial garden.' They'd acted as a middleman for hundreds of cremations.

'*Score,*' Neil said. This was accompanied by something that looked vaguely like an end-zone dance. 'I went in through the admin function on their website. Simple password script. Opened up the whole system.'

'I have no idea what that means,' I told him, then listened while he rattled off some details. What I should have said was I have no *interest* in what that means. I tuned out the rest of the techno-gibberish and changed into navy slacks and a chalk-stripe blazer. Probably wouldn't get me a lot of leering, but it did have 'urn company representative' written all over it.

A few minutes later we left the resort and climbed into the Impala, top up. We had to pass through downtown Big Knob, and I couldn't take another YouTube party.

Neil had his electronic devices out, and he was balancing a hotel coffee mug. 'This is going to be one of those three-hour-tour things, isn't it? Big Knob's the *Minnow* and you're Ginger and I'm the professor and we're never getting off the island.'

'You see me as Ginger? Really?' I glanced at myself in the rearview.

We passed through Big Knob without incident and headed south on a shady blacktop, passing lots of grazing cattle and painted barns. I turned onto a paved driveway bordered by white-fenced pastures and headed toward a long ranch house with azaleas lined up under the windows. A carport on the left side of the house held two cars. A jeep was parked behind them. I smelled a grill as soon as I opened the car door.

'Hope it works,' Neil said, and climbed into the driver's seat. We'd learned from experience that having a driver in place is a good idea. 'They're not going to be thrilled. I can tell you that.'

'Thanks for the positive affirmation,' I said, and grabbed my briefcase off the backseat.

'You look nice, by the way.' Neil leaned on the window and smiled at me. 'The business-suit thing always makes me want to mess up your hair.'

'Not going to happen.' I gave him a wink, then walked to the carport door. Front doors are for strangers. I avoided the doorbell for the same reason. It goes off, the dogs go off, and what registers is: unfamiliar person. I was hoping for a nice, friendly feeling.

I tapped on the door and waited, then cupped my hands against the glass-paned door and peeked inside – a lived-in kitchen, bags of chips on the island, a cutting board with traces of green and a couple of avocado shells, tomato seeds, lemons. A covered bowl with traces of dark green guacamole, some empty beer bottles. Beyond that, a den with heavy wood, very traditional décor, glass doors with the grill I'd smelled behind them, a few people in patio chairs with puffy cushions.

I walked around the side of the house. The first thing I noticed on turning the corner was the big, square, black head lifting up off the wood deck, then the growl, then the bark. The rottweiler was down the steps in two seconds flat and loping straight at me. I heard a couple of people yelling at him through a rush of pure terror. Coarse black fur stood up in a ridge down his back and glistened in the sunlight. He had a head about the size of a mailbox.

'Tank, *halt*!' A male voice broke through his frenzied charge. Tank stopped on a dime three feet away, licked his lips. His coffee-brown eyes rolled up at me. He started to pant.

'Hi, Tank.' My voice had a little tremble in it, and it was three octaves higher. Tank's little black nub tail made a couple of spins. 'It's okay, boy.' Voice coming back to normal. Tank's tail started to spin like a propeller, then his entire body had started to wag. I stretched my arm out. 'Good boy. Okay, come on.'

He rushed me like some kind of heat-seeking missile, jammed his nose between my legs, and practically lifted me up off the ground. He was making snorting sounds. I heard laughing from the deck. '*Tank*. Back off,' commanded a middle-aged white guy in jeans and a T-shirt who was walking quickly toward me. He had a hard beer belly, like he'd swallowed a basketball, and bright blue eyes. Tank sat down, ogled me longingly.

I tried to recover some dignity. 'Mr Huckaby?'

'Yes, ma'am, I am. What can I do you for?'

The deck was silent now, watching Huckaby greet the person who had just interrupted their cookout. 'My name is Keye Street. I'm with the Sunset Journeys Urn Company out of Chattanooga.' I said it quietly, but I let all my southern run loose so everything sounded like it had a question mark on the end. I try to keep a handle on the accent most of the time, since *southern* equals *dumbshit* to most of the world. But I'd heard Huckaby's accent, and I had the idea he'd trust me more readily. 'I'm sorry to intrude, but I was in the area and I happened to see your address on a list of people who purchased one of our urns from your funeral-care provider. I'm very sorry for your loss.'

'Could you get to the point, Miss Street? I've got rib eyes waiting.'

'Well, this is awkward, sir. We've had some trouble with that particular style of urn flaking and contaminating the cremains.'

Huckaby's smile widened. He grabbed a quick look over his shoulder, lowered his voice. 'My mother-in-law was mean as a water moccasin. *She's* the only thing contaminating those ashes. I don't give a rat's behind what happens to her.'

I tried a different approach. 'What I'm trying to say, Mr Huckaby, is that if the urn is dramatically eroding, then your mean-as-a-snake mother-in-law might end up in a pile on the carpet. Would Mrs Huckaby give a rat's behind about *that*?'

Tank whined a little. I tried not to look at him for fear he'd see it as encouragement. He nuzzled Huckaby's hand.

'What exactly do you want?' Huckaby's smile had disappeared, and so had a few of the good-old-boy layers.

'A small sample of the ashes for our lab.' I held my index finger and thumb a quarter inch apart. 'Tiny sample, really.'

Someone yelled from the deck for him to hurry up. 'Look, lady, my wife cried for two weeks. I don't want her stirred up again.' Huckaby scratched his head. 'Let's act like we're done here, and in a couple minutes I'll excuse myself and go inside and scoop some ashes for you.'

A long strand of drool hung from one corner of Tank's wide mouth and stretched toward the ground. I could hear him breathing. 'I'd prefer to collect the sample myself, if you don't mind.'

'That ain't gonna happen.'

'It's important the sample isn't contaminated.'

'You're big on the contamination theme, aren't you?' He glanced over his shoulder. 'Wait for me out front.'

Neil had his laptop out when I got to the car. He'd been using Huckaby's Wi-Fi, he informed me. 'You get the ashes?'

'He's bringing a sample out. Doesn't want his wife to know.'

'Wow. I honestly didn't think you'd pull it off.'

'His rottweiler liked me a lot.'

The kitchen door opened. I met Huckaby in the carport. He'd filled a sandwich bag with grayish-white powder. 'If you find out something's wrong with that urn, you call me directly.' He gave me a piece of paper with his phone number.

I dropped the sample into another Baggie, sealed it, then closed it in my case. Neil got my boat of a car turned around and eased down Huckaby's driveway. His hands were side by side on top of the steering wheel. He was sitting erect and close to the wheel like an old person with vision problems. Neil was a notoriously slow driver. He always seemed to be on a sightseeing tour, which made him the worst getaway driver in the world. I attributed this to the elevated levels of THC in his system.

'I finished checking out Miki's neighbors like you wanted. Inman Park must be the squeakiest-clean neighborhood in town. I mean, even on social media. They're all about kids and kittens and shit. No felons, flashers, or jaywalkers. The neighborhood association did generate a few notices Miki's way about the property. The fence needs to be painted and the yard has to be maintained according to their standards. They remind her she signed agreements on move-in. I forwarded you pretty much everything and whatever I could find on the other guys she dated.'

'You did all that while I was talking to Huckaby?'

'I've been doing it since you threw all this shit at me yesterday morning. You think I'm always on Twitter or something?'

'Or stoned.'

'I really respect the fact that you confined your drug use to huge quantities of alcohol. You're kind of a role model.'

I ignored that. 'You think you can get the speedometer up over thirty-five? I'd love to get a look at the crematorium before it gets dark.'

My phone rang. I glanced at the display, an Atlanta number. 'Keye Street,' I answered.

'Ms Street, this is Milo Stanton from the Georgian Terrace Hotel.'

Uh-oh. Milo. Black-blazer concierge with the brass nameplate. Milo – minion to the manager who hates me.

'We have your cat in our office.'

'Wait wait wait. Why would you have my cat?' Neil looked over at me. 'Pull over,' I told him. 'Get Miki on the phone.'

'She was found by a guest in the tenth-floor hallway,' Milo told me. 'To my knowledge, you have the only cat in the hotel. And some of the staff seem to recognize her.'

'Miki doesn't answer,' Neil said.

'I'm two hours away,' I told the concierge. 'I'll call someone to pick her up, and I'll be there as soon as I can.'

'We really don't have a place for a cat, Ms Street. I've been instructed to call animal control.'

'Listen to me, Milo.' Heat ripped through me like lightning. I opened the passenger door and walked around the car. Neil didn't ask any questions. He got out and gave me the driver's seat. 'You tell that manager if y'all even *think* about turning my cat over to animal control when you know where she belongs and after you've notified the owner, those big, shiny buttons on your fucking blazers are going to be all over the news tonight. You hear me, buddy? Nobody likes guys that send cats to the pound. You can expect to see my cousin, Miki Ashton; my mother, Emily Street; or Lieutenant Aaron Rauser of the APD there shortly to pick her up. By the way, her name is White Trash and she likes half-and-half.' I disconnected, cursed, handed Neil my phone. 'Get Mom or Rauser for me. Jesus, why does it have to be so goddamned *hot* in Georgia?'

I spun the Impala around, and we shot down the dirt road with a trail of dust boiling behind us. I dropped Neil at the resort with the sample from Huckaby's urn and instructions to get it to the testing lab used by the Wades. All our things were at the hotel. I didn't want to take the time to pack. I didn't want to check out. I simply wanted to get home, figure out what was going on with my cousin, get back to Big Knob, and finish the job I was hired to do.

I drove with the top lowered in the hot early evening. The air felt good on overheated skin. Whistling wind, the sound of tires on pavement usually calmed me down. It wasn't working. A million thoughts were going through my mind. How had White Trash gotten loose? Had Miki gotten drunk? Was she using drugs? I thought about the food tray Marko had handed me, then coming in and finding Miki cooking dinner. What the hell was I thinking leaving her in charge of my cat and my loft? What if something had happened to her? Had the black depression that had plagued her most of her life returned? Or the man in her window? I absolutely hated it that I couldn't take her at her word, that I didn't know what was real with Miki. She was forgetting things, using dope, alcohol, refusing to take her meds. It wasn't a good combination.

Closer to Atlanta, the traffic picked up. Exhaust burned my sinuses. My hair was blowing behind me in the chemical air. I was doing ninety as I approached the city on I-85. I barely heard my phone ringing. 'Everything's all right, honey,' my mother said in her sugar-sweet southern. 'I have White Trash and Miki. They are both fine.'

'What happened?'

'Well, we don't know exactly. Somehow White Trash must have slipped out. Miki said she went to the grocery store. White Trash was here when she left.'

In all the time I'd had my bitchy cat, she'd never once rushed the door. She seemed to prefer the loft over Peachtree to the dumpster behind it where I'd found her. On the other hand, if the door was carelessly left open, she might have gone to investigate the world beyond. I started getting mad all over again. 'Why the hell isn't she answering her phone?'

'Keye Street, you need to remember who you're talking to.'

There are degrees with Mother. Two names was a warning shot. All three and you were going to get killed. I remember Jimmy and I hiding after he'd decided to trim a neighbor's prize rosebush. To the ground. *Jimmy Landon Street*. I grabbed him and pulled him under the deck, where we waited quietly until she calmed down. I later heard my parents laughing about it.

'Miki had her phone when she went shopping and she didn't have it when she got back,' my mother told me. 'That's all I know.'

'Thanks for coming to the rescue, Mom. Rauser is so busy. I'm sorry I snapped at you. It scared me.'

'I understand, honey. You love animals like I do.' Not exactly. I'm okay with just one or two at a time. More than that and *Planet of the Apes* goes dancing through my head. I thought about Mother's cat-covered porch. 'Now just go back to your . . . work,' Mother suggested. 'Everything's fine here.'

'I'm thirty minutes away, Mom. And Miki and I need to have a chat.'

'Please don't be too hard on her,' Mother whispered. 'Bless her heart. She's been through a lot.'

11

I felt the manager's hawkish eyes as I crossed the lobby at my hotel and walked toward the elevators. I was a loose cog in the complicated internal architecture at this gorgeous, historic hotel, which he commanded with the synchronization of a water gymnast. I glanced at the time display on my phone. It was after six. I had hoped the hard-working rascal would have gone home by now.

I heard my mother's voice when I opened the door. I saw her on the couch with Miki, White Trash sprawled across her lap.

Miki stood slowly, turned to me. 'Keye, I'm so, so sorry! I swear, she was fine. We were playing earlier. I was teaching her how to roll over for treats.'

Now I was sure she was lying.

'You have a trick cat, honey,' my mother added.

'I saw her before I closed the door,' Miki said. 'I *know* she was inside. I *know* she was. I'm so sorry you had to come back.'

My cousin's eyes were wide. She looked sober. I saw the

worry and dread on her face. It totally took the air out of me. 'Look,' I said, 'it's been a really stressful time. I shouldn't have piled more stuff on you.' I moved past her and looked at White Trash. She was on her back with her back legs spread, totally relaxed, looking up at my mother adoringly, clearly unfazed by her adventure.

'I know she was here, Keye,' Miki repeated. 'Seriously, I saw her.'

'So she got out when you got home with groceries. Did you see her when you got home?'

'No.' Miki shook her head.

'Aren't we just happy everything worked out?' Emily Street said. 'My little Snowflake is just fine.'

'It's not Snowflake,' I said. My mother absolutely refused to call my cat by her given name.

'I'm going to take off, Keye,' Miki said. 'Aunt Emily said she'd come by every day and check on White Trash. I know you. You won't be able to relax with me here now. And frankly, I lost my phone and your cat in one day. I'm not feeling very confident. I've got some time off. Maybe I'll mow my grass and make the mommy association happy.'

I wasn't going to argue. 'I'll drive you when you're ready and make sure the house is secure.'

'That would be great,' Miki said. 'I have a friend coming by tomorrow to change the locks.'

'I'll go too,' Mother piped in. 'It'll be fun. I'll make something special. We could have a pajama party.'

I followed them to Miki's Inman Park home after changing out of the fake urn-company uniform and into some jeans. Not surprisingly, Miki had decided to ride with Mom. The sun was low, the last bit of orange light hitting the top of my cousin's grand Victorian as we headed up the weedy walkway. The house looked like a piece of candy, like it was made of iced gingerbread – pink and blue, with elaborately carved railings in white around oddly shaped porches and balconies. As lovely as they are to look at, Victorians never made sense to me – so many nooks and crannies, like afterthoughts. It felt chaotic. I live and work in loft space for a reason. A busy mind does better in open quarters.

We stepped up on the big wraparound porch. Mother was chattering. I was thinking about Miki walking up those steps and hearing someone in her house. I stepped in front of her and took the key, turned it in the lock. Miki leaned in and reached for the wall switch.

An ear-splitting scream erupted from my cousin. I heard my mother saying '*oh my god, oh my god.*'

A corpse dangled from the hallway door frame as if from the gallows.

I pushed them out the door and onto the porch, pulled the front door closed. 'Get in the car, lock the doors, and call the police.' I said it calmly, though my thoughts were racing. I was trying to make eye contact with Miki. She looked like she was checking out.

'Mother, take Miki and get to the car. Do you need my phone?' She didn't move. They seemed cemented to the porch. '*Mother*, I need backup. Do you have your phone?' She nodded. 'Call Rauser. Take Miki. *Go.*'

I steadied my Glock and eased the front door open with my shoulder, took in the room. Empty. I moved in closer to the dead man hanging from the hallway door. He was elderly and slight. I saw some kind of ligature – a thin rope, perhaps – running under his chin and back behind his head. It appeared to be attached to the wall over the frame on the other side. Its function was clear. It held his head up so that the corpse was looking at the front door. Rigor will seize any position it's handed. The distortion of death had twisted whatever he was in life into a kind of Halloween mask.

The rope that affixed the old man to the door frame was wrapped around his body several times above his rib cage and under his arms. I noticed that a wound over his left kidney had leaked. Redbrick stains looked like spilled paint on a pale green dress shirt.

I wanted to explore this further, but there wasn't time. I had to secure Miki's house. I thought about her and my mother, outside and terrified.

Behind the body hanging from the doorway, a long hallway went right and left, punctuated by poster-size enlargements of Miki's most famous photographs – an Afghani girl cradling a newborn from *Time;* a single rock-hurling Iranian protester who refused to run from charging riot police, *Newsweek.* An exploding volcano, *National Geographic.*

I let air into my lungs and quietly exhaled some of the tension elevating my heart rate. Adrenaline. It doesn't matter how many bodies you've seen or how confident you are with a gun in your hands or how often you've stepped off into the unknown, it will flat-out scare the hell out of you every time.

The light switch was on my left. I hit it with my elbow and spun out into the open hallway, first left, then right. Two sets of skinny, *s*-shaped track lighting made the hall bright. The oak floors creaked as I moved past Miki's photos and inspected each of the four rooms and the closets off the downstairs hallway, then checked the bathroom, jerked back the shower curtain with my pulse hammering in my ears.

Sirens screamed into the quiet evening. Inman Park was about to be jostled rudely away from the dinner table. Minutes later I heard the front door open, voices. Fearing jumpy cops who didn't know me, I wedged the Glock in the duty holster on the back of my jeans and raised my hands. 'Keye Street. I'm coming out.'

'You're good, Street.' Rauser's voice. I loved the sound of it most any time, but especially now. I turned the corner and saw him. Detectives and uniforms were spreading out across the house. Over Rauser's shoulder, I could see cops running through the yard.

'Rooms off the downstairs hallway are secure.' I pointed toward the back of the house. 'But there's still that end of the house left, an upstairs and a full basement.'

'Where are the stairs?' Rauser asked. I pointed in the appropriate direction. 'Balaki, take two officers and secure the upstairs. You guys take the back. I'll get the basement. Where's Williams?'

'He took the shooting over at Turner Field with Thomas, Lieutenant,' Balaki answered.

Rauser looked at the dead man hanging in the door frame. No emotion. 'Where's the video guy? Oh and get the victim IDed right away. Don't wait for CSU.' He had barked at Detective Angotti, who'd just made Homicide a month ago, young, thick-lipped, and compact with dark wavy hair.

'I need to check on Miki and Mom,' I said. 'They're freaking out.'

He looked back at the corpse. 'I've got an officer with them. They see this?' I nodded. He said, 'You know what this is about?'

'No idea.'

'Show me the basement.'

I knew the house well from when Miki had let me stay here with White Trash during the most intrusive part of the renovation at my place.

I led Rauser to a narrow door in the back of the kitchen. Throughout the house, I could hear cops yelling 'clear' each time they'd secured a room.

'How many entrances in the house?' Rauser wanted to know.

'Three. Front. Basement door's under the back deck, but it's usually padlocked from the outside. And a storm door with a deadbolt off the sunroom in back.'

Rauser flattened himself against the wall and motioned for me to get behind him. He reached a long arm for the knob, turned it and let the door swing open, waited for a couple of beats, then swung out with his weapon. We started slowly down steep, narrow wooden steps.

'Light's on a string to the left,' I whispered. I'd been down these steps a few times. The washer and dryer were in the basement.

A shaft of light speared the darkness and stopped us cold. It was a cop's flashlight from outside looking into the dark ground-level basement windows. Rauser pulled the light cord and a hundred-watt bulb cast a harsh bluish-white light across the basement. We circled, weapons out front, our backs to each other, then spread out and checked behind stacked cardboard boxes with neat labels, a defunct water heater, an enormous working HVAC unit that looked new, an ancient enlarger from one of Miki's old darkrooms. Everything one expects to find in a photographer's basement. Through the windows I saw the feet and legs of cops moving around outside.

We holstered our weapons. 'We're not a bad team,' Rauser said.

'That mean you're ready to sell your soul and go private?' I asked.

'Uh-huh. And maybe Michelle Obama's gonna help me plant that garden.'

I smiled. Spring fever and too many weeks of convalescing after some injuries got the best of him this year, and he decided he would put a vegetable garden in his backyard. He rented a tiller and chewed up a ten-by-twelve space in the center, which is the only area to get full sun. But then he returned to work and Atlanta hadn't wanted to behave long enough for him to actually care for the space. The area, now a full-on eyesore, had turned into a litter box for the neighbor's cat. I'd seen Rauser standing at his deck doors in his boxers in the morning, staring at the cat doing his business while he drank his coffee. 'Little bastard,' he always muttered, but I'd never seen him make a move to run the cat off.

We climbed the stairs and went back through the length of the house.

'How long you think he's been swinging?' Rauser asked, squinting up at the body.

'I'm guessing twelve to twenty-four,' I said.

'It's cold in here,' Rauser observed. 'Nobody keeps it this cold. That'll affect it too, right?' He rubbed his face. 'So we

STRANGER IN THE ROOM — 111

gotta take the leap this may be connected to Miki's break-in.'

'I wasn't sure I even believed her. I was sending her home. I was so mad at her. I feel terrible.'

'Well, consider the source,' Rauser said. 'I looked at the report. She wasn't just drinking. Responding officers reported dilated pupils. She was clearly using stimulants with the alcohol. They ran her name – history of mental illness, nine-one-one calls, people reporting suicide attempts, calls from Miki saying she heard someone breaking in. Never anybody here when the officers arrive. Never any evidence of a break-in. We get these calls all the time from users. They get paranoid. They get lonely. Who knows?'

'So let's take another leap. What if those reports were real? What if she was hearing noises? I interviewed an old boyfriend of hers today – Cash Tilison – who admitted to stalking her.'

Rauser looked at me. 'You're gonna give me all that, right?'

'Of course.'

'You need hardware to hold that kind of weight,' Detective Angotti said. We all looked up at the wall above the door frame. 'Those anchors up there had to be drilled in.' Angotti knelt, pointed to some white dust around the door frame. 'Looks like plaster chips. That's a new installation. This guy came with tools, Lieutenant.'

I agreed. 'He had to engage in a lot of precautionary behaviors to pull this off. He's thinking about Miki's routines, when she's away, the neighborhood, about tools and hardware, about getting the body inside, positioning, staging.'

'So we'll say this guy at her window, he knows what he wants to do. He knows she's away, like you said, and he comes over to check the place out. Maybe he installs the wall anchors then, sweeps up a little, so she's not tipped when she comes home,' Rauser said.

'Then Miki comes here,' I added. 'He wants to give her a good scare so she'll leave home again. Maybe he's not finished. If he's been watching her or gaslighting her, he knows she'll run.'

'We know this guy hasn't been dead forty-eight hours. So he was planning the murder when he was here,' Rauser said. 'You think he preselected the old guy?'

'It would make sense he'd go for a frail elderly person or a child,' I answered. 'He has to have a body he can manipulate.'

'House is secure. No signs of a struggle. No blood visible to the naked eye. All clear outside. No evidence of a break-in. So we got a good lock picker or somebody with a key,' Angotti said.

'Get someone to examine the locks,' Rauser ordered.

Ken Lang and a couple of scene techs trudged through the front door, burdened with aluminum cases and cameras, looking like aliens in booties and jumpsuits. Lang looked at the dead man dangling from the door frame through small, square wire-rimmed glasses. 'Oh joy,' he said, and set his cases on the floor. 'Just how I wanted to spend Saturday night. How much time before the ME fucks up my scene?'

'I can postpone the call for a few minutes,' Rauser said.

Lang looked around, sighed. 'It's going to take all night to process a scene this size.'

'ME doesn't give a shit about your scene,' Rauser groused. 'ME cares about the body. Get what you need off it and let 'em get in and out.' Rauser was a can-do guy. And that's what he wanted from the people he worked with. A lot of can-dos. I'd seen him lose patience with Lang before. Ken always seemed to go into everything with a lot of reasons up front about how hard it was going to be.

We backed away and made room for the crime scene investigators to do their job. 'You notice there's no ligature marks around the neck. None on his wrists,' Rauser said.

And no spatter, I thought. No reason to call in Jo Phillips, the bloodstain pattern analyst that Rauser used to sleep with – almost six feet of perfect nuts-and-berries complexion.

'Hey, Balaki,' Rauser said. 'We got Keye's cousin, who is also the home owner, and Keye's mother outside with an officer. We need to interview them both. How about getting them escorted to the station. Make sure they're treated real nice. And find the responding officers for a break-in reported here night before last.' Rauser chewed his cheek. 'So he hangs a dead body from a door frame inside Miki's house. He clearly positioned the old guy's head. And he might have also turned the air down to freezing so his stiff stayed good and stiff. What do you make of it?'

'He spent a lot of time thinking about how to up the creepy factor. And to send the message that he has full access to her life and to her home. That kind of power play isn't unusual with stalkers. Killing to prove it, that is,' I said.

'Miki have any other boyfriends besides Tilison?'

'I have a list,' I said, and Rauser grinned down at me.

Rauser's over six feet tall. And me, well, I can hit five-four on my tiptoes. 'Neil ran their backgrounds. We'll send them over.'

'I saw Cash Tilison at the Tabernacle when he was just starting a couple of years back,' Rauser said. 'He's good.'

I wondered whether the singer's celebrity might affect the interview process. I didn't say it, of course. Cops are as human as anyone else. A little brush with fame can be a lot of fun. I imagined detectives volunteering to interview Cash. And they would interview him and everyone else in Miki's world.

The scene techs were working on and around the body, carefully vacuuming and bagging hair and fiber evidence off the victim's clothes and shoes. The floor around him was vacuumed clean. We stood in the center of Miki's living room, where the big picture window looked out onto the wraparound porch and tree-lined Elizabeth Street. I saw police cars and the CSU van outside. A few neighbors had come out on the street to watch. I thought about how frightened Miki must be right now and felt another pang of guilt.

Ken Lang photographed the body from several angles. He then slipped bags over the victim's hands and rubber-banded them on. He placed a sterile crime scene blanket on the floor.

One of the techs got up on a stool. 'Toggle anchors and eye hooks,' she said, and tapped on the wall. 'In a stud.' Her accent was southern. But not Georgia southern. Something twangier. Arkansas, maybe. She sliced carefully through twine that was positioned under the victim's chin and ran up behind his head. His head bobbled a little but didn't completely droop. I saw the deep ligature the twine had made in his skin. 'Almost no discoloration,' she said. 'This guy wasn't breathing when he was hung up here.' She placed the twine in an evidence bag and handed it down. 'Okay, y'all. Timber.' She sliced through the rope that held the body. The CSU team maneuvered the body onto the blanket.

Detective Linda Bevins came in. She had worked the strangled-boy scene. I remembered seeing her holding back the grieving mother on television. 'We have an ID on the victim.' Her blondish hair was pulled back. She was in jeans and an APD T-shirt, looked fit. 'Name's Donald Kelly. Yesterday was his birthday. He was ninety.'

'Well, that would explain this,' Ken Lang said. He'd pulled a crumpled piece of wrapping paper from the victim's pant pocket. He bagged it.

'Jeez,' Rauser said. 'That's depressing.'

Ken Lang began speaking into a tiny digital recorder clipped to his collar. 'Gunshot wound,' he said. He cut open the victim's shirt and it fell to each side of the body. We were treated to a view of the old man's chest and stomach. No muscle. Just skin and ribs and bone sprinkled with sparse silver hair. Lang took some pictures. Clipped some fabric and bagged it.

'Nine-one-one call came in at six-fifteen last night,' Bevins said. 'Mr Kelly was being chauffeured to his birthday party on Fifteenth Street next to Colony Square. A volunteer with Dignified Elder Transport.' Bevins paused and looked at her notepad. 'Driver's name is Abraam Balasco. He picked him up at Sunrise Oaks Assisted Living.

They went into the lobby of this condo building. There's a guy reading the paper. Balasco doesn't see his face, but he thinks he may be a waiter or something because he's got black shoes with thick soles and black pants. He notices the cut is inexpensive. Not dressy. Says his father was a tailor so he notices things like this. He's not sure but he thinks he was wearing a white shirt. He says the guy looks big even sitting down. They had been discussing Mr Kelly's reluctance to go to his birthday party. The old man told Balasco his daughter was a bitch and the family was waiting for him to die. That's a quote. Balasco says the elevator opened and he was nailed from behind. Kelly never made it upstairs, and the volunteer's Honda Element is still missing.'

'See if we can get a copy of the will, and check out the family. Honda's probably the primary crime scene,' Rauser said.

'I'd agree with that,' Ken Lang said. 'Angle looks right for a bullet coming from the driver's side. And we don't have blood here consistent with a gunshot wound. Distance looks about right too.'

'Mr Balasco is on his way to the station,' Bevins said.

'Yeah, it would be nice if my detectives would jump on interviewing the only goddamn witness.' The level of irritation in Rauser's tone caused me to look up at him. It was nothing new for his detectives. Respected as he was for his investigative skills, Rauser was equally known for a tendency toward aggravation.

'He was interviewed at the hospital, where he's been under observation for a concussion, but that's when it was a missing persons,' Bevins answered patiently.

'This guy Balasco, he the one that reported old man Kelly missing?' Rauser wanted to know.

'Family members,' Angotti answered. 'Nine-one-one call. When Mr Kelly didn't come up on the elevator, some of them went downstairs and found the volunteer, Mr Balasco, had been injured. Kelly was gone.'

'Balasco unconscious when the family found him?' Rauser asked.

'Yes, sir.'

Rauser scratched the back of his head, a quick, irritated movement. 'And then Kelly ends up here. Hanging. In Miki Ashton's house.'

The male technician opened up his aluminum case. A CrimeScope that looked like a black box nested in gray foam along with a row of colored filters and forensic goggles. In the back of the case, SceneScopes, pocket-size, like small flashlights, each made to project a certain light on the spectrum. Investigators used them according to their needs – body fluids, latent prints, fibers, drugs.

'Somebody wanna give me some mood lighting?' Lang asked.

Rauser went to the switch at the front door. Bevins headed for the kitchen light. I took the lamp and pulled tall vertical blinds across the wide window. The room went dark. Blue spotlights from a high-intensity UV moved evenly inch by inch over the door frame, the floor. We stood there in the dark, watching as smudges appeared under the black light. Lang's techs scraped samples and tweezed them into vials.

'Angotti, start talking to the neighbors,' Rauser said. 'Probably looking at a guy who's been hanging around. Run with Balasco's description until we get something better. Maybe somebody remembers him. And Bevins, get Kelly's daughter and the rest of the family down to the station in the morning. We'll see how bitchy she is. Family and profit. Sounds like a good place to start.'

'A family member wouldn't hang him up like that,' I said. 'And how would that connect back to Miki?'

'It's not hard to hire somebody that's happy to hang up a family member,' Rauser said. 'Maybe he happens to have a thing for your cousin.'

He was grasping at straws. But theory generation was just part of getting to something that made sense in the face of unreasonable violence. I didn't say anything. I felt his hand on my shoulder. 'Need you to come to the station too, Street. We get everybody's statement all laid out, this'll be a lot easier.'

Lang ran light over the body. Small spots and large smudges lit up on the victim's face and clothing. 'Whadda we got?' Rauser asked. 'Some kind of body fluid?'

'Pretty good bet we know what the big one is down there. Guy pissed himself. Most guys do,' Lang said. I thought about the strangled boy, the unidentified fluid on his back and shoulders. And Lang's words. *Most guys do*. A reminder of what a messy business murder is. And about all the ways the body betrays both killer and victim.

'What about the small spots?' Rauser wanted to know.

Lang shrugged. 'Semen, salvia, urine, vaginal fluids, they can all fluoresce just like blood. Lot of variables, though. Humidity, temperature, equipment. May fluoresce one time and not another. No such thing as scientific certainty, Lieutenant. But generally if it comes from the body, it's gonna give us a light show. Under the right conditions, anyway.'

'Any other fluids that might fluoresce like that?' Rauser asked.

'What did you have in mind?'

'Fuck if I know,' Rauser said. 'What's left?'

12

Almost midnight on a Saturday and Midtown was humming when I pulled out of the parking garage at 675 Ponce de Leon Avenue at City Hall East – two million square feet of pollutant-faded brick and coughing ventilation. Atlanta's police department used the building, along with some other city services and businesses. The inefficient giant had been sold to developers a few months back. Word was the tenants who hadn't already moved out had been told to pack their desks. It was a good bet Midtown would drop dead from exposure to lead paint and asbestos when they renovated the obsolete hulk. The department had long petitioned for improvements. No one liked the building. But at least it was a devil they knew. Rauser resisted this kind of upheaval. Change is change. Even when it's good it's inconvenient. Adding to his anxiety, the Homicide Unit still hadn't been told where they would set up shop next.

In my rearview mirror, I saw my father in the driver's seat of his Ford Taurus. Miki was in front with him. Mother was in the backseat. It had been a long night for everyone. Dad had showed up at the station, big-eyed and drawn with worry, after Mother had called him crying. He was determined to take Miki home with them after the interviews. I thought it was a terrible idea. No one had a handle on what was going on. We didn't know who this person stalking my cousin was. All we knew was that he had probably carried out the murder and ritually displayed a body in her house. I'd argued with my father that my hotel has surveillance cameras, security, ten floors to get to my loft. But even as the words were coming out of my mouth, I was thinking about that terrible night last winter when I woke to a killer standing over me. It occurred to me for the first time that the scar from that night didn't look so different from the scars up and down my cousin's arms.

My father balked at the idea he couldn't defend his castle. Rauser had finally convinced me it was a good idea. The Winnona Park neighborhood where my parents lived in Decatur was close-knit and quiet. Rauser figured the neighbors would notice someone out of place on the street, unlike the in-town neighborhoods or the hotel, which was full of new faces. Decatur Police Department had promised increased patrols. But I didn't want them going home alone. And I hadn't had a minute alone with Miki since we'd pushed open her front door and seen the corpse.

I called Neil as I drove down Ponce toward Decatur. I'd practically shoved him out of the car at the Big Knob Resort & Spa after White Trash had been spotted wandering my hotel. He sounded groggy. Briefly, I explained what had happened at Miki's house.

'So you're just leaving me in Hicksville? Alone?'

'At a resort and spa. I'm a monster.'

'I have one brick of coffee, two joints, and a Baggie with somebody's ashes.'

'It's not ashes,' I said. 'It's pulverized bone fragments.'

'By the way, it's a holiday weekend. The lab Billy and Brenda Wade used is closed until Tuesday.'

'Shit.' Of course it was closed. It was nearly the Fourth of July. Ponce veered right, and I drove into downtown Decatur. Wreaths with red, white, and blue ribbon decorated the lampposts lining the street to remind me. I thought again about the weekend Rauser and I had planned and the fireworks on the square, something my parents had done each year for as long as I could remember. We'd pack up folding chairs and picnic baskets and wine for the adults. Jimmy and I sat cross-legged on blankets and listened to bands play in the gazebo until the fireworks exploded off the top of the courthouse.

'See if you can get back in touch with somebody from that lab,' I told Neil. 'A bribe never hurts. Larry's dime.'

'I've got some ideas.'

'What kind of ideas?'

'About the ashes. Don't worry about it. Get some rest.'

I turned off South Columbia into Winnona Park and pulled up behind my dad's car as he parked on the hilly driveway on Derrydown Way. We all walked to the front door. Two cats from Mother's feral colony lounged on the porch in doughnut-shaped beds, each with one open eye on our every move. I'd been treated to this kind of suspicion from animals all my life, thanks to my mother's attraction to wild things. But her love of nature and the desire to rescue the things it abandoned was, to her children, a glorious excursion into a heart she could not always freely share. My brother and I grew up with dew-covered grass slapping our ankles as we trailed behind our mother on early-morning treks through the rolling acreage behind the Methodist Children's Home just a few blocks from our house. We followed her down the hill to the pond, where a pair of blue herons became so still at our arrival that we mistook them for driftwood at the water's edge. But we always looked for them. Blue herons never fall out of love, Mother had told us. We tossed bread crumbs to the ducks and geese, and watched the fog lift up out of the reeds, then burn off the lake in the early-morning sun. Jimmy and I know the songs of mockingbirds and the sudden stillness of a meadow at the shrill warning of a red-tailed hawk. Our mother, a child of the Albemarle Sound and pulsing marshes and tundra swans and striped bass, had searched for and found the secluded marshes and private seascapes in her city life. And because we had been witness to this delicate beauty in her humanity, it was all the more confusing when her touch turned arctic and her tongue caustic.

I glanced at a huge metal vase in the opposite corner of the porch behind the porch swing. Tall metal flowers, some rust-covered, some polished steel, rustic and beautiful, bloomed out of it. Dad followed my eyes. 'I'm getting better, aren't I?'

'They're gorgeous, Dad. Will you make something for my office?'

'You bet, kiddo,' my dad said, and wrapped a long arm around my shoulders as we walked into the home where Jimmy and I had grown up and where Miki had spent most of her time as a child. My father had practically lived in the garage back then, tinkering with engines and anything else with moving parts. Howard Street's natural talent for understanding the mechanics of a thing had put two kids through college and supported my mother's rather expensive taste in antiques, cookware, stand mixers, food processors, and knives. And to think that all those years he'd welded and oiled and pieced back together whatever the community towed in or carried in boxes, his secret artist's eye was mentally sizing up the shapes a gallery would later commission him to craft. I loved the idea that my parents were finding something that made them happy. And I found it all surprisingly unsettling. It wasn't that they had found their passion, but that they *had* a passion, that their interior life had been hidden and completely unseen by their children. Or at least by me. Jimmy might have been privy to the dreams of adults. Jimmy had always been more plugged in.

Mother put a kettle on the stove. Hot tea for me. For everyone else she prepared her special toddy – hot milk, cognac, and honey, guaranteed to take the edge off. I waited at the kitchen table for my parents to leave, then looked at Miki. 'You okay?'

'Some freak is hurting people and stringing them up in my house. So no. Not so much.' Her shoulders were scrunched up like she was cold on this hot July night.

'I want to help,' I said. 'Look, I was pretty pissed about White Trash. And I was scared, Miki. I didn't know what had happened. I couldn't get in touch with you.'

Miki nodded, her face pale.

'Can we talk about what happened today with your phone?'

'I went to the store. I had my phone in the pocket of that little boyfriend jacket. I know it was there. I used it on the way. I felt it when I walked into the grocery store. When I got back to your loft, it was just gone.'

'You drive your Spitfire to the store?'

'Of course,' Miki said. 'Oh shit. My car. I'll have to get it tomorrow.'

'Don't,' I said. 'Leave it in the garage at my place. Classic cars are too easy to spot.'

Miki sipped her toddy and shivered. 'You think he's going to try something else?'

'It's a reasonable assumption.' My phone pinged to let me know a text had arrived. I saw Rauser's name with a note. He'd sent a composite operator's rendering of the man seen by the volunteer driver. APD and many other departments had begun using computers for composites rather than old-fashioned police sketches. The software allowed the victim to sit with an operator, choose from and tweak head shapes and facial features. It also allowed for quick access to facial-recognition systems and automatic comparisons to the databases. I clicked on the attachment. It wasn't much – a head, shoulders, hairline, no details on the face except an eyebrow and ridgeline. The driver had apparently seen only a split second of profile as he walked by. I slid my phone across the table. 'Anyone familiar?'

Miki took the phone in her hands and sat back hard. 'So that's supposed to be him? Just some faceless monster? The stranger in the room grabbing at me.'

Miki's penchant for fully and publicly indulging her darkness always undid me a little. Emily Street had drilled it into us that we should not show it when something was wrong. And we certainly did not talk about it. In my mother's world, that's dirty laundry.

'He wants to ruin it,' Miki said.

'Ruin what?' I asked her.

'Everything. My house, because I love it. My life, because it's good now.' Tears spilled from one blue eye, then another. Miki wiped them away hastily. But she was so fair that any emotion instantly reddened her buttermilk complexion. She looked at me with red eyes and nose, and I remembered a moment from our childhood when I'd come upon her sitting, alone, on the edge of the little creek behind the park, hugging her knees. She'd looked up at me the same way, and I'd known she'd been crying. I thought about the strangled boy and his sobbing mother. Not for the first time. Something about it was eating at me just like it was at Rauser. And neither one of us could put our finger on it.

'This guy isn't some indestructible phantom from your nightmares, Miki. He's not the bogeyman. He's a plain old criminal. Don't give him any more power in your life. Thursday night when you saw him in your house after you went out for dinner, was that dinner planned for a while?'

Miki shook her head. 'Last-minute.'

'Remember where you were when you made the plans?'

'Home.'

'How about the restaurant that night? Notice anything off? You said it felt like you were being watched at the gym. Anywhere else?'

'No. I'm sorry.' She yawned. Mother's magic toddy was working.

'You've got a penlight on your keychain. You used it that night, right?'

Miki thought for a minute. 'I *did*. I heard a noise just as I was going to put the key in the lock. I recognized the sound of the floorboards inside. It scared me. I went down the porch really quietly and pressed the light against the window. I saw the couch and some stuff I'd left on the table and then the light just kind of blacked out and I realized someone had stepped in front of it.'

'How did you know it was a man? What did you see?'

'I don't know. His stomach, maybe, and his height. He was wearing black. No buttons. Some kind of pullover. He wasn't fat, but he wasn't buff either. His belly filled the shirt out.'

I thought about Cash Tilison in those jeans. Definitely buff. 'And then he pointed at you like this? Thumb and forefinger?'

She shook her head again. 'He didn't just point. He pointed, then squeezed the trigger. Like a gun. Or like gotcha. He had on gloves. The kind germophobes get in the box at the pharmacy. They seemed really white compared to his clothes.'

'And then you looked up, right? You told me he stood there looking at you. Was the penlight still in your hand?'

'I dropped it and then I ran off the porch.' She stared down into her drink. 'I threw up.'

I nodded. I'd seen the reports tonight at the station. The officers had found her keychain under the window. Poor Miki. I wanted to reach out to her now. Why is it so goddamn awkward for me? Why the hell didn't my mother teach me this stuff? I brooded over that for a moment. My mother, the feral cat rescuer. Any kind of animal, really, but the wilder the better. For as long as I could remember, my mother had humanely trapped, vetted, and released back into our neighborhood some very confused cats with missing private parts. The free-roaming, mostly untouchable colony had become a fixture in Winnona Park. The numbers had dwindled over the years. New cats wandered in occasionally, and mother began her voodoo-like seduction with chicken livers and mackerel before the trapdoor slammed and they found themselves at the high-volume spay/neuter clinic up the street. To this day, my mother had wild cats on her porch waiting for breakfast each morning, standing back four feet until she cleared out. They returned to the sound of her voice and clinking bowls each evening. She kept track of them and worried over them, these creatures she could never lay hands on or hold.

A thought hit me for the first time – a full-on head-slapper. I made a mental note to share this with Dr Shetty. My mother wanted to rescue things without having to get too close – love without intimacy. It's what she'd done with Jimmy and me – her feral children. She read to us and made us read to her after school when we'd pile up on the king-size bed she shared with my father, taking turns reading our way through her favorite books. She had snacks waiting when we came in from school. She treated our scrapes with peroxide and made sure we were educated and well dressed. She tucked us in and captivated us with stories of growing up on the pungent marsh-scented shores of the Albemarle Sound. I had forged a connection to water, to the low country, before I had ever seen sound or sea or salt marsh. Her stories and her rich voice had mesmerized and altered me. But I could not remember Emily Street throwing her arms around me in a spontaneous display of affection. Not ever. It's a special kind of restraint one learns at the hands of a southern woman.

I thought about my brother, Jimmy, and me lying on our backs as kids in pajamas staring at the glow-in-the-dark solar system on the ceiling and saying what we wanted to be. Jimmy thought if I was going to be a superhero, I'd have been born one, so I settled on being a cop. Every night when the lights went out, I could hear Jimmy's little voice say 'Wow' as the stars lit up on our ceiling as if he were seeing them for the first time. He'd leave his twin bed and climb into mine, and we'd whisper ourselves to sleep. Jimmy wanted to be a dancer. I wondered how he got from that to becoming an adman. Since he'd left years ago, our relationship had been reduced to holiday visits, quick phone calls, and emails. There was so much I didn't know about his interior life now. I missed my brother. Reaching for him was second nature. I'd never had to work at it. So why was it so hard with everyone else in my life? Why was I struggling now with my fragile, tormented cousin? I blamed my mother and her detachment. I blamed alcohol and all the ways addiction changes you. Addicts are natural saboteurs.

'Miki, listen, I . . . I'm sorry. I didn't get it. I didn't get how real this was.'

'I understand. I haven't been the most stable person in your life.'

'You remember when you first started hearing noises in your house?'

'What do you mean?'

'Was it when you started making nine-one-one calls?'

Her expression hardened. 'So the cops are looking at my records?'

'They were aware of the nine-one-one calls, Miki, of course. Records are kept. You cut yourself around that time, didn't you?'

'It was before I met Cash. That's when I moved my bedroom upstairs. I was afraid there was someone at the window. I had all the trees cut back so the branches wouldn't touch the house. I still heard noises. Finally, I couldn't take it anymore. Everyone kept telling me nothing was going on. No one was in my house. No one was outside my house. Take your meds, take your meds, take your meds. That's all I heard. I didn't want to live like that anymore.'

'What happened then?'

'Another month of my life lost to the hospital. What a fucking waste. Magazine gave me a couple easy features to shoot until they knew I was okay. That's how I met Cash. Then, when I wasn't traveling, Cash was at the house. When he was gone, there was Jake, Greg, Ben. You get the picture.'

I patted her hand, got up. 'Go get some rest, okay? We'll talk tomorrow.'

Miki got a glass of water, and I watched her head upstairs. She looked especially frail to me tonight. I found my parents sitting side by side on the back deck, talking quietly, nightcaps under the stars.

'Come sit with us,' my dad said. 'It's a clear night.'

'You were brave tonight, Keye,' Mother said – lavish praise from Emily Street. 'I felt safe because of that.'

I pulled a deck chair close to them. We sat there in silence. 'I want to ask y'all something. It's about my adoption,' I said, and Mom nearly toppled her drink.

'Where on earth did that come from, Keye?' she exclaimed.

'What's the big deal?'

'We've told you everything we know about your parents and your grandparents already,' she said.

'Why do you hate talking about this, Mother?'

'Honey, you know we wanted children,' my dad said.

'But why did you pick me?'

'I fell in love with you the instant I saw you,' my father answered.

'I heard you arguing when I was little,' I told them. I looked at Mother. 'About how life with a white kid, a kid that wasn't damaged, would have been better.'

'It would have been easier,' my mother agreed. 'But not better. You were a broken little girl. Some days my heart ached for you. And some days, Keye, I didn't know how to get through to you. And the community. So much gossip! This neighborhood was stark-white at that time. But everyone who met you put away their stupid notions and loved you just like we did.'

'I heard you say that day that it was Dad's fault.'

Mother took my father's hand. 'Sometimes I just need to yell at Howard. It usually just means I'm overwhelmed.'

'I remember that children's home. And I remember the first time I saw you.'

'You were so beautiful,' Dad told me.

'The white children were getting homes,' Mother said. 'We wanted a child who needed us as much as we needed you. It wouldn't have mattered if you were purple.'

We sat for a few minutes, leaning back in our chairs, looking at the stars.

'Remember those blue herons at the pond?' I asked Mother.

'Of course.'

'I haven't been down there in years,' I said wistfully. 'I used to love those walks with you and Jimmy.'

My mother's voice was soft when she answered. 'I did too, darling. Let's take a picnic down there soon.'

I got up and bent to kiss them both. 'I'll call and check on things in the morning.'

'He never left her, Keye.' Mother's voice stopped me as I reached for the kitchen door off the deck. I turned and saw her lean into my dad. 'That male heron. They got old together down there at that pond.'

13

saw him when I came off the elevator. He was talking to one of the housekeepers we'd gotten to know at the hotel pool party. Her name was Bogdana, forty-five, thick accent, a big cart loaded with housekeeping supplies, and a whole lot of junk in her trunk. He saw me and smiled. He was wearing ash-colored pants, a charcoal blazer with a white dress shirt, stiff collar, no tie. I could see his Adam's apple and a hint of chest hair at the top button. I tiptoed to kiss him and smelled his aftershave. He put his arms around me.

'Did you get any sleep?' I'd managed to get in bed by three.

'Is it showing?' he asked. 'I knew I should have put on my makeup this morning.'

We walked through the lobby. 'So how is it I get breakfast with the busiest guy in town?'

We passed through the gleaming polished doors at the Georgian and the eighty percent humidity slapped us in the face. Rauser's Crown Vic was parked in the valet area. Cop privileges. Barely nine in the morning and the sun was cooking already. Steam rose up off the pavement on Peachtree. Rauser opened the car door for me. I saw a fast-food cardboard cup holder with two full coffees and some breakfast sandwiches in yellow paper.

'I should have known,' I said. 'Where are we really going?'

Rauser got behind the wheel. 'Thought we could hang out for a while before the day gets nuts.' He peeled the wrapper away from a biscuit and bit into flat eggs and fake cheese.

I found a wad of napkins in his glove compartment and handed him one. 'You're a bad liar, Aaron Rauser.'

'Okay, so I thought maybe we could poke around a couple of crime scenes.'

I smiled, lifted the plastic lid on one of the coffees. 'Sweet talker.'

Rauser did this sometimes, when he had a case that was really bugging him. He'd return to the scene again and again, try to make sense of it. I'd accompanied him many times. He liked having another set of eyes. He liked talking it out.

The scanner was turned down to a mumble. Rauser was a classic-rock guy. Hendrix was on, 'Hey Joe.' We took Tenth Avenue past Piedmont Park. The windows were down. The Crown Vic sputtered at the light at Monroe; Rauser gunned it to keep it running.

'I miss you when things get busy like this, Street,' he said, and grabbed another biscuit. I reached across with a napkin and got a crumb from the corner of his mouth. I wanted to kiss him. Okay, to be honest, I had the urge to climb all over him. I didn't, of course, but only because he was working and we were on our way to a crime scene.

We twisted through Orme Park toward Amsterdam. Blotches of warm sunlight landed on the car between the maples and oaks. Rauser's cop's eyes took in the neighborhood. At King's Court, he pulled over in front of an empty lot skirted by a vinyl mesh construction barrier, bright orange. House numbers ran in the nine-hundreds. Behind the orange mesh, a major renovation was under way at the bottom of a slope, nothing left but a foundation. Judging from the weeds and vines and ivy and kudzu that had taken over, it had been like this for a while. A piece of heavy equipment sat at the bottom of the hill with huge, mud-caked tires. Not an unusual sight in Atlanta right now. The housing market that went up in flames a couple of years ago still had not staged a comeback. Projects like this had slowed to a crawl.

Rauser took a stack of photographs from the inside breast pocket of his jacket, then got out and tossed the jacket on the seat. He came around the car, rolling up his shirtsleeves, the long muscles in his forearms flexing. Pheromones were leaping out of him and tap dancing my way.

We followed the sidewalk past the tear-down. The smell of gardenias hit me. The flowers are as delicate as rose petals, but the smell is layered and complex – almond cookies with a touch of vanilla and brown butter and that first whiff of rain when it hits the concrete. A long row of them bordered the next property. I realized where we were. I'd seen it on television from another perspective – the medical examiner's gurney coming out of the shrubs that night with a little boy's body, a mother shrieking. She'd never feel the same way about a gardenia. I knew that. Smells and trauma are a bad combination. I still can't get near cranberry anything without my stomach doing a full twist, though it has been many years since that jug of juice shattered on a grocery-store floor where my grandparents lay dying.

Rauser stood with his hands in his pockets, looking at the shrubbery. The yellow tape had been removed, and all the markers the techs put down for photographs. There was nothing at all that said this had been the scene of a violent murder except that in this one small area all the trash and debris had been collected. One perfectly clean area where a thirteen-year-old boy had been strangled.

Rauser handed over the crime scene photographs – my best chance to see the scene as the killer had left it. I looked at them in a new way. I'd thought about this scene many times since Rauser had plopped the photos on the bed while I drank my coffee. I'd thought about it again last night after walking into Miki's and finding an elderly man hanging in the doorway.

I looked at the chalk circle on the sidewalk, found the corresponding photograph. Rauser watched me. 'Dog treats,' he explained. 'The kid was walking the dog. Young dog. No protection.'

I went through each photograph – the dog treats, a vague impression in pine straw on the other side of the vinyl mesh, drag marks in the dirt, the boy facedown, the ligature, the rope used as a garrote left on his neck, trash and debris. 'The dog walk routine?'

Rauser nodded. 'Every night. And get this. The kid's

mother said their mail had been opened a couple of times in the last few weeks. So I asked if any of the mail was related to the boy. She says yeah. A letter from his baseball coach saying he thought Troy had mad talent. Coach recommended some famous trainer. Apparently, every sport this kid got near he turned to gold. He was set to try out for the Junior Olympics. Their trash was dumped out a couple times too. Mrs Delgado thought it was a raccoon or something, but the neighbor's trash, neighbor's mail, all fine. Parents cooperated, by the way, sailed through polygraphs yesterday.'

I stood there for a minute, looking at the scene. I closed my eyes and breathed in the gardenia, imagined that night, the boy coming down the sidewalk with his dog. 'He hid over here,' I told Rauser, and he followed me from the line of evergreens back toward the construction lot. 'Where you found the impressions. It's dry, so there's not much detail. He knows this. He's not worried. He just waits. He's been watching them. And he's riffled through their mail and their trash. He knows their routines, where they shop, buy gas, use ATMs. Receipts have date and time stamps. He knows the dog walk is going to happen. He knows the route. And he knows that child will be alone.'

'That's pretty much how I see it too,' Rauser said.

We stood facing the vinyl mesh. 'He drove the neighborhood and preselected this spot,' I said. 'It provided cover, but he'd have a good line of sight through the mesh. It's private enough to do what he wants to do, but not so private that the body wouldn't be discovered. That's important. He could have pulled the boy back there in the lot and left him hidden. But he wanted his body discovered.' I stood there for a moment, thinking about that.

'So he's not just a mean asshole,' Rauser said. 'He's a fruitcake too.'

'Pretty much.' I nodded and looked back at the crime scene photographs. 'The motivation could be a hundred things. Maybe he doesn't want the boy's body left in a bunch of construction trash. This could point to a relationship. Maybe he just wants him discovered because that's part of the thrill. He doesn't want to wait too long for the news to hit. Maybe he was just in a hurry.'

Rauser stepped over the fencing. He crouched down behind it just as the killer must have done while waiting for Troy Delgado.

'So he puts out the dog treats right here.' I pointed to the circle on the sidewalk. 'Maybe he knows the dog already too. Is the Delgado backyard fenced?'

Rauser stood up. 'Yep. Dog was out there when I was talking to the parents. Christ, that was hard.'

'Who's to say he hasn't been warming up the dog when he's over there going through mail and creeping around? That's what I'd do if I didn't want to startle a dog, get 'em used to my scent and hand out rewards for good behavior. So he puts the bait down, climbs over the mesh, and when the dog stops for the treats, he comes up and over and grabs the kid.'

Rauser acted out what that would look like. He's an imposing guy, square-shouldered and over six feet. He had the physicality to make you believe it when he reenacted a violent scene. It gave me an unsettling jolt, watching him. 'Perp pulls him over here where it's flat, puts a knee in his back, wraps the rope around his neck. Little dog runs home. Killer finishes the job and drags the body over to the line of shrubbery.'

'A jogger found him, right?'

Rauser nodded. 'He came from that direction. Something caught his eye. He realized he was looking at reflective strips on sneakers. Then he saw the body. He has a jogging pal two blocks over. They run five nights a week. He sent a text to his pal saying he was on the way out the door.'

'He checked out?' Some killers like reporting their own crimes. They call in to say they've discovered a murder so they have the thrill of watching the crime scene tape go up, cops arriving, maybe some reporters.

'It all adds up. Kid was wearing reflective shoes. Porch light was on over there, and the streetlights work. We tested it. If the jogger looked that way when he was running, he could have easily spotted the kid's shoes. Also, he'd been home all night. Cooked dinner for a neighbor and his wife.'

'Something about this boy really set him off,' I told Rauser. 'The super-athlete thing?'

'He saw a letter from the coach saying this little boy was going to be a big star, talking about his career and shit. Perp's a big zero, so the thought of some thirteen-year-old star probably does really piss him off.'

I nodded. 'He knew Troy. He'd seen him play. You know how sporting events are. No one questions grown-ups hanging around. It's a pedophile picnic.'

Rauser glanced over at me as we walked back to the car. 'That's how you see kids and sports?'

'You know me. Ray of sunshine.'

'Uh-huh,' Rauser said, and drew it out. We got in. He threw the car into gear. 'And maybe Oprah will give me a network. The Aaron Rauser Network. I like it. Or maybe just *Aaron*.' He made quotation marks with one hand when he said 'Aaron'.

'Or just *A.*' I smiled and looked out the window. 'For ass.'

'How 'bout just the Ass Network? Be even better.'

'Pretty sure they have one of those.'

Rauser pressed numbers into his phone. 'Mrs Delgado, it's Lieutenant Rauser. I'm sorry to disturb you, ma'am. I wanted to let you know I'll be outside your home with another investigator. Didn't want to startle you. We don't need to come inside and bother you.' He waited. 'Yes, ma'am. Thank you.' He disconnected and looked at me. 'This kid, he was their pride and joy. They're pretty broken up.'

The Crown Vic pulled alongside the curb in front of a bungalow on Amsterdam. There were a lot of them in neighborhoods around Atlanta – American Craftsman style, built in the early nineteen hundreds, when the middle class was thumbing its nose at the extravagances of the Victorian era. The Delgado bungalow was pale yellow, with an above-ground basement and an overhang roof covering a wide front porch. All the houses on this side of the street were elevated, with driveways on a steep incline. Across the street, a six-foot-high granite retaining wall, a sidewalk in front of it, a stretch of trees behind it. It was one of the nice things about Atlanta neighborhoods. We love our trees here. Though the vibrant heart of Midtown was only a couple of minutes away by car, I had the sense of being miles from the city.

I stood next to Rauser's car, looking at the street, taking in the neighborhood, the quiet. A couple walked their dog in front of the granite-slab wall. I closed my eyes.

'Where'd you go?' Rauser asked.

'Imagining coming here, coming here the way he came here.'

'What do you do first?'

'Drive by a few times,' I answered. 'I notice when their cars are here, when their neighbors are home. The driveways are long. Almost no one parks on the street, so it's not safe here. But I want to get closer. I need time to watch them. I need to be on foot.'

'So maybe he parks on the next block,' Rauser said. I opened my eyes and we both looked at the nearest cross street. 'It would put him out in the open, but he's a cocky guy, you know? Maybe he comes down the sidewalk real casual-like, crosses the street, tosses their mail. Maybe he's wearing a meter reader T-shirt or something so nobody pays attention. 'Cause he has to get the mail before they come home. So he's had to be here in daylight. We've talked to most of the neighbors on the block. You're right. He didn't park here.'

We were quiet for a minute. 'I think he'd want to get closer.' I glanced at the Delgado house. 'You can't see anything from here. What's behind the house?'

'Little strip of woods, more backyards. I think it's San Antonio Drive. Their family room looks out onto the backyard.'

'Okay if I walk around?' I asked Rauser.

He gestured for me to lead the way. We walked up the Delgado driveway and alongside the house. The backyard was flat, with a steady downward slope. We moved along a chain-link fence the length of the yard. We then passed through the tree line, and another backyard, walked to the street. A *For Sale* sign was hanging shingle-style on a white post in the front yard – new construction, infill housing dropped into the lot. It was oddly out of place on the block, a big square house with olive siding in a neighborhood built mostly in the 1920s.

'These people have been living with contractors and strangers,' I said. 'They've grown accustomed to traffic and noise and vehicles. He'd have relative freedom. He could park here without raising questions.'

We walked back to the strip of trees that separated one backyard from another, gazed up at the back of the bungalow, at wide uncovered windows that looked out over the property. A woman stood staring out at us from inside, arms folded over her chest.

'Mrs Delgado,' Rauser confirmed.

In daylight, I couldn't make out her features at this distance. But at night with the lights on, different story. 'In the dark with binoculars, he's practically in their living room,' I told Rauser. 'There's a lot of power in that. Watching. It's sexually charged.'

'Why don't people cover their damn windows?'

A pine tree had fallen. It looked like it had been down for a while. Georgia woods are full of fallen pines with shallow roots. It was lying parallel to the fence. I sat down on it and looked up at the house. Rauser sat beside me, kicked at some dirt. I felt something against my ankle, leaned over and saw a red cardboard box about the dimensions of a paperback novel. It was faded and dirt-covered. There was a picture of some kind of shaggy white terrier on the front. Dog treats. I touched Rauser's arm and he followed my eyes, pulled gloves from his pocket, picked it up.

'Well, look at that,' he said. 'Those little pigs-in-a-blanket-shaped things. Same kind we found had been used to bait the dog.'

'I'm betting this is where the dog developed a taste for them.'

A noise like a flap swinging got our attention. I looked up to see a dog door swinging and a sable-colored sheltie blasting down the back steps and through the yard toward us. Barking, panting, tail wagging.

'Hey, there,' I said, and stuck fingers through the chain link. The dog turned some circles and barked the way shelties do, pressed his face into my hand, sniffed. He was still a puppy. I got hold of the tag on his collar and turned it so I could read. He pressed his nose through the chain link and tried to kiss me. *Joey,* the tag said, with a phone number and address. I thought about Troy Delgado going out to walk his dog, about how easy it would be for a stranger to stop and make a big deal over the dog while flipping that tag around, memorizing the address, the dog's name. 'Hi, Joey, you had a buddy back here, didn't you?'

Rauser ordered an evidence tech, and we waited for the techs to arrive while walking around with our eyes to the ground, hoping to find something else. Joey stayed at the fence, tail wagging. Rauser had hoped for prints on the dog-treat box, but it had been rained on and half buried in the dirt and leaves.

'He probably wasn't wearing gloves when he shoved his hand in that box. That means skin cells,' I told a quiet,

brooding Rauser on the way back to the car. He wanted something easy. Just once. He wanted a print. He wanted results
now. The prospect of waiting for a jammed system to
analyze the evidence infuriated him.

He took Monroe to Piedmont, then turned right onto
Westminster, and curved past Winn Park to a private lot
next to a condo building on Fifteenth. It was posted with
tow signs for residents and authorized guests only. We got
out in the shadow of a Colony Square. Here on the shady
concrete the air was ten degrees cooler.

'I appreciate you doing this with me.' Rauser didn't trust
those outside his own unit easily. It was easier with me.
We'd built professional confidence on previous cases, and
we felt personally safe with each other, which meant that
the theory-generation phase of an investigation was
comfortable and productive. Without judgment, we could
let ideas fly. I liked it. I missed the work that challenged
me. It was why I'd spent eight years at the Bureau. And
it had pressed every button I had. Something happens
inside you, or it did in me, when you perform psychological autopsies on murderers, something gritty and
compulsive that really feeds my dark stuff. I tell myself I
grew up dreaming about the FBI's Behavioral Science Units
because a pair of killers touched me at such a young age,
that I wanted to help families who had suffered that kind of
fracture to find closure and justice. That may be true too.
But I'm realistic. It's also permission to obsess. It feeds my
addict, which means I get to be a hero and a victim – perfect
for a southern woman.

We crossed the lot toward the building where Donald
Kelly had been abducted, and later murdered and hung up

in my cousin's house. I was talking about the phone she'd lost, the food order she hadn't remembered, White Trash escaping. 'What if the food, the phone disappearing, the noises she reported to police – what if it's all connected? The sounds stopped when her boyfriends were around. I didn't even really believe she'd seen someone in her house. I feel terrible about that.'

'Why are you taking on guilt over this? You answered her distress call, you opened your home to her, and she thanks you by losing your damn cat. I'm thinking that's about the best she can do when she's not slicing herself up or jet-setting and star-fucking or sticking something up her nose.'

'Seriously, Mr Sensitive?' We stopped at the lobby door.

'I'm just pissed off she came back into your life with a shitload of baggage. *Dangerous* baggage. This doesn't even qualify as baggage, Street. It's more like a Hummer.'

'I shouldn't have to remind you that Miki is a victim. And she will always be in my life, Rauser. Always.'

'Well, at least she's out of your house.'

Rauser's a good man. Most days I'm not offended when he's protective. But today I had to swallow down the urge to yell at him. Preconception taints investigations. It had already prevented me from fully comprehending the danger Miki was in. And Rauser was just as human as anyone else.

'If this guy has been staging events to psychologically sabotage her, he's been stalking her for a long time. The noises were first reported over two years ago, right? Miki has been in three or four hospitals in the metro area over the years. Maybe they met there. He might have a history of mental illness. He clearly has a healthy dose of narcissism,' I said.

'We can subpoena records, cross-check her inpatient dates against other patients and staff. In the meantime, we'll check her phone. If it's still on, we can GPS it. If not, the provider will have a last location.'

He typed a four-digit code into the panel outside. The door buzzed, and we heard the scraping sound of metal swiping as the latch withdrew. The heavy wooden door popped open an inch and we stepped into a small unattended lobby. I looked around at a staircase, elevators, real estate pamphlets on one of the antiqued walnut tables, marble floors, a couple of nice armchairs.

'According to the volunteer, he and Mr Kelly come into the lobby,' Rauser told me. 'The guy's sitting in that chair. We know he's our perp. He's the only one here, and the volunteer didn't hear the door opening.' Rauser pointed to a wing-backed armchair. 'Guy has a newspaper, barely lowers it when they come in, so this volunteer driver doesn't really catch his face, except he's white. Guy took it with him, by the way. The newspaper. The driver notices his shoes. Black with thick soles. It registers somewhere he might be a waiter and the clothes are inexpensive. He knows he was wearing black pants. The shirt might have been white, but he's not positive on that point.'

'A waiter, a chauffeur, hotel staff,' I said, and wondered if the driver's recollection was accurate. Memory is not a recording device. It's corrupted by our own bias. We want to fit the pieces together. So we do. And then we convince ourselves it's true.

STRANGER IN THE ROOM — 147

'Figured he walked here or took MARTA, probably planned to steal a vehicle. One of the cameras at Colony Square catches a good section of the bus stop on that corner. We'll review the tapes and interview everyone we can that might have a view of this building. He would have had to conceal the weapon he used to hit the driver. Probably a steel pipe of some kind. Tire iron, most likely.'

'So he hid the weapon at a more convenient time,' I suggested. 'He came over and planted it out front somewhere. He'd obviously surveyed the building, had the entry code. He would have known there was no video. He didn't want to use the gun inside and attract attention.'

'He's careful,' Rauser said. 'He took the newspaper with him.' We stared at the chair where a killer had sat as if we were waiting to hear its side of the story. Rauser sat down, reached for a newspaper on a marble-top side table between the Louis XV chairs. The newspaper had a label on it with the name of the condo, identifying it as a complimentary lobby copy. The killer had taken the paper with him. He was wearing gloves at Miki's. He thinks about evidence transfer. I wondered if he'd actually been reading the paper, relaxing, waiting. It could happen. Some offenders don't even experience elevated blood pressure during the commission of a crime. Was this the kind of monster that had fixated on Miki? He'd killed to shock her, terrify her; perhaps he fantasized it would also subdue her or bring her around. I wasn't sure yet what motivated him.

I stepped outside and came back through the door, glanced at Rauser in the chair, walked toward the elevators, turned back to look at him. The paper was up.

'What do you see?' Rauser asked.

'Clothes, forehead, hair. Caught the side of your face, but who's to say the killer hadn't turned away.'

Rauser refolded the newspaper, dropped it back on the table, and walked around the lobby, glanced out one of the windows. 'You can see the parking area from here. He could have seen them coming. Then he goes to the chair and waits. Kelly's old and the driver's in bad shape, sixties, overweight. Pretty easy to take 'em.'

'Need to establish some context. When and how was Kelly first exposed to the offender? Was there a prior relationship?'

'I'm saying he preselected Kelly. Something about the old man fit this guy's agenda. Maybe it was all about how freaky it would be for Miki. I mean, who could forget that scene? Pretty fucking dramatic. Wonder why he didn't go for a kid? Would have been easier, physically.'

A thought hit me like a ton of bricks. 'Seventy-seven years between them,' I said. 'It doesn't make sense.'

'Between who? What doesn't make sense?'

'It was Donald Kelly's birthday,' I said.

'And?'

'How about Troy Delgado? It wasn't his birthday, was it?'

'No. It wasn't.'

'No, it wasn't,' I repeated, and thought about that. 'You have those photos on you?'

Rauser pulled the copies from his shirt pocket. I went through them one by one, stopped at a long shot of the body shown in its environment – the pine straw, the bits of trash, the clenched fist, the outstretched fingers. I showed it to Rauser.

'Something's been bugging me about this scene. It just hit me.' I pointed at the red plastic lying near the body, two inches long, bright against the dirt, no discoloration. 'Everything else belongs here. We've got all the stuff on the ground you expect to find near a builder's site – napkins, a fast-food bag, a cup and straw, cigarette butts. That's a balloon. It doesn't belong here. Just like the wrapping paper in Donald Kelly's pocket.'

Rauser was looking at me as if I'd just pulled a trout out of my ear. 'It was Kelly's birthday, Keye.'

'But he never made it to his birthday party. Why would he have wrapping paper in his pant pocket?'

'Maybe somebody at the assisted-living joint gave him a gift.'

'And he opens it and puts the paper in his pocket?'

Rauser raised his shoulders and palms. 'So he was a sentimental guy.'

'It's possible,' I said. I didn't sound convinced.

'You said it yourself. There's seventy-seven years between the two victims. What possible connection is there?'

'I don't know,' I admitted, frustrated. 'Or why on earth this would be connected to Miki.' I had lectured Rauser in the past about the dangers of working on a gut feeling rather than simply analyzing the physical evidence. But I had a hunch big-time, and it wasn't letting go of me. 'Who's working on your victimology?'

Getting to know the victim is essential in understanding the offender and motive. And it's the most difficult part of an investigation. You can no longer label them merely as 'victim' once you learn the details of their lives. You're no longer psychologically protected when they become real, when you look right at their pain or terror. But it's just as indispensable as physical evidence in establishing a correct pool or class of suspect and determining who had access to the victim's life, when, and why.

'Bevins and Angotti are doing vic on both cases.'

'Look how red this balloon is, Rauser. And clean. No dirt. It's not faded. It's new to this environment. And think about the body fluids on both victims. And the rope. Jesus.' My mind was racing. 'The rope that was holding Kelly's head back. The thinner one, the twine. It's about right for the gauge used to strangle Troy Delgado.'

Rauser scratched the back of his head and scowled down at me.

'Oh come on,' I told him. 'This is why you brought me, right? What's the harm in having your fiber guys compare them? And the fluids at the lab. Either the evidence will support the theory or not.'

His phone rang. He answered and listened. 'Where?' A pause. 'I'm on my way.' He clicked his phone off hard, like he wanted to punish it. 'The volunteer driver's missing Honda turned up. It's in the garage at the station.'

'At the police station?'

'You believe that shit? Blood on the passenger's seat. Probably shot the old guy as soon as he forced him into the vehicle. They dug out a nine-millimeter slug. Showy bastard put it right under our nose.'

14

White Trash met me at the door squinty-eyed and stretching, plowed into my ankles, herded me toward the kitchen. I dutifully pulled the Reddi-Wip can from the fridge. She sat up on her hindquarters like a kangaroo. I harrumphed, remembering my mother saying Miki had been teaching her tricks. *Riight.* As if this animal were trainable. Absurd. The only reason she even consents to using her litterbox is that she prefers it.

'You want some whipped cream?' I used my high voice, the one reserved for animals and babies. White Trash rolled over. 'Sonofabitch. I do have a trick cat.' I couldn't believe my eyes. She then sat like a trained dog and gazed up at me. I doled out a generous tablespoon on a saucer.

I leaned against the counter and watched her. The last couple of days had settled in my shoulders and neck. A shot of something strong would have been nice. I squirted some Reddi-Wip into my mouth, tried not to think about Troy Delgado facedown in dirt and trash. I thought about him anyway. And his mother watching us from that window.

Her house must seem so quiet now. I thought about the man in the lobby with thick soles, about Donald Kelly's body dangling in Miki's doorway, about the Delgados' mail and trash being inspected, the dog treats, drills and toggle anchors, surveillance, location selection, timing, gloves, lures, tools, scene staging, and weapons carried to scenes. So many more commonalities. An old man. A young boy. And my cousin. What was the connection? Was there a connection? I thought the physical evidence would confirm what I felt in my gut. I rubbed my eyes. I needed to let go and trust Rauser and his investigators to follow up. I needed to get back to Creeklaw County and figure out what was going on at Northeast Georgia Crematorium. I needed to collect my big fat check from Larry Quinn so I didn't have to worry this month.

I reached back into the fridge, and that's when I noticed the bottle of Jameson sitting on my counter. I looked at it for a few seconds, then cupped my hand around it, just to feel it alone here in my kitchen, the smoothness of the bottle, the shape. It was all part of the ritual of addiction. It's not just about the product inside. When I want it, my whole body wants it. My eyes and nose and mouth and fingertips.

I unscrewed the top, brought the bottle to my nose, closed my eyes, inhaled it slowly. It had been so long. And still so familiar. My entire body was alive to the warm, woody scent.

Just one. What's the big deal?

I took a glass from the cabinet, set it next to the bottle, then poured two fingers and swirled it around, watched it coat the glass, cling to the sides like liquid gold. I could feel it in my throat and in my chest, all the way to my stomach.

I didn't lift it to my lips. I didn't pour it out either.

I wandered into my living room, where I have a workstation overlooking Peachtree Street, the only piece of furniture I've added to my rambling, nearly empty loft in the last year. I buy a piece here and there when something looks right and there's money in my pocket. The two don't always happen at the same time. It's sleek and white, kidney-shaped, with a pull-out tray for my laptop, a modern extravagance I couldn't resist.

I sat down, pulled a pen from a cup on top of the desk. All I could think about was that glass sitting on my counter, that aroma still fresh. *Damn Miki.* She had to be the one who left it there. And me, what the hell was I doing? I wasn't drinking it, but I wasn't saying no either. I was dangerously close and I knew it. I'd left that glass on my counter, beckoning, inviting. I told myself I was postponing that drink. I wasn't. I was giving my drunk's brain time to make it okay. Because if you want it bad enough, you can find a way to justify it.

I remembered Miki's drunken behavior at the bar and her shitty defensive attitude, all her excuses about why it was okay to stay fucked up all the time. As long as you get your award nominations. I felt my temper spark. I walked back into the kitchen, emptied the glass in the sink, then tipped the bottle into the drain and watched it empty out. I turned on the faucet and ran water until I couldn't smell it anymore. When do the cravings stop? I needed a plan for these moments. I needed to go back to AA and make nice with my sponsor. I remembered when I could pick up the phone and call him – the voice of reason. He'd been sober for twelve years.

White Trash followed me back into the living room. I glanced at the Fox Theatre across the street, another beautifully odd and elaborate piece of construction on the National Register of Historic Places. A limo was parked at the entrance, blocking one lane on Peachtree Street, flashers blinking. I glanced at the marquee. Janet Jackson. I strained to get a look. Come on, it might have really been Janet Jackson out there in the limo, smoke-and-mirrors Jackson, every bit as mesmerizing as her brother had been. I waited to see if a limo door would open. It did. And there she was in bleached-out, ripped-up blue jeans and a white shirt with the tail tied up – abs breaking out everywhere. Someone on the street must have yelled, because she smiled and waved. Even ten floors up, the cheekbones and white teeth nearly toppled me off my chair. Rauser would have lost it. He adored her. Almost as much as he loved Jodie Foster, which was too much. It was a little creepy. I think he was secretly convinced he'd meet Jodie one day and she'd realize that she had been living a lie. I'd opened his laptop one afternoon at his house to look for something online and been confronted with wallpaper of Jodie Foster in a wife beater, hands running through wet hair, intense blue eyes, biceps sculpted, and so porcelain perfect I immediately had to wrestle down a million juvenile tendencies just to keep from spewing insecurities all over him. It was one of those moments when you realize that no matter how good the man, how devoted, how madly in love he is with you, he has an interior life full of sexual fantasies about women you will never physically measure up to, and he will never, ever understand why it bothers you.

I pulled out my legal pad and titled a line *Physical/*

Behavioral Evidence, then skipped a line, titled the next one *MO, Signature, Location, Time of Day, Victims.* I remembered Rauser grouching about what could link the victims, about the seventy-seven years between them. Bevins and Angotti were doing a victimology, getting to know the victims' preferences, lifestyle, sexual habits, professional life, family unit; the person they are with friends, with family, at work; piecing together all the contradictions that make up a human being. But what could connect a sheltered thirteen-year-old and a supervised elderly man who lived in an assisted-living facility?

I started filling in what blanks I could – ritual display of corpse, surveillance, shoe print, blood in Honda, shell casing in Honda, wall anchors, dog treats, unknown fluid. I stared at the legal pad, then wrote *balloon. Wrapping paper. A calling card?* This is the way I organize my thoughts – make lists, think, ask questions. Getting to the right questions was the trick. Donald Kelly, Troy Delgado, and Miki Ashton. Were they connected? I believed it more as each moment ticked by. But how? Something about them had caught his eye. Three victims, one living. What was it? A place they'd all visited? A restaurant? A grocery store? Something they all had an affiliation with, perhaps. Could it be something the Delgado parents were involved in, rather than the child? A political group? A club? The man in Miki's window had the opportunity – perhaps many opportunities – to kill her. But she was alive. Another big question mark.

I glanced back at the Fox. The limo was gone. I am privy to a lot of the comings and goings of performers across the street. Celebrity buses and limos unload their big shots hours before showtime and I see them striding in importantly while personal assistants and security personnel hurry them toward the dressing-room tower, all five floors of it. Tractor-trailers unload equipment in the alley, then flood the cafés and coffee shops and hotels along the street with stagehands and groupies who entertain everyone with their superstar stories. And from these windows I've witnessed beggars being picked up by cops in the early mornings when Atlanta needs to put on its makeup for a Super Bowl or the Olympics or some big conference. Lord knows where these people are dropped off. Not one cop I know will admit to the practice, including the one who shares my bed several nights a week, even though I have seen it with my own eyes. Cops are like that. It's a loyalty that surpasses other allegiances.

My phone rang. Neil's name came up on caller ID. 'When are you coming back?'

'I'm leaving in the next hour. I've been with Rauser at crime scenes all day.'

'Oh joy,' Neil said. 'That always works out so well.'

Neil and I had agreed to take on a consulting job last year with APD, and it ended up flipping our world on its head. 'Lot of weird stuff happening here,' I told him.

'Yeah, well, lot of weird stuff happening here too. There's something funky going on with these ashes.'

'Please tell me you didn't mess with that sample.'

'Here's what happened,' Neil began to explain. I braced myself. When Neil starts out that way, it almost never ends well. 'I went into Big Knob earlier. Man, this place is a trip.'

'Uh-huh.' I checked White Trash's food and water bowls, then adjusted the air conditioner. White Trash likes it warm. 'How much marijuana was involved?'

'Okay, so I got pretty high after breakfast, but hey, there's fucking nothing to do.'

'So we still have the sample from Huckaby's urn, right? I was molested by a rottweiler for those ashes.'

'Oh yeah. We have a sample, all right. But it doesn't look much like it did.'

'What's that supposed to mean?' I said good-bye to my cat, locked up, and headed for the elevators.

'Well, see, I saw this store that has all kinds of hobby shit. Model airplanes, stuff like that. So I got this idea and, well, I might have decided to add water to the ashes and pour them in an ice tray.'

'You have got to be kidding.' Finding out Neil got stoned and acted on some harebrained notion was not nearly as shocking as discovering I had a trick cat, but it was supremely annoying. Another craving for a drink slapped me hard a couple of times. It was also my week to see Dr Shetty, I remembered. For the last four years, we've had a Thursday appointment twice a month. I don't know how she remains professional while listening to the same whiny crap over and over. This is a classic example of why I'd never even once considered having a private practice of my own. I'm so me, me, me when I'm in her office. I'd be screaming at patients, *Shut the fuck up*. But there seems to be no statute of limitations on my crazy or on her patience. To be honest, I use her for many things, a sounding board, a way to stay sober and avoid the AA meetings I've neglected and the sponsor that held me together early in my sobriety. Dr Shetty does not require an intimate connection. Our intimacy is achieved through the psychodynamic therapy process, which doesn't make me feel like I'm choking. She does not look at me with soft eyes or try to hold my hand like they do at AA. The program saved my life. But sometimes the very last thing I want is for someone to be sweet to me. How can you hold together in the face of that? Dr Shetty maintains a professional distance. As far as I can tell, she has absolutely no feelings whatsoever. It works for us both.

'At what point did it make sense to you to pour water on Huckaby's ashes?' I asked Neil.

'It's not like it was evidence the cops could use anyway,' he said sheepishly.

'What's your point?' I pushed through lobby doors and walked to the garage. Miki's Spitfire was parked where she'd left it. My car was parked next to it. I got in.

'They have this stuff at the hobby store in little paper packages like flour, but it's called decorative cement or something like that. So I bought some. Then I got a mini-ice tray and brought it all back to the hotel. And guess what? First of all, the craft cement-mix stuff looked just like the stuff in Huckaby's urn when it's dry.'

'*Really.*' I waved at the attendant and pulled out onto Peachtree Street with the top down.

'I'm telling you, Keye, side by side you could not tell them apart. That's why I decided to add water. The lab isn't responding to email or phone calls. I thought it was time to get this party started.'

'And?' I was beginning to appreciate Neil's peculiar genius.

'It set up. I've got two hard-as-a-rock cement ice cubes sitting here. One made with Huckaby's ashes. You can't tell them apart.'

I let that sink in. 'Why on earth would he fill an urn with cement mix?' I wondered aloud. 'Unless you don't have cremains. I'll be there in two hours. I think we should have a look at Northeast Georgia Crematorium before the sun goes down.'

15

The Kirkpatrick family had been part of Big Knob's history since Creeklaw County was mapped out and named back in 1823. The Internet was loaded with their history, because Joe Ray Kirkpatrick's great-grandfather was the first black man to own a business in Georgia. Somehow the Kirkpatrick family had managed to prosper even during the years with the most violent racial unrest. The Kirkpatricks had found their own Switzerland in Creeklaw County, where hooded men and torches had once terrorized the non-white population. In 1937, Northeast Georgia Crematorium opened for business. It was the oldest in Georgia, a kind of wholesaler that served the tristate area. The client base: morticians and funeral homes. No walk-ins, please.

'You see these road names?' Neil wanted to know. He had a mapping program on-screen, and he was rolling two miniature cubes he'd made with cement around in his hand like marbles. 'Loretta Ann Kirkpatrick Lane, Bobby James Kirkpatrick Drive, Kirkpatrick Road. What's next? I Own the Fucking Road Road?' He snickered his sneaky, wet little George W. Bush laugh. 'Jesus, why don't they just pee on everything? Turn right here on Crematory Road.'

'A lot of roads in rural areas are named after residents,' I explained. 'Mail carriers in the early days needed—'

'Keye,' Neil interrupted. 'Whatev, okay? Keep your eyes on the road. I don't want to have an accident out here in the sticks and wake up to banjos playing.'

Gravel popped under my tires and red dust rose up behind the car like a jet trail. Half a mile down, we took our first far-off look at Northeast Georgia Crematorium and the property behind it, where the owners lived.

I pulled over and reached across Neil for the binoculars in my glove box. The crematory was brick, reddish brown, one level, *L*-shaped, with rows of narrow tinted windows in the front. Looked like a million cheap office buildings I'd seen in small towns – uninviting, meant for work, not for visitors. A gravel road split off the front parking lot and curled around the building.

No cars at the crematory. No lights, no sign of life at all. Not surprising on a Sunday. I wondered what happened if one was unlucky enough to need a crematorium on a weekend.

The house rose up beyond rolling fields, flanked by woods, then mountains. There was a small lake, a few acres at most. Behind the house, I saw a red barn with white *X*-shaped braces on wide double doors. Equipment storage. The fields were mowed. Sixteen acres, Quinn had told me. They would need a tractor. I moved the binoculars around slowly, surveyed the property. No horses or cattle or dogs. Good news. The last time I'd met a field of cattle, they'd turned on me. More recently, the encounter with Tank, Huckaby's rottweiler, had cured me of crotch-level dogs. I saw a couple of cats stretched out near the house. A partially enclosed chicken coop built with raw wood and wire was next to the barn. The framed-out wire door was open. A few chickens pecked around in the dirt. I saw a small room built onto the coop, also raw unpainted wood. The door was closed. Food storage, I assumed. A padlock hung off a steel hasp. 'Who padlocks chicken feed?' I wondered aloud.

Brenda Wade had been right about the way the property was laid out. The story about the crematory employee mixing the cement mix with the chicken feed made even less sense to me now. Northeast Georgia Crematorium sat on the frontage road at the end of the lane, a substantial distance from the house and barn and chicken coops. How would an employee manage this without being seen from the house? The land had leveled out here – a holler, as the locals call it, a nestled-in valley. My binoculars showed me bits of flaking paint around the window frames on a dated but stately eighteenth-century Georgian farmhouse with a slanted roof and stone chimneys running up each end, all the rage in the pre-Civil War South. French and Roman architecture wowed us a bit later, and the influence remained through Reconstruction. Then huge plantation homes with giant pillars and sprawling porches – Tara on steroids – began to dot the landscape. We are a mishmash of styles, a full-on architectural identity crisis. The South had reinvented itself many times since the Civil War turned previous incarnations to ash.

I had once lived in a two-room apartment with a round bedroom on the top floor of a Victorian. I remember having a very hard time deciding where to put my bed. I'd rented it for two hundred and thirty dollars a month my last year at Georgia Southern. The owner, who lived on the ground floor, had liked me. She made warm flour tortillas from scratch in the mornings, and waking to that scent, like baking bread, warmed me each day. We smeared them with butter and homemade fig preserves and talked over coffee before school. She had felt some kinship with me, I think, because I'm Chinese and she was Hispanic. We'd both had the experience of growing up looking different in the South.

'So why would a guy who's clever enough to use cement mix to replace the spilled ashes go all the way to the house where the chicken feed is stored to refill the urn?'

I handed Neil the binoculars. He studied the property. I saw something moving on the dirt lane that ran between the house and business. 'There's someone on the road halfway between here and the house.'

'It's Kirkpatrick,' Neil said. 'Looks just like the picture on their website. Except he's sweaty.'

'What's he doing?'

'Digging,' Neil said, and handed the binoculars back to me. I saw a pile of dirt and weeds and debris in a wheelbarrow. I watched Kirkpatrick shoveling out more debris into the wheelbarrow.

'Rain comes pouring off the mountains when there's a thunderstorm,' Neil said. 'If you don't keep your ditches clear, you flood.'

'Really, Mr Green Jeans? Wow. I didn't realize you were up on irrigation.'

'I did a lot of reading about the area while you were gone. Do you want to know how Big Knob got its name?'

'Definitely not,' I said, surveying the area. I inspected a small brick house with a screened porch, located fifty yards dead ahead, off the frontage road and across from the Kirkpatrick property. Through the magnification, I spotted a ceiling fan making slow turns behind the dark screened porch. 'Holy cow,' I exclaimed. 'We've just been made by the local snoop.'

I was looking at a slight, white-haired figure in a chair. She had a pair of old military-style binoculars about the size of two thermoses. She was looking right back at me. I put the car in gear and eased up the road, pulled into the driveway. The mailbox was decked out for the upcoming holiday with a red, white, and blue foil cover.

'What's the plan?' Neil wanted to know.

'How about we say we're house shopping,' I suggested.

'Together?' Neil snickered at that. 'We don't have rings.'

'We'll wing it,' I said, as we walked toward the house and the dark screened porch, and the American flag on a pole mount at her front door.

Neil seemed to freeze up on me. I took the lead. We had been looking at a property close by, I told the small, wiry figure who stood at her door. She had white hair and quick brown eyes, the same woman who had been watching us through binoculars. We liked the area but had concerns about living so near a crematorium, I explained. On that, the door flung wide open and we stepped into Mary Kate Stargell's small, immaculate, doily-covered home.

She waved for us to follow her to the kitchen, where she filled tall glasses with ice cubes and poured us sweet tea from a pitcher, then wrapped a cloth napkin round the bottom so as not to leave a ring on the broad, flat armrests of her white rocking chairs on the front porch. She left us for a minute, then returned with a platter of lemon bars with powdered-sugar tops. Chilled lemon bars were the perfect companion to iced tea on a hot day, Mrs Stargell informed us. Neil didn't need to be sold. He was all about it.

The rockers were in a straight line across her front porch, facing the Kirkpatrick pond, rolling fescue fields, and Joe Ray's dirt lane, where he was still working with his shovel.

'It's so quiet up here,' I remarked, after we had settled into our rockers and stared at Joe Ray for a while. Apparently, Mary Kate Stargell wanted to keep it that way, because she did not respond.

'That's one reason we're thinking about living up here.' I elbowed Neil.

'Right,' he managed with his mouth full of lemon bar. 'We love the country.' Bits of graham-cracker crust sprayed my arm. I brushed them off.

'I guess that's one of the neighbors? Or is he hired help?' I nodded in Joe Ray's direction.

'You watched him long enough. What was your opinion?' Mrs Stargell's voice had a little age wobble in it.

'I think he lives there,' I replied, without letting her know she'd surprised me. I was getting the feeling Mary Kate Stargell was a little bit more than I'd bargained for. Something about old women can be a little chilling anyway, in the same way a cat that attacks is scarier than a dog. She was sizing me up now.

'Where you from, honey?' There it was, loaded with subtext, southern style with a smile.

'I'm Chinese American, Mrs Stargell, if that's what you're asking.'

'So's that kudzu out there. It's taking over everything too. Lordy, lordy.' She snorted. 'If you ask me, you got to pick one. Chinese or American. Which is it?'

I felt myself coming up off the chair. Neil grabbed my arm. 'These lemon bars are the best I've ever had, Mrs Stargell,' he said in a good-ole-boy voice I'd never heard him use. Sugar always brought him to life.

She smiled at him with teeth too big and too perfectly sheared off on the bottom to be real. I was betting they slept in a glass of water next to the bed. 'You're a polite young man.' She offered him the platter, and he helped himself. 'You remind me of my Frank. God rest his soul. He's been gone since '97. We bought this property thirty-five years ago.'

'Bet you've got some stories,' Neil said, and finished off his treats. They'd cut me completely out now, which was fine. I'd never seen Neil quite so charming. He actually seemed to like the old windbag.

'Do I ever,' Mary Kate told him. 'That one right there worries me a lot.' She was watching Joe Ray Kirkpatrick. 'He's always digging and planting something or another. Does what he feels like doing. Leaves his mama to take care of the place most days. He brings kudzu from the woods and plants it along the road to keep the bank in place.' She huffed at that absurdity. The wild-running vine had practically swallowed up the South. 'Takes a hired man and a machete just to keep it off my black walnut trees once a week. If you ask me, anyone caught planting it deserves a good beating. But you know how stubborn blacks can be.'

My, the Confederate flag was flying high today. Neil must have noticed my fingernails digging into the armrest, because he put his hand on mine and asked Mrs Stargell what it was like living near the crematorium. 'Is there smoke?'

Mary Kate shook her head. 'Never was like smoke, really. When Frank was alive, he called it the vapors. We'd see it coming out that metal stack pipe like steam. Especially in the winter. Joe Ray's got the vapors, my husband used to say, and we'd just laugh and laugh.' She thought about that, rocked her chair a few times. 'Joe Ray, Senior, of course. That rascal out there in the ditch took over when his daddy died a few years back.'

'So he's a rascal?' I tried to insinuate my way back into the conversation.

'That's the nicest thing I know to call it. Chases every skirt in town. And he's lazy.'

Neil and I looked across the Kirkpatrick property to the man in the distance who had not stopped working since we arrived.

Mrs Stargell seemed to read our thoughts. 'Oh, don't be fooled by that. It's the only work he cares about doing.'

'How about the crematorium?' I asked.

'I ain't seen the vapors for a good year. Last winter I could see my breath out here even with a space heater, but I didn't see nothin' venting out of that place.' Her voice got low, like she was telling a ghost story. 'I saw him let in a hearse this morning and then he closed back up and was gone. That place is more closed than open.'

'Interesting,' Neil said, attempting to appear only casually concerned and not quite making it. 'What's your theory?'

'Lordy, I hate to think of why.'

I leaned back in my rocker and watched Joe Ray. 'How's the traffic from the employees on workdays? Does it bother you? I wouldn't want to live on a road with a lot of traffic.'

'Always been a family business,' Mary Kate answered. Neil and I exchanged a glance. 'I don't think I've ever seen anybody work there except the senior Joe Ray and Joe Ray Junior. Lordy, that place has got to be a mess in there. I know he didn't have time to take care of those bodies this morning. I bet they're just sitting there waiting for somebody to give two hoots. When I'm gone, I want somebody to do me right. I ain't lying around on some gurney in one of Joe Ray's cold rooms. We have to give up enough of our dignity in life.'

16

Big Knob had a little Niagara Falls in it – a carnival plopped down in the middle of eye-popping geography. I fully expected to find a house of wax wedged between homemade fudge shops and Jet Ski rentals and restaurants that buttermilk-battered lake fish and hush puppies and served them with offerings from local breweries. I'd come into town to get a general feeling from locals about Georgia's oldest and, by volume, largest crematorium. Something still wasn't adding up. The chicken-feed-and-cement-mix story seemed even more implausible now that I'd seen the property, just as Brenda Wade suggested it would. And something Mary Kate had said about the 'vapors' stuck with me. I didn't want to speak with Joe Ray Kirkpatrick just yet. I knew his story. And I sure didn't want to tip him off to an investigation.

Neil had stayed at the lodge to follow my hunch on Rauser's case. I'd asked him to search police blotters, which most of the local papers carried, for any violent crimes where wrapping paper or a balloon or anything similar was reported as part of the scene. It was a shot in the dark, I knew. But I'd come so close to overlooking the clues I now believed were being left at each crime scene, perhaps the police had too. Perhaps this important evidence had ended up on some inventory sheet just like the wrapping paper in Kelly's pocket. And even more troubling, perhaps Miki's stalker had killed before. As much as Rauser had not wanted to discuss the possibility of a serial killer, he was a good cop. I knew he'd follow up, run the signature and MO through the databases and order comparisons from his fiber and trace specialists on the twine. I kept thinking about a grieving mother looking down at us from her window, Donald Kelly's twisted old face, the brick-red stain on his shirt, the bright splotches that came to life on his body under a forensic light source. Rauser had given me that look when I'd suggested a connection. He hadn't wanted to think about it at that moment. No one would. The implications are too great. But I knew he'd thought about it anyway. That's the kind of guy he was.

Big Knob's restaurants and taverns were busy. I had to search for a place to park. In most parts of the Bible Belt, liquor stores are closed on Sunday. But restaurants are allowed to serve alcohol from noon on, which coincides with church letting out so that God-fearing southerners can start drinking right away. But that kind of thinking is about as welcome on a Sunday in Georgia as a flock of pigeons on the runway.

I stopped at a narrow two-story tavern wedged between storefronts in the main strip with crowded tables sitting on a flat roof and tiny white lights strung around the railing. I went through a propped-open wooden door and took a stool at the empty bar. A couple of booths had customers. One of them was eating a good-looking salad.

'I'll have one of those,' I told the bartender, a curly-headed brunette with a spatter of freckles across her nose and an easy smile. 'And club soda with a lemon twist, please.'

What arrived on a plate in front of me was nutty mache and peppery arugula with toasted pecans, split red grapes, and an air-light Danish bleu vinaigrette that made me rethink pub food. I watched the bartender fill orders and thought about the perfectly good bottle of Jameson I'd poured down the drain earlier.

Servers ran up and down the stairs with trays to the rooftop crowd. When the bartender looked like she'd caught up, I called her over and asked her if she was from Big Knob. She was. 'So what do you do if you're bored? Any scandals, deceptions, gossip?'

She grinned at me. 'In Big Knob? Relationship drama, maybe. That's the most that happens here unless the tourists get drunk.' One of the servers slapped a ticket on the bar and unloaded a tray of used mugs. 'You a reporter or something?' the bartender asked while she filled the order. The waitress glanced over inquisitively.

'Me? No way. Just looking for some dish,' I said.

The waitress and the tray disappeared upstairs. The bartender dried her hands on a white hand towel. She smelled like the lime she'd just squeezed into tequila, and I had a vivid recollection of the way Cuervo Gold melts through the slush and citrus and lands at the bottom of your frozen margarita. That's how a drunk remembers drinking, I reminded myself, through a soft-focus lens. We want to waltz with those memories, whisper in their ear – just one of addiction's dirty little tricks. But even with all its pressures and temptations, I still loved a bar – the low light and glistening bottles, rows of clear, spot-free glasses, the smell, the chatter.

'We had a drought and then the economy went south,' she told me, and I finally pinpointed her accent, southern Appalachian, a confusing, quick-stepping rhythm with a hint of a brogue – the Clampetts go to Scotland. 'So I guess the big news up here is for the first time in four years, we can make a living without having to leave the county for work.'

'I hear there's a big crematory up here.'

She nodded. 'Handles three or four states, I think. I'm no expert. My family plants their dead in the ground.'

I thought about Brenda and Billy Wade and Huckaby. They all had urns full of something they didn't pay for.

She pushed a fresh club soda in front of me. 'You hear any stories about the crematory?' I asked.

She laughed. 'We used to get drunk in high school and sneak around out there. Scare the shit out of each other. It's still going on. You can't have a crematorium within a couple miles of a high school without there being stories. Nothing else for kids to do in a tourist town in the off-season. Crematorium and the funeral homes get broken into about every Halloween. My little brother still swears he saw the crematory owner carrying out bodies on his shoulders in the middle of the night and throwing them in a truck.' She chuckled and shook her head. 'Now, just why in the hell would anybody do that?'

'Crazy,' I said, going back in my mind to Mary Kate

talking about the vapors and Joe Ray digging on a dirt lane.

The kitchen door swung open to my left and I felt the heat from the ovens. A red-faced young man in a chef's hat came out with two enormous shrink-wrapped trays. I glanced over at them as he set them on the end of the bar. Raw veggies and dip, hummus and pita, jalapeño poppers, and a bunch of fatty pub food. 'Stewart order,' he told the bartender. 'One more tray coming out. They're picking up any minute.' He handed her a ticket, disappeared back into his hot kitchen, came out again with the third tray.

'We cater a lot of parties,' the bartender told me. 'People like the food here.'

'The vinaigrette is excellent,' I said, and finished my salad while she rang up the order and collected money from a couple who'd showed up for the trays.

'Tell Mr Stewart happy birthday,' the bartender told them.

I watched them leave. A thought hit me. I reached for my phone. 'Rauser, was Donald Kelly's birthday party catered?'

'Who is this?'

'Hilarious,' I said. 'Just never gets old.'

'Kelly's daughter gave us a list of everyone at the party,' Rauser told me. 'No caterers on the list. And we've interviewed everyone there.'

'It would have given him access to the building. Service people would have a code. He'd have opportunity to hide a weapon.'

'And it would explain why the guy might have been dressed like a waiter. But I got nothing in any of the interviews about caterers.'

We were quiet for a minute. 'Maybe they weren't there,' I told him. 'Maybe they delivered and left.'

'We asked about service people, anyone that might have access to the building.'

Of course they had, I thought. Rauser had a top-notch team. But I couldn't let it go. 'Did you ask specifically about a catering company?'

'I wasn't present for every interview, Keye. I've got five other cases open.' He sounded annoyed.

'Okay. Sorry.'

'No, no. I'm sorry. Long day. We'll double-check and I'll let you know. I got some other stuff I wanna talk to you about later anyway.'

'Thanks.'

'So how's it going up there in God's country? Figure out why there's no ashes in the urn?'

'Not even close,' I told him. The door opened and a group filed in. The sun was going down and the bar was filling up.

'Where are you? It sounds like a bar.'

'That's because I'm in a bar.'

'Great,' Rauser said. 'Good to know I don't have to worry about you at all.'

'Bye, Rauser,' I said, and smiled.

'Bye, darlin'.'

17

'Jesus, it's pitch black out here.' Neil stumbled over gravel and rocks. It was almost midnight on Crematory Drive. I'd parked the car a quarter mile or so back and we'd started up the dirt road on foot. The cicadas were buzzing this year, worked up by July's smothering heat. No moon. No stars. The mountains, black waves against the clouded, charcoal sky, were our only point of reference other than raggedy treetops. They'd looked different during our daylight visit. We had bright LED penlights, but I didn't want to use them. I had a feeling Mary Kate Stargell didn't miss much. For all I knew, she slept on that porch where she had served us sweet tea and lemon bars and insulted my ethnicity. And the ground was flat here. Maybe a penlight would look like a firefly from a farmhouse window. Maybe it would just look like a prowler on the road.

I felt my phone vibrating. I saw Rauser's name before I blocked the bright display with my palm. 'I need to take this,' I told Neil.

'What am I supposed to do? I can't see my hand in front of my face.'

'Just wait here.'

'Don't leave me alone out here, man.' I heard him skid, then curse.

'You were right,' Rauser told me. 'Caterers dropped off party trays forty-five minutes in advance. Kelly's daughter didn't want them around when the old man got there. We're running down several angles. By the way, last location for Miki's phone was the Whole Foods in Midtown where she shopped. So no way to know if she lost it there and it went dead or if somebody lifted it.'

'You sound tired.'

'Closed three cases today. Probably open five more tomorrow. For now we're looking good enough so that I can bring another team in on the Kelly and Delgado killings.' He paused. I heard the foil sound of his nicotine gum pushing through the package. I knew that sound by heart now. He was totally strung out on the stuff, a couple hundred bucks' worth a month. But he wasn't smoking, which was pretty good for a guy who had learned his high-stress job with a cigarette in his hand. 'You were right about a couple things. The balloon hadn't been exposed to the elements. It's fresh out of the package. And Fiber matched the twine. It's exact. We're probably looking at the same lot. I think we can trace it to an individual store. Looks like you can get it at about any building supply, and a lot of drugstores and grocery stores too.'

'Miki's house, the condos where Kelly was abducted, the neighborhood where the Delgados live, it's all in a pretty tight area,' I suggested.

'Yep. The assisted-living place too. All in Midtown.'

'He had to buy more than twine,' I said. 'He needed toggles and drill bits and whatever. Big building supply right in the heart of Midtown. He'd shop where he's comfortable, and he'd go where he's just a face in the crowd. I'm sure they have some kind of cameras operating.'

'As soon as we confirm the origin, we'll start looking at security tapes. I got someone going over cold cases too, looking over the inventory sheets and shit. Maybe we got some stuff that didn't seem important at the time.'

'Exactly what I've been thinking. Neil's been going through old newspapers with police blotters.'

'I appreciate the help. And your help today. You might have blown it wide open for us. And you're right. It's why I drag you to crime scenes with me.'

'I'm happy to do it,' I said.

'How you doing, darlin'?' He always dropped the *G*. Like a country singer. 'You feeling okay?'

'I'm worried about Miki. But I'm okay.'

'You know, we went through a lot, you and me, with the Wishbone cases last year.'

'Where did that come from?'

'We were hurt bad. And you went right back to work as soon as you were physically able.'

'I have a huge mortgage. Of course I did. You would have too if APD would have let you.'

'I had to go through weeks of psych stuff before they'd let me carry a gun again.'

'Are you suggesting I give up work or my ten-millimeter?' I said it lightly, but I had an uncomfortable feeling Rauser had more on his mind.

A slow second ticked by. 'I bumped into Tyrone today. Said you seemed wrapped up a little tighter than usual last time he saw you.'

'Why? What did he say?'

'Said you went all Chuck Norris on some kid, then drew down on him.'

Had my response been inappropriate? I didn't think so. I'd felt threatened. I'd protected myself. I felt my temper spike and that tic pumping at the corner of my eye.

'I just want to know you're acknowledging what happened to us was a big deal,' Rauser was saying. 'I want to know you're dealing with it and not stuffing it. You don't talk to me about your feelings.'

'I don't need you to be my shrink, Rauser. I pay Dr Shetty to insult me every other Thursday. We pick the same scab off the same wounds. I get to be utterly self-absorbed, and she gets five hundred bucks a month. Everyone's happy.'

'I'm the guy that sees you put your gun under the pillow every night. I see the night terrors and sweats.'

'Early menopause.'

Rauser was silent.

'What do you want me to say?'

'How about something real?'

'Okay, I'm standing in the pitch dark on a country road with Neil, and this is not a great time to have this conversation.' Everything inside me had always risen up against Rauser's daddy tendencies. It made me feel crowded and watched. I didn't like it. When I wanted advice, I'd ask for it. I took a minute before I continued to adjust my tone. And my attitude. 'Okay, the truth is I almost never feel safe anymore. And I miss drinking. God, I miss it. I came so close today. I think I might need to start those whiny-ass meetings again if my sponsor is still speaking to me.' I hadn't shown up for so many meetings I'd promised to attend. I hadn't talked to my sponsor since it was my turn to help clean up afterward. I didn't mean to blow off the meeting. I just forgot. There's always some emergency in my business. A fire that needs putting out always gets in the way. I'd gotten an angry message from him that night about commitment, about putting recovery first, about learning not to let down the people who counted on me. I hadn't had the guts to go back.

'It makes me happy you're considering AA again.'

'They usually have doughnuts.'

'I wish I didn't know you were on some dark road in Bumfuck.'

'Well, I have a gun and a bad temper so . . .'

Rauser laughed. 'I love ya, Street. Get to a meeting. I'm sure they have them in Creeklaw County too.'

I didn't move for a minute after I hung up, just let the heavy air fall down around me. Rauser wanted me to talk more or cry or something. Because I'd been a victim of violence. Because we both had. Dr Shetty gives me prescriptions to manage anxiety around post-traumatic stress. I never fill them. I can manage my own goddamn anxiety without a pill. I just wanted to move on. I didn't want to *keep* being a victim. I remembered Miki arguing against her meds. *Fuck.* I didn't want to deal with this.

'Hello?' Neil's voice broke in the darkness.

I couldn't see him, but I heard him milling. 'I'm coming, you big baby.'

'Everything okay in paradise?'

'Rauser's acting like a wife. It's a pain in the ass. I kind of want to run away right now.'

We walked for a minute. Gravel and sandy fine clay under our soles felt like walking on marbles. 'Doesn't that cop have enough drama in his life?' Neil chuckled. 'Let's face it. You're a magnet for the shit. You're the whole fucking cast of *Glee*.'

'Gee, thanks.' I slipped and almost went down.

'Some people like that, though. I have a friend down in the Keys. He says when the hurricanes come the howling is so constant and so eerie you think you'll lose your mind. And then it stops. You walk outside and everything is torn all to shit and totally silent. And suddenly you miss the howling. Because you're so used to it. Like you're empty without it.'

'Wow. Are the serial rights available to that? Because it was *absorbing*.'

'You obviously missed the point,' Neil said. 'The analogy was to love and drama, the way it howls, the way you get used to it.'

'Again, fascinating. Thank you.' I squinted in the darkness. 'Hey, there's the fence. We're close.'

'That means Mrs Stargell's house is just up the road.'

'*Aww*. You miss her? Want me to drop you off there? She can tell you stories and rub your head.'

'You're just jealous because she didn't like you.'

'Because I'm Chinese. Doesn't that offend you on some level?'

'Not really. I was there for the food.' We walked with only the electric buzz of cicadas, dirt and rocks grinding under our feet. I heard frogs and remembered there was a lake on the property.

'What's with the double names?' Neil asked out of the blue. 'Joe Ray. Mary Kate. I guess it's a southern thing. Billy Ray. Bobby Joe. Wally Bubba. Bubba Bubba. I think we should do that. What's your middle name?'

'No way.'

'You don't have a second name?' Neil turned his penlight on my face. 'Come on. What's the big deal? You know mine.'

'Turn that off. And it's no big deal to you because yours is David. Neil David Donavan. Could you be any whiter?'

'You can call me Bobby Jane if it makes you feel better. Come on. I won't tease you.' He punched my arm. 'Tell me or I'm turning the interrogation lamp back on.'

'Lei,' I answered, against my better judgment.

'Lei? Oh my God. Your name is Keye Lei? You *rhyme*?' He started to laugh. 'Is that a family thing or what? What were your parents' names? Pee Wee and Kiwi?' He laughed so hard he snorted. 'Oh Jesus, I'm going to wet my pants.' I thought I saw him grab himself in the dark, then I heard shoes skidding on gravel and a *fump*. '*Sonofabitch*,' he cursed loudly into the night.

'Could you maybe be a little quieter? The whole undercover thing. Remember?'

'It hurt, Kiwi,' he fake cried, then sniggered some more.

We found the sloped driveway and hurried to the front of the building. Neil used his body to block the flashlight while I checked the door and windows. Didn't look like there was an alarm system. I pulled my lock-picking kit out of the front pocket of my black hoodie.

'Seriously?' Neil said.

'You have a better idea?'

'No.'

'Then hold the light and make sure the old fossil up the road doesn't see it.' I examined a standard cylinder lock on the front door. 'She probably doesn't sleep. Probably lives off the blood of children.'

A few seconds later, the bolt withdrew and I pushed open a squeaky door into what looked like one of those walk-in doc-in-the-box clinics – commercial tile floors and a long Formica counter. But none of the tools normally found in reception areas – appointment books, magazines. No pencils or notepads. We stood there with the penlights in our hands, keeping the light low and away from the windows.

'Not very welcoming,' Neil whispered.

'No point, I guess. Visitors come in a coffin.'

'Oh Jesus,' Neil moaned. It seemed to hit him for the first time that we were inside a crematorium.

We slipped behind the reception counter and opened the door. The same tile met us – ash, with sparse blue and charcoal flecks. Metal doors with a square of reinforced glass at the top and center lined a hallway. Five of them. All closed.

'What are we looking for?' Neil wanted to know.

'I don't know exactly. Tax files. See if he's ever reported an employee. Utility bills and whatever else you can find that might make this place run. Suppliers' invoices. I need his utility accounts.'

'I'm shocked you'd think I'd invade someone's privacy. What will I be looking for?'

'Fluctuations.' I pushed open the first door to my left. Two adjustable gurneys. A metal table in the center. No windows. My flashlight swept over two rows of cabinets, upper and lower, a counter between them. There was a dock door, garage-style, with ridged metal, and a standard door next to it. A clipboard with a pen attached to it by a chain hung on the wall next to the dock door. I checked it out. *Receiving Room Log*. It was columned and lined, spaces marked for date, time, name of deceased, and funeral home delivering the body, and a column for the receiver's initials. I flipped back through one page at a time. Same initials on each line. JRK. Joe Ray Kirkpatrick had checked every corpse into the receiving room – more evidence he was lying about an employee. A quick count of pages, then lines per page, told me the crematorium had accepted more than four hundred bodies since the log began at the first of the year. I went back to the front page and checked today's date. Three lines. Mary Kate's eagle eye had seen a hearse pull in this morning. Now I knew why. I looked over the counters, opened a couple of drawers, didn't find anything that would help.

We crept back out into the hallway. I chose the door across the hall. Neil was hot on my heels. If I'd stopped suddenly, I'd have had to see a proctologist. We stepped into an office with a messy desk, an ashtray piled with Black & Mild butts, and the stale stink of pipe-tobacco cigars. I saw stacks of paper on the floor, a braided throw, dusty like everything else, coffee-stained paperwork on the desk.

'This is exactly what we need,' I told Neil.

'Guy's a total slob. Be no order to it. Makes stuff harder to find.'

I heard a sound, metallic, familiar – the squeaky door hinge in the front room. *Crap!*

Neil grabbed my arm at the biceps and squeezed. I guided him to the wall behind the door, cut my light. I could hear his breath quicken. 'Just stay really still, okay?' I hissed. 'Whatever this is, we'll be fine.'

We stood there in the dark and silence. No, not silence – footsteps, soft with a little drag. A sliver of light played under the door, then vanished. Neil's breathing was coming heavier, and my heart was starting to tap-dance. How would we explain ourselves? And to whom would we be explaining ourselves to at almost one in the morning? Doors opened and closed. A one-inch gap between floor and door let the light in again, a quick sweep, then another. The door cracked open. There was nowhere to go. The only other door was being opened by a stranger. I reached for the Glock I had in the duty holster attached to the back of my jeans and gripped it by the barrel. Whoever it was, they were going to have a hell of a headache in a few seconds, because I was not about to wind up in a Creeklaw County jail. Larry Quinn would never let me live it down.

I saw the tip of the flashlight. The beam bounced around, explored the room. I raised my arm. Neil sucked in a breath. Then the barrel of the flashlight came into view. I took a step forward. Mary Kate Stargell's petite frame spun around with impressive dexterity for a woman her age. She aimed her flashlight at my face. I squinted, lowered the gun, and retaliated with my bright LED, pointing it at her beady little brown eyes. Not wanting to be left out, Neil switched on his penlight and moved it back and forth between us.

'Mrs Stargell, what are you doing here?'

'What am *I* doing here? *Ha!* Why, I'm just being a good neighbor, watchin' out after Kirkpatrick's property.' She wagged one of her scrawny fingers at us. 'And wouldn't they like to know I found you in here? I knew there was no way in blazes you two were house shopping up here. You got the city written all over you.' Her voice was shrill with accusation and excitement, dark eyes glittering like a rodent's in the light of so many penlight batteries. 'You're investigatin' that rascal Kirkpatrick, and you better let me in on it or I'll blab to everyone I know.'

'You're interfering with an investigation. Go home.'

'If I have to leave here before you leave, then I'm going straight up to that Kirkpatrick house and knocking on that door.' White skin, thin as parchment, creased into hundreds of little lines. The woman must have been in her eighties. Her eyes narrowed. 'On the other hand, if we leave here together with me knowing everything you know, why, then it's a whole nuther story and I won't feel the need to discuss it with anyone.'

I moved my light over her – silver-white hair, pink quilted bathrobe, and hard-soled moccasin-style slippers. 'Neil, fill her in and you two get busy looking for those accounts. I'm going to check out the crematory. Nice outfit, by the way.'

'I used to come up here and keep Joe Ray Senior company. God rest his soul. That's the crematory room two doors down. Across from that are the coolers. 'Cause there's a waiting period and they got to keep them cadavers good and cold.'

'*Eeww,*' Neil shuddered.

'Keep that flashlight down and away from the windows, please.' I could hear the irritation in my own voice, but I didn't care. I was aware of the waiting period. Twenty-four to forty-eight hours in most states. It was a safety measure in case an investigation was launched. Cremation prevents determining cause of death in most cases. There are exceptions. Bone fragments can tell the story if certain poisons and toxins contributed to death.

'Why are you being so mean to her?' Neil asked in a loud whisper. His nerves seemed to be fraying a bit too.

'Because I don't want to spend the night in jail. And because she may actually be Satan.'

We looked at her standing at the large antique desk sucking her false teeth and tsk-tsking at the papers and stains and empty Coke cans and dirty ashtrays. Mrs Stargell pushed the eyeglasses hanging around her neck onto her nose, plunked down in the desk chair. The glasses pulled up at the corners like Catwoman's. 'If he had a grave to roll over in, why, then Joe Senior would be rolling.' She looked up and added earnestly, 'He was cremated, of course.'

'Of course,' I said.

'Of course,' Neil said.

She opened a drawer and began riffling through Kirkpatrick's private papers with the fervor of a Cold War operative. Neil, penlight stuck between his teeth, went to a pile of papers on the floor in front of a paper shredder.

I left them and went to the door leading to the crematory chamber. Same Formica counters and cabinets I'd seen in the receiving room. There was a clipboard on the counter and a ballpoint on a chain. A wide, glistening stainless-steel chamber seemed to tunnel into the far wall. A *Caution* sign with warnings about high temperatures hung over it. A stainless conveyor system about five feet long was positioned in front of the oven. A gurney was pushed up to the conveyor.

I studied the crematory log. The top sheet was blank. I checked the next page. Not one entry. Then, one sheet at a time, I went through the stack. Not one recorded cremation. What did it mean? At the very least, Joe Ray Kirkpatrick wasn't keeping up his paperwork. The records were required by law. A corpse has to have a paper trail. It cannot simply disappear. Maybe Mrs Stargell was right about him being lazy. Lazy, careless, and greedy. He'd probably dropped the urn himself and decided to stuff it with fake remains so he could get paid. It came back to bite him, though. He'd had to reimburse the Wades for everything.

Neil and Mary Kate appeared at the door big-eyed and grinning – Starsky after gender reassignment and Hutch on pot. Mary Kate waved a wad of papers. 'We got 'em right here. Power bills and suppliers just like you wanted.'

'Excellent.' I was examining the control panel mounted on the right side of the crematory. 'See if there's a copy machine, and let's get copies.'

'I peeped at the federal and state tax files too,' Neil said. 'No employee reported. But he said he was paying cash under the table, right?'

'Never was no employee,' Mary Kate griped.

'Let's find a copier and get out of here,' Neil urged. 'I'm getting the creeps.'

I pushed a button on the panel labeled *Crematory Light*. I'd never been this close to one. I wanted to see what the inside looked like. Something was blocking my view – a huge container that looked like heavy-duty cardboard, the kind often used in cremation. It took up nearly the entire space. I could see edges of the ceramic lining inside the chamber, but that was about it.

'What's that?' Mary Kate asked. She and Neil took a couple of steps forward.

I pressed a green mushroom-shaped button and heard the whir of fans. Arrow buttons pointed up and down. I pressed the down arrow; the conveyor wheels began a backward rotation. The container didn't budge. It was too far into the chamber. I glanced around the room. A metal pole with a hook on one end stood in the corner. I grabbed it, stuck it in the chamber, pushed it up under the lid, and grabbed the edge. I pulled as hard as I could, moved it a few inches.

'Give me a hand,' I told Neil.

'Do you know what you're doing?' He took hold of the pole, reluctantly, and helped me pull. 'I Don't Like This.'

We got the container far enough back for the conveyor to move it. The casket-like box backed evenly out of the oven. When it was out far enough so that I could lift the lid, I pressed the big red stop button. The rollers kept turning. I hit it a second time. Nothing. A third time. The coffin edged nearer to the end.

'It's gonna fall out.' Mary Kate had an excited wobble in her scrawny old voice.

I tried shutting down the power. No luck. I banged on the stop button with a balled-up fist. The back half of the container came off the conveyor, an inch, two, three. I was hitting all the buttons. Another foot, two. I backed up. Nothing was going to stop it. In retrospect, we should have at least attempted to give it a soft landing. But we stood there watching it, morbidly, dumbly holding our little flashlights. Three feet out, the back half tipped toward the floor, started a slide on the tile. Then the front half came off the rollers and landed with a thud. Mary Kate closed the distance by a couple more steps. We stood there staring at it.

I put my fingers under one edge and flipped the lid off the box. An open-eyed, bluish pale and ghastly swollen naked corpse stared up at me.

'*Holy crap!*' Mrs Stargell shrieked.

I bent for a closer look, swept my light over the box. 'There's more than one body in here. Christ, there's three or four of them, stacked one on top of the other.'

Neil and Mary Kate bolted for the door like Lindsay Lohan at rehab, just asses and elbows and a wad of Joe Ray's power bills. They tried to push through at the same time. Mary Kate did a sideways move and slipped under Neil's arm, squirted out into the hallway like she'd been squeezed out of a toothpaste tube. Neil ran after her. I heard them giggling like kids at a slasher flick. The little traitors never even looked back.

18

Now, I'm no expert in crematorium procedure, but I knew this wasn't how it worked. I studied the bodies at my feet. Why weren't they in the refrigeration unit? Why were they piled up? Like nothing. Like they were disposable. Tonight while I stared down at them naked, completely exposed and powerless, someone was grieving their death, their absence – empty chairs and beds, unanswered phones, all the routines broken by death. And here they were in a cardboard coffin on a scuff-marked tile floor.

Mary Kate's explanation would have been that he's a lazy rascal, that he just didn't take the time to store them properly. But this was worse. Not only was it incredibly disrespectful, it was irretrievably stupid. If a death investigation was necessary on any one of these individuals, it would reveal his poor handling of the corpses, which are considered evidence during the waiting period. Mishandling a corpse is a serious crime. Fraud is a serious crime. Was this why urns were filled with fake ashes? Were there more?

And why wouldn't he be performing the cremations? Surely bodies in this condition are much harder to deal with than they are when simply reduced to bits of calcium and bone. I wanted to test the oven. Maybe something was wrong with it. But first I needed to get a few pictures.

I used the camera on my smart phone, a pretty good twelve-megapixel. The auto-flash popped in the dark room and fully illuminated an obese, white, midlife female. Underneath her, white arms and legs, brown ones under that, male. Three bodies of varying race and gender, funeral home customers delivered for cremation on a holiday Sunday. Stacked.

I ran my flashlight over the body on top. No visible signs to indicate cause of death. She was wide with a lot of fat. I tried to move her a little so I could see underneath, but she was big, and secondary flaccidity had replaced rigor. I considered splitting the box down the side. But then I'd have three dead bodies spilled out on the floor, fluids leaking out. And in the end, I couldn't subject them to any more mishandling. Not even to find the truth. It felt like a violation. There's no privacy in death. It's disturbing.

I stood there deciding what to do next. I had a mess on my hands. Even if I could get the rollers turning the right way, I had no chance at getting the box back in the oven so that Kirkpatrick wouldn't know he'd had a break-in. Neil and Mary Kate were probably still sprinting up the gravel road.

I returned to the receiving room. I grabbed the log, took it with me back to the crematory chamber where the corpses had fallen, held my flashlight, and read the names. Faye Milner, Demetrius Trite, and Joseph Wagner, the last three names on the list. I looked back at them stockpiled here in one of Joe Ray's rooms. Flipping back through the log, I found the name Wade, Shelia Marlene. I noted that the same funeral home that delivered the three bodies at my feet had also delivered Billy Wade's mother a month ago. I took a picture of both pages.

My phone vibrated. I pressed the tiny button on my earbud. Neil was breathy. He'd seen headlights coming down the lane from the farmhouse.

Joe Ray. Had he seen something, the flash from my camera, maybe? I quickly propped the metal hook back up where I'd found it on the off chance he'd assume his equipment had gone nuts on its own, set off a flash, and dumped out some bodies. Hey, I'm trying to be an optimist. I cut my flashlight and groped my way through the dark, palms out like a bad mime's, the receiving room log under my arm. The receiving room had a standard door next to the dock. It was my best bet. Hurriedly, I reattached the log to the clipboard. Kirkpatrick should be busting in the front door any second.

I have to admit I moved pretty fast, considering the surroundings were unfamiliar. I'm not exactly saying I did it with catlike agility, but let's just say I was out the back door and stepping onto the metal steps next to the loading dock in a matter of seconds.

Have you ever had that empty feeling of just stepping out into nothing? I mean literally, like you accidentally go two steps down instead of one? Well, only moments after congratulating myself on my natural feline grace, I missed the bottom step entirely. I might have stayed upright if gravel wasn't the main fucking industry up here. Everything was covered with it. My right foot started to slide, and I went down hard. My phone flew out of my hand; rocks punctured my knees and palms.

. . . Then, tires on the gravel. Close. Kirkpatrick was driving around back. I looked at my phone. It had landed right in front of the dock. Red taillights, yellow reverse lights lit up the corner as the rear end of a pickup truck came into view. He was backing in? He hadn't seen. He was here for something else.

A line of trees behind the crematorium and twenty feet to the right of the dock offered the only cover. I looked at it, looked at my phone, back at the tree line. If he found my phone, I was screwed. I'd broken in, spilled bodies out on the floor, taken pictures of them and his logs, and left a cranky conveyor running backward.

I went for it obstacle-course-style on elbows and bloody knees, praying I was low enough to stay out of Joe Ray's side mirrors. I grabbed my phone one-handed and rolled out of the way, tires so close to my ankles I felt a rough wave of gravel pushing against them.

I made it to cover and hunkered down in the pine straw. The mosquitoes liked the heat this year too, and they were having their way with me. Kirkpatrick stepped out of his pickup truck and ambled toward the big dock door, unlocked a brass padlock with the key. He was in no hurry. That was going to change once he saw the cardboard coffin on the floor. I needed to clear out, fast.

Just then, the passenger door opened and a woman stepped out. 'I got it, Mama,' Joe Ray called, and pushed open the garage-style receiving door. 'Won't take long.'

She walked to the steps, a slow, rocking walk like one leg

was too short. 'I don't want to be up all night again.'

Again? What the hell was going on? I waited for her to disappear inside, then hightailed it down the gravel drive and through the front parking lot without wiping out. I was finally getting my gravel legs. I looked back over my shoulder. No lights on inside. Joe Ray and his mother show up in the middle of the night and use flashlights inside their own business. Something very weird was going on at Northeast Georgia Crematorium.

A flicker of light got my attention, a loud whisper. *Over here.* I found Neil and Mary Kate on the other side of the road in a dry ditch facing the building. I jumped in with them. My favorite jeans were ripped, and my knees were on fire. I was covered in mosquito bites. Mrs Stargell and Neil were slapping at them too.

'What's that rascal doing in there?' Mary Kate wanted to know.

Lights came on inside, then the floods mounted on the side of the building lit up the parking lot. We all ducked down, came back up slow. Joe Ray pushed through the front door. He had a rifle. Walking from one corner of the building to the other, he checked around corners and behind the line of azaleas planted up against the building. Then he kicked around in the parking lot for a while. Finally, he turned and went down the drive he'd backed into a few minutes before.

Neil let out a breath and so did I, but Joe Ray wasn't done. He showed up a minute later with a handheld flood-light, kicked around some more. Mrs Kirkpatrick opened the front door and told him to check up on the road.

'They're gone, Mama. Probably kids again. Not even a tire track out here.'

Fortunately, the local high school kids had paved the way. The mind works that way too. It searches for safe explanations. Joe Ray would want to believe it wasn't serious. I thought about the bartender's kid brother seeing Kirkpatrick carrying corpses out on his shoulder in the middle of the night. Everyone had laughed it off as a spooked kid's imagination. I desperately wanted to know why he was here so late tonight and why he'd backed his truck up. If we could see the docks, would we see Joe Ray carrying bodies out tonight? And to where? And why?

'Check it anyway,' Joe Ray's mama ordered, and hobbled gooselike out into the parking lot. She knew they had a problem, kids or not. Someone had seen the bodies and knew they were being mishandled.

'*Fuck,*' Neil said.

'All you can see in the dark is movement,' I whispered. 'Just stay still.' I reached for my Glock.

Joe Ray's light bounced around us. Flat in the ditch, we could hear his boots on the gravel road. Mary Kate sucked in air. The mosquitoes were relentless suicide bombers. Neil had talked me out of buying anything with Deet in it to repel them, said the chemicals would cause cancer. This from a man who puts hashish in desserts and pulls rolled-up dollar bills out of his pocket at cash registers.

'Nobody out here, Mama.' His voice was so near I felt Neil jolt. I held on to his wrist. Kirkpatrick started back for the crematorium. 'You gotta let me spend a little money and get that alarm system.'

He went back to the building and to Mrs Kirkpatrick. They were talking as they passed through the front door, but I couldn't make out what they said. We stayed put.

Whatever they'd come for, they would be leaving with. And none of us wanted to get caught on the road.

'Well, I just cannot believe Loretta Ann is involved in whatever's going on in there,' Mrs Stargell hissed, and slapped at a mosquito. 'Joe Ray Senior loved that woman.'

'Maybe the senior Joe Ray was involved in whatever this is too,' I said.

'Hush your mouth,' she scolded, just as the truck came around the building. We ducked back down in the ditch. I was praying they'd head back to the house rather than down the road where the Impala was parked on the shoulder. They did. Our heads came up and we watched the truck take the lane to the house. I raised mini-binoculars and watched them pull up to the barn. The driver's door opened. Joe Ray separated the big double barn doors illuminated by the headlights. Mrs Kirkpatrick must have slid into the driver's seat, because the truck went evenly into the barn.

'What's happening?' Mary Kate demanded.

'They're pulling into the barn,' I said. 'We need to see what's going on up there.'

'We?' Neil squeaked. 'I don't think so.'

'You can count me in,' Mrs Stargell said. 'As long as it ain't tonight.' She climbed out of the ditch in her pink robe and hard-soled moccasin slippers, brushed herself off. 'Y'all come on.' She started up the road. 'I'll feed ya.'

She scrambled eggs for us, southern style, large curd finished in a butter toss and a sprinkle of chives and black pepper, exactly the way my mother had always done them. She piled them on sourdough toast and set a glass of milk and a chewable Flintstones vitamin next to our plates. We didn't ask. We just took our vitamins and drank our milk and used our napkins and remembered our yes-ma'ams and thank-yous, which is what's expected down here when you've been invited to someone's table.

Mrs Stargell drove us to my car in a money-green Cadillac Fleetwood, spanking clean and boxy like they made them in the early nineties. Her head barely made it over the steering wheel. I glanced at the mileage. Sixty-four thousand. It must have been parked for the better part of twenty years.

It was past three when we returned to the hotel. We'd agreed to start new after a few hours' sleep. I sat up in the big bed with my back against a hardwood headboard and my notebook in my lap. I started a list. *Urn, unrefrigerated bodies, waiting period, flashlights, bartender's brother.* I stared at it. The clouds didn't exactly part. Why would he leave the bodies out like that? I wrote: *Motive?* How hard would it be to move them into the refrigeration unit? Whatever was going on, the mother appeared to be in charge. I added her to my list. *Loretta Ann Kirkpatrick.*

I thought again about what Mrs Stargell said, that we suffer indignities enough in life. The prospect of being devalued that way had frightened her. I'd seen it in her face when we sat on her porch talking about the vapors while we watched Joe Ray plant kudzu. Country people take death seriously. Plus, she was old. She'd no doubt begun to contemplate the inevitable. Perhaps we are just shells after we die. I don't know. But if for no other reason than the fear people have in life about being mishandled in death, they should be treated with respect.

I added to my list. *Vapors. Utilities.*

I looked at the pictures I'd snapped earlier, almost as shocking now, so brightly lit on my camera phone as that moment in the chamber room. I remembered Mary Kate's face when the lid came off the box and I chuckled. Hey, funny is funny.

I attached the photographs of the stacked-up corpses to an email to Quinn and hit the send button, then pulled the sheet up to my chin and reached for the bedside lamp. So far this July Fourth weekend had been about as much fun as PETA at a backyard barbeque.

19

I woke to my phone ringing, hints of sunlight under heavy hotel curtains. I glanced at the clock. Nine-fifteen. 'I'm seeing this email you sent, but I don't know what the heck I'm looking at,' Larry Quinn complained. 'Is this some kind of joke?'

I got out of bed, pulled the cord on the draperies, looked out at a dark blue day, thunderclouds but no rain. 'That's what was sitting in the oven last night in Kirkpatrick's crematory.'

'Okay, first of all, I have zero knowledge of how you obtained these photographs.'

'Relax, Larry. It's not like I'm wearing a wire. Hang on a second?' I slipped into jeans and a pale blue blouse and knocked on the door leading to Neil's room, braless. He opened it smiling and handed me a cup of coffee, which was why I was there, of course. He looked wide awake. Bare chest, pajama pants with a gathered elastic band under his navel.

'I heard you moving around,' he whispered, seeing the phone in my hand. I gave him an air kiss, took a sip of coffee. It was good, strong but not bitter, black, exactly the way I like it.

'We found three uncremated bodies stacked one on the other sitting inside the crematory chamber,' I told Larry Quinn. 'According to a neighbor, the last delivery to the crematorium had been early yesterday morning. She says the owner left and never came back. The last entry on the receiving log was three names: Faye Milner, Demetrius Trite, and Joseph Wagner. I also found the entry where the Wades' mother was logged in. So if that's not weird enough, Kirkpatrick and his mother show up. It's the middle of the night, Larry. He pulled up to the docks in back so I couldn't tell what they were doing.'

'You think he forgot to turn the oven on?'

'No. I don't think whatever's going on there has anything to do with forgetting.'

'Maybe he's doubling or tripling up to save money,' Larry suggested. 'He just collects the remains and splits them up. Who would know?'

'That doesn't explain the chicken feed. And I'm pretty sure there was never an employee. Also, those ovens are *designed* to do one body at a time. Even at twenty-one hundred degrees, it wouldn't work if they were stacked up. I guess he could do it without a container, but there's body fluids and leakage to consider. It would be messy.'

'Okay, okay. I just had breakfast.'

I drank some more coffee, found a room-service menu, and handed it to Neil. 'Order us something? Also, Larry, they're supposed to be kept in a refrigeration unit during the waiting period.' I then told him what the bartender had said about her brother seeing Joe Ray carting bodies out at night.

'I knew something was going on up there,' Larry congratulated himself.

Neil was on the hotel phone with room service. I wandered back into my own room. 'Kirkpatrick has already violated the law about six different ways. If he's not cremating them, that's theft by deception and improperly handling a corpse right there.'

'I want to show a pattern of noncompliance and neglect.'

'At least one other urn had cement mix instead of ashes,' I said, and told him about Huckaby and the ashes that had turned to craft cement when they got wet.

'I want more. And stay away from the local cops, okay? We don't know what kind of network Kirkpatrick's got up there. Any theories?'

'I'm stumped.'

'I really don't understand why he would fill urns with cement mix rather than cremate the bodies.'

'Tell me about it.'

I hung up and headed for the shower. Mrs Stargell's scrambled eggs had worn off and I was hungry. She was expecting us later. I did not particularly want to include her, but her house was a perfect vantage point from which to watch the Kirkpatricks. And she'd promised us lunch. My hopes were high. The passionate southern cook I'd grown up with regularly put her own flair on regional delicacies like spicy shrimp and grits. She grew poblano peppers in her own garden and stuffed them with cheese and cubed acorn squash she'd sautéed in garlic. She skewered fresh peaches on cinnamon sticks and bathed them in bourbon and honey on the grill until their meat was sweet and smoky. She filled tiny pastry cups with goat cheese and homemade lime curd and glass pitchers with sweet iced tea and fresh thyme. Southern cooking gets a bad rap. But when it's done right, it's a beautiful thing.

I opened a tiny, overscented bottle of shampoo I found in the bathroom. I'd forgotten mine. My knees and palms stung under the hot water after last night's fall, and I used the towel carefully on my sore body.

Neil wheeled in a room-service cart as I squeezed Kinerase from a hundred-and-fifty-dollar bottle on my face, then brushed on a little blush and mascara. He glanced at me. 'That's hot.'

'Yeah, well, don't get any ideas.'

'I have Joe Ray's gas and electric bills for the last couple of years,' he said. I heard dishes rattling as he set our breakfast table. 'Doesn't that turn you on a little? Twenty-two months without a spike or sharp decline.' He sat, picked up a small silver pitcher, drizzled syrup over his plate.

I let my hair down, picked up my coffee cup, and took it with me to the table. Under the silver lid on my plate, I found poached eggs nested in wheat toast and potatoes, two pancakes with blackberry butter on a separate plate. *Perfect.* Neil had a spinach omelet with vegetarian sausage, hash browns, and a tall stack of pancakes. We dug in.

'Something interesting, though,' Neil said. 'Twenty-three months ago the bills were seventy percent higher than they have been for the last twenty-two months.'

I looked at him. 'And before that?'

'I went back as far as they had records online. Five years. Monthly usage was pretty consistent. Then it declined and never went back up.'

I thought that over while we ate, watched the window

for a minute or two. Golf carts moved up and down paved paths over the fairway. Dark foliage lined the nooks and crannies of the nestled-in lake, and pine trees without branches for the first hundred feet towered over it with lime-colored needles.

'How about sales figures?' I asked. 'Volume or whatever they call it in the cremation biz.'

'Joe Ray Junior is doing about the same volume as his father did.'

'Maybe he upgraded to a more efficient system.'

Neil shook his head. 'Thought of that. No big expenses. I remembered the name and model number on that crematory and checked it out. It's almost thirty years old. Shit should be breaking. And replacement parts are expensive. The new ones are modular, state-of-the-art, but the old ones are slower, overheat, have to be cooled down in between customers or you have visible emissions.'

'Vapors,' I said, and Neil nodded. A pair of golfers selected a club from their cart down on the green, shaded their eyes, sized up the course. 'Did you happen to find a bank account?'

'Sure did. Joe Ray pays himself seven hundred a week. Automatic deposit. No other deposits. Mrs Kirkpatrick gets fifteen hundred.'

'So Joe Ray Senior dies a couple of years ago, business stays about the same but overhead drops significantly?' I picked up a knife, spread blackberry butter over a pancake, held it like a piece of toast, and took a bite.

'Yep. Overhead's way down. Prices are higher too. The business is definitely more profitable now. Doesn't sound good, does it?'

'Sounds like maybe the equipment isn't being used a lot.' I wished again I'd had time to test the oven.

'But the bodies are still rolling in.'

'And the Wades and the Huckabys have urns full of cement mix.'

We worked on breakfast in silence. The potatoes were white and cubed, seasoned with rosemary and fresh lemony thyme, cooked with red and green bell peppers with a little crisp on the skin.

'This is really getting weird,' Neil said.

'No shit. You get any sleep?'

'I had trouble. All that creepy stuff. This is my fourth cup.'

'I want to see what's in that barn. You think you can make Mary Kate behave?'

'Sure,' Neil said. 'I think she has a little crush on me.'

'Or vice versa.'

'Well, the old broad does have an ass kinda like a sixteen-year-old shotputter.'

'That's disgusting.'

'You started it.'

We pulled into Mrs Stargell's gravel driveway a little after twelve and parked behind the house. I didn't want to leave my Impala in plain sight. The Kirkpatricks would be jumpy after last night. The green barge Mary Kate called a car was parked in a freestanding carport. Ridged vertical panels were held up by metal poles attached to a frame. It was just wide enough for her huge Fleetwood and a bit of an eyesore here in beautiful Blue Ridge Mountain Valley.

'There she is,' Neil said. 'The old hottie.'

I followed his gaze up stone steps to a back porch where Mary Kate Stargell gripped the railing with one hand and waved with the other like the Queen Mother about to set sail, a royal wave punctuated by perfect bridgework on full display. A knee-length yellow cotton dress was belted at the waist. Blue veins snaked down bony shins into slippers. I smiled. I couldn't help myself.

She held the back door open and showed us to a kitchen that smelled of garlic and herbs and baking chicken, then buzzed around us like a woman who'd spent her life cooking for others and had relished it. I wondered how often that opportunity arose. Perhaps Mary Kate Stargell had a rich social life, but somehow I doubted it. She was a bit crusty round the edges, after all, and she had glommed on to us the way lonely people do.

Neil and I were seated on pine chairs with yellow tie-on cushions. I had absolutely no appetite after the enormous hotel breakfast. But Neil was ready. Neil is always ready to eat.

Mrs Stargell placed a loaf of homemade bread in the center of the white-tiled tabletop. I smelled the yeast and saw flecks of rosemary. Fresh bread. It doesn't matter if you're hungry when there's fresh bread.

A bony hand rested on Neil's shoulder. She asked if he wanted anything else as she set his plate in front of him. I eyed it – chicken, skin on, browned, roasted asparagus with sprigs of thyme that had caramelized in the oven, potatoes whipped smooth with a little pat of butter melting down the stack. We had both been making a halfhearted effort to eat in a more humane and thoughtful way, local and free-range products mostly, and less meat in general. But let's face it, Neil and I are the poster children for the flesh being weak. One piece of crispy chicken and our ethics cave like Anna Nicole Smith at a Vicodin lab. I placed my napkin in my lap and waited. After all, I didn't want to be impolite.

'There you go, honey,' Mrs Stargell said to me. 'I hope you enjoy that.'

She had placed a single bowl of sticky white rice in front of me. I looked at it. I looked at Neil. I looked at her deceptively cute little face, the short white hair that hugged her tiny head, the overapplied blush to her fragile skim-milk cheeks. But her brown eyes were hard and mean and held mine easily. She smiled. I zoomed in on the row of fake teeth that I knew would outlive her.

'What's wrong, Eggroll? Isn't that what your people eat?'

Neil nearly blew an asparagus spear through his nose.

'Mrs Stargell, I grew up right here in Georgia just like you did. Christ. How far up your own ass is your head, anyway?'

Mary Kate snatched a gravy boat from the table and tilted it over my bowl. About half a cup of light brown, gelatinous liquid rolled slowly out and plopped on top of my rice. I looked down at the mush. 'That southern enough, Miss Potty Mouth?'

Indignant, I pushed away from the table.

'Oh, no,' Mrs Stargell said, fanning herself theatrically with a veiny hand. 'She's gonna leave hungry. Hide the house cats.'

Neil's hand came down against the tabletop and shocked the shit out of all of us. My little rice bowl jumped about an inch. Gravy slushed down the side. 'Mrs Stargell, you've got to stop being so ornery. And nobody's going to cower to your blackmail anymore. You're nice, you're in. You're mean, you're *out*. And Keye, Mrs Stargell is twice your age. You owe her a little respect.'

'She's more than twice my age. I'm just sayin'.'

'*Please*, both of you shut the hell up and let me eat my delicious goddamn lunch.'

Mrs Stargell sank into a chair. Her pale skin had blushed to match the color of her overbrushed cheekbones. She was swooning over his outburst, I realized. I couldn't believe my eyes. 'Sorry about the house-cat remark, honey,' she said demurely.

I slid my chair back to the table, tasted the rice, and shuddered. They were both staring at me. 'What?' I brought the napkin to my mouth. 'Oh right. I'm sorry too.' Neil's eyes narrowed. 'Okay, okay.' I looked at Mary Kate. 'I'm sorry I said you had your head up your ass.'

Mary Kate gazed at Neil while he shoveled food in in a way that made me uncomfortable. I entertained a vivid fantasy of her in a pointy witch's hat, cackling over a steaming pot of children. A couple of minutes crawled by.

I stood up. 'I need to see what's in that barn.'

'I figured that's why you dressed for maneuvers,' Mrs Stargell commented. I was wearing army-green cargos and lace-up boots, appropriate, I thought, for an investigation that included chickens and barns. 'Women didn't dress like that in my day.'

'Did they have pants back then, or did y'all just throw a bison skin over your shoulders?'

Her little eyes narrowed. She pointed a bony finger at me. A smile played on her lips. 'Good one, Eggroll.'

20

We left the dishes on the table and went out the back door. I stretched out across the backseat of the Cadillac. It was hot in the car. I lowered the rear windows. In the front seat: Neil, Mary Kate, and a nine-by-thirteen baking dish that had been used so often it was dotted with amber flecks. It belonged to Mrs Kirkpatrick. Mary Kate planned to use returning it as an excuse to barge in and introduce Neil as her nephew from Atlanta.

'Keep her busy for a few minutes and text me if something happens,' I said to the back of their heads. 'Like if Joe Ray comes home early.'

'Sure,' Neil said. 'I'll text you. That won't look suspicious at all.'

'She won't think twice about it,' Mrs Stargell said, easing the spotless Cadillac up the dirt lane. 'All y'all come up here from the city with your heads down and one of those things in your hands. We wouldn't be able to pick one of you out of a lineup. And Joe Ray almost never comes home before four. I think he's seeing a married woman in town. He has to leave before her kids and the husband come home.'

I watched them for a second, smiled to myself. 'Hey, maybe when we're done the two of you can go out for a drink or something. Hook up.'

I saw the skin crinkle just a little at the corner of Neil's eye. 'Jealousy is an ugly emotion, Keye.' We were easing nearer to the house. Neil looked at Mary Kate. 'I do have a little magic weed, though. You ever tried weed, Mrs Stargell?'

Mrs Stargell stopped, put the car in park. 'You know, I have always wanted to try that, but my husband, God rest his soul, wouldn't do it.'

'Well, then we're on,' Neil promised her. They got out of the car. Neil grinned down at me in the backseat, made a goofy face, crossed his eyes.

I waited there, still in the midday heat. The sun cracked through the clouds and roasted me. I could hear them knocking, Mary Kate's raggedy little voice calling out for Mrs Kirkpatrick. Finally, muffled introductions. I peeked out and saw her invite them inside. Not that she had a choice. Mary Kate was clutching the baking dish and squeezing in sideways. I slipped out the opposite door as soon as they disappeared inside, and hurried to the barn, pulled open one of the double doors just enough to get inside.

A small tractor was parked in the barn. It was cool inside. The half hayloft was good insulation. And it let in just enough light from its open doors upstairs so I could navigate. There was an empty space for Joe Ray's truck. It smelled like hay and machinery and earth, exactly the way you'd expect it to smell. I had feared finding something else. I had a feeling they'd carried bodies back here last night. But why? I had no idea except that from the accounts Neil and I had spent the morning looking at – suppliers and utility companies – the crematory wasn't using enough of anything to keep it operational. Utilities were low, no spikes in usage. Expense accounts that would normally be full of maintenance items for the business were almost non-existent. Even office supplies, copies, postage was way off what would be normal numbers for most businesses. I wondered if the refrigeration unit even worked. Maybe that's why the bodies had been improperly stored. I wished I'd been able to spend more time inside the crematorium, and then was struck by the sheer bizarreness of that thought. Another question nagged at me: If he wasn't cremating those bodies, where were they?

My phone vibrated. A text from Neil. Had Joe Ray returned early?

O dear God, this woman's wearing a muumuu and toe socks.

I typed back. *Way to stay focused.*

I saw a light switch at the door and outlets for tools, but I couldn't risk turning on a light. There was a length of yarn hanging on a screw-in hook. A small gold key dangled from the center, the kind that fits a padlock. I remembered seeing the padlock hanging off the room attached to the chicken coop. I took the key and put it around my neck.

My phone again. Neil: *J.R. meeting alarm company about break-in. Mrs S. milking story about hearing wild kids last night.*

The clever old snoop was a natural. She was buying me time, carefully reinforcing Joe Ray's theory about kids breaking in.

I looked around the barn. One of the walls was covered

in Peg-Board from a long countertop up. Tools were hung neatly, organized. Nothing like the messy office at the crematory or the undone records or the uncremated bodies. Urns were lined up neatly. *Urns in the barn.* I peered inside one. Empty. Turned it upside down and realized it had a handwritten label on the bottom, the type used on file folders. It had the name *Trite*. The next one was labeled *Wagner*. The next, *Milner*. The same names I'd seen on the receiving-room log. A bench was pulled up to some oily bolts and engine parts. A chain saw was in some phase of reconstruction – the blade was off, the carburetor was out. I looked at the chain lying on the counter. It was flecked with something deep brown. I zoomed in with my camera phone and snapped a picture, then studied it. The bright flash had illuminated what I couldn't see in the dim light – dried blood and tissue matter. Or a very close facsimile. I scanned the tools hanging off the Peg-Board. Teeth on a hacksaw were tipped with brick-colored stains.

What kind of slaughterhouse was this? I didn't see any spatter on the Peg-Board, on the counters. No smell. What had they been sawing and where? My brain searched for explanations. Kirkpatrick was a hunter. He probably did his slaughtering outside. I remembered the rifle in his hands. It made sense. Backing up to the crematorium receiving room in the night did not. What if he was delivering something rather than picking something up? I hadn't thought of that. But what? I looked around the barn for cement mix. He had urns lined up. Maybe this was his filling station. The light wasn't strong enough to detect concrete dust.

A battleship-gray four-drawer file cabinet stood at the end of the counter. Now, I'm no expert on barns, but I didn't think a file cabinet was standard farm equipment. I ran a finger across the top and saw the track it left in dust. The cabinet was locked. I found a pry bar among the blood-tipped tools and forced the lock to give. The top drawer opened smoothly – army-green hanging files, letter size, with manila folders and plastic tabs for each letter of the alphabet – another example of organization not seen at the crematorium. The drawer was full and went only as far as the letter *H*. I removed the first file – *Abbey, Jeff*. Inside, two eight-by-ten-inch satin-finish photos, black-and-white, high-contrast. The man in the photographs looked to be about seventy. He was sitting in a straight-backed chair, feet flat on the floor, forearms rested on unupholstered walnut, black suit, white background, staring into the camera. It looked like something you'd find framed in an antiques store. The guy had a dead stare. I looked closer. A very dead stare. And pale as tilapia.

I felt a spurt of excitement. I didn't know where this was heading, but I had a feeling I'd just found one of the corner pieces on the jigsaw. I clicked a couple of pictures and put Abbey's file back, removed the next one. *Abbott, Alana*. Two more satin-finish black-and-white photographs, same chair, same positioning, black dress, white pearls, same backdrop, same antiqued finish, another hollow gaze. I photographed the Alana Abbott file too, and pulled out the next one. *Abbott, Carl*. Same suit Jeff Abbey had been wearing, same chair, same everything. I grabbed the stool from the work-station and pulled it up to the file cabinet, opened up the second drawer and searched for Milner, Faye, the woman whose body had been stacked on top of two others and stuffed in a cardboard coffin and whose empty urn sat on the counter. I took the file folder from the cabinet and opened it. Same positioning and props used in the other photographs of dead women – black dress, pearls, an unoccupied, taped-up set of eyes. Faye Milner didn't seem as big propped up in the chair as she had last night when the bodies hit the floor. I photographed the contents of her file, then looked for the others: Demetrius Trite and Joseph Wagner. And, finally, Shelia Marlene Wade, Billy Wade's mother, Brenda's mother-in-law. They were all there. I remembered Brenda saying they just wanted to know what happened. They needed to be sure Shelia Marlene was at rest. And here she was dressed up in undertaker grim clothing. I photographed her file, looked at the photographs for a few seconds. I don't know what happens to us after death, but I do know something leaves the eyes. It's like finding an empty birdcage after the dove has flown away. There's just nothing there. Shelia Marlene Wade's eyes were absent of all the things that signify life.

In the early days of photography, it wasn't unusual for families with money to have their loved ones posed for this kind of portraiture after they'd passed, especially babies and children. These photographs had the same feel. Creepy as that idea is now, it was seen as a way to honor and remember the dead, a sign of love and respect. I didn't think Joe Ray or his mother shared that respect for the dead. What I'd found sitting in the ovens last night was evidence enough of that.

What was going on at the crematorium and in this barn? I thought about Joe Ray and his mother driving into the barn last night. Is that what they do in here at night? Photograph their customers? And then they fill urns with cement? I thought it was interesting that the reception and receiving room at the crematorium were neat and everything out of sight seemed only half done, in some state of neglect. But the barn was different. Here, someone took time to hang things up, make repairs, keep the file cabinet alphabetized. Had Joe Ray Senior and his son had problems? Was this a payback to dear old Dad for some hurt, some perceived injustice or disrespect, trashing his business, turning it into whatever it was now? Rauser would say I was overthinking it. *Follow the money.* And that would lead me where?

Outside, chickens milled around, pecking at invisible things in the dirt, looking busy. The chicken coop was open, shelves of wooden crates filled with straw, the sleeping quarters, I assumed. I have no experience with chickens. We don't get a lot of them on Peachtree Street. I'm okay with that. One of them was checking me out. She was big, red and brown. She walked right up to me, pumped her neck a few times. I didn't think I deserved the attitude. In the distance, a low rumble of thunder got my attention. I looked up to see clouds gathering to the west. A breeze had started to cool the air. Not necessarily a good thing during midday heating. When a cold front sneaks in from the north and slams into buckets of hot, tropical air pumped up from the Gulf, we've got ourselves a thunderstorm that can detonate in one hot second. Georgia in summer can be as violent and unpredictable as our capital city, and even more so in the last few years. Something about El Niño, which apparently especially dislikes the United States. Take a number.

I used the key I'd found in the barn. It slid perfectly into the padlock. The shank popped up. Big Red crowded next to my ankles. I moved her out of the way gently with my foot as I opened the door. It didn't go over. She threatened to make a scene, started squawking and flapping. She was a big bird. Kind of freaky. I let her inside simply to shut her up, though having not spent time with a chicken before, I was uneasy about the prospect of the two of us locked up together in a feed shack. Do chickens fly? A scene from a Hitchcock movie ran through my head. I saw bags of chicken feed stacked up. I was in her treat closet, I realized. There was a barrel full of feed with an empty Maxwell House can inside. I scooped some grain out, cracked the door, looked around, then tossed it on the ground outside. Big Red squeezed out clucking, started pushing the other chickens around right away – an extortionist *and* a control freak. I closed myself back inside.

Bags of birdseed and cat food and chicken feed were all stacked up on a couple of pallets. The floor was coated in an ashy-gray dust. I moved some seed and animal food around, and there it was – sixty-pound bags of quick-setting masonry cement, ten of them, enough to fill a hell of a lot of urns. *For commercial and decorative projects,* the bag read. *Just add water.* It said nothing about its value as a counterfeit replacement for pulverized bone fragments.

Also stored in the feed closet: cardboard tubes with fifty-foot rolls of two-mil plastic sheeting. I thought about that for a second.

My phone vibrated. Neil: *Truck coming. And Miss Muumuu's ready for us 2 go.*

I blasted out of the storage room, snapped the padlock back in place, and dashed behind the barn. A few drops of rain hit my arm. I could hear the truck coming around the house. At the closest point, the tree line was fifty, sixty yards away. I'd have to go through an open field to get there, to get to cover. But then I'd be able to work my way around the property to the main road.

I'm little, but I'm fast. I was a sprinter in high school. Coming out of the blocks in the hundred-meter, I could medal most of the time. You never forget how to accelerate like that once you've learned it.

The path was well worn. The ground was dry. The grass had been flattened by tires. My lungs were letting me know how they felt about cardio without a warm-up at thirty-something when I tumbled into the packed-down layers of leaves and pine straw on the forest bed.

The very next thing that hit me was the smell.

21

t registers in some deep place. One never forgets. Investigators use different methods for pushing through the stench of decomposing flesh. It is one of the services the living must perform if they want justice for the dead. I had always reminded myself of this at the Bureau when we arrived at an especially horrid crime scene. Me, I try not to fight it. Accepting the organic realities of death makes you a better investigator. I never wanted to have to turn away from a scene, or from a victim.

I followed my nose, and thirty yards deep into the woods I nearly fell over something encased in leaves and pine straw. I used a stick to gently rake away debris. I found myself staring into the cavernous eye sockets of an eaten-away face – mostly skinless, jawbone intact, a perfectly formed skull. All the parasites and bacteria and animals that live off decay had done their job. Some of them were inside, doing it still.

I took a picture, stood there for a few seconds. I was beginning to realize I was inside a crime scene. Was this a disposal site for uncremated bodies?

Tall pine trees without lower branches made it easy to move through the dense forest. I began to pay closer attention to bumps and mounds in the pine straw. I found an arm, a hand, bones of a skinless leg. I saw tracks, impressions on the straw. Small tires, like those of a wheel-barrow. I followed them and heard the thick buzz of flies before I found a mass grave that the seasons hadn't had time to blanket with leaves and pine needles. The smell here was stronger, like mill pulp and rotting animal and overripe fruit. It hung on the humid mosquito-infested air. Body parts, piled up and swarming with flies, thousands of them. Human debris was strewn recklessly, arrogantly, as if they were exempt here to the law, to moral borders – bodies without eyes, heads without bodies, arms and legs. When I spotted a leg with long patches of skin removed from the knee up, I was certain for the first time what this gruesome graveyard was all about and why. The Kirkpatricks had performed dark deeds in their barn while their neighbors and friends slept, the community that had entrusted them with the bodies of sisters and children and friends and fathers. The entire horrible scene finally made sense – the two-mil plastic that must have been strung up to prevent spatter, the bloodstained tools, the tissue in the saw chain. They were hacking, dismembering bodies for profit, selling the organs. Follow the money, Rauser always said, and that's exactly what was happening here. The scene was so massive, the smell so overpowering, the flies and other parasites so thick, I could barely comprehend it.

I'd seen tissue-trading cases when I was with the Bureau. It's a brutal practice in a field where safeguards like tracking and oversight have not caught up to the trafficking. Illegal tissue brokers don't have an ethics issue when it comes to selling improperly harvested body parts. Death certificates, origin and source certificates can be faked so that tissue banks don't know when they're buying diseased organs from decomposing bodies. Larry Quinn and Neil and I had laughed about the chicken feed in the urn when he called to offer me this job. I didn't feel like laughing now.

I should have called this in immediately, but the investigator in me wanted to do what I'd been hired to do first. I moved carefully through the woods, trying to disturb as little as possible, getting what ghastly photos I could. I found more disposal sites. Each one made it seem less real. By the time I attached a couple of photographs of the carnage to an email for Quinn, my spirits were somewhere in my boots.

My phone jiggled in my hand a minute later. It was Larry. I told him about the dirty chain saw, six hundred pounds of cement mix in the storage room, empty urns in the barn with labels on them, the photographs, the body parts, hundreds of them tossed so carelessly in the woods it was impossible to estimate the numbers. 'Are you okay?' he wanted to know when I'd finished. 'We need to get you out of there.'

'Rauser has contacts at the GBI,' I answered. 'Can you catch him up and let him make the calls? I'm going to start emailing the rest of the pictures to you both before my phone is toast. The rain is picking up.'

I moved closer to the edge of the tree line. Here there were more tire tracks forking out from the barn to the lake and from the barn to other sections of forest – more disposal sites. I'd lost the ability to even estimate the scope.

I thought about the families who had grieved these people, about the Wades, about the people who had just begun to heal from their loss. They would have to confront this barbarism – the Kirkpatricks stripping bodies of organs and skin and eyes, and not only selling them but recklessly putting the recipients at terrible risk. Someone had to be held accountable. My stomach rolled for the first time, came all the way up to my throat.

Heavy clouds had turned the day to charcoal blue. The drizzle had morphed into a steady rain. My spirits sank even lower as lightning popped and an earthshaking clap of thunder rumbled under my feet like an aftershock. I moved back into the woods where the trees would provide some protection from weather and from Joe Ray and his creepy toe-sock-wearing mama. Lightning again, too near. The trees had started to sway. I shivered.

I could barely hear Rauser's ringtone over the rain. 'I forwarded the pictures to Mike McMillan at the GBI. A warrant is forthcoming. It looks like a fucking nightmare, Street. Are you safe?'

'Yes. They don't know I'm here. Rauser, there's death everywhere you look.' I couldn't even hide the darkness in my voice. 'I'm standing in the middle of some madman's cemetery.' I came up on a row of aluminum vaults, eight feet long, three feet wide, four feet deep. Latches on each end, three latches on the long section. Didn't take a genius to figure out what was in them. The only questions were how many were piled up this time and in what stage of decay. I kept moving. I needed to get deeper into the woods for shelter. I said good-bye to Rauser and answered an incoming call.

'This is Special Agent Mike McMillan from the Georgia

Bureau of Investigation. You're on speakers, Dr Street. I'm with Deputy Director Freed.'

'You'll have to speak up, Agent McMillan,' I said. 'Bad storm up here.' The rain was rolling off the trees now.

'Looking at it on radar. It's moving northeast pretty fast. Clear skies here. We're going to fly in.'

'Good,' I said, and left it at that. I didn't tell McMillan the rain wasn't helping to wash the smell away or that I didn't want to be out here alone anymore.

'I'm looking at these pictures from Lieutenant Rauser. I've worked with Aaron. If he wasn't a friend of mine and if I didn't know you'd been FBI, I wouldn't believe this.'

'Being here doesn't make it more believable.'

'You're still on the property, then? Do you know if they have firearms?'

'I've seen a shotgun. I don't know what else they have.'

I gave him my location, explained that I'd been hired to find the truth behind the fake ashes. I told him where to find the file cabinets and the photographs of the dead. I explained the photograph of the chain and the hacksaw, the cement mix, the body parts, and the tire tracks, which probably led to more disposal sites, all pictures Rauser had forwarded to him.

'We're almost wheels up, Dr Street. Flight time is one hour. Hunker down until we're on the ground and the structures are secure. I'll let you know when to come out.'

'Agent McMillan.'

'Yes.'

'You're going to need to drag the lake too.'

A beat passed. 'Affirmative.'

22

I moved deeper into the woods, sat with my back against a tree trunk, and hugged my knees, pelted by the rain. Neil had called twice, then fired off a series of increasingly panicked text messages. My phone was starting to misbehave. And so were my muscles. Nerves had them coiled up tight as a rattlesnake.

I got a text off. *I'm okay. GBI on the way. Wait for me.*

Fifty-three minutes later I heard chopper blades whipping the air, echoing off the mountains like drumbeats. The rain was back to a trickle. I imagined Mrs Stargell's huge old binoculars lifting at the sound of the helicopters. That image brought on the smile I didn't think I had left in me.

McMillan's call came four minutes later. His team were on their way to meet me. I moved toward the tree line. The agents came around the barn. They walked through the meadow in black cargo pants that gathered around their boots, jackets, three men, two women.

McMillan introduced himself, then his team. I'd

forgotten their names a second later. The shock was setting in. McMillan handed me a Windbreaker with *GBI* in big white letters. I pulled it on gratefully over soaked clothes.

'You mind leading the way, Dr Street?'

A few yards into the woods we came upon the fleshy half-decayed skull I'd tripped over. As I led them deeper, McMillan stuffed his forearm under his nose. A couple of the other agents made coughing sounds and did the same thing.

An arm sticking up through pine straw with long fingernails and blackened rotting skin caused one agent to spin away and vomit into the leaves. 'It's just the beginning,' I told them. 'It's a study in how the elements affect decomposition. I think you need to prepare yourselves.'

The agent with the video moved in close to the arm. Then we all slogged forward. My boots were caked with rotting leaves and mud and God only knows what else. I folded my arms over my chest, shivering violently.

'Holy Christ,' McMillan murmured after a few more yards. The agents made a slow circle, struggling to get some context. We were dead center in one of the Kirkpatricks' bone yards. They hadn't even bothered to bury this shame.

'According to the receiving-room log,' I told them, 'almost four hundred bodies were checked in just this year. I have a feeling they're all here. Or parts of them. And maybe more. I found vaults on the north edge.' I didn't explain how I'd happened to have access to the crematorium logs, and no one asked. It didn't matter now. They had their warrants. They'd find admissible evidence. Plenty of it.

McMillan got on his radio. 'Big Knob cops on the scene yet?' An affirmative crackled back through his radio. 'Have the Kirkpatricks held at the city jail for now. Let's start with theft by deception, abusing a corpse, suspicion of illegal tissue harvesting, and fraud. We got body parts everywhere out here. We're going to need every agent and every technician we can pull in. And we gotta have heavy equipment.' He looked at me. 'You ready to get out of here?' I nodded. 'We have a civilian coming out of the woods behind the barn,' McMillan said. 'Have somebody meet her, get a preliminary statement, then release her. She's had a helluva day.'

The driveway was full of black SUVs and Crown Vics. The chopper sat in the meadow on the other side of the dirt lane. Two Big Knob black-and-whites were on hand. So was a Crime Scene Unit van. Collecting the evidence was going to take weeks. Sorting out and testing what they collected, even longer. I wondered what this would do to the logjam the labs were facing already.

I watched Joe Ray and Loretta Ann Kirkpatrick marched out in handcuffs and pressed into the back of a cop car. Mrs Kirkpatrick peered at me through the window, her eyes sad and glassy. She was probably in some stage of disbelief at her weird world crumbling. I had no sympathy for her. If I felt pity at all, it was simply for how stupid and greedy they'd been.

'I'm Special Agent Cushman.' A woman with a service holster and a GBI cap and Windbreaker shook my hand and handed me a towel. The drizzle was dripping off the brim of her cap. 'I was in the chopper with McMillan, so I'm up to speed. I'd like to get a partial statement from you for the record. Just the basics. We'll finish up in Atlanta once we figure this out.' We started toward the Kirkpatrick house. 'It's pretty bad out there, huh?'

I threw the towel around my shoulders and raked back wet hair with my fingers. '*Bad* isn't a big enough word for what's out there,' I said.

She led me inside to a big sit-down kitchen and a long farmhouse table, tossed me a dry towel. I saw cookies on a plate and evidence Mrs Kirkpatrick had entertained Neil and Mrs Stargell. Cushman put her recorder on the table. 'You need anything?'

'I'm fine,' I answered, but I knew I was pale as rice paper. I was still shivering.

'Any idea how many corpses are out there?'

I shook my head. 'They're in pieces.' I felt tears burn my eyes. Tension, sadness, shock, disgust. Understandable, I knew, and probably even healthy, but embarrassing nonetheless.

Cushman had the decency to ignore it. She continued the interview. When we were done, I called Neil and asked him to meet me in the car at the end of the dirt lane. The property entrance had been blocked off to anything but official business, I was told. All sixteen acres were now a crime scene.

I walked along the edge in the GBI Windbreaker as a convoy of law enforcement vehicles passed me. The rain had moved on, as Agent McMillan had promised. The July sun beamed through breaking clouds. Steam rose up off the fields and ground that had been cooked by summer sun. Our southern saunas.

I stopped and looked at the place where we'd watched Joe Ray planting kudzu and suddenly realized it wasn't kudzu he was planting at all. I made one last call to McMillan, then climbed into the passenger's seat of my

Impala at the end of the drive. Mrs Stargell waved at me from her porch. I waved back. I could hear Rauser's ringtone. But I didn't answer. All I wanted was a shower. An endless, boiling-hot shower.

I sent a text. *I'm fine. Heading to hotel now. Need to decompress.*

He'd understand. Rauser was maybe the only person in the world who would understand completely. The benefits of dating a cop sometimes outweighed the hazards.

At the hotel I stripped and tossed my wet clothes in the wastebasket, then showered until the Big Knob Resort and Spa ran out of hot water. I thought about those agents in the woods hauling in excavators and backhoes. Trying to guard and protect that huge scene when the sun went down tonight. The media would descend on that place soon, if they hadn't already, and the GBI would have their hands full. I wasn't ready to turn on the television.

I twisted my hair up and slipped into one of the hotel robes. I couldn't face the drive home to Atlanta right now. I didn't feel like I could face anything. Except maybe a nice cognac swirling round a brandy snifter, sending heat down my throat to my stomach. Yeah, I could face one of those.

Neil ordered room service – cream of broccoli soup and warm bread, a pot of tea. Comfort food. He knew I hadn't eaten since breakfast. Neither of us was counting the dish of sticky rice Mary Kate Stargell set in front of me.

I called my mom to check on things in Decatur. The neighborhood barbeque was under way. They'd scheduled it for late afternoon, when some of the heat had passed. Dad had strung up lights and sprayed everything in sight with chemicals in an effort to defeat the mosquitoes. Miki had been a big help and seemed to be enjoying the distraction, Mother reported. I smiled at that. My parents had been more parents to her than her own had been. I was glad she had that right now. I think maybe Miki had felt terribly alone a lot. Still, I felt a pang of resentment that she had brought her waist-deep crap into our lives.

I picked at my food. My appetite was on a rare furlough. I talked to Neil about what those agents were digging up out there. All the charges they'd slap on the Kirkpatricks would be multiplied by the number of bodies they could identify. Joe Ray and his bossy mama might end up with a thousand counts against them. I wondered aloud when a respected family had made that first critical decision to cheat and if it had escalated slowly, step-by-step, until they were so deep it didn't matter anymore. Perhaps it was thought out, but I didn't think so, I told Neil. I thought something went wrong with the crematory along the way and someone couldn't stand to turn the business away. How easily this could have evolved to selling the dead rather than just tossing them away. How easily they could have convinced themselves they were actually contributing something valuable, filling a need for organs and tissue.

'It's totally sick,' Neil said.

'At least one of them felt guilty. I think that's what the photographs are about.'

Neil brought his napkin from his lap, touched his mouth. 'What do you say we forget about this for a while? I mean, we're here for the night. It's early. Let's do the town.'

I shook my head. 'Take the car. Have fun. I'm beat.'

He didn't push it. He touched my shoulder as he passed by and picked up the car keys. 'Call if you need me.'

I sat at the window after Neil left, hotel robe wrapped around me, no lights on inside my room. Hand-holding couples crossed the fairway below and families with children and blankets had gathered on the hilly green. The long dock at the shore was lined with onlookers gazing out at the dark lake.

I thought about Rauser, about his voice, about how nice his wide shoulders would feel against my cheek right now. I wanted to call him. But I didn't. What would I say? That I'd spent the day in greed so dark and soulless that I'd been literally ankle deep in human debris?

I heard the first high-pitched whine of fireworks darting into the night, the hiss and crackle of one lit fuse after another, and the sky exploded in thunderous booms of bright gold and red and blue to the delighted cheers of the crowd outside the hotel.

I pulled the robe closer around me and felt as utterly alone as I ever had. My phone rang. I wanted to ignore it. It rang again and I retrieved it from the table where it sat next to my uneaten room-service dinner. I saw my cousin's name on the display. But Miki's phone was lost, wasn't it? Rauser had tracked the last location to the Whole Foods in Midtown. Had they found it?

I answered and heard voices. Lots of them. Chattering. Music in the background. And then I heard my mother's voice. She was talking cheerfully to someone.

'Miki, are you there? Mom, can you hear me?'

No answer. Just the same chatter. I went from zero to eighty-five in one second flat. I hit the end-call button and pressed my mother's mobile number. Four long rings. 'Mom, thank God! Did y'all get Miki's phone back?'

'You have to speak up, honey. Half the neighborhood is here. We just had the most beautiful fireworks show.' I heard the sangria she loved to make for parties in her voice.

'Mom, did you get Miki's phone back?'

'Why, no. We're going by the Verizon store after my audition to pick up a new one.'

'Do you see Miki?' I started getting dressed, tossing cosmetics into my bag.

'I'm looking at her right now. Keye, honey, what's wrong?'

'Mother, listen to me. Find Dad and y'all take Miki and get inside the house. Keep your cool, but do it now.' I didn't know if the call had been intentional. I knew my number must have been on Miki's call log. Maybe it had been accidentally pressed. But not by Miki. And that was the problem. I burst into Neil's room, started gathering up his things too.

'Keye, what in the world—?'

'I just got a call from Miki's phone. The one she thought she lost. He's there, Mom, and he's close. I could hear your voice.'

23

'**M**iki, sweetheart,' I heard my mother saying, so nonchalantly she might have been about to discuss the weather, 'I need you to help me with something inside for a minute. I'm so sorry to interrupt, honey. Will you excuse us?'

'Perfect, Mom. You're doing great.'

'I have Miki, and I'm trying to find your father,' my mother said in my ear. '*Howard.*' I could hear the rising tension in her voice. 'There you are, Howard! Would you help us bring out some more trays, please? Now.'

'Well done, Mom. I'm calling Rauser. Stay inside until you hear from him.'

'But Keye, the party—'

'Lock yourselves in,' I snapped. 'Tell Dad to get his gun and check the house. I love you. The cops will be there soon.'

I called Rauser. I told him about Miki's lost phone calling my number. He disconnected without saying good-bye. I didn't know what he'd do, but I knew he'd do it fast. The

Decatur cops could be there in minutes. I fired off a text to Neil. *We have to leave. Emergency.*

Neil blew through our connecting door fifteen minutes later as I was making a last sweep of the room for personal items. He was carrying the suitcase I'd packed for him, a shaving kit, and a belt. We raced through the lobby and to the car. I told Neil about the phone call. I was on edge, waiting for my phone to ring again, waiting to hear they'd found him, this stranger who wanted to harm Miki in ways I wasn't sure I understood, this killer who might be at this very moment milling around with my parents.

Neil put his head back against the seat and closed his eyes. He smelled like beer and cigarettes. 'You know, it's out of our hands now,' he said. 'Rauser's there by now. The Decatur cops were probably there in five minutes. And I'd like to get there in one piece too.'

I glanced at the speedometer. 'Sorry.'

I heard Rauser's ringtone. 'Everyone's safe,' he reported. 'We found Miki's phone on one of the tables outside, bagged it, locked the place down.'

I sucked in air. 'He wanted us to know he was there. Jesus, he was so close to Mother I could hear her voice.'

'Hopefully she remembers seeing somebody she didn't know. Look, we got Miki out of there, and we did it in the wide open. If he was anywhere close, he knows she's not at your parents' house anymore. Bevins and Angotti drove around for a while, but they never picked up a tail. She's at my place for now. Wherever we end up putting her, she'll have a detail twenty-four-seven.'

'Thanks for that. Where are my parents?'

'Emily and Howard are in the house with a group of

their friends. Balaki's taking statements. Someone had to have noticed him. Unless he's one of them, somebody that grew up in the hood with you guys. Maybe had a thing for Miki.'

It was worth thinking about. I told him I would.

'Street,' Rauser's voice sharpened, 'he knows who you are. He picked your number to call. Christ, there's a lot of people here. We broke them up into four groups of twenty. Williams, Thomas, and one of Decatur's plainclothes are helping get statements outside. That's gonna take awhile. Decatur City is on the street too. By the way, the caterers checked out clean. Everyone that delivered food to Kelly's party came and went together. Pretty clean bunch.'

'Shit.' I sighed. 'Right now he's just toying with Miki. Again, he had an opportunity to harm her and he didn't.'

'Maybe he wants it to be just right,' Rauser suggested.

'Maybe. We need to understand it, Rauser, before she gets hurt.'

'We won't let her get hurt.'

'Can you get me access to the evidence? All of it, I mean. The crime scene analysis, the victimologies, whatever your detectives have pulled into the files so far, interviews, anything the labs have with regard to the Delgado and Kelly cases.'

'I could if you were, say, a psychological consultant.'

'I want in.'

'I thought you'd never ask, Dr Street.'

A couple of hours later, Rauser parked on the street. I pulled in behind him. There was a Crown Victoria in his driveway, a much later model than the one Rauser drove. And much cleaner. It shone under the outside flood. He used his phone to call inside from the sidewalk as we walked toward his always-in-some-stage-of-renovation two-bedroom in the Virginia Highlands section of Atlanta. He'd knocked down walls and put in windows and built a deck off the master bedroom and screened in half of it. He was planning to convert the unfinished attic to a master loft overlooking the living room when he had time. Rauser would have been a carpenter, he'd once told me, if he hadn't gone into law enforcement. He loved working with his hands. He was a project guy. I liked that about him. Watching him banging nails in a wife beater with a tool belt hanging off his waist wasn't bad either.

Detective Angotti opened the door for us, his shirt bunched under a double shoulder holster, his S&W forty tucked up near his rib cage, right side. Angotti was a lefty. The snap was open.

I saw playing cards on Rauser's coffee table. The TV was on, but the volume was low. Angotti was doing things to keep them both busy – games, TV – while making sure he could hear outside noises.

Miki came from the kitchen, saw me, and ran into my arms. I hugged her tight. We went to Rauser's couch. She gripped my hand. Rauser sent Angotti on his way, then checked the doors and windows, made coffee while Miki and I talked, put mugs and cream and sugar on the antique coffee table, then took a chair facing us.

Miki poured cream into a mug. I took a cup black. 'You need anything?' Rauser asked. 'Want some food or something?'

Miki shook her head. 'Aunt Emily stuffed everyone within reach all night. Oh God, she must hate me. She worked so hard to make everything perfect.'

'She's fine,' Rauser said. 'She was serving drinks and snacks and shit while we were getting statements.'

'That's Mom,' I said. 'She really knows how to throw an interrogation.'

'Anybody at the party look suspicious to you?' he asked Miki. 'Someone who didn't fit in? Somebody alone, not interacting? Someone you didn't recognize. Someone you recognized but couldn't place.'

'That pretty much describes the whole experience. I mean, it's a different neighborhood now. I only go back for holidays. I didn't know most people there. Or they looked vaguely familiar. Jesus, we've all gotten so fucking old!' my thirty-four-year-old cousin told Rauser.

'How about you just tell us everything you remember from the first folks arriving,' Rauser suggested.

Miki took us through the party. She was holding together just fine. No frazzles. Miki had fought her way through life. For the first time, I was beginning to see the survivor in her, the one who had to have emerged these last couple of years, the one who had kept her out of the hospital. She was completely sober as I looked into her eyes, clear and turquoise, even though I knew Rauser's bottle of bourbon was on the kitchen counter and that booze had been flowing freely at the party. For these get-togethers, Mother fills punch bowls full of white sangria with orange and lime slices that have absorbed liquor for days.

'Well, I guess the good news is it's not Cash.' Miki sighed. 'Cash can't go anywhere without being recognized. And I would have spotted him. I'd know that walk and that voice anywhere.'

'Two of my guys paid him a visit today,' Rauser told us. 'He cooperated fully. He had a house full of celebs for most of last weekend. The twenty-four hours after Kelly was killed, he was home. Lot of witnesses to that.' Rauser didn't mention that I'd been to visit Cash Tilison. I was glad. I wasn't ready for that discussion. 'He had a big bash planned on the lake.'

'I was with him and his friends last Fourth of July.' Miki smiled at some private memory, looked down into her cup. 'I appreciate you offering me protection. But I can't stay locked up here. Aunt Emily's audition is in the morning at the TV station. I promised I'd be there.'

'I'm sure Emily would understand,' Rauser said.

'I'm keeping my commitment to Aunt Emily.' Miki said it like she wanted a pat on the back. 'And after that, I'm flying out. I have an assignment.'

'I can't hold you here,' Rauser told her. 'But we can't protect you once you get on a plane. We'll move you to a nice hotel, if that's what you want. You don't have to stay here. I have a uniform coming at seven in the morning. I'd like you to stay here with us tonight.'

We were quiet for a minute. Then Miki nodded and said, 'There's severe weather cutting through Texas. They're predicting a super-outbreak. Tornadoes. I'm meeting a storm chaser in Birmingham, then we're driving to meet the storms. I fucking cannot wait to get out of here. Besides, this asshole never follows me.'

'She has a point, Rauser. I don't think he has the resources to follow her. You can't fly around the world unless it's your job or you're loaded. Remember, that volunteer noticed his clothes aren't expensive. Think your unsub has trouble holding a job. Plus, he's probably not the most charming guy in the world, probably has a lot of trouble getting along with coworkers, thinks he's always right, argumentative, egocentric, and we know he's violent. We're probably looking at a borderline personality. I bet there's a lot of anger and panic when she's away. The loss of control would set him off.'

'I wish you wouldn't talk about me as if I weren't here,' Miki said. 'But I had to change my number last year. Hang-ups, text messages. *You can't hide. You can't run.* Shit like that. I thought it was Cash. Then, one day when both Cash and I were in LA, we met for lunch. I was planning to tell him I was going to get a restraining order if he didn't stop harassing me. One of those messages came in while we were together. Went on and on about me disappearing.'

Rauser sat forward. 'Why is it I never heard anything about text messages or phone calls?'

'APD hasn't exactly taken me seriously, Aaron,' Miki shot back, with a little flare of anger. 'I told the officers about the calls when I got back in town and started hearing noises. The calls stopped when I changed my number. But the noises didn't.'

'I'm sorry,' Rauser said.

'Nothing personal, but I'm safer out of town. '

'I don't like it,' Rauser said.

'He took your phone, so he has the new number,' I said. 'Maybe he'll try to communicate. We'll get you a replacement with a new number and APD will keep the old one.'

'I never responded to any of the messages,' Miki said.

'You did the right thing,' I told her. 'It would just fan the flame. Rauser, you have access to the hospital records yet?'

'Records of subpoenas were easy enough. But we're dealing with four different institutions and it's a holiday weekend,' Rauser groused.

Miki got up and went to the kitchen, called out to Rauser, 'You mind if I make a drink?'

'Only if you bring me one. Bourbon. Neat.'

She returned with two glasses. 'Thanks for letting me stay,' she told Rauser, and touched her glass to his. She sat down and knocked back the bourbon. Three fingers in one long drink. We'd all had a hell of a day. If I was drinking I'd have done the same thing.

I heard my name. Rauser hiked up the volume on the television. A chopper hovered over the dirt lane I walked only hours ago, its spotlight illuminating the flat earth below.

A Fox Five journalist reported over the footage: *'Private detective Keye Street made the first grisly discoveries behind the home where crematory operator Joe Ray Kirkpatrick lives with his mother. Street was hired to investigate the operation by Atlanta attorney Larry Quinn.'*

Rauser shook his head. 'Quinn went straight to the media. He's such a whore.'

I leaned forward and switched the ringer on my phone to silent. Miki glanced at me, then back at the television. The pond was in some stage of being drained, the reporter said. The GBI had erected barriers to protect their scene, but their generators had it lit up like a football field. Super-zoom lenses and enterprising reporters doing fly-bys gave us a close look at the scene. Investigators carried big sheets out of the muck. They'd covered them to defeat surveilliance, but I knew what they were hauling out of that lake. I wondered how hard it would be to identify the dead after being immersed in water. I thought about what must be happening in the minds of thousands watching this report. A blizzard of phone calls would follow broadcasts like this one. They'd want to know if their funeral provider used Northeast Georgia Crematorium. They'd want to know if a piece of someone they'd loved was being dredged out of that nasty pond.

'What the hell is wrong with people?' Rauser fumed.

'Investigator Street famously made headlines during the Wishbone serial murders last year . . .'

'Uh-oh,' I said and groaned, dreading whatever was coming next. My relationship with Atlanta's press corps had not always been cordial.

'That's where you were all day, Keye? Jesus. Why didn't you tell me?' Miki demanded.

'When did I have time? It's been high drama all night.'

Miki nodded. 'Well, even when it's quiet you play it pretty close, Keye. No one ever knows what's up with you unless you totally blow. Isn't that right, Aaron?'

'I'll take the fifth,' Rauser said.

'Thanks for the support,' I said.

'A source says Street gained access to the property with the help of a neighbor who was there by permission. . . .'

A source? I smiled. Mary Kate Stargell had been busy too.

'. . . Street contacted GBI agents from the property when she allegedly discovered mass graves littering the surrounding woods. . . .'

While the reporter talked, stock footage began to play of me crossing Peachtree Center Avenue last year dressed for an appointment at Suntrust Plaza with one of my biggest clients.

'Nice shoes,' Miki remarked, with that talent for detachment that runs in our family.

'*According to the attorney, Street emailed photographs of the carnage to GBI officials after she stumbled over a severed head. . . .*'

'You like the skirt?' I asked.

'*The GBI will attempt to piece together and identify what authorities say could add up to several hundred dismembered bodies. . . .*'

'Hot,' Miki said.

'Christ,' Rauser muttered, and drained his glass.

24

ongbirds. I heard them as soon as I opened my eyes. I never hear birds at The Georgian unless one of them careens into the palladian windows. But that's not a happy sound. More of a tragic little thump, really.

I was lying on my side in Rauser's bed with a white sheet tangled around me. The door to a screened porch was open. The sky was just beginning to brighten. I could see Rauser sitting on the porch. His hair was wet. I smelled coffee and wondered how long he'd been up.

I slipped into one of his shirts and a pair of boxer shorts that had to be rolled at the waist to keep them up, brushed my teeth, splashed cold water on puffy eyes. Four hours' sleep wasn't enough for me anymore. Rauser had clearly had even less.

I stood over the gas stove, looking down into a saucepan of liquid the color of tar. Rauser's I-don't-give-a-shit cowboy coffee. He could not contain his sarcasm when he visited my office and saw all the devices Neil uses to achieve the perfect cup. But he never turned down Neil's coffee.

I poured black coffee through a sieve into my cup, set the microwave for thirty seconds, then found my phone in the living room where I'd silenced it last night. Twelve missed calls. Six messages. I knew they weren't from prospective clients. These calls had all come in after the report on the crematory aired. Oh joy. Fortunately, I had a great reason not to talk to reporters. I did not want to say anything that could damage the GBI's case against the Kirkpatricks. GBI would have someone handling the press by this morning, I was sure, someone with a tone more measured and a head cooler than mine.

I stepped out on the screened deck. I kissed Rauser from behind and smelled aftershave on his skin. He reached an arm back for me.

'Been up long?'

'Nah,' he said, but I knew that wasn't true. He was showered and shaved and he'd made coffee and dressed. He was dreading the day. The Major Crimes Division had a new addition today, Major Herman Hicks. Rauser's new boss. Hicks was coming in from Internal Affairs. He'd have a lot to prove, Rauser had told me, and that worried him. Rauser would have to reveal the details to Hicks of an investigation that was more complicated and more expensive each day.

I sipped coffee and looked at the place he'd tilled for a vegetable garden and never planted. In the early-morning light, it was a mess of dirt and weeds. It was humid as hell already. No air was moving through the screen.

Something scuffled at the fence and we both turned, instantly uneasy. Rauser's hand went to his weapon, then slid away when we saw the gray tabby from next door pulling himself up and over the fence. He balanced on top for a couple of seconds, then jumped to the ground and sauntered over to the patch of neglected garden. He dug around, sniffed, turned a few circles, sniffed, dug, then laid back his ears and did his business.

'Little bastard,' Rauser growled, watching the cat with Wile E. Coyote eyes. 'Fucker's looking right at us.' I had to bite my lip and look away. Rauser had unintentionally built a giant cat box in his yard.

He sighed. 'Officer here in forty minutes. Time to wake Miki up and make sure we're straight on everything. And I want to get someone out to your mom's. I don't want to risk her picking up a tail and leading him straight to the TV studio.'

I didn't want to think about Miki or Miki's safety or the baffling murders of a child and an elderly man. I wanted to sleep it all away – the murders, the stalker who had gotten too close to my parents, the crematory. All of it. I stood up anyway and prepared to start the day.

Rauser was behind glass in his office, the phone pressed against his left ear, when I walked into the station. It was ten a.m. Miki and my mother had been escorted safely to the television studio Miki had arranged for Mother's taping. White Trash was fed, and I was showered and changed. Brit Williams spotted me coming up the hallway from the elevators and met me as I turned the corner. Rauser had let his team know I was coming onboard. It wasn't the first time we'd worked together. They'd waded through distrust and resentment the previous year, when I'd been hired by APD as an outside consultant. We'd worked it out. Trust has to be earned. I understood that. Brit Williams had stepped in for Rauser last year when he was on injury leave. It had earned Williams a promotion to sergeant when Rauser returned and he graciously stepped back down. There were seventeen investigators in Homicide. A couple of them had become good friends. Williams was one of them.

He showed me to a low-sided cube in the room where the Homicide Unit worked as part of APD's Major Crimes Unit. He was in camel-colored slacks, a white dress shirt, tie loosened. His forehead was glistening, but the shirtsleeves hadn't come up yet. Mid-morning and it was eighty-eight degrees outside. Gulf air was streaming into our already unstable atmosphere. I think down South we actually enjoy the volatility of the weather. Straight-line winds come in on the afternoon thunderstorms and whip up a lot of drama. Huge fallen trees with shallow roots cause chaos at intersections and street closures. Darkened traffic lights swing in the wind. At lunch tables all over the city one hears terms like *wind shear* and *barometric pressure*. El Niño and Atlanta's red-hot summers will educate you in a meteorologist's vocabulary. We're all experts now.

As usual, the air-conditioning wasn't keeping up at City Hall East. A couple of pieces of metallic ribbon had been tied to one of the rusted registers, but the whiff of air was so faint coming up from somewhere below two million square feet of decaying brick and plaster that the ribbon lifted and twisted sporadically.

I sat down inside the gray cube. Williams leaned over me. 'I've got you logged in to the system so if it's entered, you can access it. I jotted down the case numbers for you, but you can keyword access too. If it's real cold, I can get it from Records downstairs.'

'Victims' families and the volunteer driver is where I'd like to start.'

Williams nodded. 'Help yourself. Recorded interviews are part of the official report.'

Rauser came out of his office. 'Shooting outside lottery headquarters downtown. Officers on the scene. A suspect has been detained. Thomas, Velazquez, you take it. Angotti, you work the crowd for overhears,' he said, instructing his detective to listen for whispers in a crowd that may not readily be reported to police.

'On it,' Detective Thomas, one of two female detectives in the Homicide Unit, said. All three detectives pushed away from their desks.

'Close one and open two more,' Rauser said, and raised his voice. 'Just a reminder: everybody in the War Room at five so everybody knows what everybody else is doing, please. Also, Major Hicks would like to introduce himself.' Scowling, he turned back to his office. Rauser hated having unsolved cases. He was a good cop. He'd been entrusted with a profound duty to the families of victims, and he felt the weight of that with every investigation. He'd sit in his office and study the files for hours, go back to the scenes, brainstorm with his team, push them, push himself. He stopped and turned back to me. 'You got what you need?'

I nodded. 'All set.'

'Gimme fifteen to finish up some things. If you're going over interviews, I want a second look with you.'

Twenty minutes later we were sitting in front of a wide flat-screen monitor. Rauser was leaned back with his ankle propped on one knee. I had my legal pad in front of me – yellow with wide blue lines. Easy for rereading notes. On the screen, I watched Troy Delgado's grief-stricken parents being interviewed. It was hard to watch. Then Williams and Balaki interviewed Donald Kelly's daughter and grand-daughter and her husband, a grandson. Those closest to the victims had to be excluded first. The detectives carefully reconstructed the hours leading up to the killings, gently pushing the same questions at people who did not want to submit to an interview, who simply wanted to be alone with their anguish. This is just one of the tightropes walked by investigators every day. They are often seen as the enemy by the families. This couldn't be further from the truth.

Rauser told me the grandchildren and great-grandchild stood to profit most from Kelly's death. He got up, stretched and made a kind of growling noise, left and returned with cold water in two mugs. 'Too damn hot for coffee,' he complained, as I went back over the recording of Brit Williams's interview with Abraam Balasco, Donald Kelly's volunteer driver.

'He didn't want to go,' Balasco was saying. His hair was cut short, thin on top, gray with strands of brown. 'He was quiet the whole way. Wasn't himself. I shoulda just taken him to the park instead. He liked it there.'

'Did you have any prior contact with the Kelly family?' Williams asked.

Balasco shook his head. 'Only when I took him over there. Sometimes the daughter would be waiting. But mostly I just put him on the elevator. Christ.' His head tilted down. His hand came to his forehead. This interview had been taped only hours after Kelly had been abducted.

Balasco had spent most of the time in the hospital. Hard to know when you were looking at real grief and confusion or performance art. But I couldn't see what Balasco had to gain from Kelly's death. The man appeared genuinely disturbed, even blaming himself for delivering Kelly to the place he would be abducted, then murdered. 'He said, "My daughter's a bitch." Said they were just waiting for him to die. His great-grandson was the only reason Don bothered with them.'

'Had he ever said anything like that before?' Williams wanted to know. 'Did you ever get the feeling he was in danger?'

'He was a disappointed man,' Balasco answered bleakly. 'Not a frightened one.'

I clicked on the left arrow at the bottom of the screen and rewound. *'He said, "My daughter's a bitch." Said they were just waiting for him to die. His great-grandson was the only reason Don bothered with them.'*

'What was Kelly's place like, Rauser? Retirement community, right?' Rauser nodded and kept his eyes on the screen. I was playing catch-up. This investigation was five days old already.

'Assisted living,' Rauser said. 'Monitored pretty close. Nice little apartment. Sparse. Not a lot of personal items, clothes, a few pictures, TV, bedside clock radio, typewriter. No computer.'

'You have the personal items?'

Rauser got up. 'In my office. Haven't returned them to evidence yet.' He came back with a box labeled with Kelly's name and case number. He lifted the lid, and I saw a keychain, a wallet, a typed manuscript held together with binder clips titled *Call Me Monday* by Donald A. Kelly.

'Been reading it,' Rauser told me. 'Not bad. It's about baseball and a hot chick. What's not to like, right? Some of the pages are old, some are newer. Looks like he'd been working on it for years.'

My phone went off. I saw Neil's name on the display.

'Hey, Keye, remember when you told me to look for anything similar to balloons and wrapping paper?' I put him on speaker. 'Found this in the nightly police reports in the Stone Mountain newspaper. About a year ago, a woman was found with a gunshot wound to the head in Stone Mountain Village. She was found in the gazebo. No ID. No personal belongings apart from what she was wearing – skirt, blouse, underclothes, one silver bracelet, and a ribbon tied like an ankle bracelet.'

'What's the date?' Rauser asked Neil, then jotted it down. We moved into the Homicide room. Rauser handed the note to Bevins. 'Get hold of Stone Mountain PD. Find out what they ended up with on this Jane Doe case. And let's see if we can get a look at her.'

'That gazebo is in the heart of the village,' I said. I'd been there shopping dozens of times with my mother. She loved the village, with its quaint row of restaurants, stores full of antiques and folk art. I remembered going there with her to a German restaurant and watching her flatter and flirt her way into the kitchen. She fully understood the intricacies of authentic German buttercream by the time we left. Mother was a student of restaurants. 'It was a disposal site, not a primary scene,' I added. 'You can't fire a gun there and get away with it. The killer would have known leaving a body there would have drawn a lot of attention.'

'Yeah, sounds familiar, doesn't it?' Rauser said.

'Be consistent with his MO,' Williams commented. 'But way out of our perp's strike zone. And a ribbon hasn't been part of the other two scenes.'

'Lieutenant,' Bevins said. She'd been on the phone with a detective from Stone Mountain PD. 'I have a picture from the Gwinnett County ME's office.'

'Can you get it up on the main monitor?' Rauser asked, and a very brightly illuminated photograph came up on the overhead. In television shows they have sharp, modern-looking autopsy suites with lots of dim mood lighting in different hues. In life what you get are harsh lights in a sterile hospital environment. The equipment may be state-of-the-art, but it's not pretty and it doesn't look or feel like the romantic atmosphere it appears on those shows where some twenty-year-old forensic scientist is so accomplished she's an expert in every discipline. We all looked up at the body on the screen, laid out on a stainless-steel table. The dead woman's clothes had not yet been removed – skirt, smudged with what looked like red clay, torn blouse, a silver bracelet. A bedraggled ribbon was tied around her ankle like a shoestring. Scars crossed and crisscrossed her arms.

'You can see it in several of the crime scene photos. The investigators didn't focus a lot of attention on it,' she said.

'What kind of weapon we talking about?' Rauser asked Bevins.

'Nine-millimeter, Lieutenant.'

Rauser rubbed his hands together like he was standing over a campfire. 'Now we're getting somewhere. Have 'em email their tool-marks reports to our examiners pronto.' He picked up a landline and dialed an internal code. 'Lang, we got a ballistics report coming in from Stone Mountain PD. I need a tool-marks examiner to compare it to the slug you dug out of the Honda where Kelly was shot. Pronto, okay?' Rauser put the phone down. 'Won't take long,' he said. 'It's not like DNA. We won't be in walkers before it gets here.'

I went back to the War Room and the box of items taken from Donald Kelly's apartment. I picked up the manuscript. It's about baseball and hot chicks, Rauser had told me. Baseball was Troy Delgado's game, wasn't it? Or one of them. His parents said during their heartbreaking interview that their son had excelled at most sports. I read a few pages before Rauser stuck his head in.

'You wanna come out here, Street? Tool marks line up on the overlaps. Probability is the bullet that went into Donald Kelly and Jane Doe were fired from the same weapon.' We stepped into Homicide and he briefed his detectives. 'Williams, get a police courier out to Stone Mountain. And tell 'em we're coming. They have any issues, let them know we'll keep them apprised of anything that affects their case. Keye, you got any thoughts?'

'Three disposal sites now,' I said. I was willing to bet everyone in this room had considered that already. There was still a lot of argument about standard definitions of serial killing, but the basic accepted criterion is three victims with a cooling-off period between murders. No one in law enforcement wants to hit that magic number three. The press goes ape shit. 'And every scene was meant to be found. The scenes were staged. He had to manipulate a body into a gazebo in the center of town, in and out of a car and into a home in Inman Park. And Troy Delgado's body was found just a few yards off the street. The offender has to have some understanding of the neighborhoods, the routines of the community. And of local police. Offenders hunt within their comfort zone. Why is he intimately familiar with both areas? I think he moved from Stone Mountain to Midtown since Jane Doe was killed. Or his profession requires him to frequent both areas.'

'If he moved,' Balaki said, and started tapping at his keyboard, 'we can look at DMV, voter's reg, real estate records.'

'What do both areas have in common?' I asked.

'Restaurants, for one,' Williams answered. 'And we already have a witness who thought our perp was a waiter. Stone Mountain Village has that little strip with a half dozen restaurants right there.'

'Good,' Rauser said. 'Follow that.'

'The fact that he's leaving some kind of party favor at the scenes is interesting. It might have to do with some obsession with parties. Or maybe birthdays. Kelly died on his birthday. But it could also be a behavior that developed over time,' I said.

'You're saying he was killing people *before* he was decorating them.' Bevins was frowning. 'Or leaving party favors.'

'I'm saying it's possible.'

'Street people and hookers.' Balaki shook his head. 'That's usually where it starts. Easy targets.'

I nodded. 'Prostitutes are more likely to experience exploratory wounds. And their disappearance is slow to get reported, if it's reported at all. Fewer intimate relationships. Predators count on this.'

'Be nice to know about the fluids, wouldn't it?' Williams

said. 'I was in the morgue. I saw that stuff all over the kid. Working without DNA is like being hurled into the goddamn dark ages.'

'Listen to me, people,' Rauser snapped. His fuse had frayed a little. 'All that DNA shit, it's gonna be great in court. But it's good old-fashioned police work that closes cases. Don't ever forget that. The district attorney can use it to convict. It's not our problem. Our job is to act like detectives and bring in suspects.'

'My bet's on urine,' Bevins said quietly. We all looked at her. 'The fluid, I mean.'

'We have a fluid pool?' Balaki asked. Cops are competitive by nature. They'll bet against one another on just about anything. 'I'll take semen for ten bucks.'

'Stone Mountain ever get an ID on Jane Doe?' Rauser wanted to know.

Bevins looked back at her computer, tapped a few keys, then nodded. 'Her name actually *is* Doe. Fatu Doe. Twenty-one years old. She was a prostitute.'

25

Rauser knocked the volume back on the blaring police scanner and pushed a piece of nicotine gum through the foiled back of the package. 'This stuff tasted like crap at first. But now when it starts to get peppery and release that shit, and I'm like, oh yeah, baby.' He looked behind him, swung out of the parking spot in his Crown Vic. We were about two inches from one of the huge support columns. His car was banged all to hell already. Rauser drove like somebody who had spent his life rushing. On a straightaway, I loved it. I'd grown up with redneck boys in muscle cars, after all. I have a chemical reaction to hot guys in fast cars. But in the garage at City Hall East, not so much. I squeezed my eyes shut.

He turned right onto Ponce de Leon Avenue and hit the first red light. Deep fryers from the Mexican restaurants that dotted Ponce cranked out tortilla chips for the lunch crowds and oily air mixed with exhaust fumes – Atlanta's summer scent. I had my elbow propped on the lowered window. Rauser's fan was out in his car again. I could feel the heat coming up from the pavement on my arm. The sun was hammering us. The motorcycle shop on our left was buzzing with perspective buyers. Georgia's hot summers trick us into thinking this is a good idea. We long for wind in our hair. Lot of bikes on the road this time of year, scooters are all over the city streets. We ditch our gas guzzlers. We suddenly care very much for the environment. I know. I was once seduced by a little red Vespa. And then the blistering sun cooks you inside your helmet at stoplights. Or you run over your own toe. Or winter moves in. Folks with real winters and heavy snows think it's funny that we complain about winter down here, but let me tell you, when the windchill hits you on a little scooter doing thirty-five in a business suit in January, your friggin' lips will freeze to your teeth. I lost five pounds just by shivering. My concern with America's dependency on foreign oil stopped there.

Ponce de Leon Avenue bustles and quivers and mutters through Midtown Atlanta – theater, art, shopping centers, strip malls, liquor stores, street people, men's bars – then crosses North Highland and meanders through the historic district lined with southern mansions and landscaped parks. It veers into downtown Decatur and great restaurants, passes MARTA stations and farmers markets before it narrows into a two-lane that runs along weedy railroad tracks past little frame houses and brick apartment buildings. We followed it ten miles into the heart of Clarkston.

I had spent the morning going over Troy Delgado, Donald Kelly, and Fatu Doe's death investigations, learning the details of their last moments. Pin drag and other distinctive marks on the 9mm bullet that had stopped short of Fatu Doe's skull wall and lodged in the cranium cavity matched tool marks on the slug that had ripped through an old man's kidney and ended up inside the volunteer's 2010 Honda Element. A twenty-one-year-old hooker and a man who didn't want to celebrate his birthday. Why had the killer chosen them? I didn't think it was random. But I still didn't know why they'd been selected.

The trajectory told the ME the killer had been standing behind Fatu Doe. The exterior entry wound was relatively small, between the temple and right ear. The muzzle was pushed against skin and bone, which made a clean entry. But when the bullet was blown in, all those gases exploded inside the wall of her skull and tore a lacerated path through the brain in a millisecond. A rape kit had been done. No ejaculate had been detected. There was blood in the lining of the uterus that was not menstrual in origin and a sizable laceration in the vagina. Medical examiners and coroners avoid legal terms like *rape*, but there was little doubt Fatu Doe had been sexually assaulted before her death. She had blunt-force contusions and abrasions on her arms and face. Deep color in the wounds. She was alive when she was raped and beaten. Her parents had told the detectives that Fatu had been in a rehab facility for a meth habit and was no longer using drugs or hooking. Toxicology had shown trace amounts of THC in her bloodstream. Marijuana hangs around a long time. It's not an unusual find in someone who has been drug-free only a few weeks. Doe's parents had told investigators their daughter had an on-again-off-again relationship with someone they'd never met, someone she called Mister and sometimes Mister R. Still, the Stone

Mountain PD had uncovered no suspects. The initial was a lead that led nowhere.

Rauser glanced at me as we crossed the tracks. He turned left on Church Street in Clarkston, a community vibrant with immigrants and refugees. It's the original home of the Fugees Family, an organization dedicated to child survivors of war, an estimated half the population here.

We drove east a few blocks, then turned right on a side street that looped in a circle, punctuated by potholes and *For Sale* signs in yards where home owners had forgotten to keep up the landscaping in a down market. Half the houses in the neighborhood were vacant. Lanky, dark-skinned boys kicked a soccer ball around in an empty lot. They stopped and stared at us as we passed. Rauser's Crown Vic was unmarked, but it was obviously a cop car.

We parked in front of a mint-green house. Shingles had peeled away from the roof, exposing black patches of tarpaper underneath, an unrepaired reminder, I guessed, from one of the big storms that had roared through this year. The house was a decade past due for pressure washing and priming and painting, but somebody loved it. The window boxes were bulging with petunias that had lifted their velvety heads to the hot midday sun. Ferns hung from hooks under porch shade, and containers with red geraniums stood on each end of the wooden steps leading to the screen door. A white oak towered over the front lawn and shaded one end of the house. The windows were open. Everyone tries to save those cooling dollars. By the end of July the heat is so heavy and thick, you don't have a choice but to close the windows and strain the budget for an extra couple hundred a month through September.

Before Rauser had folded up his knuckles to knock, a figure appeared in the doorway. Wearing a long skirt in washed-out orange and yellow, she had rich brown skin and eyes, high apple cheeks, hair cut close to her head, a white linen shirt. She was tall. She looked at Rauser, then at me, but said nothing. 'Good afternoon, ma'am,' Rauser said. 'I'm Lieutenant Aaron Rauser from the Atlanta Police Department, and this is Keye Street. Are you Mrs Doe?'

Her eyebrows pulled together almost imperceptibly. 'I am Tomah Doe. This concerns Fatu?' she asked in the Liberian English that is both rhythmic and beautiful and requires concentration. The words *this* and *concern* sounded like *dis* and *cone-sir*.

'May we come in and speak to you?' Rauser's years as a cop had programmed him to answer questions with questions. 'I tried to call, but there was no answer.' He pulled out his identification and held it up to the screen.

She ignored the ID but stepped outside and let the door bang shut behind her. 'We've been outside. My husband is still in back,' she told us. We followed her down the wooden steps and around the house. Clothesline cord was stretched out from one corner of the house to a small freestanding building that had probably once been a one-car garage. Wooden birdhouses and feeders hung from the line, hand-made, hand painted, beautifully fashioned. Dolo Doe was bent over a sawhorse in the center of the garage he'd obviously converted to a workshop. He was working with a tool, a small chisel. His hands looked too big for such delicate work. The floor was covered in wood shavings that smelled sappy and clean. He lifted his eyes, looked at Rauser and me, put the chisel down on the thick plywood table.

'Tomah?' he asked, simply, but his eyes hadn't left us. He was a tall man, taller than Rauser, who was six-two.

'Police,' she told him. 'About Fatu.'

He brushed his hands off on dark blue jeans. Sweat was glistening on his face. 'Come in out of the heat.' He motioned for us to follow him up cement steps into the back of the house. In the small kitchen, the appliances looked old, but they were scrubbed spotless. So was the floor and the sink. The room smelled like banana bread, which my mother bakes, and when I said so, Tomah's cheekbones rose in a polite but reserved smile.

We sat down at a square kitchen table with four chairs. Dolo washed his hands at the sink and dried them on a blue towel. I found myself thinking about their daughter on that stainless-steel table. I could see in her mother the features nearly lost behind the bruises on Fatu's face. Dolo's arms were long and muscled – working arms. He joined us and waited silently while Tomah took a pitcher from the refrigerator and filled drinking glasses without ice. She then removed cloth from a loaf of bread and sliced four thick pieces and placed them on white plates. She put them in front of us with cloth napkins.

'Rice bread and juice,' Dolo told us, and took a long drink. A trickle of sweat ran down his temple. He had a wide forehead and nose, with prominent ridges over his eyes.

The juice was pulpy and icy cold – pineapple, mango, orange. The bread was moist and dense with mashed bananas and nuts. We broke it off with our fingers. Rauser complimented them. We were patient.

'You have discovered her killer?' Dolo Doe asked finally. Tomah was sitting straight, muscular arms on the table, hands clasped.

'We think we're close,' Rauser replied. 'When your daughter was killed, she had a piece of ribbon around her ankle. Do you know why?'

Mr Doe shook his head. 'Our daughter's life was largely a mystery.'

'Had you seen it before?' Rauser asked.

'No,' Dolo answered.

Mrs Doe sat to my right. A tear came to the corner of her eye, balanced there, then cut a streak down her cheek. She didn't try to wipe it away. She did not lift her eyes from the tabletop. 'Fatu had just come from the addiction center. She was just beginning life again.' Her heartache was palpable. Some wounds never heal.

'What was the name of the facility?' I asked.

'It is Peachtree-Ford. Fatu was in the aftercare program. She returned each morning for two-hour meetings.' Peachtree-Ford Hospital was one of the institutions where Miki had spent quite a lot of time. 'Our Fatu loved going there. Many kinds of people.' She smiled faintly.

'In the statements you gave police, you mentioned a man your daughter had been seeing. Can you tell us about him?' I asked.

Mrs Doe shook her head. 'We never knew this man. Fatu had ended this relationship before she came back home to us. This man said she belonged to him. 'I am the only one who cares for you out here in this world,' he told her.' She lifted her eyes. 'He told the truth. No one cares for a black-skinned girl. She is only a prostitute to you. Only a drug addict. But she is also our daughter . . .' She choked on her final words.

'Tomah,' Dolo scolded her. 'They are here to help.'

But Tomah Doe wasn't finished. I imagined how many times she'd longed to express her anger in words. 'The police will tell you how many times your daughter is arrested for prostitution and for drug possession,' she told us. 'They will tell you prostitutes put themselves in harm's way.' Tears flooded her eyes. Her chair scraped the linoleum floor as she tried to push away from the table. Dolo's fingers caught her wrist.

'Fatu was lost for so long to the streets,' he told us. 'One day she was a small child and the next she was lost.' He released Tomah's wrist, patted his wife's hand. 'When our daughter was murdered, she had only been home two weeks.'

'I have children,' Rauser said, surprising me. He wasn't the kind of guy that shared. 'They're grown up now, but it would just about kill me if I had to go through what you've been through. I give you my word that I'll use every resource I have to find the person who murdered your daughter. Anything you remember might help. Anything. You can call me night or day.' He pushed his card to the center of the table.

'This man, he did not wish to go away,' Tomah said, quietly, the silk in her voice restored. 'He called many times. Fatu refused to take his calls. Or she would hang up.'

'Did she have feelings for him?'

'No. He promised her things. This was the attraction. But it was a lie. He had nothing, this man. He was a bother to her.'

'You know what kind of work he was in?' Rauser asked.

'No. My daughter never said.'

'Do you know how they met?' Rauser persisted.

'We were careful what we asked. We were often afraid of the answers.' Dolo said it quietly.

'Can you tell us about the last time you saw your daughter?'

'She was walking fast up our street with her phone against her ear,' Dolo replied. 'We wanted her to stay home and get well. But she was young. She wanted to go out and see people. We were afraid it meant trouble again, and drugs.' He shook his head. 'So many times with Fatu, we begin talking and end up shouting.'

'There was no record of a phone recovered,' Rauser told them. 'We didn't find any telephone records either.'

'Mr R gave her the phone,' Tomah answered. 'Another thing we argued over. It was a way to hold on to her. But she wanted things that we could not give her.'

'You have the phone?'

'We never saw the phone again,' Mr Doe told us.

Rauser and I exchanged a glance. It was a good indication that Mr R was her killer. He would have taken the phone and destroyed it, knowing its records could lead to him.

'When she was on the streets,' Rauser said carefully, 'do you know where?'

'She called us to pick her up only once,' Dolo said. 'When she was ready to accept help. We went to the Majestic Diner. She met us there. She was so thin. And her eye was swollen. Someone had struck her.'

The Majestic in Midtown, I thought. Midtown again. The common thread. His comfort zone. 'Was your daughter celebrating anything special when she died? An anniversary or birthday?'

'On the day she died,' Tomah told us, 'they had given her at the meeting just that very morning a special orange key tag to commemorate being drug-free for thirty days.'

'Is her bedroom intact?'

They shared an uneasy glance. 'We waited for some time,' Dolo said after a moment. 'We had to grieve Fatu's life. And then we had to recover ours. We cleaned out the room in order to do that.'

'I understand,' Rauser said. 'Was there anything of Fatu's you decided to keep?'

'We have a box,' Tomah said. 'That's all we have left. Just a box.'

26

We left Clarkston with a photograph of Fatu Doe, which had been entrusted to Rauser by a reluctant, heartbroken mother. She was smiling in the picture, brown eyes lit by laughter. I saw the high cheekbones she must have inherited from her mother, masked in the crime scene photos by the brutal beating. I didn't know how Rauser dealt with the grief of suvivors day in and day out. The Bureau and my position in the Behavior Analysis Unit had mostly shielded me from dealing with families. I typically worked with other law enforcement agencies. I'd seen my share of crime scenes. I'd met my share of monsters and learned all about their terrifying interaction with their victims. But I didn't want to look at the wounds of the living with the zoom lens used by local law enforcement. I was intimately familiar with that kind of wreckage.

Visiting the Does and sitting in their kitchen, waiting for their story, we had learned much about their daughter. She was impulsive, stubborn. She wanted nice things. She had a prior relationship with a man who had stalked her, possibly beaten her, who refused to let her go. And she was willing to maintain some contact with her stalker. I thought about Tomah Doe talking about her daughter's attraction to the trappings. Fatu wanted to start over. She'd received help from an addiction center, fought a meth addiction. But there's a lot of shame in addiction. It tears away at your self-esteem. She'd sold her body to support it. Getting clean or getting sober doesn't take away that feeling that you're pretending. Because that's how addicts live. We pretend we're present, that we're clean or sober, that we're okay when we're so far from okay on most days. We hide. We lie. Addiction sticks with you even after you've crawled back from it. A smart predator could take advantage of this.

Fatu's parents had put a box in front of us, sealed with red duct tape. Rauser was careful when he looked through her things, respectful. The world wouldn't have seen much value in the contents, but the Does had kept what was meaningful to them. A couple of handmade leather and beaded bracelets, a pair of silver earrings. A to-do list – *driver's license, open bank account* – and an unfinished job application for The Home Depot, some poetry scribbled on an envelope, a piece of recovery literature from Peachtree-Ford.

We drove toward Stone Mountain Village, only a few miles from the house in Clarkston, discussing scenarios. Her killer knew Fatu was an addict. Perhaps he'd even been a john. It was easy for him to devalue her, given her choices. He'd tried to emotionally isolate her, I told Rauser. *I'm the only one who loves you.* When he could no longer control her and when he discovered her only interest in him had been for material gain, his rage simmered. Perhaps she'd called him that day after she'd argued with her parents. He'd lured her back in, then beat, raped, and shot her. Perhaps the ribbon, whatever it had meant to him previously, was some symbol of his triumph over rejection. In death, he owned her.

'Probably planned to kill her all along,' Rauser said. 'If she got outta line. I mean, like you said, he tried to isolate her. She didn't have friends except the new ones at the addiction center. And we're all over that.' He fished around for his nicotine gum. 'So what if this guy's in one of these institutions where your cousin happens to be, he gets a thing for her, feels rejected by her? Later, he meets Fatu. Maybe she somehow reminds him of Miki. The scars on her arms? Then something about the kid and the old man set him off. He's got an appetite for killing by then. He's bolder.'

'Dime-store psychology, Lieutenant,' I said. I looked out my open window so Rauser wouldn't see my smile. We crossed the railroad tracks and passed the German restaurant I remembered from my childhood.

'You're just jealous, Street. You're jealous 'cause I can figure this shit out without a bunch of degrees.'

'It was Donald Kelly's birthday,' I said. 'Fatu Doe's thirty-day orange key tag. Troy Delgado was on the cusp of something too, wasn't he? A huge career, an expensive private coach, qualifying for the Junior Olympics. And Miki. What is it about Miki?' I wondered aloud. 'Is she connected somehow? She cut herself, just like Fatu did, but she hasn't been in a hospital in two years. Her career is surging again. She was short-listed for a Pulitzer and actually won other major photography awards. She's received tons of recognition for her work. She's also landed in the tabloids for relationships with famous singers.'

'Maybe it's success that freaks him out,' Rauser suggested.

'Maybe,' I said. 'Or transitions. Moving on. Maybe he was unable to move on from something significant in his life.'

We passed shops with canvases from local artists on sidewalk easels, cupcake makers, gift shops, cafés and restaurants, antiques stores, and a pub with tables and chairs on its roof. Rauser found parking near an old Charleston-style home turned restaurant. It was called the Sycamore Grill because for years a huge sycamore tree had overhung the veranda. It had served as a hospital during the Civil War. We didn't have a lot of those old places standing. Sherman's torches had lit up everything in sight.

'Something about each of his victims set off their killer. That motivation's what we need to figure out.'

'That's what *you* need to figure out,' Rauser said. 'Me, I'm just a cop. I deal in whens and wheres. Not whys.'

We stepped out of Rauser's fanless oven and felt a breeze. The gazebo where Fatu's body had been left was fifty yards to our left. The Sycamore Grill and several other businesses sat on a slight incline above railroad tracks that split the village in two. There was parking on both sides of the tracks, which made the gazebo more accessible than either of us remembered. We discussed this. The offender could have easily come into the village without using the main drag and parked above, rather than below, the tracks. No one had seen him. Again, this indicated familiarity with the area – where to enter, where to park, the routines of local cops and business owners. It was important to him to leave her in a public place. Why? A final act of dominance over her? He'd pulled her skirt up to her waist before he walked away from her. He wanted to degrade her. He'd raped and beaten and murdered her elsewhere but dragged her here and pulled up her skirt – he wanted her humiliated, even after death.

As we crossed the park, I told Rauser about having seen the gazebo full of microphone stands and musical instruments when the city of Stone Mountain was having events and the lawn was covered with blankets and coolers and folding chairs and kids running wild. This seemed too innocent a place to be a disposal site. I tried to imagine what the atmosphere in this quaint little village must have been when Fatu Doe's body was discovered and the word of her murder spread from doorway to doorway, shop to shop. Fatu's body was found by a startled shopkeeper who had her coffee in the gazebo on nice mornings before opening.

We wanted to come here to get a feel for the location. The toughest thing about crime scene photographs is understanding context – how and where the scene falls within its environment and where the victim is within the scene. Neither of us expected to find new physical evidence at this late date, but there was still a lot of information to be gathered regarding offender behavior. In order to satisfy his needs regarding placement of the bodies, he had taken risks by operating in public. Calculated risks, however. The killer had used the cover of darkness to stage the scene; he'd worn gloves as always; he was careful about being quiet, where he parked. But he wasn't careful enough. We knew he carried a 9mm, and Rauser's specialists had concluded it was an S&W. We had fluid samples, which hopefully would hold enough skin cells for DNA typing. The twine found around Troy Delgado's neck matched the twine that helped hang Donald Kelly. We weren't dealing with a mastermind or someone well schooled in evidence collection like the Wishbone killer, who had taunted police last year and terrorized the city. But this killer was careful enough, intelligent and erratic enough to be dangerous.

Rauser's phone went off. Mine followed as he was answering. I didn't recognize the number. Miki. 'Hey, this is my new number. Log it in. I'm at the gate at Hartsfield. So weird walking through the airport with a cop.'

'Are you okay?' I asked, and wondered how she was handling the fear. I wondered if she was clean and sober.

'Really fucking glad to be leaving Atlanta,' she said. 'I'd appreciate you and your boyfriend solving this shit while I'm gone. Hey, they're boarding my plane now, gotta go. Really I just wanted to say thanks for everything and tell you Aunt Emily totally rocked her audition. I mean, we were just shaking our heads. She is the most uninhibited person I've ever seen in front of a camera. They're going to love her. She's a natural actress.'

'This explains why she and my ex-husband are so crazy about one another.'

'I think she really is going to be the next Paula Deen,' Miki said.

'Only prettier,' we said at the same time.

'Be safe, Miki. Tornadoes don't care if you've got a camera.'

'No kidding,' she said, laughing, and she was gone. I looked at Rauser. 'That was Miki. She's getting on the plane.'

'I just got the same report. And your mom is home safe. How'd Emily's thing go?'

'She blew them away.'

'Of course she did.'

We crossed the manicured center of town and headed back to Rauser's car. His hands were dug into his pockets and he was watching his feet as he walked. 'I gotta powwow with Major Hicks when I get back. See how the new boss handles all this in his first week in Homicide. Nobody's gonna like it. Multiple homicides without a viable suspect. Might as well be walking on hot coals.'

Atlanta has a long and violent history. And the pain is fresh. Only a year ago a killer had tormented and murdered, then vanished. It was inevitable there would be rumors that Wishbone had returned. Police Chief Jefferson Connor had nearly been tarred and feathered last year for his mishandling of the Wishbone cases. While Rauser and I were convalescing, we'd watched the chief skewered daily in the media with utter, unremorseful joy.

'I don't mean to make this all about me, but I went through hell with Chief Connor last year over the Wishbone investigation. I don't want to go through it again,' I said. 'You sure Hicks is okay about my being on board?'

'Connor learned his lesson about meddling. He stays quiet now unless there's a press conference and he can grab the credit for something. And Hicks won't bother you. He has no reason not to trust my judgment. I've got a good record. And he knows they offered me his job first.'

Rauser stopped and looked at me. He has a way of showing emotion without doing anything at all. It starts with a tiny crinkling at the corner of his eyes that makes you think he's going to smile. I stepped in closer. His big hands touched my waist just above my hipbones. 'Why don't we sneak away for dinner tonight? Williams can handle whatever comes up.'

I leaned in to him. 'I want you first. Then dinner.' He kissed me and I felt his hands move up my back. I felt them all the way south to the Everglades.

On the way to the station, we stopped in the Majestic Diner, where Dolo Doe told us they had picked up their daughter one evening. Rauser showed Fatu's picture to the manager and cooks and anyone else who would look at it. No bells went off. Rauser's detectives and the uniforms would have copies of her photograph too, in case someone on the street recognized her and remembered her boyfriend. But a year is a long time in the hazy, transient world of Atlanta's streets.

We tossed out theories on the drive, Rauser's favorite being this man Fatu called Mister was actually her pimp. Her parents knew this, that it was the real reason they'd argued that night when Fatu took off up the street with the phone against her ear. We also discussed the possibility he was a john or in some other position of power – counselor, sponsor.

We returned to the station. Rauser got me the box of personal possessions from Donald Kelly's room in the assisted-living facility, and I hauled it to the cubicle they'd loaned me. It's astonishing what our lives get boiled down to in the end. I thought about the box we'd picked through so carefully at the Does' house.

I opened a black leather billfold and saw credit cards, a state identification card, a debit card, insurance card, forty-seven dollars, a yellowed, dog-eared folded note: *Honey, don't forget your lunch*. There was a fading photo-booth picture of a couple. I looked at the inventory sheet, which described the photograph of Kelly and his wife. She had been dead for over ten years. I found a school picture of a little boy grinning at the camera, tooth missing just right of center, lots of dark hair, eight or nine years old. And another one with the same dreamy-blue school background and the same boy, slightly older. *Great-grandson Levi Sobol*, the sheet told me.

Williams was sitting in the cube in front of me. 'No other family pictures in Kelly's apartment?' I asked.

'Just in his wallet. Wife and grandkid.'

'This must be the boy Kelly had talked about to the driver. You know if this picture is current?'

'The last one is two years old.'

'That would put the great-grandson at about the same age as Troy Delgado, wouldn't it?'

Williams nodded. 'Different schools, though, different neighborhood.'

'How about the summer baseball leagues? Delgado played in one. I think we should take a closer look at the grandson. Maybe there's a league roster or something. Social media might be the fastest way to check out sports and other extracurricular activities.'

'So you're thinking our perp sees Kelly's great-grandson while he's watching the Delgado kid and that somehow led him to Kelly? How do you figure?'

'I don't figure.' I sighed. 'I'm just looking for a way to put your victims in the same location at the same time. Kelly didn't have many pictures. Just his dead wife and this boy. Both obviously meant a great deal to him. And he was a baseball fan. The novel he'd written was about baseball. He told the driver how much he cared for the kid. He'd want to see him play.'

I needed to know how and where he met his victims. All four victims, one living, three murdered, had been celebrating something, at some turning point. Even Miki had stopped cutting herself. It said something about his psychology, but what did it tell me about where he'd seen them, met them, selected them? Fatu worked on the streets. He could have easily picked her up in Midtown. Perhaps they'd met at the hospital where both she and Miki had once been patients. Was he part of the hospital staff? Or a patient? Could he have met Miki there too? Or had he formed his attachment to my cousin through tabloid stories or her photos in magazines? Maybe he'd simply spotted her somewhere and latched on. The hospital was one of the largest mood disorder and addiction centers in the Southeast, with several clinics. It was a good bet that most of the addicts in the area who needed inpatient rehab had been in the Peachtree-Ford system at some point. That Miki and Fatu had been in the system was not necessarily the smoking gun I was looking for. And where would that leave Donald Kelly and Troy Delgado? Neither was in recovery. Nor had either suffered from mental illnesses, as far as we knew.

Williams turned back to his computer. I continued looking through a dead man's things. I thought about him hanging there in Miki's house, chalky and cold.

'Check this out,' Williams said. 'Levi Sobol's Facebook page. No privacy controls. Somebody should teach these kids how to do this safely.'

I got up to look at his monitor. There was the nice-looking boy from the wallet photos. But he was wearing a red baseball cap, and white uniform with red stripes. *Cardinals,* it said in thick red screen-printed letters. Williams started clicking through Sobol's Facebook photo albums. He found a team picture – three tiers of boys in uniform, the bottom row sitting cross-legged, steadying a sign that said *Atlanta Summer League Association.*

On the far wall next to the enormous combination dry-erase and corkboard that listed open cases and relevant details added by the investigators, photographs were posted of victims before they were victims, when they'd simply been student or mother or baseball player or dog lover. I walked to it and looked at Troy Delgado standing on the pitcher's mound, glove on, hands at his sides, goofy kid smile that said he was indulging a parent and couldn't wait for the photo shoot to be over. Blue script on his uniform said *Blue Jays.* I remembered the letter from the coach that had been opened. The one that said Troy had extraordinary talent.

Rauser appeared and stood watching me. 'Which teams are in that league?' I asked. 'If they have Blue Jays, can we get a list of players?'

'Both teams are in the same league,' Williams reported a minute later, and our first connection was born.

'Let's see if we can put them on the same field the same day.' Rauser was chewing his bottom lip, which meant his nerves were popping. You could feel the energy coming off him. 'Balaki, call that driver. See what he knows.'

'Schedule's online,' Williams said. 'And look at this. Delgado's team played Levi Sobol's team twice already this season.'

'Lieutenant,' Balaki said, and covered the mouthpiece on the APD landline. 'Mr Balasco says he took the old man to the field a couple times to watch the kid play. He thinks one of the other drivers did too. He's gone to get his schedule.' Balaki scribbled on his notepad. 'Thank you, Mr Balasco. Yes, sir. Have a good day, sir.' He hung up. 'May twenty-first and June third Mr Kelly was driven to the ballpark.'

'That's a match on the schedule,' Williams said. 'June third. Blue Jays versus the Cardinals.'

Rauser clapped his hands together. 'There it is, people. Two victims in the same place at the same time. Nice work, everybody. Okay, let's have a second look at the volunteers for Dignified Elder Transport. Any other drivers that took Kelly to the ballpark, this Balasco guy included. See if he'll take a polygraph. Let's get records from the assisted-living facility on Kelly's coming and goings. Residents or their caretakers have to sign in and out. Find out who's in charge of this summer league, and let's figure out how big the organization is. Do they have people that work concessions or are they outside vendors, things like that, assistant coaches, anybody comes in contact with the kids or the property. That includes maintenance people. Get a list and start checking 'em off. Is it just one field?'

'Two fields, same park,' Williams answered. 'It's the sole location for the league to compete. Near Piedmont Park in the Saint Charles neighborhood. Close to Grady High School.'

'Somebody get the Midtown grid up on the main monitor,' Rauser said, and we all looked up at the flat screen mounted on the wall, the same one I'd seen them laughing at with Miki and the Booger Bandit video. 'Now give us marks on the Little League field; Inman Park, where Miki lives; fifteenth, where Kelly's daughter lives; Kings Court and Amsterdam, where the Delgado boy was killed; and the assisted-living place on Monroe, where Kelly lived.'

A red pushpin icon appeared on the screen at each location. It was shaped like an *F,* if you marked the four points and added one in the center. Miki's house was farthest away and at the bottom of the *F,* the condos near Colony Square at the top. The ballpark was dead center. Delgado's neighborhood and Kelly's home would be at the points of the two forks.

'So the Little League fields mark the center of the area our perp's been working. It's a residential area, so let's start talking to the neighbors. What have they seen, et cetera. Keye, you want to add anything?'

'It's been days now with no credible tips,' I said. 'That means whoever he is, he's blending in. He has knowledge of the area and the area is used to seeing him. But most important, this is our Stone Mountain connection. All kinds of events in the village that require concessions and vendors. Including a baseball field on the outskirts of the village.'

'Lieutenant,' Williams said. 'Levi Sobol's team is playing tonight.'

Rauser looked at me and smiled. Our dinner date had just moved to the ballpark. I wouldn't have had it any other way.

27

My phone went off – the standard ring, the one that meant unknown caller. I'd been ignoring it all day. So many calls were coming in about Northeast Georgia Crematorium. Tyrone had called twice too, but I wasn't ready to speak to him. I looked at the display. Media? Or possible new business? I sure couldn't live on my consulting fee from APD.

'Keye Street,' I answered. I'd left Rauser at the station to deal with bosses and seventeen investigators and six open murder cases. I'd come home to take care of my cat before hitting the office to take care of my business. Larry Quinn would be waiting for a full report from the crematory, I knew, champing at the bit. Now that I was looking at a ball-game date, hair and makeup would be a snap.

'Dr Street, it's Mike McMillan. How are you?'

'Well, I'm out of Big Knob, which means I'm probably doing better than you are, Agent McMillan.'

'I wanted to thank you for the excellent detective work and for notifying us right away. And not speaking with the media. I imagine you've had plenty of opportunities.'

'A few,' I agreed, and poured black coffee into my cup. Steam rose up off an espresso grind, a gift from Neil. It smelled like dark chocolate. White Trash strode in importantly, stretched out at my feet.

'I thought you'd want to know what we've found up here so far. Strictly confidential, of course, until after the court case. But you certainly deserve some closure on this.'

'Thank you,' I said, and meant it. I wondered if there was such a thing as closure for something like this. Not like I could ever un-see Joe Ray's disposal sites. 'I keep thinking about the families.'

'It's about the worst thing I've ever seen,' McMillan said bleakly. I didn't know him, but I recognized exhaustion when I heard it. 'Those photographs have been a big help in estimating the number of bodies we may be dealing with, since the files were all labeled. We've begun the process of contacting families in hopes we can get DNA samples to match what we're digging up here. There doesn't appear to be many other records. As you already noted, the crematory log was empty.' I sat down on one of the stools along the kitchen bar with my coffee. 'The photography studio was located inside the crematorium in a nonworking refrigeration unit,' McMillan continued. 'Lights, backdrop, the clothes you saw in the photos. Loretta Ann Kirkpatrick has confessed to assisting her son in removing the bodies from the property, body harvesting, and falsifying documents so the buyers did not know they were buying illegal, partially decomposed, and/or diseased body parts. We have people following that trail so that patients and families can be notified. We found almost three hundred thousand dollars in cash in the farmhouse and another two hundred thousand in a crawl space. We are talking about suitcases full of money, Dr Street. They were afraid to bank it. We have reason to believe this extends beyond the Kirkpatricks to a local funeral home director and a local physician. Joe Ray isn't saying much.'

'I had an opportunity to observe them.' I didn't mention that I'd been hiding in a ditch with Neil and Mary Kate Stargell, getting eaten by mosquitoes, after we'd broken into the crematory, turned on the conveyor, and dumped a box of corpses out. 'Didn't look like Joe Ray was the one giving the orders,' I told McMillan.

'Yeah. Kind of what we're thinking, but she's putting it all on the son. And he's taking it. Interesting that she says she told him to stop taking the pictures over a year ago. She thought it was *disturbing*. This woman was able to help or supervise the dismemberment of bodies and throw leftovers in the woods, but her son photographing them was over the top.'

'Different requirements,' I told him.

'Psychologically, you mean.'

'Joe Ray wants to remember them,' I said. 'Honor them in some way. It assuages his guilt. If I was the one questioning him, I'd use that. Poke at that spot enough, he'll talk. And Mrs Kirkpatrick, she wants to depersonalize the whole experience. They've both probably convinced themselves they were performing a service. That way they don't have to look at the deadly implications for the recipients or at their own deception.'

'We have seasoned agents up here that are barely getting through this. It's bad.' McMillan trailed off. Hours of excavating the Kirkpatricks' body farm was catching up.

'What happened, Agent McMillan? Do you know how it started? If they'd simply used the crematory after harvesting the tissue no one would have ever known. There wouldn't have been body parts to stumble over or cement mix in the urns.'

'Greed, pure and simple, Dr Street. The crematory chamber needed an overhaul. Almost twenty thousand dollars.'

'Let me guess,' I said. 'They planned on making the repair and somehow never got around to it.'

'They had enough cash in that place to replace that old crematory chamber many times over. But profit has a way of blinding people.'

It was exactly what I'd begun to suspect after Mrs Stargell talked about the disappearing vapors and Neil had uncovered the low utility bills – no working crematory and a refrigeration unit that had been turned into a photography studio.

'Agent McMillan, I have to complete my report for the attorney. I can't really withhold it. He has a good relationship with the media and a way of tossing gas on the fire. Be forewarned. He won't withhold anything he thinks might benefit him personally or help the civil case.'

'I noticed. We'll talk soon, Dr Street.'

I finished my coffee and put a piece of smoked Gouda on top of a cracker. White Trash squinted up at me. She was never happy when I left her alone. I was usually treated to a lot of attitude afterward. 'Don't be a hater,' I told her, and gave her a piece of cheese and some Reddi-Wip. This was probably doing nothing to extend her life, but it did make her a slightly more pleasant roommate.

My phone played Body Count's 'There Goes the Neighborhood' – Tyrone's ringtone. Great song. I waited as long as I could to answer.

'Hey baby, what up?' Tyrone asked.

I grabbed my briefcase and headed toward the elevators.

'Hey Keye, you don't need to return calls now that you're in the news again and shit?'

I pressed the down button and didn't bother to hide my irritation. 'Sure. Channel Five's going to pay my mortgage for the year.'

'Sometimes I got time-sensitive issues. Know what I'm saying? I offer you jobs before anybody else 'cause I like you.'

'Really. Is that why you told Rauser I came unhinged or whatever you told him? What exactly did you say to him?'

'Is that what this is about?'

I stepped into the elevator and nodded at two men in business suits. Their suitcases sat next to their ankles. They both straightened, sucked in their stomachs. One of them slid his hand in his pocket, leaned on one hip like a department-store model. I was in a black pencil skirt, a clingy white Elie Tahari button-closed V-neck, hair down. Works every time. I tried to keep my voice down. 'I felt threatened by those guys, Tyrone. I don't have to take that from anyone. And I shouldn't have to explain why I don't like being grabbed.'

'All I told the man was that you seemed really stressed. I said it out of love, Keye. Come on, now. Don't do me like that. Don't pull some little-baby pouty shit and stop returning calls.'

'I *was* stressed. I'd just been threatened by a gang of

thugs.' I glanced at the guys on the elevator. They both found something very interesting on their shoes. 'And you have no right to speak to Rauser about anything that concerns me. Really crosses the line for me. I don't need the men in my life trying to be my daddy.'

'You need to learn to go with the flow,' Tyrone advised. 'That's your problem right there.'

The blood-pressure bell started to ring like someone had just whacked the mallet on one of those carnival strength tests. 'Thank you so much,' I said with false politeness, and heard my mother's southern influence in my voice. 'I'll be sure to call you the next time I need to know what my fucking problem is.'

'Don't get me wrong. I love me some anger. It brings me a lot of bail jumpers.'

'I'm not angry,' I snapped, and clicked the phone off. My elevator companions were staring at me. '*What?* I'm *not.*'

First McMillan and then Tyrone. Maybe later I'll slam my finger in the car door just for fun.

I saw the Blue Marshmallow when I pulled down into the sunken lot for our offices. Anyway, that's just one of my names for Neil's car. It's a convertible Smart Car, midnight blue with silver detailing. He hadn't had it long, but it had made him smug as hell. I'd noticed his vocabulary now included terms like carbon footprint and greenhouse gases.

My office is located on North Highland Avenue in a row of once forgotten warehouses that have been transformed to fit into the current urban landscape. The landlord gave us some color and slapped on a lot of shiny things – railings and lights, a breezeway with a severe metal *V*-shape top that looks like a really stoned Metallica fan went on a bender with a torch and a few slabs of nickel. *Modern*, he told us, when the exteriors were overhauled. *Hip*. Sure, it's hip now. Just wait until the next trend in commercial office space hits Atlanta's loft districts. We'll be about as hip as a forty-year-old tattoo. The neighborhood is mostly thirty-something professionals, cool restaurants and row houses, brunch lines and chocolatiers, elaborate tacos and my favorite pizza at Fritti. We're three minutes from downtown if you use Glen Iris. In the opposite direction, three minutes to the heart of Midtown, where Rauser's office was located. I can be home in less than seven minutes, unless it's rush hour. Then, all bets are off. No way to time that. We slip into doggy years every day at four.

The parking lot sits down low in front of what were once the loading docks, and you have to climb metal steps to get to the office. It can get a little tricky during the freezing rains in February. And the lot floods in the pop-up thunderstorms of spring and summer. All the tenants in the front row – me, a gay comedy theater troupe, a hair salon, and a tattoo and body-piercing studio – still have a dock door. We lift them in fall or spring before or after the bloodthirsty, Volkswagen-size mosquitoes descend upon us. It's the only time I have natural light in my office. And the simple act of raising our doors turns us into a neighborhood. After air-conditioned summers and locked-up winters, we hear one another again and we wander outside and talk. Smells from the street up the hill where something is always cooking drift into our rambling spaces.

The air was heavy, gray sky. Showers in the forecast. I thought about Miki and knew she would be in Birmingham by now, probably on her way to meet the weather with a professional storm chaser.

My phone rang. Another unavailable number. What's with reporters and their blocked numbers? I didn't want to talk to them. *Crap.* I had to start dealing with this stuff. I couldn't let my voice mail stay stuffed. I had a business to run. I pushed through the urge to avoid another call. The bills don't get paid that way. But avoidance is my natural tendency.

'Keye Street,' I answered into the Bluetooth device on my ear. What I heard was something akin to an oxygen tank or an asthma flare-up. For a moment I thought that it was the hissing dead air you sometimes get when a call is dropped. I tried again. 'Hello?'

'Where is she?' The words were amplified, slowed down – an old record on warped vinyl. *Where . . . is . . . she.* Chilling.

I stayed in my car, glanced around the parking lot. 'You must have the wrong number.'

'I know who you are. I saw you go in her house. The rest was easy. Where you live. Where you work. Where you used to work, *Doctor* Street.'

If he wanted to scare me, he was doing a fine job. There's something so unearthly about voice disguises. It kicked up a kid's fear in me.

'*Where is she?*'

He'd yelled it. The device blasted into my ear. I jerked out my Bluetooth and adjusted the volume.

'Why don't you give her a call?' I suggested, as I reattached the earbud. 'Or text. You're into texting, right?'

More electronic wheezing through the device. 'I know

the cops have that phone. I'm not stupid.'

'Are you wearing a Darth Vader mask? Because that's kind of what it sounds like.' I said it with a smirk I didn't feel. I hoped refusing him my fear, refusing to give him anything back, would be the hook that would keep him talking. I imagined his childhood full of lukewarm women from whom he'd begged attention. I didn't want to make myself a decoy. You have to be careful with guys like this. But the more he shared, the closer we were to knowing his identity.

I looked again at the parking lot, looked for anything out of place. I recognized my neighbors' vehicles – the hair-cutter's Malibu, the tattoo artist's Wrangler, the usual mix of clunkers from the theater company. No movement. Nothing off. 'You know what that voice disguiser says about you?' I asked. It was a cheap cell phone device. He'd probably spent ten dollars in the mall. What it actually said to me was what I'd already theorized – he was scraping by. He probably couldn't hold a full-time job. He's a big loser with a lousy attitude and a scar on his life he's making everyone else pay for. But that's not what I said. 'It tells me you really think things through. You're a careful guy.' I didn't mention the DNA he'd left at the crime scenes. Or that Kelly's driver had seen him, noticed him because he stuck out in the lobby of an upscale Midtown address. A suit and some decent shoes would have made him practically invisible. But even that was beyond his reach. 'So I have to wonder where you think this is headed.'

'I'm going to kill her. She's going to die. That's where it's headed.'

'You had an opportunity. Why didn't you?'

'Sometimes it's just more fun to watch her kill herself.'

A chill skipped over me. How long had he been watching Miki struggle through life? How many times had he contributed to her insecurity? Noises, things out of place, messages, that feeling of being followed – he'd dogged her for months. 'If you turn yourself in now, you'll be safe. Just tell me where you are.'

His breathing rushed through the disguiser like a static-filled storm. 'You're just like her! You arrogant, lying cunt. I'm saving you a seat at the table.'

I dislike that word. It really sets me off. I resisted the bait. 'We can get you help. I give you my word. Let us help you. Let me help.'

He laughed, and the device made him sound like the monster he was. 'You'll help? You're a drunk. You think everybody loves you now just because your cop boyfriend gave you some big case last year? You think that made people see you as respectable? You're not moving out of the gutter. You're not going *anywhere*. You're *nothing*.'

I let it all sink in for a moment. He'd watched us walk into Miki's house that night we'd found Donald Kelly hanging. He'd probably watched the cops arrive and the chaos that followed from whatever creepy perch he used in the neighborhood. He would have seen me draw my Glock, push my mother and Miki out of the house. He would have wondered who I was. It wouldn't have been hard to find out everything. There were so many stories put out there during and after the Wishbone investigation. They'd started out as harsh, biting exposés about my alcoholism and dismissal from the FBI. But after I had identified the killer and nearly paid with my life and Rauser's, a writer for

Rolling Stone had come to my loft and interviewed Rauser and me. My story was written for all to see, from my grandparents' murder to the stint in the FBI, the fall from grace, getting sober, tracking the Wishbone Killer when Rauser and APD took a chance on me. It was all there. The press began to use words like *recovery* and *strength* and *the power of love* when they talked about me. My business had boomed. All of it was more than enough to infuriate a guy who seemed to hate watching people rebound. 'Tell me why you killed them.'

'You're so fucking smart, Miss Ex-FBI. You tell me.'

'I can tell you that I know how it feels to be in love with something that hurts you,' I said, and meant it. I thought about that drink I wanted and talked myself out of every day. I thought about my ex-husband, Dan, in all his impossibly sexy, toxic glory. I thought, too, about how many times I'd been warned never to let the bad guy see your soft spots. But I needed him to keep talking. 'What happened with Miki? How did she hurt you?'

No answer. Just creepy, mechanized breathing.

'I want you to know something,' I told him. 'Miki's not malicious. She's just a little clueless. She wouldn't have tried to hurt you. She's not like Fatu.'

'No, she's not.' His voice boomed like a lion's roar through the device. 'She's a different kind of whore. You're late for the party, Dr Street. And you're a whore too.'

The car window exploded. The sound came a millisecond later. *Pop, pop, pop, pop.* I dove down in the front seat as gunfire danced across my dashboard.

I scrambled to the passenger's door, opened it, fell out, crouched behind it. Where was he? He had to be up on the street somewhere, looking down, a clear advantage. Was he on the street? Or in one of the buildings? North Highland Avenue was wall-to-wall restaurants and pedestrians. I couldn't even attempt to return fire.

I edged toward the front of my car. The five-foot cement wall that had once served the loading docks was at my back.

Pop, pop, pop. Bullets chewed up warm asphalt, pinged around my car.

I needed better cover. He could move. I couldn't. I didn't want to be pinned here. I glanced right. The metal steps were fifteen feet away. They might as well be a mile away. I'd never make it.

Pop.

My office door swung open. I jerked my head around. *'Neil. No!'*

Two more pops. I saw Neil spin, saw his body hit the ground. Seventeen rounds in that S&W 9mm, I was thinking. How many had the shooter used? *Shit.*

Neil was half inside, half outside the building. His head and shoulders were exposed. I had to get to him.

I kicked my shoes off, put a bare foot on the front fender, and used it to hike myself up on the concrete ledge, then took off, zigzagging over the concrete landing, a strange, terrifying ballet to the staccato burst of a semiautomatic.

Pop, pop, pop, pop, pop.

I launched myself at the half-open doorway like I was trying to beat an outfielder's arm to home base, grabbed Neil's arms and pulled him inside, slammed and locked the door. My heart was pumping so fast I sounded like I was the one in the Darth Vader mask. Eight months since Rauser had been hit, since a bullet exploded into him while he was in my arms. Thirty years since my grandparents were killed. *Give me the money, old man.* Time was the great narcotic, I'd been told. But it had never numbed the memories.

I dialed 911, misdialing twice. My hands were shaking. There was blood at my front door. Neil's blood. And drag marks where I'd pulled him inside. I dropped to my knees and checked his head and neck, calling his name. I found the wound on his upper thigh. He was bleeding like crazy. I grabbed his belt, tore it off, and strapped it above the wound.

A recorded message came into my ear, telling me to hold or call the emergency center back. *You have got to be kidding.* Atlanta's lackadaisical response to 911 calls had been criticized so publicly that the call center's director and several operators had been fired recently. I cursed.

'Neil.' I touched his face. 'You're going to be okay.' His eyelids lifted weakly, revealing pale, watery eyes. I hit redial. 'You're okay. Can you hear me?'

A steady male voice answered my call. 'Nine-one-one, what is the nature and location of your emergency?'

I gave him the street address. 'There's been a shooting. One victim with a gunshot wound. I think the shooter was in the three-hundred block of North Highland. He shot at me in my car. We're inside a building now.'

Blood was seeping into Neil's pants. He was as white as an onion.

'Are you carrying a weapon?' the operator wanted to know.

'Yes. Ten-millimeter Glock model twenty, registered.'

'Have you discharged your weapon today?'

'If you mean did I discharge my weapon into my friend who's lying here fucking bleeding, no. You dispatched the ambulance, right?'

'Help is on the way, ma'am. What type of vehicle are you driving?'

'Sixty-nine Impala, white.' I gave him my plate number.

'Do you know the person with the gun?'

'He's a suspect in a homicide case. He just called me at this number. I had him on the phone for a couple of minutes. I'm working with Lieutenant Aaron Rauser at APD Homicide.'

'Can you see the shooter from your position?'

'No. We're locked inside now.'

'Please stay on the line with me until the officers arrive.'

'Sorry, pal.' I disconnected. I had better things to do. I'd given him what he needed. I knew cruisers were on the way. And the ambulance. I wanted to call Rauser. I wanted them to locate the number that had dialed my phone and location-track it. I wanted them to find the freak who'd done this and put him away.

Neil's eyes fluttered. 'You're okay,' I promised him. I hoped it was true.

'What?'

'You were shot. And you hit your head pretty hard.'

He tried to move his wounded leg. 'It burns.'

'I know. Stay still. Help's on the way. I told them to hurry. I left a very expensive pair of shoes in the parking lot.'

He gave me a crooked smile and said, 'Fuck you. I quit.'

28

I was sitting in the waiting room at Emory University Hospital in Midtown with a spiral notebook I'd found in the hospital gift shop when Rauser walked in carrying the shoes I'd left in the parking lot. I had ridden in the ambulance with Neil, shoeless. I slipped them on. Rauser glanced at the notebook.

'Making good use of your time, I see.'

'I need to organize it a little and get it in the computer, but it's the most complete psychological sketch I can give you considering the evidence we have. And don't have.'

He took the notebook and looked it over. 'Dog owner, huh?'

'He'd want that kind of adoration. He's unable to maintain human relationships.'

'No dog hair in the Honda. No dog hair on the victims or in Miki's house where the techs vacuumed up,' Rauser said. 'Usually, if we have an offender with a dog—'

'Then he has a dog that doesn't shed,' I interrupted. Stress bled into my tone. 'Trust me on this. There's a big pet store right next to the building supply, where he probably bought supplies to hang Kelly. It's also the same shopping center where Miki's phone was lifted. He's sticking to the area he's most familiar with.'

'They make dogs like that?' Rauser asked, lightly. 'Nice.'

'He's probably totally obsessed with the dog. Buys lots of toys and treats, clothes, photographs the dog, makes videos. He may post them on social-media sites or on YouTube. And he's a reader. He needs to escape into something during long stretches of alone time. Everything he needs is in that center – the pet store, the bookstore, the building supply, the grocery store.'

'Can I run with this?'

I nodded. 'I feel good about it.'

'I put a detail on your parents until we figure out where this is going. I don't want to take any chances. And I talked to the doc. They wanna keep Neil a couple of days to make sure there's no infection. He'll be sore as shit. But he'll be okay.'

'Thank God.'

He held up a plastic bag. 'Here's what came out of him. Nine-millimeter. It's mangled. Entry point was an up angle, and there's wound damage reduction, which means it ricocheted off the concrete. Bad timing he opened the door, but he's lucky it wasn't a direct hit.'

'I have a feeling Neil's not feeling lucky right now.'

'How are you doing?'

I was rattled. I was angry. And I didn't want to talk about it. 'How's my car?'

'Three broken windows. Messed up the dashboard pretty good. And the inside of the passenger's door.'

'Shit.'

'We've been following up on the ballpark connections all day too, narrowing down the list. Several hundred people when you factor in fund-raising booths, umps, coaches, vendors, and parents. What time can you be ready?'

'Are you serious? I want to stay here and see Neil.'

'Doc says he'll be sleeping awhile. They'll let us in later.'

I was silent. Walking around in the open at a ballpark wasn't really my fantasy at the moment.

'You gotta get right back in the saddle, Street. You know that. You get scared and this guy wins. And we might turn up something that will nail the sonofabitch tonight. That'll cheer you up.'

'Good point,' I said.

'And there's junk food,' Rauser added.

An hour later we snaked through a Midtown neighborhood two blocks from Piedmont Park. It dead-ended at a dirt parking lot. Beyond it, a ballpark with two fields, bleachers, covered dugouts, a sprawling wooden canopy. The lot was packed with vehicles. Whoever was in charge of fund-raising for the league was clearly on it.

Rauser was driving my Neon, knees spread so they didn't hit the steering wheel. We'd gone to my place to change. We left Rauser's cop car in the garage. My Impala was a mess. Again. I dreaded telling my father. He'd had my car completely restored a couple of times already.

We had slipped into shorts, our usual uniform for baseball in or out, and Rauser had jammed a Braves cap on his head. He had good legs and he knew it. He'd worked out his entire life as a way to fight the stress of cop life. It had paid off.

'I had no idea this ballpark was here,' I said.

'Saw it on the map.' I had half his attention. He was cruising the crowded lot for a parking spot. 'Never had a reason to drive back here.'

'And why would you? Unless you're a parent or a coach or a vendor.'

'Yep. Bet our perp fits into one of those categories.' He gunned it toward an empty space, but an SUV coming from the other end of the parking lot got there first. Rauser cursed. He wasn't accustomed to searching for parking in his own jurisdiction. It's one of the perks he fully exploited. He could park on the sidewalk if he felt like it. But tonight he didn't want to look like a cop. 'By the way, there's no criminal background checks in Georgia on coaches and umps. And the people working out here pretty much run the gamut as far as day jobs. Musicians, a broker, insurance salesman, couple of teachers, techies, route drivers, business owners.' He finally found a spot he liked, whipped the Neon in, jerked the emergency brake up, and we got out.

'That means vendors don't have any special requirements either?'

'Licenses and permit is all they need. Stupid. You don't know who you're turning loose with your kids.'

Rauser and I crossed the dirt lot to the ballpark. We stood there for a moment, taking it in. Rauser squinted at the fields to see where Kelly's grandson's team was playing. He needed glasses but so far had resisted the idea. I don't argue. He thinks I'm gorgeous, so I'm okay with his blurred vision.

Vendors with T-shirts and mugs, and bottled water and soft drinks in metal ice tubs, sat behind card tables with metal cash boxes under a wooden canopy with a raised concrete floor. Outside, a mobile food vendor in a silver trailer had a long line of customers dressed for summer baseball, a busy grill, and a sign up top that said *Burger Dog Bob's Flaming Grill*.

'I never could resist a hot dog at the ballpark,' Rauser told me. That might have been true, but I knew he wanted to check out the vendor inside the trailer. We lined up, took a step at a time, until he was forking out eight dollars to the guy inside with the brown eyes, a cap that showed brown hair at the temples, late twenties, early thirties, wide shoulders.

We squeezed mustard and dill relish on fat hot dogs. Me, I'm not really a hot dog fan, but some food is about the experience. Like popcorn at movies. Rauser said what I was thinking. 'He fits the body type and the coloring. And he's parked right here where two vics frequented.' He got on his phone. 'Anything come up today on a food vendor called Burger Dog Bob?' He waited. 'Okay, double-check his event permits for the Stone Mountain/Clarkston area. And send me a picture. I want to know if the guy that made my hot dog owns the business.' He disconnected.

We balanced food and drinks, headed toward the bleachers at the field where the Cardinals were about to take on the Midtown Bulldogs. 'No felony record on the owner. I'll know in a sec if that's him on the grill. He's registered a thirty-eight. No nine.'

'What's his name?'

'Robert Crammer.'

'Robert? Fatu's Mr R?'

'Let's hope.' He looked around. 'It's organized out here.

Takes a lot of people to pull this off. Kept us busy all afternoon.'

We found space at the end of the fifth row and sat down. 'Have you noticed almost everybody's white?' I whispered.

'I don't look at race, Keye.' He stuffed about a third of a hot dog in his mouth, then proved he had no problem talking with his mouth full. 'I've evolved past that.'

'I can see that.' I smiled. Why his bad manners were attractive to me can be explained only by a flood of pheromones. Or a chemical imbalance.

He washed his hot dog down with iced tea from a red plastic cup with a Coca-Cola logo. He rattled the ice in the cup, then elbowed me. 'Kelly's granddaughter's down there with her husband.'

I recognized them from the interview tapes. They were two rows below us. They'd both been there that day waiting for Donald Kelly to arrive for his ninetieth-birthday party. They said the volunteer driver, Abraam Balasco, had rung up to say he was in the lobby with Kelly. They'd waited in the hall for the elevator with everyone else, fifteen or twenty people with plastered-on smiles prepared to sing happy birthday as soon as the doors split open. But the elevator never came. Finally, Phil Sobol, who is married to Kelly's granddaughter, had gone down to the lobby. He'd found Balasco unconscious and his wife's grandfather missing.

Boys in clean uniforms and baseball mitts sprinted onto the field. The coaches shook hands, then went back to their caged-in wooden benches. I gave Rauser the rest of my hot dog and we sat for a while just taking it in – the vendors, the parents, the coaches, the kids. Was this where a killer had first noticed Troy Delgado and Donald Kelly? What was the attraction? Troy Delgado's exceptional talent? But what about Kelly? And how did they connect with Fatu Doe? And my cousin, whom he had chosen not to kill? *Sometimes it's just more fun to watch her kill herself.* How long had he watched Miki coming apart, then piecing it back together? The fact that she was out searching for twisters spoke directly to her suicidal tendencies, in my opinion. I'd been caught in a tornado once on the highway. I had made it to an overpass, parked underneath, got out of my car, and climbed up a concrete incline to a covered ledge. Two more cars stopped, and I found myself waiting on that ledge with four strangers – a man and his young daughter and a sixtysomething couple that looked like they'd just left the buffet at Shoney's. We'd all seen the funnel cloud barreling toward the interstate, gaining width, swirling debris. And then hail the size of walnuts spattered the ground. My ears started to pop a moment before it sounded like a seven-sixty-seven was sitting down on top of us. The air turned black. I couldn't catch my breath. The man next to me was fighting to keep his little girl from being sucked out of his arms. Sixty seconds of terror and uncontrolled chaos reminded us all how small we were, how fleeting our time. Come to think of it, that was the first time my father had to put my car back together, but it would not be the last.

We moved down to an empty space next to Levi Sobol's parents. The welcome mat didn't exactly roll out. 'Lieutenant. What are you doing here?' Phil Sobol asked. Neither of them smiled. A follow-up visit from a cop after crime and violence rocks your family must feel like the other shoe dropping. The Sobols had that look on their faces.

Rauser feigned disinterest, said he was here on another matter, just wanted to say hello. He introduced me casually, no explanation.

'Is it about that boy on the Blue Jays?' Virginia Sobol wanted to know. 'It's horrible. You think someone out here did it?'

Rauser was looking out at the game, tapping crushed ice into his mouth from the cup. Mr Casual. He side-glanced Virginia Sobol. 'You knew him?'

'Everyone did,' she answered. She was brown-eyed and a little plump, dark hair tucked behind her ears, and wore a Cardinals cap. 'He was *the* major threat out here. There wasn't a batter in the league that wasn't terrified of him.'

'The kid was a machine,' Phil Sobol told us. 'Thirteen years old and he's consistently throwing at eighty miles an hour. Everybody that wasn't a Blue Jay fan hated that kid.' His astonished wife slapped his leg.

'It gets a little competitive out here. Parents don't like seeing their kids lose,' she explained defensively.

Phil Sobol clapped his hands. 'Show 'em what you got, Levi,' he bellowed.

'It can get heated from time to time,' Mrs Sobol told us. 'But I don't know one person who would have laid a hand on that child or any other child.'

Wood cracking against a ball turned our heads. Once you've heard it, you never forget the sound – music to a baseball lover. Levi had sent one flying into left field. We were on our feet. It was easy to see how you could get caught up. As we held our collective breath, he rounded first and slid into second base. One set of bleachers roared; the other heckled. He strayed a few yards from base. The pitcher looked over his shoulder, faked a wind-up, then spun and hurled the ball to the second baseman. Levi slid in, hands first.

'*Out,*' the base umpire yelled. Levi Sobol's coach was on the field and in the ump's face in fifteen seconds flat. The umpire's hat came off and hit the ground, revealing a shiny clean-shaven skull. He scooped up his cap, banged it angrily against his pant leg, then shoved it back on his head. Both bleachers were on their feet. It felt like a schoolyard just before a fight breaks out. Phil Sobol and other parents were yelling suggestions at the field and generally impugning the umpire's vision. The coach kicked sand at the ump's shoes. The umpire pressed a pointed finger against the coach's chest. Their faces were too close. Someone ran out and tugged the coach off the field. Levi Sobol walked calmly back to the dugout. The kids, it seemed, were the only ones who hadn't totally lost their cool.

'Friendly game, huh?' Rauser whispered.

I thought about my dad putting my brother and me in his pickup truck and hauling us to games long before we were old enough to understand the sport. But we did understand the vibe, the food and the crowds, the over-the-top excitement from a normally quiet and unemotional father who'd leap to his feet and cup his hands around his mouth and offer loud, unsolicited advice to both players and coaches.

I leaned forward once the drama had subsided and spoke to Virginia Sobol. 'I understand your grandfather was a baseball fan. I'm sorry for your loss. He must have really enjoyed coming out to see your son play.'

'Oh he did,' she said. 'Mother didn't really want

Granddad getting out too much. She worried he'd fall out here. But we couldn't keep him away. If we couldn't pick him up he'd just find another way. He'd call a volunteer or take MARTA or call a cab.' She shook her head, smiling. 'I think Levi was the only one who could get along with my grandfather. He was sick, and he'd gotten mean. But he and my son loved one another.'

Rauser was staring out at the field, but I knew his cop's brain was doing sixty-five. Had Kelly's family arranged the old man's murder? What would connect Troy Delgado to that scenario? Had one of the parents gotten too heated up over Troy Delgado's super-charged pitching arm? If so, what connected Donald Kelly and Fatu Doe and Miki? I knew he'd put cabdrivers on his mental list. His detectives would soon discover what companies and which drivers came out to this ballpark and when. No one, no possibility had been excluded.

His phone went off, and he looked at the screen. 'Robert Crammer,' he whispered, and handed it to me. I looked at the photograph of the man who had served us the hot dogs.

We said good-bye to the Sobols and ambled around a little. Rauser wanted to get a feel for the place, work our way casually back to the food vendor. I struck up a conversation with the woman behind a collapsible table covered with folded T-shirts. She had a metal cash box open on the table, flimsy, drugstore variety. Clearly, security at the ballpark wasn't a big issue. She was a volunteer, she told me, along with several of the parents. Everything sold under the wooden canopy was to help buy new uniforms. I shelled out seventeen dollars for a T-shirt and watched Rauser talking to one of the parents who was selling canned

Cokes and bottled water from a cooler of ice.

'I heard one of the players was killed,' I whispered in a gossipy way as she handed me change for a twenty. She then explained how awful it was for everyone to think something like that could happen in a 'good' neighborhood.

I felt Rauser's hand on my shoulder and noticed he'd turned his baseball cap to the backward position, which meant he was feeling cocky. He gave the T-shirt seller a winning smile. And she gave him one back. I let him have the moment.

We crossed over the poured concrete of the pavilion. A man in a stained white apron and a Braves baseball cap that matched Rauser's was leaning against the concession trailer watching the field where Levi Sobol's team played. I noticed Robert Crammer's shoes right off – thick-soled and black.

Brown eyes cut from the field and tracked our approach. Was this the man who had twisted a piece of fine rope around a child's neck, the man who had murdered a sick old man and hung his body from a door frame? Was this the man who nearly killed me and Neil today?

'Must get hot in that hot dog trailer,' Rauser remarked in a friendly way.

'Y'all ready for another?'

'You Bob?' Rauser asked.

'That's me.' The man shook a cigarette out of a red-and-white box, lit it, dropped the match. His eyes landed on me, then back to Rauser. He was close to Rauser's height, doughy but powerful.

'I'm thinking about a burger this time,' Rauser said.

Bob crushed his cigarette under his heel and opened the

trailer door, went up metal drop-down steps to go inside. He pulled the door closed behind him.

'You make 'em yourself, Bob?' Rauser was still shooting the shit with him.

'Every morning.' Bob opened a big cooler, the kind ice-cream vendors use. He pulled out a hamburger patty wrapped in paper and dropped it on the grill. It sizzled like bacon in a skillet.

'Must be hard to make a living,' Rauser said. 'You gotta do a lot of these events, I bet.' He covered his burger with pickled jalapeños and yellow mustard and ate it while Bob bragged for five minutes about how successful he was. The mobile vending business was impervious to downward shifts in the economy, he claimed. He owned two concession trailers and two stationary versions of Burger Dog Bob's in shopping malls. He handled events all over the metro area.

Rauser demolished his burger in about five bites. Rauser ate like a cop – fast, on the go, never sure when he'd have time for another meal. He balled up his napkins and burger tray and tossed them into a bag-lined event bin. 'Hey, honey, how 'bout taking my picture with Bob here before he gets too rich and famous to be bothered? Come on out, would ya, Bob?'

Crammer came out of his trailer, wiped his hands on his fry-cook apron. Rauser threw an arm around him. I backed up so I could get the whole package, Bob head-to-thick-soled-shoes, the trailer, the logo. Robert Crammer was a thick, powerful man. The victims shared a certain physical vulnerability – young, elderly, female. So the killer's selection process was designed to satisfy not only emotional needs and fantasy behaviors but certain practicalities as well. He wanted to be able to physically dominate them.

I held out my camera phone and looked at the two of them through the display. Rauser crossed his eyes just as the tiny shutter opened and closed. It was not only the picture Rauser's detectives would later enlarge and circulate through the department as a way to torment him, they'd hang it on their suspect board. The cropped version along with the driver's-license photo Williams had sent to Rauser's phone would be shown to Balasco, the Kelly family and their neighbors, everyone at the assisted-living facility, drivers, cabbies, the Delgado family and their neighbors, the staff at the Majestic Diner, the Midtown building supply. I messaged both photos to Miki's new number before we had reached the car.

My phone rang. Neil's name came up. 'You're awake,' I said. 'How are you feeling?'

'What happened, Keye? They took a bullet out of my leg.'

'I'll explain everything. I'm on my way.'

29

I found Neil's room and peeped through the door just in time to see a woman leaning over him with her lips pressed against his. Women always seemed to like Neil. He had an artsy, shaggy boyishness about him, something that said he was probably brilliant and needed gas money, which was a joke. I think Neil makes more money than I do. And for less work. But the whole package really seemed to attract female caretakers. Pretty ones, apparently. I waited outside until the door opened. I watched her walk down the hall, a girly girl with a ribbon holding back sandy hair.

'Hey, looks like somebody has good insurance.' I set flowers from the hospital gift shop on the window ledge. 'Nice digs.' I pulled a chair close to his bed. 'Who's the blonde?'

'Tammy. Cathy's on the way. They forgot they were mad.'

'Do all your girlfriends have cute names? When do Misty, Mandy, and Sandi plan on showing up?'

'Keye, what the hell happened today?'

I told him about the phone call, sitting in my car listening to Miki's stalker rage at me through a voice disguiser. 'Then my window shattered and all hell broke loose.'

'I was at my desk. You know how the office is. The AC was blasting. I had music on. I heard something. I couldn't tell if it was a gun. I went to the door and that's pretty much all I remember.'

'Just a suggestion: When you hear shots, don't open the door.'

'I should have opened it sooner. You could have been killed. Jesus. I could have called the cops or done something.'

'I'm sorry you were hurt,' I told him.

'Ah, well, they have great drugs here.' He peeled plastic wrap off a plate of cookies on the hospital overbed table. He took one and handed one to me. They were chewy, with chocolate chips that were still warm and velvety.

'I think you and Blond Tammy should get married so I can have cookies more often.'

'They're both blond, by the way, and blue-eyed. And sweet. So let out all your snarky shit before Cathy gets here. Hitler's dream girls. Aryan Nation. What else you got?'

'That pretty much covers it.' I took another cookie. 'I've been thinking about something. The business is growing so fast I can't keep up. When the whole story comes out about this crematory thing, it'll get worse. We'll have more clients than we'll know what to do with. The business has been in a place for a while where it could grow. I'd like you to be a partner and help me figure out how to make it happen.'

Neil's eyes searched my face. 'Is this about me saying I quit?'

'So you do remember.' I smiled. 'I don't know. Maybe a

little.' Something about bullets flying around had made me take stock. 'I just realized today it just wouldn't be fun without you.'

'Well, since you put it that way,' Neil said. 'But listen, Keye, we have to have some agreements going in. We've both proved we suck at the office stuff. And you've been putting off hiring someone for a really long time. I know it's hard to let people in. It's understandable you'd have trust issues, but we have to do it. Half the new business gets turned away or doesn't get a return call. You need someone to manage all that and to get your schedule under control. And we need to think about hiring another investigator too.'

He was right. I had been putting things off. We didn't have time for the day-to-day grunt work, what with frequent trips to Southern Sweets and Cakes & Ale. Plus, Neil needed to smoke a couple of joints a day. So we were *busy*. It's just so hard to bring in a new person. I dreaded it. Whom can you trust with your business and your life? Who's going to have a crazy girlfriend or a kid that calls all day or bad habits? I mean, what if they sucked their teeth or moaned when they got up and down? Just the thought made me twitch. And there were baskets full of unfiled invoices on top of the file cabinets, and unreturned messages, and the billing piled up, which meant cash flow was lousy.

'Agreed,' I told Neil. 'But it has to be a good fit. We can't just hire the first person who comes along. And I want you to agree to not bring pot into the office. I don't care where you do it or how much you do it, just don't smoke at the office.'

'Okay,' Neil said. 'I can respect that. How about this consulting thing? On the table or not?'

'No.'

'You like dodging bullets? Because I don't.'

'If it makes you feel any better, he wasn't shooting at you. The bullet ricocheted.'

'Doesn't make me feel better.'

'It's not on the table, Neil. Look, you're doing what you love. But this business, it wasn't my dream. It was just a way to keep the lights on. I miss doing work that matters. Consulting is a way to make a difference. And maybe get back a little of what I lost.'

'You can't relive the past, Keye.'

'Well, thank you very much, Dr Shetty.'

I heard the door open behind me. Neil hastily handed me the cookie plate. I turned and saw another pretty young woman, pale, short hair, perky, a Carol Channing bob. She was carrying a gift bag bristling with glossy ribbons. She rushed to his bedside. 'Oh my God! You poor thing!'

'I'm fine.' Neil patted her hand. 'I'll be out in a couple of days.'

'You're going to have to have crutches. You'll need a lot of help at home,' she told him.

Neil began to squirm. I stood up. 'You must be Cathy. I've heard so much about you. I'm Keye Street. I work with Neil.' There was not a hint of recognition on her face when she shook my hand. I was as much a surprise to her as finding out Neil had two girlfriends was to me. 'Well, I'll leave you two alone.' I shoved the cookies at Neil. 'I made them myself.'

'Stay safe, Street,' Neil called, as I left the room.

I left the hospital knowing I had a bull's-eye on my forehead. On the phone, the killer had gone off like a road flare, then unloaded a 9mm. *'I'm saving you a seat at the table.'* Don't have to be a genius to know what that means. *'You're late for the party.'* He was raging, hated women, felt his control slipping with Miki. She'd been out of psychiatric hospitals for a couple of years. She was more confident. She'd stopped cutting herself. Fatu had been moving forward too, I thought. She was clean. She was off the streets. Could that be the connection?

I walked in and bolted my door. White Trash came trotting to see me. I went to the front windows and looked out on the street. The Fox Theatre had been running a summer classic film series. *Casablanca* was on the marquee. To my left, a constant stream of headlights twisted into downtown. I could see the hospital, where I hoped Neil was resting, and the pale light under the filigreed dome at the Bank of America building glowing in the checkered skyline. I lowered myself into my desk chair, jotted down on a legal pad: *Transition. Shifts. Change. Attachment. Obsession.*

White Trash jumped on my lap. I reached for my phone and called the one person on earth who could always pull me up out of a sinkhole.

'Oh my God!' I put on my best Paris Hilton. 'It's you.'

'Oh my God! It's you too,' my brother shot right back, and proved he was a much better Valley girl. 'I was going to call you first thing in the morning. I have something to talk to you about.'

'That sounds mysterious.'

'I know how you love a good mystery.'

'So tell me.'

'You tell me what's wrong first. I hear it in your voice.'

'Long day,' I said.

'Want to talk about it?'

'I hardly know where to start, Jimmy.'

'Start anywhere. I've got time.'

'Miki has a stalker. He's dangerous. He shot at me, and Neil got hurt. He's okay, but he's in the hospital for a couple of days. Miki's in Mississippi or Alabama or somewhere chasing tornadoes. I'm consulting with APD on murders this man committed. I have the willies. I wanted a drink as soon as I hit the door. And our mother thinks she's the next Paula Deen.'

'Okay, wow,' Jimmy said. 'Wow.'

'Sorry.'

'This bastard is shooting at you? Is APD close to making an arrest? No wonder you're upset, sweetie.'

'Getting closer. Big break in the case.' I told him about a possible connection to events held in Midtown and Stone Mountain, the ballpark, Mr R. I told him everything I knew so far. I'd always talked to Jimmy. Apart from my shrink, he might have been the only person on earth who just listens without judgment. I poured grape juice in a whiskey glass, three fingers, and curled up on my couch. I told him about Mother's audition for the cooking network, and we laughed about our parents as we always did behind their backs. White Trash joined me on the sofa. She was really needy. I'd been away more than usual this past week.

'Paul's been offered a promotion.' Jimmy gave me his news when I'd finished. 'If he takes it, we would transfer back down South.'

'To Atlanta?' A flicker of sunshine crept into my glum mood.

'His office would be in town. But I think I want to look for something outside the city.'

'That's fantastic! Please tell me he's going to take it. God, I'd love to have you guys here.' Jimmy's silence felt like it was coming through a loudspeaker. 'You don't want to come,' I said.

My brother is not as romantic about our southern roots as I am. The streets were too narrow here for a boy of color and undetermined heritage. The dewy breezes, the dogwoods and cherry blossoms and blackberry vines – all of it, in Jimmy's opinion, was just camouflage for a racist heart. I had begged him to come back from Seattle over the years. He'd left Georgia immediately after graduation and headed for Stanford on scholarship. Paul was a coppery redhead from Missouri who watched sports on weekends and liked to strum the guitar and sing at parties after a few beers.

'I'll make peace with it if it's what he wants,' Jimmy told me.

'It's a different world here now, Jimmy. It's not like it was when we were kids.'

'And you would know this because you're black, male, and homosexual? I don't think you get it, Keye. Do you know that our mother informed me that one of my birth parents must have been either white or, I don't know, Afghani or something? Because I have light eyes. She told me this with a lot of excitement. She's been looking at pictures on the Internet. Can you imagine? Our mother is Googling things like "black people with light eyes." You don't feel the undercurrents like I do. It's different for you.

Everyone just always assumed you'd be a scientist or something. And I'd beat my wife and wind up doing time.'

'I wish you'd tell that to the TSA agents at the airport. I'm pretty much guaranteed a hot date every time I fly. You should see the stares I get when I work up in the sticks somewhere. I don't always get a free pass, Jimmy.'

'I'm getting misty,' Jimmy fake cried. 'You're a hero, Keye.'

'Walk a mile in my shoes, my brother.'

He laughed. We were quiet for a moment. 'We've lived here for nine years,' he said, quietly. 'Our friends are here. It's not an easy decision. On the plus side, you're there and I miss you *so* much. And we both want our child to grow up knowing you.'

I sat up. 'Child?'

'We've registered with an agency and started the process of searching for a surrogate mother.'

'That's terrific! You'll make such a great father.'

'It will take awhile. The call could come tomorrow or it could take a couple of years. But we both want children.'

I laughed. I could barely manage my cat. Thank God I'd never wanted kids. A niece, on the other hand, might be really fun. I had convinced my brother when we were little that your eyes change sockets when you cross them. He'd spent a lot of time in front of the mirror testing it. Pliable little minds. Big entertainment. 'What happens when the call comes?'

'We jump on a plane to wherever, meet the mother, spend some time, see if we're a good match.'

'This is the best news I've had all year. I'm so happy for you guys. When will you know about Paul's job?'

'He hasn't decided. So no pushing, okay? Don't you hang up and call him.'

'Would I push?'

Jimmy laughed. 'It's a big promotion, Keye. And a lot more money. It makes financial sense. Especially since we're starting a family. Hey, I love you, big sister. Get some sleep. I'll update you soon.'

'I love you too.' I reached for White Trash. 'Jimmy's a sucker for cats,' I told her, and she yawned.

30

I felt for my Glock as soon as my eyes opened. My security blanket. It had saved my life once because it was there under my pillow when I reached for it. I had learned a couple of lessons that night. One: You don't really know the people in your life. Not really. Not below the surface. Not ever. And two: Keep up with your gun.

I put the Glock on the bed table and picked up my phone. No emails from Miki. No texts. No missed calls. I'd sent her the picture of Robert Crammer, Burger Dog Bob, and never received a reply. I found her new number in my contacts list, called it. Five rings and it went to voice mail. I left a message. White Trash leapt off the bed and huffed off with a few fuck-you tail twitches, miffed I had dared to move my legs. I heard her scratching a couple of minutes later, kicking litter all over my wood floors, no doubt. The box has not been built that can contain White Trash's grave digger–like enthusiasm. I think she has a little shovel stashed somewhere, or a tiny backhoe and a hard hat.

I pulled on a summer robe, filled the teakettle with

water, and dumped coffee into the French press. There was a love note from Rauser on the counter. I squinted to read his backward-tilted scrawl. White Trash skidded around the corner, batting at a catnip-filled mouse with the dexterity of a midfielder. Later, she'd carry it back under the table, where she hoarded all her toys and occasionally circled them menacingly. My alley cat had the heart of a predator.

Rauser called. I put him on speaker while I fed White Trash and made my coffee. 'When did you leave? You were so quiet.' I barely remembered him slipping into bed with me. I didn't remember him getting up to leave.

'I tried not to wake you. You had a rough night. You woke me up talking about the men yelling again,' Rauser said. 'I guess getting shot at has a way of stirring up memories.'

I sat down on a stool with my coffee. 'I was dreaming about my grandparents again. And then I woke realizing there was only one male voice that day. He kept yelling at them to hand over the money. The second man didn't come into the store until later. I think the second man tried to stop it. Then I heard the shots.'

'So maybe the second guy was just a customer who walked in.'

'Maybe. I don't know. Why would he run?'

'Man, would I love to snag the sonsofbitches that did this to your family. No statute on murder. You've been having weird dreams since I've known you.'

'It's only been thirty years,' I said, and poured more coffee. 'I could probably stretch out the misery a few more years.'

'And your mother says you're afraid of commitment.' Rauser laughed. 'Hey, wanna know about the phone that called you yesterday? It's a no-contract prepaid with a couple thousand minutes. Purchased at Lenox Square Mall, which is coincidentally where the hot dog man happens to have one of his two stationary locations.'

'How about GPS? Can you location-track it?'

'Phone must be powered down. Maybe he dumped it already. Emergency location tracking can't be disabled, but if there's no power to it, you can't find it. Last location was right where you thought he was. Up on North Highland over your office parking lot four minutes before your call to nine-one-one.'

'I was trying to keep him talking. I told him Miki wasn't like Fatu. I might as well have fired a detonator in a wad of C-4. He lost it completely. Screamed at me that she was a different kind of whore. That's when my window shattered. The bastard.' I took my coffee and headed for the television. 'I can't get that creepy voice disguiser out of my head.'

'We've got Crammer coming in later this morning. He thinks he's coming to look at photos to see if he recognizes anybody from the ballpark.'

'You still like him for it,' I said, and clicked on the TV. I wanted to check on the weather where Miki was.

'Don't you? Opportunity, location, timing, physicality – what's not to like? He's divorced, lives with a couple rescue dogs, drives a two-year-old forty-five-thousand-dollar BMW, which he still owes a ton on. And get this: He leased an apartment in Midtown a couple of years ago. Leased it for a year. Didn't renew. Unclear at the moment what he used it for. But he was going through a divorce at the time.'

'Nice car, Midtown apartment. Might have looked like a way out to someone like Fatu. On the other hand, I don't think his moods are manageable enough to run a business. The guy is incredibly torqued up.'

'We'll see which way Crammer bounces in the interview room. By the way, big storms came through Mississippi, Arkansas, and Missouri last night. Alabama's in the cross-hairs now. Towers are down. Power's knocked out.'

'That explains why I haven't heard back from Miki, I guess. I sent her Crammer's picture.'

'There's another line developing to the southwest. That one's coming this way. Maybe by tomorrow afternoon. All emergency services and personnel are on alert.'

I glanced at the window and saw blue skies in Atlanta. I clicked the remote, found the Weather Channel, and was immediately bombarded with images of storm-ravaged land-scape. A forecaster explained why atmospheric conditions were perfect for the first super-outbreak in forty years. Tornado warnings and watches covered the entire southern United States. I switched to CNN and watched bobbing, grainy cell phone video of a giant, filthy cloud chewing up and spitting out everything in its path. Fourteen people had been killed and hundreds were missing in Mississippi. As many as sixty tornadoes were currently on the ground in Alabama. *Sixty*. One of them was a real bad boy.

'Jesus, an EF-Five hit Tuscaloosa.' The city looked like it had been shelled. Houses, mailboxes, street signs, office buildings, hospitals – everything was leveled.

'Don't worry,' Rauser said. 'Miki's a pro. She'll call when she has service. Hey, I gotta head downstairs. Televised briefing with the new boss. What's your plan?'

'I'm going to take Neil's computer and stuff to the hospital. Then I'm coming to the station.'

I sipped coffee and watched a storm chaser's video on television. It was shot from a moving vehicle. I wondered if Miki was somewhere in that truck with her shutter humming. They were tracking the EF5 while trying to stay out of its path. Wide strips of landscape looked like a toothpick forest. The tiny things that people cherish had been sucked out of drawers and closets. Photos and memories. Gone. Clothes, furniture, pieces of houses and cars had been sent swirling, then dumped in piles that looked like rubbish. Whole lives in little pieces.

I muted the television. 'Rauser, these nightmares I've had on and off all my life. I think he has too – the man Fatu called Mr R. The stuff he's leaving at the scenes – the ribbon, the red balloon, the wrapping paper. They're linked to something for him, some trauma. He's reenacting it in his own way, I think.'

'Honestly, Keye, I could give a shit about the crazy fuck's childhood traumas. Not all of us grew up in Happy Town. I damn sure did not, and you had a shitty start. But neither one of us has the uncontrollable urge to fuck someone up.'

'Speak for yourself,' I said.

'You're saying I should talk about that evidence?'

'The items could have been present in other situations. Maybe someone noticed. Maybe they're all over his house or his dog. I don't know. I'm just asking you not to overlook that aspect of the profile.'

'Opens the door for copycats when I start talking crime scenes.'

'I get it. Do what you need to do.'

'I gotta run. Be careful out there, darlin'. Eyes open, okay?'

I pressed in Miki's number again. Straight to voice mail. 'Hey. Just weather-watching. I guess you're in the thick of it. This is what you like, right? Jesus, you're a freak. Call your cousin. I'm worried. I love ya.' I pushed the phone off and thought about that. I did love her, my complicated, brave, self-absorbed, strung-out shutterbug of a cousin. Introspection not being my specialty, this was a bit of a revelation. I had loved her when we were children. But our lives had forked off in very different directions.

I switched to a local station and caught the breaking news banner across the bottom of the screen, then APD's pressroom and a walnut lectern with the official emblem on the front. I turned up the volume and sat back with my coffee. The voice of an unseen reporter told me in the hushed tones of a golf commentator that the Atlanta Police Department had an urgent announcement. He stressed the hurried nature of the press conference, then speculated on its meaning. In the background, other whispers from other journalists to other cameras, the occasional cleared throat, a cough, the rustle of paper or the clang of equipment, a metal chair leg scooting forward or back on tiled floors.

APD's press liaison and official spokesperson, Jeanne Bascom, walked to the lectern flanked by Major Herman Hicks and Lieutenant Aaron Rauser. All of them were in their dress blues, gold piping, the embroidered APD emblem on their shoulders, gold buttons and cuff links. All of it sending an important message: *We're competent and professional, and you're safe in our hands*. It was the first time I'd seen Rauser in uniform since we'd attended an officer's funeral a couple of months ago. He stood military straight.

Bascom pushed reading glasses onto a small, straight nose, glanced around the room, then at the notes she'd placed on the lectern in front of her. She straightened them. I'd seen Jeanne Bascom manage Atlanta's hungry press corps during Olympic bombings, Super Bowl threats, serial rapists and killers, and a firestorm of backlash against APD's own police chief after he was accused of allowing his own political goals to get in the way of a murder investigation. I'd seen her face pinched so tight she looked like she'd been sucking a lemon. Today her manner and expression reflected the gravity of the message she was about to deliver. The press room knew it had to be big to bring Bascom to the lectern in a hastily scheduled conference. She was a stickler for the regular briefings.

The glasses were removed, folded, and placed on the podium. 'A Q-and-A will follow a brief prepared statement. Please withhold your questions until that time.' Bascom always set the ground rules first. 'Through exhaustive investigative efforts and in coordination with the state crime lab, the Atlanta Police Department has linked the homicides of a Clarkston woman to two male victims in the Midtown area.' The pressroom erupted. 'Major Herman Hicks and Lieutenant Aaron Rauser will take your questions.'

Hicks was five-ten, African American, with the pock-marked skin of a man who'd had ravaging acne as a boy. The questions came in a bombardment. *What are the victims' names? Is there physical evidence? How much time between murders? What is cause of death? Is this linked to other serial murder cases?*

'The first homicide took place approximately eleven

months ago,' Hicks told the pressroom. 'The first victim appears to be a twenty-one-year-old female named Fatu Doe, a resident of Clarkston. The second and third known victims are Troy Delgado, a thirteen-year-old male, and Donald Kelly, a ninety-year-old male. Both are – were – Atlanta residents. Physical evidence at all the crime scenes has been collected and sent to the state crime lab. According to witness statements, the unidentified suspect is a Caucasian male between six feet two and six feet four inches tall, with brown hair. He wears black thick-soled shoes, size thirteen. They may be worn in his profession or because of an orthopedic condition.' Hicks gave his Homicide lieutenant a nod, then stepped aside.

This was a part of Rauser's job he absolutely hated. He took in the room, leaned forward to a microphone that was set too low for him. 'Think about your friends and neighbors. Ask yourself if someone has had unexplained absences lately. Have their habits changed? Have they become erratic? The suspect may exhibit obsessive behaviors, some of which could be focused on these images.' He held up a photograph of the ribbon that had been tied like a bow around Fatu Doe's ankle and the balloon from the Delgado scene, then continued reading off the psychological sketch I'd prepared in the hospital waiting room. 'The suspect is between twenty-five and thirty years old. He might have had a severe trauma as a child and been in a neglectful or violent situation. The suspect may exhibit symptoms of paranoia, thinks he's being criticized, judged. He's hyper-sensitive. He's an introvert and prefers working alone. He may have an inappropriately explosive reaction to perceived insult or disrespect. He has periods of depression. He likes to read. He has difficulty in social situations. He's good with dogs and may frequent places like dog parks or dog-friendly settings, such as public parks or sidewalk cafés where dogs are allowed. One of the victims was sexually assaulted, and we believe the suspect has sexually assaulted other women as well. If this man sounds familiar in any way, please contact our tip lines immediately. Your identity will be protected.' Rauser's eyes raked the room. 'He owns or has access to a nine-millimeter Smith and Wesson M-and-P. He's known to have recently driven a blue 2010 Honda Element. We believe he works and may live in the Midtown area.'

The pressroom exploded with questions. Rauser remained vague. He stood for five minutes and answered follow-up questions. There was a lot of panic these murders might be connected to the Wishbone murders last year or other known active serials working in this country. Rauser dispelled this notion unequivocally.

'Lieutenant Rauser, has the FBI been brought in?' a reporter asked. 'Who prepared that profile you're reading from?'

Uh-oh. I sucked in my breath. Major Hicks stepped to the lectern. 'The FBI is not currently involved in the case. As you are well aware, we rely on forensic scientists to analyze the physical evidence. It's not unusual for this department and other departments to seek out qualified analysts to compile psychological profiles. We've done that in these cases in an effort to reveal sooner the identity of the offender.'

'What about DNA evidence?'

'Budget constraints and the high volume of cases now

depending on DNA evidence mean lab results take anywhere from a few days to a few weeks.' Hicks turned on his heel, and all three of them left the pressroom. The door behind the lectern had barely closed before my phone rang.

'This is Monica Roberts, WXIA-TV. Are you profiling on these cases?'

'I've consulted with APD in the past, you know that, Monica.' I'd met Monica Roberts in a parking garage last year. She'd chased Rauser and me wearing high heels. And caught us.

'Did you compile the profile they're working from?'

'I think it's APD's call to release the names of their consultants. Or not.'

'That's not a no,' she said.

I didn't answer. Okay, so maybe there is a little ambition in me. Favorable speculation from someone like Roberts would bring in a lot of business. Big business. Paying business. Not just bail jumpers and background checks and subpoenas. I'd lost my biggest client last year, a big-money law firm that paid me a few thousand every month. I'm one of the little guys. A few thousand makes a huge difference in quality of living. I was feeling it.

'Listen, how about we get together and talk?' Roberts pressed. 'About everything. On camera. The alcoholism, what went wrong at the FBI, consulting on the Wishbone cases and what that cost you, Northeast Georgia Crematorium, these new cases, your relationship with Aaron Rauser, your life sober. Even better – how about the two of you do the interview? You and the lieutenant together. You're a fascinating couple.'

The thought of an on-camera interview with Monica

Roberts was terrifying. How do people do that? Just walk on television, I mean. I tend to obsess about the little things. Big surprise, right? Me obsessing. Is that really my posture? I look kind of slouchy. My eyes are too far apart. My nose is too narrow at the bridge and turned up at the end. And what's up with the freckles? Don't Asians get a pass on freckles? My parents promised I'd grow out of them. And Rauser put media interviews right up there with the opera on Sunday as a way to screw up a perfectly good day. I knew he'd never go for it. I'd had to beg him to sit through the *Rolling Stone* interview. He'd done it because he loved me and he wanted the truth to come out. And, if he was being honest, because *Rolling Stone* magazine was *the* coolest, in his mind.

'Can I think it over?' I wasn't ready to light a fire under this bridge. Not just yet. I wanted to see what it felt like to be on Roberts's good side for a change.

31

The good news is: Even stalkers can't stalk twenty-four hours a day. It's how he'd lost track of Miki. He had a job. He had to buy groceries. He had other responsibilities. Maybe he had to walk his dog. It was a comforting thought. Not comforting enough. I had the hotel valet get me a cab rather than use the Neon. Then I checked for a tail out the back window compulsively.

The driver waited while I ran into my office and collected Neil's things, then dropped me off at the hospital. Neil was having a bad morning. Lots of pain. Lots of pain meds. He was in and out, seemed barely aware of me there. I tucked his phone and iPad under the blanket next to him and pushed his laptop under his pillow. At the front exit, I hailed another cab.

'Where to?' The driver was dark-skinned. Indian, perhaps.

'City Hall East,' I answered, and glanced instinctively at the driver's ID clipped to the visor. There was a pink ribbon hanging off the rearview mirror, tied in a droopy bow.

The driver watched me in the mirror. What he could not see was my hand coming to rest on my Glock. 'Today is my birthday,' he told me. 'My daughter made lunch for me this morning and put a ribbon on it. I'm a sentimental man. You have kids?'

'No.' I studied him. He was too small and fine-boned for the man who'd left a size-thirteen shoe print at the Delgado scene. I relaxed a little, but didn't take my hand off my gun. My eyes went back to the bow. *Ribbons, wrapping paper, presents, birthdays, baby showers, Christmas.*

'Ma'am?' We'd stopped. 'I'm sorry to say the garage is too busy. I'll have to drop you in front.'

The businesses and other city offices that had used the City Hall building for years had stuffed the garage with moving trucks. Rauser had mentioned the neighbors were moving out. Major Crimes would be the last to go. There was talk of shiny new offices off Peachtree. I paid the driver and got out on Ponce de Leon. Detective Bevins was in her cube when I got upstairs to Homicide.

'The lieu wants me to make sure you have access to what you need,' she told me, smiling. 'Want some coffee? I'm headed that way.'

'Absolutely.' I nodded. 'I take it black.'

'That's easy. By the way, the lieutenant's in interview room one with the burger guy.'

'We have video?' I asked.

'Pick a monitor.'

I turned on the monitor in the empty cube I'd used before and pressed the appropriate button for the interview room I wanted, plugged in earphones. Bob Crammer was sitting across a table from Brit Williams, Ken Lang, and

Rauser. Rauser had rolled up his shirtsleeves. It was probably hot as hell in there. He liked to cut the air to his interview rooms just so no one got too comfortable. Crammer had his arms folded over his chest and the metal chair tilted back on two legs.

'He turned surly once he figured he was a person of interest,' Bevins said, and put a coffee mug in front of me. It had a Starbucks logo. Fivebucks, Rauser always called it.

'What? No confession?' I took a sip from the mug and shuddered. 'They get anything out of him?'

'Not much once he realized he wasn't here to look at pictures. Lang's in there for a cheek swab. I think Crammer's going to lawyer up. He's got that look.'

Bevins was right. Crammer refused to answer more questions, and he refused the cheek swab. They had to let him walk.

'Do you have time to search some archives?' I asked Bevins.

'Sure. What you got?'

'I'm looking for anything involving a living child found at a crime scene or a child pulled from a severely abusive situation. Time frame twenty to twenty-five years ago. I'll start the same process with news reports online.'

'Log-in passwords change every day. I'll get you logged in. I don't know what you got in your case' – she nodded at the laptop case I'd come in with on my shoulder – 'but this new system they gave us can really fly.'

'Great. I'll use it. Thanks.'

I felt eyes on me and turned in my chair. Bob Crammer stood, watching me. He'd just left the interview room. He paused, then left. Ken Lang, Rauser, and Brit Williams came out. 'What do you think, Lieutenant?' Bevins asked.

'I want to stay all over this guy until we can either bring him in or exclude him,' Rauser said. 'Street, the tip lines are ringing. Lot of folks responding to your profile. Williams, get someone on Crammer. And let's have Balaki and Thomas work tips. Bevins, you on something?'

'I'm running with an idea,' I said. 'I could use Detective Bevins.'

Rauser nodded. 'We'll let you have her as long as we can.'

Bevins and I worked for the next ninety minutes. She cruised archived police files. I looked at quarter-century-old headlines that had been converted from microfilm to online archives. APD's system had access to everything I needed. No logging in to databases to find information. This was never an issue for Neil. Passwords, log-in info, none of it seemed to trip him up. We do subscribe to software programs that allow me access to some databases, but without Neil's code-cracking brain and expert navigation skills, it was still a painstaking process.

I'd typed in keywords *murder, murder-suicide, double homicide, homicide, child found at crime scene, child at murder scene, neglected child, abused child, killings at Christmas, murder at parties*. I ended all the queries with 1980–1990. The volume of information was overwhelming. I sorted through the slush with dying hopes until one of the articles stopped me in my tracks.

Police: Murder-Suicide at Child's Birthday Party

My heart rate accelerated.

A man and a woman were found dead in an Atlanta home Saturday afternoon, according to the Atlanta Police Department. Police said it was a murder-suicide.

Emma and Jackson Richards were found in a single-family dwelling on Moreland Avenue. The couple were married but had divorced, said Atlanta police spokesman Evan Bell.

Emma Richards previously filed a family violence complaint against her ex-husband in April 1980. It resulted in a temporary restraining order.

Emma Richards was last seen greeting guests at a children's birthday party outside her home at noon. According to witnesses, her estranged ex-husband, Jackson Richards, entered the premises at approximately 1:45 p.m. and shot and killed Emma Richards, then shot and killed himself.

When police arrived, the couple's eight-year-old son, Jesse Owen Richards, who had witnessed the murder-suicide, was outside under the supervision of adult guests and neighbors. Six children and three adults were present during the shooting. The dead couple's child was taken away from the scene by child protective services. Police later located the grandparents, who will assume custody.

A witness at the party said the party was well under way and the gifts were being opened when Jackson Richards walked in the front door and drew a gun. 'It happened so fast,' the witness, the mother of an eight-year-old classmate of Jesse Owen Richards, sobbed. 'No one had time to move. He just shot her. Then he put the gun to his temple.'

I read through the story again. 'Gotcha,' I whispered. 'Hey, Bevins, can you run May third, 1980? Jackson and Emma Richards.'

Bevins typed in some information. 'It's in Records. A hard file. Closed. A murder-suicide. Hasn't been put in digital yet.'

'Can you get it?'

'Sure. You think our guy's in there?'

I felt a rush coming up from my toes. Every investigator gets one when they know they're close, a little flutter, a slightly elevated heart rate, a split-second blast of chemicals. 'It's him,' I said.

32

We used the big conference table in the War Room and spread out the case file. The scene photos showed Emma Richards with a dark, wet pool under her skull. She lay only feet away from where her husband, Jackson Richards, had collapsed. He'd shot her, shoved her body aside, then shot himself. I studied the photos. The table was littered with paper plates and the remains of a white birthday cake with blue icing, melted ice cream in little pools on plates, paper cups. Nine chairs. Four of them matched the oak veneer table, five of them appeared to have come from other parts of the house. At the far end of the table, the plastic forks, paper plates, the tablecloth, and the presents were spattered with a fine spray. Emma's eight-year-old son would have been sitting on that end at the head of the table where the presents were clustered. He must have been covered with his mother's blood. I thought about that night at Miki's house when Lang turned on his UV and blue stains appeared on Donald Kelly. I picked up another photo of Emma Richards and finally understood.

'It's tear fluid,' I told them. 'And probably semen.' Rauser, Balaki, Williams, and Bevins gaped at me as if I'd just pulled up in a hovercraft and declared myself a Vulcan. 'The mystery fluid,' I explained. 'Tears and semen.'

'You saying he's crying and whacking off at the scenes?' Williams asked. Silence had settled over the room.

I nodded. 'It's the only time he can cry. It's not about remorse. It's a release. And masturbating gives him back control. It's not necessarily sexual. It's about power over his victim. And his lack of power in life.' I pushed the photo of Emma Richards to the center of the table. One arm was straight out from her body, palm up. She'd been holding a blue ribbon when she fell. 'This is why he's leaving ribbons and balloons and wrapping paper.'

'Look at that,' Rauser said. He'd turned a little pale. 'In the mother's hand. All over the table. Little hand-tied ribbons everywhere. And presents.'

'And red balloons,' Williams said.

'Miki said something to me about how it felt like he wanted to ruin everything just when she was piecing her life together. I don't think she's far off. I think the killer's selection process is somehow connected to transitions. To life changes. Every one of these victims was on the cusp of something. Fatu Doe was recovering, clean, getting strong. Miki's not cutting herself. She's not depressed. She received a very public award nomination. She's moving forward.'

'Troy Delgado was a superstar. He was gonna have a contract before he finished high school.' Balaki was still staring at the picture of Emma Richards.

'He was moving on,' Williams said. 'Leaving. Everyone leaves the killer behind.'

'The old man. Kelly,' Bevins added. 'He was sick. Not expected to live much longer. Dementia and lymphoma. He was transitioning too.'

'Okay.' Rauser pushed back his chair. 'Let's get to work, see if this is our guy. Balaki, get on the hospital records. Jesse Owen Richards shows up at any of the institutions we have down for Miki, cross-check the dates. Bevins, find out where Richards is now. And get a recent photo. We gotta connect him to the Doe girl, Kelly, and Delgado. Get everything. Credit cards. Bank accounts. We want to know where he eats, lives, walks his dog, who he sleeps with. And take another look at the personnel out there at the ballpark.'

You could feel the energy in the room take off. My heart was hammering. Rauser's phone jingled as we all moved back to the Homicide room. He answered, plugged his free ear with a finger, and wheeled away. He was biting his bottom lip when he came back. 'GBI lab,' he told us. 'Full reports have been emailed, but you were right, Keye. It's tear fluid and semen. The tears didn't come from the vics. Williams, get that report downloaded. Run the sequence through CODIS.'

Ten million or so offender DNA profiles had been logged into the CODIS system. It was not a hundred percent for positive hits even when an offender's DNA was actually in the system. But technology and software were constantly improving, and more and more law enforcement agencies were taking the time to log in offender profiles. As a result, the system had become increasingly effective.

Rauser pulled pages of reports Williams had printed off the printer and handed them to me. I scanned the details as fast as I could. 'They amplified the samples from the clothing using PCR. DNA is confirming your witness statements. The offender is male. It's likely he's also white. It's possible his eyes and hair are brown.'

'But it's not certain?' Williams asked.

'Gender is definite. They've identified the XY,' I said. 'Race has certain ID markers. The probability is he's Caucasian. But we've confirmed that with witness statements already. Eye and hair color are less certain.'

'Got a hit on CODIS,' Williams announced. 'Matches the sequence in the samples Stone Mountain PD submitted from offender skin samples under Fatu Doe's nails.'

'Okay, now we've got a physical link for all three victims,' Rauser said, and smiled. 'DA's gonna wanna kiss my face. Balaki, you get anything on the hospital records?'

'Affirmative,' Balaki answered. 'Four instances in two hospitals where Jesse Owen Richards and Miki Ashton were both on the inpatient register.'

'Okay, that's it right there. Richards is our guy. Let's track him down.'

'Got the last driver's-license photo on record,' Bevins said. 'It's six years old, though. He hasn't renewed. I don't see any vehicle registrations in his name either. I'll put it up.' We all looked up at the big screen. A white, overweight man with a thick neck, a jowly face, and brown eyes and hair looked back. 'Six-three,' Bevins told us. 'Three-twenty.'

'He could have lost the weight in six years,' Balaki pointed out.

'Miki said he was a big guy, soft. She saw his stomach under his shirt,' I said.

'Where is he now?' Rauser wanted to know.

'Missing,' Williams said, and the energy in the room took

332 — Amanda Kyle Williams

a dive. 'A missing-persons report was filed three years ago by the grandparents, Fred and Melinda Etheridge.'

'Find out where they are and stake 'em out. Front and back. I don't want anyone slipping out the back door. This feels a little too convenient. Once we're set up, Keye and I will go in and have a chat with the grandparents.'

'No work records for him. Nothing,' Williams said. 'He never resurfaced.'

'Oh yes he did,' Rauser said. 'And he started killing people.'

'How about bank records?' I asked.

'Bank account was closed,' Bevins said. 'A week before the missing persons was filed. Two hundred and thirty bucks.'

'So, he knew he was going to disappear,' I said.

'Looked suspicious then too,' Bevins said. 'He was an adult with a history of mental illness, and he'd emptied his bank account. Notations from the detectives indicate their conclusion was he left of his own free will.'

I spotted a package of cookies in cellophane on Balaki's desk and picked them up. 'Blood-sugar emergency,' I said. My nerves were running laps and I couldn't remember if I'd eaten. Hey, don't judge. Vodka would have been nice, but cookies was what I had.

'Go for it,' Balaki said.

I ripped the package open. The cookies were hard and stale. I popped one in my mouth. My phone lit up, a 205 area code. I hooked on my earpiece.

'Hel-woo,' I said, which is what you get when you answer your phone with a mouthful of old, dry chocolate-chip cookies. Balaki snickered.

'This is DCH Regional Medical Center in Tuscaloosa, Alabama. Is this Keye Street?'

'Yes.'

'We have Miki Ashton here under observation.'

'What happened?' Rauser must have heard something in my voice. He looked up at me with concern. 'Is she okay?' I thought of the devastation the storm had wrought.

'I'll let her tell you.'

'Keye, I'm fine. It's my leg. And I lost my new fucking phone.'

'What happened? Is it bad?'

'Broken in a couple of places. I'm out of commission for a while.'

'Oh no, Miki. I'm so sorry.' I mouthed to Rauser that Miki had broken a leg.

'It got totally crazy here,' Miki told me. 'Looks like there was a war. Seriously. I was in Beirut after a bombing and there was less infrastructure damage and fewer people hurt. I've already uploaded the pics to the magazine. They're stunning, Keye. What happened here, it's beyond description. Biggest tornado I've ever seen, stayed down for about three miles. We were right behind it. We came through this neighborhood that was just leveled in about two minutes. All you could hear was crying and screaming. It was horrible. Except one house was standing all alone. The roof was sheared off, but the rest of it looked strangely perfect and beautiful among the rubble. I heard a woman calling for help. I went in and found her, then one of the walls came down.' Miki asked me to hang on, and I heard her being a brat to the nurse. 'Can I please get some painkillers over here? Do you have any idea how fucking bad this hurts?' Then back to me in a different tone entirely, 'I have a friend from Birmingham getting me to the airport when I'm released in a couple of hours. Will you pick me up at Hartsfield-Jackson?'

'Of course,' I said, and took down her flight info. 'Miki, what about the woman?'

'What woman?'

'The injured woman in the house.'

'Oh yeah, yeah, right. She's fine. She had a bathtub on top of her. They got her out. I think she's down the hall. Keye, they're saying maybe a couple hundred people died. I've covered some bad shit, but this is right up there.'

I heard stress in her voice. I didn't have the heart to tell her about the creepy phone call or the threats to her or the shots at me or that Neil had been hurt. Not yet. 'Miki, does the name Jesse Richards sound familiar?'

'No. Why?'

'I'll tell you about it when I pick you up.'

33

We stood in front of a sandy brick home with a second-story clapboard addition. Rauser knocked on the door, a cop knock, too firm, too official. I knew he had detectives on the street already. I'd spotted the car, another Crown Vic, with a driver and passenger two doors up. He'd wanted them front and back, but the house backed up to the golf course. I wondered how they'd decided to handle that.

The woman who opened the door wore dark pink pants, sneakers, and a polo shirt. Her hair was silver and thick, tucked behind her ears. We knew she was seventy-two and her husband was three years older. But she didn't look it. Not even close.

'Mrs Etheridge, I'm Lieutenant Aaron Rauser with the Atlanta Police Department, and this is Keye Street. May we come in?'

Alert green eyes went from Rauser to me. 'Of course, Lieutenant, Ms Street. Please come in. May I offer you a glass of iced tea?'

'No, ma'am. Thank you.'

She led us through a tidy house to where a white-haired man was sitting at a table, gluing back together a model airplane that looked like it had some age on it. He didn't lift his head when we entered the kitchen. She touched his shoulder and spoke loudly. Behind him, outside the window, the Candler Park Golf Course stretched out. 'Fred, these people are from the police department. They want to speak with us.' I saw the hearing aid in his ear when he raised his head.

'Well, pull up a chair,' he told us. 'Did my wife offer you something?'

'Yes sir, she did,' Rauser answered. Melinda Etheridge sat down with us.

'You here about Owen?' Fred Etheridge asked. 'Can't be good news or a phone call would have been sufficient.'

'He doesn't go by Jesse?' Rauser asked.

'His mother called him Jesse,' Mrs Etheridge told us. 'She was killed when Owen was seven and we were awarded custody. He wouldn't let anyone call him Jesse after that.'

'We'd like to speak with your grandson. Is he here now?' Rauser asked. I thought again about the stakeout on the street and the wide open green of the golf course. I imagined a door being flung open and Richards running. It didn't happen.

'Why, no.' Mrs Etheridge looked shocked.

'Where can we find him?'

Mr Etheridge frowned. 'I assumed you were here to tell us where he is.'

'No, sir. We're trying to locate your grandson. It's very important.'

'We're not even sure Owen is alive,' Mrs Etheridge said. 'He disappeared about three years ago. We filed a report.' Irritation crept into her voice.

'Yes, ma'am. I'm aware of the report,' Rauser said. 'We believe your grandson is very much alive and in the Atlanta area.'

Melinda Etheridge reached out, squeezed her husband's hand on the table. 'Before he disappeared, Owen had moved back in with us. He couldn't seem to hold a job,' she told us. 'And he could be very difficult to deal with. It started in high school. The moods and gloominess could turn violent when things didn't go his way. He'd break things, yell and scream. He gave up the things he loved, put on a lot of weight. He was so angry. It would break your heart to see how angry he was.'

'What did he love?' I asked.

'Baseball, for one,' Mr Etheridge answered. 'And he was good at it. He liked girls, though he wasn't good with them. Our daughter, Owen's mother, and his father were killed right in front of him. He never seemed to be able to get over it.'

'So you haven't seen him in three years? Not even a note or a phone call?' Rauser asked.

'No,' Mrs Etheridge answered.

'Did he have any friends?' I asked. 'Anyone he spent time with or trusted?'

'Owen had trouble keeping friends,' Fred Etheridge said. 'He was too unpredictable. He'd blow up at them. But there was the guy with the landscaping crew who picked him up for work. They went out a few times and seemed to stay friendly. You remember his name, honey?'

Mrs Etheridge shook her head.

'Please, anything you can think of, Mrs Etheridge,' Rauser pressed.

'I don't mean to appear rude, Lieutenant,' she replied, evenly, 'but you've asked a lot of questions. You've come into our home and told us our grandson is alive and that you're looking for him. But you haven't bothered to offer an explanation. And you seem completely oblivious as to how this might affect us.'

Rauser calmly removed his phone from his pocket. Too calmly. He wasn't in the mood to be polite. He touched the screen a couple of times, then slid it across the table. Mrs Etheridge's hands came up to her face. But her eyes stayed locked on the pictures on Rauser's phone. He'd framed them all on one screen – Fatu Doe brutalized in the gazebo, Troy Delgado face-down in the dirt, Donald Kelly hanging.

'God in heaven,' Mr Etheridge said.

Rauser pointed at the photo of Kelly. 'This man was abducted, shot, and then hung like this in the house of a woman your grandson spent time with at Peachtree-Ford Hospital. He was also an inpatient at a facility for mood disorders at the same time she was a patient. We believe he's been stalking her for at least two years. There was a piece of wrapping paper in this man's pocket.' He pointed to Fatu Doe's picture. 'She had a ribbon tied like a bow around her ankle.' He pointed at Troy Delgado's body. 'This little boy right here. He loved baseball too. Body fluid on this little boy and on the old man, it matches semen found inside this young woman. She was beaten and raped before he killed her. Now, I realize this may come as a shock, and I hope you'll forgive me if I don't have time to sugarcoat it, but we believe your grandson did these terrible things. And we think he wants to do the same thing to the woman he's been stalking. Dr Street here has profiled the killer and all roads led to your grandson. If you withhold information from us, it's blood on your hands. Do you understand?'

'Is the woman being stalked blonde, and is her name Miki?' Mr Etheridge asked.

I fought a shiver.

'I'd love to know how you know that,' Rauser said evenly.

'Last two times he was in the hospital we visited him. . . . They were long stays, weeks. He'd checked himself in both times. He talked about a young woman. He said they'd met and fallen in love. He talked about how pretty she was, how smart she was. He said she understood his darkness,' Mr Etheridge said. 'When he came out and moved back in with us, he wouldn't talk about her. Not in a way we approved anyway. He made disparaging remarks each time we raised the subject. He'd had these infatuations before. His response to rejection was always anger. He got that from his father. We didn't want our daughter to marry that man. When he was violent with her even when she was expecting, we begged her to leave him. She finally did when Owen was about five. But he wouldn't leave her alone. . . .'

Mr Etheridge was veering off track. His wife took over gently. 'After Owen disappeared, we went through his things. We'd hoped maybe he'd left a note. He'd hurt himself before. Cut himself. It was always our fear. That we'd get a call or we'd find him dead. So we went through everything. We found dolls. *Barbie*-type dolls. Male and female. They were hanging from clothes hangers in his closet. They all had strings tied around their necks. And they were all *naked,*' she added venomously.

'We found letters,' Mr Etheridge added. 'Letters about what he was going to do to someone. A woman. He didn't name her. Sexual things. Violent things. It was too horrible to read. We burned them in our fireplace.'

Rauser sat back in his chair and looked at them. 'Everything? You destroyed the dolls too?' The Etheridges nodded mutely. Outside, thin white clouds passed over a pale blue sky. Inside, Rauser's nostrils had flared and his jawbone was busy. 'Did it occur to you that you might be destroying evidence? You knew he was violent and dangerous, didn't you? You were afraid of him, weren't you? And you stayed silent?' Again, the elderly couple didn't answer. 'How about pictures of your grandson just before he disappeared?'

'He stopped letting us photograph him years ago. He could not bear seeing himself.'

'Do you remember how many dolls you found in the closet?' I asked.

'I'll never forget it,' Mrs Etheridge told me. 'Four male and four female.'

'Can you describe how they were positioned? Were they all hung alike?'

'Three male dolls and three female dolls were hanging by their necks. Each one of them on an individual hanger,' Mr Etheridge told us. 'The other two were attached to one another by the arms, facing one another on the same clothes hanger.'

I let that sink in. Rauser asked, 'Did Owen use a computer?'

'Oh yes,' Mrs Etheridge answered. 'He was very good with them.'

'I'd like to see it,' Rauser said.

'We never found it. It disappeared when Owen disappeared.'

'You mind if we have a look around his room?'

'It hasn't been his room for two years. We got rid of everything. There was too much darkness in this house for too long.' Melinda Etheridge sounded indignant.

'If Owen was close to this friend who picked him up for work, maybe he's been in touch,' I suggested to her. 'Can you try to remember his name?'

'I don't remember the man's name. He was about Owen's age. The work was good for Owen. He started losing a lot of weight. Owen didn't talk much about his day at work or what he did when he went out. And he didn't like to be questioned. We felt we'd walked a tightrope with him his whole life. His threats were always hanging over us. That's what he'd do the moment something went wrong. Threats. He would rage and scream, and then he would threaten to kill himself. It was manipulative. We knew that. He controlled us with those threats. But we were still terrified he'd follow through one day. And he knew we couldn't bear the thought of that.'

'You remember the name of the landscaping company?' Rauser asked.

She shook her head. 'It was an architectural landscape service. They designed and maintained golf courses and parks, places like that. It had "commercial" in the title. Maybe Commercial Landscape and Design?'

Rauser jotted the name down on a tablet he pulled from

his pocket, then put his card on the table. 'Thank you for your time.'

'What'll happen when you find him?' Mr Etheridge wanted to know.

'I can tell you this,' Rauser answered. 'The longer this goes on, the worse it's gonna be. He gets in touch, you tell him to turn himself in to me now. It's the only way I can guarantee his safety.'

'One last question,' I said. 'Did you ever celebrate his birthday after his mother died?'

'She was our daughter!' Mrs Etheridge exclaimed. 'How could we celebrate the day that monster took her from us?'

We walked together to the car, leaving the Etheridges silent and ashen-faced at their table. 'Fucking great,' Rauser grouched. 'Little strung-up dolls and destroyed manifestos and some friend with a landscape company nobody remembers the name of. You buy any of it?'

'Jury's still out,' I said, and opened the passenger's door, got in. 'They were weird about his room. Something felt off. But they looked genuinely shocked by the photos. Of course, that doesn't mean they don't know where he is. The description of his manipulations, the threats without regard to the effect on them, lack of empathy, violence, anger, rage, blowing up when he doesn't get what he wants or expects, his inability to connect – it's all part of a cluster of psychopathetic behaviors. I believe they were sincere in how helpless they felt. You were hard on them.'

Rauser threw his battered Crown Vic into gear. It lurched forward away from the Etheridge home, sputtered.

'They knew the sonofabitch was dangerous. He was under their roof with all these weird behaviors while he was playing Fatu Doe, saying he would get her an apartment or whatever and planning how he was gonna kill her. I mean, what the fuck? They're either hopelessly clueless, in deep denial, or they're liars. We'll see what they do now. I can show cause for a listen on their phones.'

'Three years and he hasn't been in the workforce,' I said. 'But he has to have food and shelter. He has a dog. He's not begging on the streets. He's working or he's getting support. Can you get their financials too?'

'Hell yeah we can. Statute in Georgia allows us access as long as it's a criminal investigation.'

Rauser stopped at the traffic signal at Ponce and Clifton. The afternoon rush was revving up. We were jammed in bumper to bumper.

'He could be living under an assumed name,' I said.

'Three, four years ago, it wasn't that hard to do. If you know the social's available, you're pretty much home free. Next stop, the DMV.'

'Especially if you *make sure* the social is available,' I said.

'So maybe he offs somebody,' Rauser said, and continued playing with that idea. 'The guy he worked with, you think? I mean, Richards is a real manipulative sonofabitch, right? So he buddies up with this guy, gets his sympathy or whatever. Let's say he's about the right size and type physically. Owen gets the right haircut, claims he lost his license, shows his social. Piece of cake. Old licenses don't have the thumbprint either. If he gets his print on that new driver's license, he's good to go. New life. I like it, Street.'

The car behind us laid on the horn. Rauser ignored it and got on his phone. 'Williams, we need the bank records for Melinda and Fred Etheridge. We're looking for regular payments going to an individual. And we need somebody going over all the missing-persons cases starting about the time Jesse Owen Richards dropped off the grid. Start with local cases and branch out. We wanna make sure Richards didn't swipe somebody's identity, okay? Narrow it to males at least six-two or -three. Hair and eye color can be changed, but let's start with brown. Also, he worked for a landscaping or landscape design company that didn't come up when we looked at him. Something like Atlanta Commercial Landscape. Let's see what they have to say.' Rauser finished catching Sergeant Williams up on the Etheridge visit and got the ball rolling on the warrant for the phone tap. He looked at me. 'That scenario fit the cluster-fuck of behaviors for psychopathy?'

I smiled. 'Your vocabulary has improved since you've been hanging out with me.'

'Uh-oh,' Rauser muttered. The engine had started to knock. Loudly. The car shimmed.

'You know these things use oil?' I asked, and got a sideways glare. 'Sounds like you're about to throw a rod.' Growing up with a fix-it guy like Howard Street, both Jimmy and I had learned how to keep a car running. Rauser knew how to start them, drive the hell out of them, and bang them into things. And he'd been incredibly stubborn about accepting what anyone else in the department would have appreciated – a new car. He'd chain-smoked in this one for six years before he gave up smoking last November, and it permanently smelled like cigarettes. He didn't even like the car. It was about resisting change, in my opinion. But Rauser wasn't particularly interested in my opinions regarding his motivations.

'Might as well hang on to it until it quits,' he said.

'That should be any minute now.'

'What do you have against my car?'

'Let's see. It stinks. Oh yeah, and it's ugly.' I saw the skin at the corner of his eyes crinkle. 'And it's unreliable. What if you need to catch a bad guy? You ever think about that?'

'You're pretty fast, Street. I'll just kick the door open and you can pursue on foot.'

'And I'm low-maintenance. I run on Krispy Kremes.'

'Yeah. Sure. Low-maintenance.' We drove for a minute. Rauser pulled into a gas station with a convenience store and went in for a couple of quarts of oil. He threw open the hood, took the cap off, and poured them in. Both of them. No checking the level with the dip-stick. I watched this with amusement. He got back in but didn't start the engine. 'So you're not talking about the dolls. That means you're deciding how to translate the psychobabble shit, right? You asked about the number of dolls they found in this freak's closet and the positioning. How come?'

'Eight of them,' I said. 'One for each year leading up to his eighth birthday, and that momentous day – the murder-suicide.' I thought about my grandparents, pushed the memory away. 'Not that the day itself shaped him. But it sparks and continues to fuel what was there already. I think the dolls represent victims. Or intended victims. The male and female doll tied together, it's hard to interpret without being inside his head. But the obvious conclusion is they represent a couple.'

'A double murder with that signature. No way it happened already. We'd have found it. We been running everything every which way.'

'I'd focus investigators on couples who are transitioning somehow, on the threshold of something, some new life. I realize that in practical terms that's difficult. But it's all we have. A big event. Marriage, a first home, a first child. I think his thing is all about people on the crest of something, moving forward. Our boy's stuck in his past.'

'We could look at marriage licenses, home sales, births,' Rauser mused. 'Narrow the search geographically, since Richards only hunts in a couple of areas.' He glanced at me. 'That's good work, Street.'

I felt his energy surging. For the first time since I'd learned of Jesse Owen Richards's obsession with my cousin, I had an opportunity to get a step ahead of him, to stop him before he pulled out his party favors.

34

I rummaged for Neil's keys at my office. Rauser insisted on waiting, even though he was managing seventeen investigators, all their open cases, one very dangerous repeat offender, and a new boss. He paced around my office with one hand jammed in his pocket and the other holding a phone to his ear while I printed out a long-overdue report on the crematory for Larry Quinn, called a courier for a pickup, and taped it to my door. I didn't want Rauser waiting. I'd tried to shoo him away. His restless energy in my office was not helpful. And I wanted to be able to be there. Alone. I wasn't being reckless. I simply didn't want to be spooked all the time. It's no way to live. But Rauser didn't want to hear it. He wasn't interested in my feelings at the moment. He was thinking about his. That I had my Glock snug against the small of my back in a duty holster or that I'd spent four years in the field at the Bureau before moving into the BAU made no difference to him.

We left the office together, and I snaked through downtown in Neil's Smart Car. Sunlight streaming between skyscrapers dappled the streets. It was almost five, and the traffic was getting worse. Neil's little blue bump was like melting in a butter dish at stoplights. I passed Underground Atlanta and saw Rauser peel off a few cars back, heading to City Hall East. He had stayed long enough to be sure I wasn't being tailed. We were both keenly aware that blocking his path to Miki, that my story, my life, had all the elements to trigger Richards's rage. My name was in the news again. This time in a favorable way because of the crematory scandal. And he had proved he was perfectly willing to train his sights on me if he couldn't get to my cousin.

I rang my parents and told them about Miki's broken leg and that Miki was going to stay at Rauser's. Mother immediately declared she would prepare meals for Rauser's refrigerator that we'd be able to heat for Miki. She surprised me by saying she'd actually enjoyed having cops hang around her house. She liked the company. My dad wasn't a big talker. And she was using the detail assigned to keep them safe as guinea pigs for new recipes.

I turned onto Mitchell Street a block from Tyrone's office. I had to take the time to make up with Tyrone. I didn't want the gap to widen. His business was an important part of my monthly income. And I liked the guy. That wasn't true for a few others I'd met in his line of work. I'd regretted the tone of our last conversation. I wanted to set it straight. It was one stressor I did not need tugging at me. And one I could actually make go away.

No thugs were waiting for me this time. They had taken Tyrone's warning seriously and cleared out. I smiled. A big Glock didn't hurt either. I finally found an empty meter and walked half a block to Tyrone's dingy yellow stucco building. Color was chipping off the building so the tips of the stucco peaks were white. The glass doors looked too new for the rest of the place. A hallway with closed doors and dirty carpet went off to the right, a staircase to the left, elevator dead center. I don't use the elevator in this building. It shudders and bumps, and I don't like touching the filthy buttons. But the staircase reeks. By level three I'd actually adjusted to the smell of urine. My thighs had started to burn, though, another reminder to get back to running. And to pick up those free weights collecting dust on my living-room floor. I'm told it makes an amazing difference in your level of fitness if you actually lift them off the ground and move them up and down a few times a week. Go figure. I stopped at the top landing and caught my breath. I couldn't walk into Tyrone's office red-faced and panting.

'May I help you?' The reception desk actually had a receptionist today. She was young. Very. And pretty. Very. The faces changed frequently at Tyrone's office. A buddy of his operated a temp agency, and since Tyrone had only enough clerical work to keep someone busy for a couple of days a week, this worked out well for them both. Plus, Tyrone could be a little bit of a rascal. I didn't think he'd learned the lesson yet about office romances. Twice last year I'd walked in and found someone crying at the desk.

I could see Tyrone in his office with his feet propped up, ankles crossed, leaning back, the phone to his ear. He hadn't seen me yet.

'I was hoping to pop in on Tyrone for a couple of minutes,' I told the receptionist. 'I'm Keye Street. I'm—'

'I know you,' she interrupted, and stabbed a long

turquoise nail at me. 'You're that Booger Bandit lady! We've watched that about a hundred times. The part where his finger goes in his nose, that's some classic shit right there.'

'Yeah. Classic. You mind letting Tyrone know I'm here?' He had spun around in his desk chair, still on the phone, gazing out over his Mitchell Street kingdom.

'Personally, I think you should have capped his nasty ass.' She reached over to shake my hand, carefully, like her nails were wet. They were weirdly long, kind of curvy on the ends. 'I'm Latisha.'

'Nice to meet you, Latisha. Is Tyrone being a good boy?'

'He's being as good as he is capable of being.'

'You're here all week?'

'Oh, I'm not one of those temp hos. I'm permanent.'

Oh boy.

She got up and went to Tyrone's office. Her skirt was turquoise to match her nails and barely covered a high JLo butt and muscular thighs. Total brick-house body. She had on white sneakers and short, fuzzy girl-jock socks that matched her skirt and her nails. Tyrone waved from his office and held up a finger, the one that meant give me a minute.

Latisha came back to her desk. 'Would you like to sit down? You look flushed. How about some water?'

'No thanks.'

'Did you come up the stairs? That's what I do. You won't see me stepping in that nasty-ass elevator.'

'No kidding,' I agreed. 'Wonder why he stays in this building. It's disgusting.'

''Cause he cheap,' Latisha said.

'Maybe he likes the pee smell,' I whispered, and we shared a giggle.

Tyrone emerged from his office in white linen, immaculate. Chocolate shirt, open collar, no tie. I was betting he'd had his nails done this week too. He smiled, and LL Cool J-style dimples cut craters in his perfectly smooth brown cheeks. *Slurp*. My knees always get a little wobbly around Tyrone. I forgot why I'd been mad at him.

'You meet my girl, Keye?' He came up behind Latisha's chair and massaged her shoulders, then bent and kissed her cheek. Latisha could not have been more than eighteen, if that, too young to handle the power imbalance that comes with a boss hitting on you. I folded my arms over my chest and gave Tyrone all the silent disapproval I could convey. 'Come on now, Keye!' Tyrone laughed. 'Don't do me like that. This here is my oldest daughter.'

Latisha smiled up at him. Dimples broke out everywhere. Yup, she was definitely Tyrone's kid. 'There's three of us, in case he forgot to mention his children. And three baby mamas. Our daddy is a man ho.'

'Don't feel bad,' I told her. 'My biological father was a drug addict.'

'Your mama too?' Latisha wanted to know.

'Stripper,' I said. 'Then some white people adopted me.'

'Oh, now see, I'd rather have to drive all over town to see my brothers and sisters than live with that. White people do not know how to have fun.'

'Yeah. We played a lot of Monopoly,' I said.

'See what I mean?' Latisha asked.

'Tyrone, I owe you an apology. I was hard on you on the phone. I'm sorry. I know you acted out of concern when you spoke to Rauser.'

'No problem, Keye. We're friends, right? I wasn't worried about it.' Tyrone smiled.

'Okay, good. Well, I need to run. Latisha, it was nice to meet you.'

'Hey, wait,' Tyrone said, as I reached the door. 'How 'bout some work? I got an absconder who needs some encouragement. Little nerdy guy. Fast.'

'What do you mean by *fast?*' I asked.

'He's a runner. Takes off.'

'I'm snowed under,' I said.

'I need him checked in by close of business Friday after next. So you got over a week. Latisha, get the Banerjee file and assign it to Keye.'

Latisha pushed away from her desk and shot her dad a look. 'A please and thank-you might be nice.' We watched her go to the file cabinet.

'Lord help me,' Tyrone whispered. 'I thought giving that girl a summer job would calm her down a little. Her mother has just let her run wild.'

'Growing up too fast, huh?' I said, as if I had a clue. I knew nothing about children. Especially teenagers. I thought about Jimmy and Paul, starting a family. I had a feeling we were all going to get a crash course in children.

Tyrone sighed. 'It's my fault. I was only eighteen when she was born, and no kinda father. She needs a role model, Keye. A woman, I mean.'

'So maybe you should settle down.'

'I was talking about you.'

'Oh no. I'm not the maternal type. And I'm not exactly a role model.'

'Neil said you were going to hire somebody for your

office. Latisha's real smart. But she's driving me crazy.'

'I can hear y'all,' Latisha called. 'This ain't no movie where you can't hear somebody in the same room.' She pushed the top drawer of a black metal file cabinet closed with her palms, careful of her painted nails. 'My daddy want me out because he can't be a man ho with his children in the office.'

'I just thought you'd like a little freedom too,' Tyrone told her. 'Be good experience for your résumé.'

'Some people should not be stuck in an office together all day,' Latisha said, and handed me the Banerjee file.

I glanced at it. The man had been charged with identity theft. His bail bond had been posted at fifteen thousand dollars. I don't do a lot of quibbling when I'm offered work. I'm mortgaged up to my eyeballs. Generally I take what I can get. If I've learned anything these last four years trying to build a new business, it's that work leads to more work. Word of mouth is huge.

'I could report for duty on Monday morning,' Latisha told me. 'Would we be going out on jobs together? Do I get a big-ass gun too?'

'No,' I said. 'I need clerical help. And someone to take messages. No gun.'

'So I got the job?'

'Let me think about it, okay?'

'You're blowing me off,' Latisha said. 'I know when somebody blowing me off. I'm a high school graduate.'

'Congratulations,' I said.

'I'd rather you just say no than try to blow me off.'

'Okay. No.'

Tyrone went into his office and came out with a Taser gun. He handed it to me. 'Fifty thousand volts and it shoots fifteen feet.' It looked a lot like my Glock, except that it had bright yellow detailing and half the weight. 'Nerdy guy takes off, let him have it right between the shoulder blades. Look, it came with a service holster.' He held out a cheap piece of imitation leather.

Leaving Tyrone's with a job I didn't have time for, a job applicant I was nervous about, and a Taser gun wasn't exactly how I'd planned it. But almost nothing was lately.

I parked in the attended lot across the street from the hospital and headed up to Neil's room. I had an hour before I needed to leave for the airport to pick up Miki. I thought about that and sighed. I was dreading it.

'Well, look at you,' I said when I walked into Neil's room and found him sitting up with his computer on his lap. 'You're so alert. How's the leg feeling?'

'Way better. They release me tomorrow. They've already slacked off on the rocking pain medication.'

'I'm sorry,' I said, and smiled. 'I know how you hate being present.'

'I know, right? Hey, thanks for bringing my stuff over this morning. I barely remember you being here.'

'I'm driving your car. Is that okay?'

'Sure. But you get it shot up, you're paying for it.'

'Ah, now, that's the generous spirit I know and love. You need me to pick you up tomorrow? Or are Cindy and Peggy competing for the honor?'

'Cathy and Tammy.'

'Whatever,' I said. 'The blondes.'

'They're making me nuts, Keye. I had a shrimp alfredo

for lunch. And look at that.' He pointed to the windowsill, which was stacked up with cookies and brownies. 'A person can only eat so many damn cookies. I have to make a decision. I can't handle both of them anymore.'

'Poor baby.' I walked over and picked up a brownie, sniffed it. 'There's nothing in these, right?'

Neil waved a hand. 'They're clean.'

I took a bite of brownie. 'Whoever's doing the baking, my vote's on her.' I pressed some brownie into my front teeth and smiled at Neil. This always guaranteed me a laugh. I handed him a brownie, and he blacked out his front teeth too. We'd had whole conversations like this at the office when we should have been working. I swallowed the brownie and swished some water from a paper cup. 'Hey, I just picked up a job from Tyrone. It's not a big rush, but if you're bored, you can do the trace for me.'

'Heck yeah.'

I handed him the file, which now had a chocolate smudge on the folder. 'By the way, Tyrone has a daughter who needs a job. She's working at his office right now, but they're driving one another a little crazy.'

'Have you met her? You like her?'

'Well, she's outspoken, I'll give her that. I'd want you to talk to her too. How do you feel about coming back to the office?'

'Great. As soon as this weirdo Miki stalker is off the streets.'

'Hey, at least he's a crappy shot,' I pointed out, and Neil chuckled. 'I'll check in on you later.'

A female voice called my name when I walked past the nurses' station. 'You're Keye Street, aren't you?'

'Yes.'

'I saw you yesterday in Mr Donovan's room. He told me you were business partners.' I waited to see where this was going. 'Someone dropped this off for you during the first shift.' She handed me a card addressed *Keye Street – visitor to Neil Donovan, Room 3301* in small, tight cursive. It was a slightly oversized white envelope of the greeting-card variety. No weight. And oddly flimsy, like there was no card inside.

I tore the envelope down the side, careful not to disturb the glue strip – old training kicking in. I tapped it. A handwritten note tumbled out onto the tiled floor. I borrowed a piece of tape from the nurse and touched the corner to pick it up.

See what you did to your friend? See the pain you caused? That bullet was meant for you. I will find her. I always find her. And then I will come for you.

I looked left, then right down the corridor. A nurse in quiet shoes turned into a patient room. The elevator doors opened and a volunteer in pink scrubs and a hairnet pushed a dinner cart stacked with meals under thick plastic domes.

'Is everything okay?' the nurse called.

My heart was hammering. I glanced at her name tag. 'Mary, you have a plastic bag back there I could borrow?'

She handed me a bag about half the size of a newspaper sleeve. I slipped the note back into the envelope and dropped it inside, twisted a knot in the end. I looked up for security cameras and found them. One pointed at the nurses' station. Another was positioned in the corner near the elevators to take in the long passageway lined with patient rooms. Those tapes might tell us what Jesse Owen Richards looked like.

'Mary, do you know who took this note?' I asked the nurse.

'It was left here, I was told,' she answered. My tone made her frown, puzzled, no doubt, by the urgency in it.

I started down the corridor, glancing at each door as I passed, seeing only vague shadows through small glass windows. A few doors were open – patients in their beds, visiting relatives or friends, flickering televisions. A gurney with a wheel that thumped on each rotation caused me to spin around. An attendant in blue scrubs gave me a nod, then pushed through a set of swinging double-doors marked *For Hospital Staff Only*. My fingers brushed the Glock that was concealed under my jacket. Security. For what it was worth.

I walked quickly back up the hall toward the nurses' station, checked the waiting area, glancing at faces, at shoes. I went to the windows and looked out onto the parking lot, a pedestrian bridge over the street. I pressed in Tyrone's number.

'I'll make a deal with you,' I told him when he answered. 'I'll consider Latisha helping out at the office, but I need a favor. And I need it right away.'

Then I called Rauser. I told him I was staying at the hospital with Neil and that I'd arranged for Tyrone to pick Miki up at the airport. I asked him to get ahold of the surveillance tapes.

I pushed open Neil's door and found him snoozing with his computer open on his lap and the file I'd given him scattered on the floor beside his bed. I picked it up, found a folded blanket in the tiny closet, sat down in the chair with my Glock, covered myself up, and clicked on the television. I didn't want to leave him alone. And it sure wasn't the first night I'd spent in a hospital with my gun in my lap.

35

When the door opened and light from the hallway streamed into the room, my hand tightened instantly around the Glock. Neil didn't budge. Rauser stepped into the room. He had two coffee cups and a folded newspaper. 'Fivebucks coffee,' he whispered, and grinned. Rauser was always snarky about Starbucks, but he always bought it anyway. Just like he made fun of Whole Foods, called it Whole Paycheck, and shopped there all the time.

It was four in the morning and pitch black outside. I could hear Neil breathing smoothly. Rauser and I walked out into the corridor, then sat down in an empty waiting area.

'Got the surveillance video. Several shots of him coming in the main entrance, walking through the lobby, and several angles on this floor,' Rauser told me. 'He wore a hoodie and kept his head down. He knew where the cameras were. So we don't have anything with a clear shot of his face. But we know one thing for sure. He's not a fat boy anymore. We're going to release the video to the news channels this morning at seven.'

I took a sip of coffee and rolled my neck. I felt like I'd slept in a chair. 'How about Miki?'

'Sleeping by the time I came in. I woke her up and showed her a picture of Richards. She remembered him as Owen, which is why she didn't recognize the name Jesse Richards when you asked her. She was completely floored. She thought he was a nice guy.'

'Something happened,' I said. 'He took offense at something. Something triggered his rage. That's how it goes with borderline personalities. He might have been completely in love until she said or did something he perceived as demeaning or dismissive. Then, all that emotion turns to fury. It can turn on a dime.'

'I've got a uniform with Miki. Cruiser parked on the street. Even if whacko Owen figures out where she is, there's a lot to discourage him,' Rauser said, flatly. 'APD officers don't play.' He opened the morning paper to the local gossip section called Peach Buzz. He pointed to a picture halfway down the page of the two of us standing in front of his Crown Vic. I remembered the setting well, a crime scene at rush hour, the murder of a former colleague last year. The caption read: *Atlanta's hottest crime-fighting duo, Lieutenant Aaron Rauser of APD Homicide and former FBI profiler Keye Street together again on another string of murders in The Atl.*

'Shit.' I looked away.

'I know,' Rauser agreed. 'It's a terrible picture. Of you.'

I laughed and slugged his arm. 'At least my eyes are all the way open. You look like a person with mental problems.'

'Yeah, but at least my mouth is closed,' Rauser said.

I looked back at the photograph. We'd been having a hell of an argument that day. I finished my coffee, stood up, stretched. 'I need to shower and change and take care of my cat and my cousin. And my business. Jesus. I'm going to see if Tyrone will babysit Neil until he's released. Then I'll head to the station.'

Rauser grabbed my hand. 'Hey, first of all, this creep Richards, he's not after Neil. Even Forensics agrees shooting him was an accident.'

'I know,' I said. 'But Richards was so close to him when he dropped off the envelope. Just right outside his room. I don't want to take anything for granted.'

'I've already got an officer on the way here. Just to make sure everything goes like it's supposed to when he checks out and goes home. If this whacko's objective is to stretch our resources, he's sure doing that. Major Hicks is starting to talk about the cost of all the extra details. I gotta make an arrest.'

'Did you guys run marriage licenses and real estate records yet?'

'We did. Big list. Over four hundred couples applied for marriage licenses just last month in the city limits. About a hundred this month and it's only the seventh. Real estate deeds, new sales, births. We're looking at all of them, looking for commonality to Richards and Richards's parents, names, addresses, comparing date of filings to his DOB, to the date of the killings. Anything we can think of.'

The elevator opened and a uniformed cop stepped out, polished shoes, hardware gleaming. No squeaks in the heavy duty-belt. We went to meet him. Rauser briefed him, introduced him to me, then took him to the nurses' station, showed ID, and introduced him again. He handed the officer his card with his cell phone number and pointed him to Neil's room.

'I'll walk out with you,' Rauser told me. 'Maybe we can make out in the elevator.'

Making out right now sounded like about as much fun as sandpapering my eyeballs. I hadn't brushed my hair. Or my teeth. I hadn't even looked in the mirror. I hoped my mascara wasn't somewhere around my ears. I marveled at Rauser's ability to think like a fourteen-year-old boy even under the very worst circumstances. Men really never grow up, which is one of the wonderful things about them, of course.

His phone jangled as we stepped on the elevator. 'Rauser,' he answered, and checked his watch. Not quite four-thirty a.m. The dark shadows under his eyes told me he hadn't been to bed that night. He listened for a few seconds. 'Okay. You call CSU and spatter already?' He waited. 'Give me the address on Pine.' He disconnected and looked at me. 'Balaki and Williams are at an address on Pine near Felton. They were just gonna do a drive-by until the sun comes up, but the dog was sitting in the front yard, and when they got closer, they saw the front door was cracked. Young couple. Both murdered. They applied for a marriage license last week. Cross-checking names raised a flag on the bride-to-be. Name's Emma Jackson.'

'Emma. Jackson. Richards's parents,' I said, as we stepped off the elevator. We crossed the lobby toward the hospital exit. Our pace had picked up. 'Emma and Jackson Richards. He targeted their names.'

'Exactly. Richards must have been looking for the right couple. Hell, you can do it online. Pretty sure it's our guy. Besides the connection to the victims' names. There's a dog there that was taken outside. Most perps don't bother.'

'If we could have just gotten to the grandparents a day earlier and known about those fucking dolls, I'd have known where to look. God.' I felt sick.

'You're not a goddamn psychic, Keye. Once we had evidence to analyze, you interpreted it correctly. That's all you can do. No one expects anything else. Come with me to the scene,' he said, and clicked a key fob as we crossed the street to the parking lot. The lights on a new Crown Victoria blinked. 'The old clunker bit the dust last night. This baby flies too. And it's midnight blue. Sexy, huh?'

I didn't answer. My thoughts were full of the two people who had died because their names were too close to the parents a damaged mind believed had betrayed him.

We turned on Peachtree Street, then hung a left onto Pine. Atlanta in early morning was lit up and still a little sleepy. The sky was as dark as Rauser's new Crown Vic. And cloudy. I thought again about the crime scene we were walking into and those old rival emotions tapped on my shoulder – excitement and sorrow – and a healthy shot of guilt at feeling either of them.

We pulled up as Ken Lang slid open the side door on the Crime Scene Unit van parked at the curb outside a squat brick home. He and another scene tech pulled covers over shoes and snapped on gloves and coats meant to minimize trace transfer. Williams and Balaki approached as Rauser and I suited up. Balaki peeled off and went to his car. I saw a cocker spaniel, its nose sticking through the cracked window. Balaki was an animal lover. He had several cats and a couple of dogs, and once stopped to pick up a dog and drive it by a vet's office to check for a microchip while a murder suspect waited in cuffs. He baby-talked the spaniel through the window, then joined us.

'What are you gonna do with the dog, Balaki?' Rauser asked.

'I'll figure it out later, Lieu. Poor girl. Something like this is tough enough for a dog without having to take a trip to Animal Control.'

Bloodstain analyst Jo Phillips, all five-foot-ten inches of swimmer body and no-need-for-makeup skin, strode toward us with an aluminum case in her hand. Rauser had had an on-and-off affair with Phillips before our friendship turned steamy. They had remained friends.

Phillips stopped at the van, where we suited up to enter the scene. 'Well, if it isn't Atlanta's hottest crime-fighting duo.' She flashed a brilliant smile at me that makes even straight girls get crushes, and bent to stretch booties over shoes. Size-tens, I thought, with no small amount of pleasure. Don't get me wrong. Big feet are fine. She's really tall. She'd tip over without them.

'That mean we can all go home and get some sleep, since Batman and Robin are here?' Lang asked. The scene tech tried unsuccessfully to stifle a snicker. Williams and Balaki found something fascinating on the ground.

'Okay, so everybody knows about the Peach Buzz piece,' Rauser said. 'Anybody else need to get anything off their chest?' He looked at his investigators. No one said anything. 'I didn't think so. Let's go to work. Williams, fill us in.'

We walked down a curved river-pebble sidewalk. 'Male

victim Jorge Wagner, twenty-six. Female victim Emma Jackson, twenty-four. ID in the house, valuables apparently intact. Female vic has a nasty knife wound. Wagner was shot in the neck at close range.'

The pebbled sidewalk had hidden how much blood had been tracked in and out of the house. But we saw it at the bottom step leading to a small porch and front door. Shoe prints, big ones, with a distinctive tread, some kind of athletic shoe. And dog prints that came from the front door, crossed the porch and went down the stairs.

'We found Pepper with her leash tied to the porch railing.'

'Pepper?' Rauser asked.

'The dog, Lieutenant,' Balaki answered, seriously. 'That bowl of water was there when we got here.'

'Careful going in,' Williams warned, and pushed open the door, then stepped aside for the spatter analyst. 'Looks like it started when the first victim opened the door.'

There was a pool of blood just inside the door, more shoe prints and dog tracks. Bloody drag marks led to the bodies. They were positioned on their backs, side by side, the male victim in boxers and a T-shirt. The dead woman wore a green bathrobe tied at the waist and open enough to expose the knife wound that had probably killed her.

'I opened the robe to check her,' Balaki said, before we could ask. 'It was closed all the way to her neck.'

Williams squatted over them and lifted their arms so we could see their wrists tied together with the same gauge twine that had held up Donald Kelly's head so he was staring at Miki's front door, the twine that had also been used as a garrote to strangle Troy Delgado. A candy '8,' like the ones you put on cakes, dangled from their tied wrists on a piece of blue ribbon.

Lang was examining the shoe prints. 'Best impressions yet. Good detail here. Should be able to identify the shoe with this. Looks like about the right size, Lieutenant.'

'So she opened the door,' Jo Phillips told us. 'And he stabs her, slices upward. She falls here.' She pointed at the blood at the door. 'Then he walks over here and gets the dog, takes it outside.' She was following shoe and paw prints as she spoke. 'He comes back in and walks straight back this way. Male victim was shot here, dragged. Then he goes and gets the woman, drags her, positions her next to the male victim. He tracked into the kitchen too.'

'No vics in the kitchen,' Williams said. 'But there's blood on the sink and counter.'

Lang's scene tech took body temps. Lang studied them for a minute. 'Time of death between eleven and midnight.'

'Male vic was in bed,' I said. 'He heard something. He gets up and comes in here with his glasses in his hand. Gunman fires. Wagner drops his glasses.' I pointed to a pair of thick-rimmed glasses on the floor where Jorge Wagner was killed, according to the spatter analyst. Spray and spatter dotted beige walls, drops on the floor, then drag marks. 'Killer positions them, binds their wrists together. Lot of symbolism there. Then he closes up her robe, goes into the kitchen, washes his hands, and fills a water bowl for the dog. And leaves it on his way out. He knew exactly what he was going to do and how he wanted to leave the scene.'

'He finds them on the list of licenses. He likes her name. And he starts watching them. Let's get some people out here to interview the neighbors,' Rauser ordered. 'Anyone on the street when you got here?'

'No sir,' Balaki answered. 'Real quiet.'

'Check this out,' Williams said, holding up a framed photograph of the male victim in a baseball cap posing with a group of young boys in uniforms.

'All roads lead back to the ballpark, huh? Maybe he didn't find them through city hall,' Rauser said. 'Balaki, follow that trail. See if Jorge Wagner's name came up anywhere on the list of coaches at the park where the Delgado kid played. And get me the names of closest living relatives for these two.' He looked down at the slain couple on the floor, fished a pack of nicotine gum out of his pocket, and pushed a piece through the foil. He'd go himself to notify the family. He almost always did. 'Williams, why aren't the cruisers here? We need this street blocked off before the news trucks do it for us.'

'Any second now, Lieutenant,' Williams answered.

The scene tech had the video going. The auto-winder on Jo Phillips's digital camera was singing. She let it hang around her neck while she swabbed pooled blood, dropped samples into vials, then sealed each with a rubber tip.

Rauser scowled at me. 'So he closes up her robe.'

I nodded. 'So different than Fatu Doe. He pulled her dress up. But this was an attempt to protect her dignity. She had his mother and father's names. He didn't want her found exposed.'

'Yeah, he paid her so much respect at the front door,' Rauser said.

'It wouldn't have crossed his mind then,' I said. 'He blitzed her at the door because it was quiet. He knew it would buy him time to get in. He'd probably watched them for some time. He waited for them to go to bed. When the dog barked, she got up. It wouldn't have mattered which one of them opened the door. He didn't see them as anything but objects to complete the fantasy. But once he had control, when he owned them, after he cried and masturbated, he felt protective, affectionate.'

'You wanna test that?' Rauser asked me. 'Hey, guys, can we get a forensic light source on the bodies for a second?'

'Jo, you mind if we cut the lights for a minute?' I asked.

'No problem,' Phillips answered, and backed away from the bodies.

Outside, sirens screamed and blue lights came whirling down the street. Balaki sidestepped past blood at the entrance and went out to meet the officers. Lang hung a box in a leather case about half the size of a car battery off his shoulder. He plugged a cord with a light on the end into the front of the metal box. I reached for the light switch.

A blue spotlight traveled over the darkened floor, showed us the blood we'd already seen, then over the victims. Blueish-white drops and smudges spattered their faces and clothes.

'He cries a lot of tears while he's jerking off,' Rauser said. 'The sick fuck.'

36

CSU put down heavy brown paper over plastic sheeting once the blood samples had been taken at the front door and Jo Phillips had made her measurements. The blood, the way it fell or dripped or sprayed, the way it flew off a weapon, would tell Phillips a terrifying story of those deadly seconds when a killer overtakes a victim. In combination with the wound pattern analysis and the physical evidence, every movement the killer had made and how each of these victims had responded would be horrifyingly clear. It would take hours to process the scene. Rauser and I could both be put to better use elsewhere. Too many chefs. The CSU team needed time to do what they do best – amass the evidence that seals the fate in court of cold-blooded murderers like Jesse Owen Richards.

I heard an unfamiliar click as I stepped out on the front porch, then light hit my face. Freestanding spotlights blazed. Voices behind them shouted my name. *'Keye Street.'* *'Hey, Dr Street!'*

Rauser stepped out behind me. 'You up for this? Richards

sees you on TV, he's gonna go off again.'

We stepped off the porch and stripped off scene clothes. 'Let him try,' I answered. Microphones came at us as soon as we ducked under the scene tape.

'Lieutenant Rauser, can you describe the scene inside?'

'Two victims,' Rauser told them. 'Male and female. Mid-twenties. Names will be released once the victims' families are notified.'

'Dr Street, is the Birthday Killer responsible for these murders?'

I was careful not to look at Rauser, but we both knew what that question meant. There was a leak in his unit. 'The crime scene is still being processed,' I replied. 'As you can see.'

'Obviously something about these murders had character-istics that raised flags or you wouldn't be here. So—'

'It's always a good idea to wait for the department in charge of an investigation to release the details when and how they choose and in a manner that won't harm an investigation,' I interrupted. 'In other words, I'm not going there.'

A ripple of strained laughter, then a voice rose above the others. *'Are you sober? What's your recovery status?'*

Microphones crowded nearer.

'The friends and families of the eighteen million other recovering alcoholics in this country would probably tell you that recovery is a process. You take it a day at a time. I've been sober for over four years now.'

'There will be a press conference at seven in the briefing room at City Hall East.' Rauser glanced at his watch. 'Less than an hour.'

'Do you have a suspect in the birthday killings?'

'We have identified the suspect in the murder of the Clarkston woman and two male victims in Atlanta. Until this scene is fully processed we can't confirm a connection.' I noticed he refused to use the name the press had given Jesse Owen Richards – the Birthday Killer. 'We'll release the suspect's identity at the briefing, along with a driver's license photo and surveillance video recorded just yesterday. We need your help in getting those pictures out. Thank you.'

We headed for Rauser's new car, got in, sat there for a minute, staring through a perfectly clean windshield. I felt a little shell-shocked. The sun was coming up, revealing a smudged sky streaked with dusty yellow. Storms were moving in today, I remembered. *Oh joy.*

'Hey, you were great back there with the reporters. Did you see how still they got? You had their attention. They like straight shooters.'

I didn't answer. I didn't like thinking about standing outside that bloody crime scene, making the story all about me. I kept thinking about those two young people, murdered and bound together in death, about their families and friends planning a wedding that would never happen. How quickly the focus had moved away from all that with one question. *'Dr Street, are you sober?'*

Rauser called the officer on duty at his house to let him know I was coming, then dropped me off in the hospital parking lot. I climbed into the blue bump, flew by The Georgian, showered, changed, tossed some food at White Trash, apologized for the neglect and promised her better days ahead. Wonder when that would happen. I'd constructed all this, after all. I'd lost control of my life, then my job. I'd decided to dig for money as a small-time PI and pimp my FBI experience as a consultant. Right now, overtired and underfed, I wasn't feeling particularly happy about my choices. It was six-thirty in the morning and I was already thinking about what a shot of Jameson would taste like in my coffee, how it would feel when it hit my throat and started to work on those muscles in my neck, the ones that slept with a gun. What I needed was salt air and a big bath towel on the beach. And sex – long, slow, middle-of-the-day sex – movies, dinners out, baseball games, a friggin' break. What I had was a cousin with a badly broken leg who would need meals and attention and twenty-four-hour protection, a killer who wanted us both, a neglected business, a hospitalized partner, piled-up paperwork, unanswered messages, and a resentful feline. And all of it by my own design – which was the real head-scratcher. Dr Shetty had some opinions about why I stack my life up this way, about why I say I want downtime and then can't handle the quiet.

Dr Shetty. It was Thursday. *Rats.* My regularly scheduled appointment was at two, right in the middle of the day, another example of really poor planning. I thought about the next few hours. I needed time to be sure Miki was okay, to deal with some paperwork and return calls at the office, phone time with Mom and Dad, check in on Neil, and an afternoon at APD to look over new reports. Once Rauser released the photos and surveillance video of Jesse Owen Richards, information would flood in.

Okay, so there was no way I was going to make my shrink appointment. That meant I'd have to deal with

Mariza, Dr Shetty's office manager, a Brazilian who pretended her English was bad so she didn't have to talk to patients. Mariza enforced a strict twenty-four-hour cancellation policy. We'd been down this road before. I imagined Dr Shetty having another hour-long lunch on my dime.

I picked up breakfast and raced to Rauser's. I didn't want Miki waking up without family. I could only imagine how vulnerable she'd be feeling, hunted, in an unfamiliar bed with a broken leg and a uniformed stranger guarding her.

A police cruiser was parked in Rauser's driveway. An officer named Jacobs opened the door, hand on gun, and asked for identification. I came in with a bag from Radial Café, the first completely green restaurant in Atlanta and *the* place for cinnamon rolls – big fat ones made from scratch and smothered in cream-cheese icing. The aroma hangs over Dekalb Avenue when they're baking. It's nearly impossible to drive by without hitting the brakes.

The television was on with the volume low. I saw the officer's smart phone on the coffee table next to his cap. 'Has she been up?' I asked.

'Haven't heard a peep,' Jacobs answered.

I shook the bag. 'Radial rolls. Want some coffee too?'

'You bet,' he said. I saw him sit down and pick up his phone. I wondered vaguely what a beat cop Tweets when he's on a protective detail. Must be boring. Maybe he was updating his Facebook status. Or texting his lover, playing Angry Birds.

The press conference had begun. On the screen, I watched the surveillance video of the suspect we now knew was Jesse Owen Richards, head down, wearing a dark green hoodie and keeping his face away from the cameras. I watched as Rauser spoke to television cameras and enlisted the community in the search. He again described the personality characteristics outlined in my profile. The hospital video looped to show Richards's physical posture, the way he moved and walked. Rauser had the six-year-old driver's license picture on a screen and reminded everyone that Richards's face would be thinner now. APD were estimating that he'd dropped eighty to a hundred pounds since the round-faced photograph had been taken.

It was only a matter of time now. Richards's face and the video would be all over the media.

I went down the hall to the guest room, which doubled as Rauser's office, and pushed the door open.

Miki's broken leg was sticking out from under the covers. The cast was knee-high. It had a few signatures on it already. I smiled at that, put the coffee and the cinnamon rolls on the bed table, sat down on the bed.

I was well aware that Miki was waking to no small amount of emotional and physical distress. What kind of mood she'd be in was anybody's guess. I wished I could take it all away, all the pain and fear. Getting Richards off the streets and out of her life was a good start. I touched her hand. 'Good morning.'

She stirred, blinked up at me, started to sit up, and then remembered there was plaster on her leg. She pushed herself up with wiry, muscled arms. I helped pile pillows behind her.

'I have coffee and some food if you want it.' She wanted the coffee. I handed it to her. 'There's a great-looking uniform in the living room. I guess that's the silver lining.'

'I only have eyes for Tyrone now,' Miki said. 'He actually carried me inside.'

There were crutches leaning against the wall. Miki was thin, but she was strong and was fit. I knew full well she didn't need to be carried. 'What a guy.'

'He's coming over later, I think. With lunch or dinner or something.'

'Really? Wow.' I didn't like the sound of that. The last thing I wanted was for Miki to get involved with Tyrone, though he might have been enough of a player to handle her.

She sipped her coffee and studied me. 'I remembered something about Owen. I had a birthday while I was an inpatient at Peachtree-Ford. I don't know how he knew, but he knew. I was so depressed. We were in this common area with a TV. They let you do that after you've been there a few days. He handed me this little tablet of paper. He'd made a cover for it. I think there was some artwork on it. I don't really remember. They take everything, you know? So you can't hurt yourself – belts, shoestrings, whatever. But somehow he'd gotten hold of some ribbon and used it to bind this paper. He made a big loopy bow for the top. He was so nice to me. I remember thinking how sweet he was. I don't get it. I don't get why he wants to hurt me . . .'

She broke off, shook her head. I was silent.

'You know, Keye, I don't even remember what I did with that gift. Or what I said to him. You saw me in that place. I could barely remember my own name.'

I imagined her casually pushing his gift aside, the one he'd worked on and decorated with something meaningful to him, something that had taken no small amount of effort to obtain. He would have fantasized about how she'd react when she received it, how grateful and smitten she would be, her affection for him amplified in his mind about a million times. But Miki hadn't followed the script. Miki rarely does. The gift meant nothing to her. Had that been the trigger that turned his infatuation to rage?

Miki was watching me. 'You think I did something to cause all this, don't you?' she asked.

'He's an egocentric sonofabitch, Miki. You didn't cause that.'

Her blue eyes smiled a second before she did. 'That your official diagnosis?'

'And just one more reason I never went into private practice.'

I helped her up and handed her the crutches. She was hurting, I could see, as she navigated the hallway in panties and an undershirt. While she brushed her teeth, I found the mega-dose ibuprofen she'd been prescribed. 'You have to eat before you take these, okay?'

'You're leaving? What am I supposed to do?'

'Read. The bookshelves are full. You have a Kindle.' I needed to find a way out of mobile home health care. I wasn't really cut out for it. Back in the guest room, I handed her the remote control. 'Rauser has every channel known to man. Have you noticed the size of the dish out back? Seriously. You can see Russia from his house.'

'Fucking great.' Miki's mood turned sour instantly at the prospect of being left alone.

'I'm sorry. I know it sucks.' I opened the blinds. Thunder-clouds were gathering. I remembered Rauser saying emergency services were on alert. 'Can you call your insurance company and see about getting some home care? I'll be back early this afternoon to check on you. The landline is on Rauser's desk right there, okay? Call if you need anything.'

'I want to go home.'

I felt that tic at the corner of my eye. 'Not yet. It's not safe.'

'It's a free country, Keye. I'm an adult. Besides, isn't Mr Uniform out there supposed to protect me? Make him take me home.'

Pain makes people nuts. So does fear. *Cut her some slack,* I told myself. 'Why put yourself and the officer in more danger?' I didn't say that she'd already put my parents at risk or that because of her Richards had added me to his creepy list. 'Give Rauser's team twenty-four hours. They're closing in. Now, eat something and take the ibuprofen. You'll feel better.'

'I'm going to call some friends to keep me company,' Miki said.

I pressed my finger against the corner of my eye. 'Miki, every time that door opens, every time someone else is introduced, you're adding risk. No one should know where you are, okay? It's not safe. Not yet.'

I poured a glass of water from a filtered pitcher in Rauser's nearly empty refrigerator and set it on the bed table. My phone jangled. My mother is the only one who calls me at seven-thirty in the morning. I looked at caller ID. It was my alarm company.

'This is Peachtree Security. Is this Keye Street?'

'Yes.'

'We have an alarm at your place of business. We've notified law enforcement.'

Now what? *Crap.* 'Miki, I have to go.' I kissed her cheek.
She refused to look at me. 'Tell the cop Tyrone's coming
over later, okay? And tell him not to bother me.'

I turned and left before the scene ended with my hands
around her neck. The diva act was wearing on me. I let the
officer know about Tyrone's visit. He'd have to call Rauser
to authorize the visit. I didn't like the idea of anyone coming
in and out. It made the officer's job too difficult, and I
believed it would have a psychological effect on his level of
vigilance. He would be at his best when he wasn't expecting
anyone, when everyone who stepped on that porch was
suspect.

37

Two police cruisers were parked at my office when I came down the hill in the blue bump. The lot was empty. The surrounding businesses didn't open until nine or ten. The metal door to my office was wide open. I could see the dents as soon as I stepped out of the car. An officer was sitting in his vehicle with the engine running, writing on a clipboard. The windshield wipers made an occasional sweep. The windows were foggy. The rain we'd been promised had turned from a fine mist to a trickle. Another officer stepped out of my office onto the landing where the bullet that hit my partner had ricocheted.

'You Ms Street?' she asked when I ran up the steps. She was standing under the tin overhang out of the rain. I glanced behind her into my work space.

'What happened?'

'Looks like vandals,' she said. 'We responded within seven minutes, but there's a lot of damage. Door was open when we arrived. No one on the premises.'

I stood there in my doorway, trying to take it in. She was

right: The damage was extensive. It looked like someone had run through our office with a huge hook and just swept everything off the surfaces and onto the floor. Our desktops, monitors, our printer and fax machine were smashed, broken, kicked. Neil's expensive chair was on its side. Glass and bits of plastic and paper littered the floor. The smart panel was shattered. There had to be thousands of dollars in damage. Hours of work and love and effort down the tubes.

'Looks like they used crowbars on the door,' the officer commented. 'Probably what they used in here too. Hope you're insured.'

Every drawer in my office had been wrenched out, dumped. My desk chair had been ripped up, vicious slits across the back and seat. The glass top that protects my desk had cracks webbed out across the length of it. He'd used a black Sharpie to write cunt on the glass. There was no question that Richards had done this. His vile energy had coated everything in our offices.

'We checked the whole strip. No other break-ins,' the officer told me. 'Looks like somebody has it in for you, Ms Street.'

I left my office and went to Neil's desk chair, stood it upright, dusted it off – a tiny island of order in the ugly chaos.

Rauser was in Williams's cube in the Homicide room. Detectives Bevins, Angotti, and Thomas were at their desks. The other cubes were empty. That meant fourteen homicide investigators were out on the streets today. I didn't have to guess their focus. Rauser waved me in. I heard Andy Balaki's South Georgia drawl on the speakerphone. 'We're heading to the job site to see if we can find him.'

Rauser pressed the end call button and looked at me. 'Monica Roberts called me awhile ago. Said you'd agreed to an interview with the two of us?'

I glanced at Bevins. She tried to hide the smile playing on her lips, looked down at her keyboard. I figured Rauser had let off some steam after the reporter called.

'Does that sound like something I'd agree to?' I retorted. I didn't even try to disguise my shitty mood.

'Well. No. Actually,' Rauser said.

'She asked. I was vague. But I did not agree.'

'You catch any news today?'

'I've been a little busy.' I didn't mention watching the press conference.

'The Fox Five morning show had a big discussion about you,' Bevins said.

'Great,' I muttered. Dread hit me like an eighteen-wheeler. Why wouldn't it? So far the day had been about as much fun as finding a hairball in my shoe. I assumed the worst, of course. On the right day with the right degree of stress and exhaustion, it didn't take a lot to shake my self-esteem.

Rauser was looking at something on the computer, typing with two knotty fingers, something I usually found cute. It annoyed me today. 'Relax, Street,' he said without looking up. 'It's like I said, they like straight shooters.'

'Looks like you have single-handedly broken the stigma of addiction by talking about recovery,' Bevins said. She didn't try to hide the sarcastic tone. Bevins had her own personal challenges with booze. I knew this from Rauser. It was private. She'd never talked to me about it.

'A few months ago they were going to string me up,' I said, gloomily.

'As long as you know how it works,' Rauser said. 'Where you been all morning?' He looked up at me. 'You okay?'

'My office was trashed this morning. Richards. He left a note on my desk using one of his favorite words. Everything was smashed to pieces. I had to deal with police reports. Insurance companies, locksmiths, landlords. I had to wait for the door to be repaired before I left.'

'Why didn't you call?'

'The damage was done, Rauser. The police were there. There was nothing you could do.'

'Seeing you talk to the press outside his crime scene and then a follow-up on the morning show probably really got his bells ringing.' Bevins was frowning.

'No doubt,' I agreed. 'So where are we? Anything from the tip lines?'

'Half my unit is out on follow-ups,' Rauser said. 'And we located the landscaping company the grandparents told us about. Big turnover in the ranks. The front office doesn't really mingle with the workers. Nobody remembers our guy. But they have him on record. They have a supervisor who's been there a few years. Balaki and Williams are trying to locate him. See what he remembers.'

Lightning flashed so bright we all looked at the windows. I did what I've done in storms all my life. I counted in my head, waiting for the thunder. It was a tactic my mother had used to distract me from the storms that had always frightened me. *One, two, three. Boom.* There it was. The lights blinked out in the old building. Computer screens went dark. Bevins cursed softly. There were twelve seconds before the lights and fans and computers came back to life. In the silence, all we could hear was the rain spraying the windows along North Avenue like buckshot.

'Christ,' Rauser said. 'Somebody find out if this shit is gonna get worse. Why haven't we heard back from Balaki and Williams? Bevins, find out where they are with that landscape guy.'

'Landscapers can't work in this stuff, Lieutenant,' Bevins answered evenly. 'They're probably still trying to locate him.'

'Find out,' Rauser snapped.

'Lieutenant,' Detective Angotti said. 'Those storms have crossed the state line. Watches are out for the city and warnings for the south metro counties.'

Ken Lang came around the corner. He dropped a photo of the bloody shoe prints we'd all seen on the floor where Jorge Wagner and Emma Jackson had been shot and stabbed. 'They're plate shoes,' he said. 'Size thirteen.'

'As in baseball?' Rauser asked.

'As in umpire.' Lang dropped another photo down on the table. 'This particular style just looks like an orthopedic. Super comfortable. But look at this angle. High-traction rubber outsole. It matches our prints.'

Bevins cupped her hand over the phone. 'Lieutenant, Balaki and Williams are talking to the landscaper now,' she reported.

'Good. Okay, everybody, go back over that list of officials in the local leagues. Find out if they have photo IDs. Look for anything that stands out. We think he's still using an R name. So start there. These people are like freelancers. They work different leagues all over the state. Bastard could be anywhere right now.'

The phone rang. Rauser hit speaker. 'Found him, Lieutenant.' Balaki sounded excited. 'At the Zesto's on Moreland. He remembers Jesse Richards real well. Said the guy was pretty strange. Pissed off a lot. Fat and real touchy about it. Only other guy that would put up with him was some guy named Rabelo who got him started jogging.'

'What happened to Rabelo?' I asked.

'Julian Rabelo quit his job here in a letter and never came back,' Balaki answered. 'Asked to have his last paycheck snail mailed. Crew chief thinks it was pretty close to the time Richards left.'

'I bet it was,' I said. Rabelo's decomposed body was probably in some stretch of forest or picked clean on the banks of the Chattahoochee so that Mister R, as Fatu Doe had called him, could steal his identity. We'd found our man.

'Crew chief is calling the front office to see where they sent his final check,' Balaki told us. 'We got Rabelo's DMV records pulled up.'

'Crew chief recognize the photo?'

'No sir. He swears it's not the guy he knew as Rabelo. So we asked if it looked like Richards and he says maybe, if he lost a hundred pounds.'

'Here we go, Lieutenant,' Bevins said. 'We have a Julian Rabelo on the list of league umpires. We took his statement in our first sweep. No red flags.'

'Run Rabelo's DMV records through face recognition

with Richards's. We get any certainty, we can go in without asking,' Rauser said. 'Who interviewed Rabelo?'

'I took his statement,' Angotti said. 'I remember him. We only talked to two umps that day. Nothing suspicious about either one of their statements.'

We heard Balaki's muffled voice talking to the landscaper on Rauser's speaker. 'We have the address,' Balaki reported. 'They sent the check to the address on the license. We're on our way.'

'Stake it out. Wait for backup,' Rauser ordered. 'Thomas, get a BOLO going on Rabelo. Now, let's get some background on this address. And let me see satellite imagery of the neighborhood. Everybody have a look. We want to do this right. That means knowing where we are and what corners the rats run to hide.'

'Face rec gives us a ninety-five percent likelihood Rabelo and Richards are one and the same,' Bevins reported.

Rauser went down the hall to brief Major Hicks. Hicks would release Julian Rabelo's photograph to the media immediately, he told us when we returned.

'Angotti and Thomas, take a car. Bevins, you ride with me,' Rauser told them.

'I want to go,' I said.

'You can follow us,' Rauser said. 'But you gotta stay off the property until it's secure.' I nodded my agreement. My heart was doing about a hundred and fifty. I could not wait to see the prick that had torn up my office this morning taken down. I hoped they made sure he accidentally walked into a few doors on the way to the station.

The lights blinked off again. The elevators were down. We used flashlights to navigate the pitch-black concrete stairs at City Hall East. Vehicle trunks were popped open in the garage, and we pulled on overt body armor – vests with Kevlar panels that would protect us from a body shot. Even with the protective plates, the vests were surprisingly light. But they were hot. Rauser tossed me an APD rain slicker and got in his car with Bevins. I jumped into Neil's blue bump. Thomas and Angotti pulled out behind me.

We curled through the Old Fourth Ward toward I-20 and Boulevard. The house was on a month-to-month lease that had been renewed many times in Julian Rabelo's name. A known slumlord owned the house. Bevins had told us APD had dealt with the guy many times. He'd never cooperated when they'd needed permission to go inside. They stopped asking. Most cops would testify they'd heard something inside that suggested a life was in danger, always weighing one oath against another.

We pulled onto McDonald Street SE and headed toward the block between Berean Avenue and Boulevard. The rain was coming in sideways sheets now. The street started out with freshly painted one-story frame houses and mowed yards and window boxes. But it quickly degenerated into sagging porches and broken fences, chipping paint, graffiti-covered walls, and overgrown lots with tires and junk cars piled up. We parked behind Williams and Balaki, in front of a house with a fallen porch overhang. A cableless trailer from a big truck had been dumped on the corner. It was covered with elaborate artwork, gang symbols, and graffiti that was both beautiful and alarming. Weeds had grown up around it. The back was open, and a group of kids were standing around inside out of the weather, smoking, laughing. The street was lined with cars. Either the residents were working night jobs or they weren't working at all. The poor had only gotten poorer in Atlanta for a while now. It was a perfect neighborhood in which to hide.

The checks on Rabelo before we'd left the station told us he'd gotten his citizenship just before 9/11 and he'd worked in either food service or landscaping. He appeared to have no family in this country. He wasn't married. He had no children. He was light-skinned and lived in a dilapidated neighborhood of transients. His neighbors probably did not even know his name. In a neighborhood of month-to-month leases, who would have noticed if he was replaced by someone else?

We all stepped out into the rain. Rauser glared at me. 'I'll stay off the property until it's secure,' I told him. But that didn't mean I wasn't going to get as close as possible. I was a big girl, and they knew it. I'd worked closely on surveillance ops last year with Rauser's investigators on a subject I'd been profiling for APD while Rauser was in the hospital.

They checked hardware and vests, turned their attention to a house three doors down, a single-level frame partially obscured by wisteria vines and clumps of privet that must have been eight feet tall. The house had once been painted a light blue, but had been weather-stripped down to raw, bowing board and sagging gutters.

Rauser's nod was all it took. Angotti and Thomas went over a bent chain-link fence to the back. Balaki, Williams, Bevins, and Rauser went in the front. I pulled up the hood on the rain jacket and positioned myself on the sidewalk in front, made sure vines and shrubs blocked me from the windows. My vest wouldn't do anything to protect the rest of me. I wanted to be close, but I didn't want to be a sniper's target.

A dog started to bark as soon as Rauser and his investigators hit the front porch, a small dog. Poodle, I thought. No dander. No shedding. No dog hair at crime scenes.

I saw Angotti and Thomas creeping around the back of the house. One week since Troy Delgado's body had been found. One week and here we were. The investigation had roared full force. Unfortunately, I hadn't understood until Richards's grandparents talked about the dolls in his closet what his next move would be, and because of that, a young couple had been murdered just before their wedding. That responsibility felt like a ton of bricks on me right now.

I drew my weapon and positioned myself with my back to a kudzu-covered tree. I could see both ends of the sidewalk this way. I wasn't going to take any chances on getting clobbered from behind.

Through the slashing raindrops, I watched Williams slam his foot into the door just above the knob. I heard shouting, the investigators clearing rooms, checking in with one another. My pulse was in high gear. I felt something at my feet and looked down. A white miniature poodle was looking up at me, wagging his tail, squinting against the rain. He was wearing a baby-blue bandanna. I bent down and scooped him up, tried to hold him still. He was soaked. His tag said *Hank*.

'Good boy, Hank,' I told him. 'Be still, buddy. You're okay.'

I heard Rauser's voice. 'All secure, Street. Nobody home.' Disappointment washed over me. I had longed to see

Jesse Owen Richards marched out in handcuffs.

I carried Hank inside and set him down, closed the front door so he wouldn't take off again. 'Hey Keye, you gotta see this,' Balaki called.

I walked through a living room with a rattling air-conditioning window unit and shabby furniture. I noticed Hank's food and water bowls were filled in a stand as I passed a small galley kitchen piled high with pots and pans and dirty dishes. The place smelled awful. On my left, a bedroom with an unmade mattress lay on the floor, sheet rumpled and stained. No blankets. I turned the corner at the second bedroom and saw Miki's blue eyes. Rauser and his detectives were all looking at the collage of photographs – Miki, seemingly unaware of being photographed, in grainy cell phone pictures, some clearer than others. Tacked and taped to the walls were hundreds of Miki's photographs from magazines. Sticky notes were attached that said *Afghanistan, New York, Texas, California, Alaska, Iraq.* The dates were written under each location. There was a single chair in the room and a lot of porn, magazines with girls too young to show their breasts showing their breasts anyway. Hand towels were all over the floor. Rauser handed me a pair of gloves.

'You're going to need those,' Bevins said. 'Cum towels everywhere. This shithole's DNA is all over the place.'

Rauser opened the closet, and we saw a single Barbie doll hanging by its neck. He looked at me. 'Miki,' I said.

'He left the dog,' Rauser said. 'So he's coming back. Looks like it's the only thing in this dump he cares about. If the BOLO doesn't get him first, we got him as soon as he gets back in the hood. Williams and Angotti, you stake out the street. Thomas, take that intersection up there. What kind of car is he driving?'

'Ninety-eight silver Honda Accord owned by Julian Rabelo with a current registration.' Balaki recited the tag number that had gone out with the Be-On-The-Lookout Bulletin to APD officers and other law enforcement agencies around the state.

'Balaki, dig through this shit and see if you can find something useful. Bevins, maybe that computer has some clues about where he hangs out early in the middle of the day.'

'What about the dog?' Balaki asked.

'Put him in my car. I'll bring him to the station,' Rauser said. We all looked at him. 'What? You want this little guy here if the shit goes down?' Rauser picked Hank up and got his face licked. 'I'll take him myself. Balaki, grab his food for me.'

I stood in the center of the room. Everwhere my eyes looked there were hundreds of photographs of my cousin, indications of a million ways this man had violated her privacy and terrorized her. There were pictures of her house and car, of Miki in workout clothes on a treadmill. I remembered her shivering, saying she felt like she was being watched at the gym. I'd had some flip answer to her concerns at the time. Guilt squeezed the air out of my lungs. 'I'm going back to check on Miki,' I told Rauser.

'She's fine, Street. Officer on duty checked in on time.'

I was silent, scanning the room once more. It made me sick. 'I want to be with her when you call to say you've got Richards locked up.'

38

Thunder shook so hard I felt it in the blue bump when I parked on Rauser's tree-lined street. Huge branches on old water oaks bounced in the wind like a rowboat at sea. The sky was blue-black – a perfect day to see Jesse Owen Richards put away where he belonged. I imagined the surprise party waiting for him courtesy of the Atlanta Police Department. I wanted my life back. I wanted my cousin safe. I hoped he dropped the soap in prison every goddamn day. I had no sympathy for him. I'd stood in the room he'd lined with pictures of my cousin, the room where he'd touched himself and planned the terrible things he wanted to do to her, to me, to others. A lot of us had seen some bad shit as kids. Most of us hadn't turned into monsters because of it.

A line of young maples bowed in the gusts, leaves blowing straight out like flags. I lifted the hood on the APD rain jacket I was still wearing and felt resistance from the wind when I pushed open the car door and stepped out into the rain. A gust nearly knocked me off my feet. The jacket flapped up behind me before I could get it zipped up. I thought about White Trash at home alone. She hated storms as much as I did. Her history as an alley cat had made her good at reading the atmosphere and seeking out a warm cubbyhole. Nothing is as miserable as a wet cat. That she now lives in dry cushy comfort apparently hasn't sunk in. She still heads under the bed at the first clap of thunder – learned behaviors, avoidance skills. I knew them well.

Lightning sliced across a dirty black sky. The air was full of juice. I felt the energy on my neck and arms. I didn't like it. This kind of storm always undoes me a little. Lightning has odd taste. It doesn't always take the path of least resistance and go for the tallest object. Nope. It indiscriminately knocks the shit out of several hundred people a year. I didn't want to be one of them.

I rushed up the sidewalk toward Rauser's house. I hoped Officer Jacobs wasn't going to shoot me when I banged on Rauser's front door like a crazy person, but I wasn't staying out here.

Something hit my foot when I opened the storm door. A cell phone had tumbled out. It must have been wedged between the two doors. It looked like the one I'd seen in Officer Jacobs's hands earlier – small, white, an iPhone. Why would his phone be out here? Had he gone in and out and accidentally dropped it? Why would he do that hours before his shift ended? He seemed too attached to his phone this morning not to miss it. Had something – someone – drawn him to the door?

The hazard lights started to flash in my brain. I pressed my ear to the wood door. Silence. I stood there for a moment, wet, listening, deciding, and forgetting about the howling wind whipping hair in my face or the strobed, lightning-filled sky.

I found Rauser's key and pushed it into the deadbolt carefully, turned it quietly. I eased the door open an inch . . . *two, three.* The chain caught. Through the opening, I saw a slice of the couch where the officer had set up camp this morning. No one there. No movement. Epinephrine lit up my bloodstream. Every cell knew something was off. My heart started to jackhammer.

I leapt off the porch, ducked under the front windows, moved fast toward Rauser's office, the guest room, Miki. The room was in the elevated rear corner of the house. I hoisted myself up on the top of the chain-link fence. Rain and wind stung my face. My foot slipped on the wet fence, and sharp metal points ripped the skin down my calf. Opiate receptors shot off their fireworks, but it still felt like someone was holding a torch to my leg. I lost my balance, fell, hit the ground on my back. Muddy red-clay rivers of rain had jumped the curb, sluicing down the yard. I was soaked to the skin. I pushed myself up, climbed back on the fence, got hold of the windowsill, raised up and looked inside. I was peering through glass and screen into an unlit room. It took a few seconds for my eyes to adjust. But then I saw the empty bed.

Where was Miki?

Where was Officer Jacobs?

I dropped down, ran under the deck behind the house, and curved up around the side where the dining-room windows were low enough to see inside. Rauser had knocked out some walls. I'd have a view. I'd be able to determine where they were in the house, and, I hoped, what was happening. A million scenarios ran through my head. None of them had happy endings.

I turned the corner and got smacked by tropical storm–force winds and debris. Anything loose – branches, leaves, blossoms, birds' nests – was being stripped off and sent flying. BB-size hail started to ping off everything. I pressed into the house, back rubbing against brick, leaned forward and tried to get a look inside.

My cousin was at the dining-room table. So was Officer Jacobs. Strips of duct tape covered their mouths. I could tell by the way their shoulders were hunched that their hands were tied behind them, anchoring them to the chairs. Both wore children's cone-shaped party hats. Candles flickered on a square white cake with blue icing.

I sucked in air, pressed against the brick, feeling sick. *The birthday party – the murder-suicide.* Jesse Owen Richards was desperately trying to relive the scene that had scarred his childhood. And I had a seat at the table. That day when he raged at me on the voice disguiser, he'd meant it literally.

Where was he?

I fumbled for my phone, trying to shield it from the weather, but it was coming down too hard. Rauser answered on the first ring. The wind was so loud I barely heard him. Tornado sirens had started to wail in the distance; recorded emergency messages were blasting out over the city. Atlanta was bracing for a helluva storm. 'Richards has Miki and your officer. He's inside. Rauser's staging the birthday party.'

Then . . . *Bang.* Lightning lit up a transformer on a telephone pole at the curb in an explosion of sparks. I felt the electricity sizzle through my phone. I dropped it. The house went dark. I fell to my knees under the window, got as close to the house as I could. Richards would come to the window to find out what had happened, wouldn't he? Hail was piling up, looking like tiny golf balls. The most dangerous part of a storm, I'd always heard.

I waited, my pulse hammering, then rose and peered inside. And nearly fell back.

There he was. *Mr R.* His face was lit up in the dancing glow of birthday candles. He wore a bright gold foil hat with pink and blue balloons, the elastic strap under his chin. Beneath the cap, his head was shaved. The child's hat seemed especially small and strange sitting on his big head. The elastic strap cut into his chin. He was sitting between Miki and Officer Jacobs. His mouth was moving. His expression was agitated, his hands flailed like he was arguing.

The umpire, I realized. The umpire on the ball field who'd yelled at the coach, the man who'd dusted his cap and stalked off angrily.

A balled-up fist slammed the table. I saw Miki's body jerk. He leaned over into her face and yelled something I couldn't make out. Her eyes were blank with terror.

I looked over at the table, saw the 9mm next to gaily-colored paper plates and napkins that matched the party hats with little balloons in pink and blue, almost exactly like the ones in the crime scene photos from his eighth-birthday party.

He picked up a knife and I froze. He cut a slab of cake, started to eat it with his hands, devour it grotesquely as if he were starving, his wide face twisted into a mask of grief. Tears ran down his cheeks as he leaned forward to blow out candles. Icing and cake were smeared on his cheeks and lips and shirt. Blue food coloring had stained his teeth. He grabbed the back of Miki's hair and jerked her head back. I saw dried blood on her face for the first time and a bruise covering her cheekbone and right eye. How long had he been here tormenting her? I looked at Officer Jacobs. He was looking back at me, but his skin was very pale and his eyes seemed unfocused. He'd been hurt, I realized. It was the only way Richards could have gotten past him.

Richards started to yell again, something I couldn't hear over the storm through the glass. He reached for the gun. I had to get inside.

I raced back under the deck off the master bedroom and yanked a wheelbarrow from the crawl space. Alarms in every octave wailed across the city – ambulances and cop cars, tornado warnings. The thunderstorm must have spawned a touchdown somewhere in the city. I hoped Rauser had heard me. I hoped some of those cops were on their way here. But I couldn't wait. Richards had started to cry – his ritual, his letting go. He was going to kill them.

I scrambled up on the wheelbarrow and saw the blood that had seeped into my pant leg, but I wasn't feeling any pain now. Stress hormones, training, instinct; they were all doing their job.

I grabbed onto the deck railing, closing my eyes against pelting rain, pulled myself up. The screen door was latched. I punched out the mesh and reached in, lifted the hook from the eye, then pushed open the wooden door. The wind roared. And I knew the pressure had shifted too. He'd know a door had opened somewhere in the house. I left it open, hoping he'd blame the storm. Maybe he'd come to check it out.

I stopped, listened. No crying. No raging. No sounds to support the sickening scene I'd witnessed through the window. Richards's fucked-up birthday party, with its little plates and napkins and cone-shaped caps with elastic bands and cake, was silent now.

I kicked off wet shoes and pushed them under the bed, waited, shivering, behind the bedroom door. I'd started to consider the odds. Richards was a big guy. I couldn't handle him physically. He'd have his 9mm and Officer Jacobs's service weapon too. I closed my eyes, breathed out some tension, waited.

Five seconds, ten, fifteen. Not a sound.

I came around the door and started down the hallway, sidestepping an old floor register on creaking 1950s hardwood floors. My clothes were heavy and dripping wet. I looked into the guest room where Miki had been propped up in bed. The covers were half off the bed. She'd been dragged out. I peeled off the soaking APD windbreaker and kept moving, Glock steadied.

I leaned around the doorway to the living room and took a quick look. Jacobs's handheld scanner was on the floor, smashed into pieces near the front door. The scanner had squawked and annoyed Richards. Or frightened him. Police dispatch would have tried to contact Jacobs as soon as Rauser received my call. Richards had probably run into the living room on hearing it. I imagined him crushing it under the heel of his big shoes, raging around Rauser's house. Miki must have been frightened to her core.

I turned the corner into the living room, first right, then left. Nothing.

I moved down a long wall toward a wide archway, part of

the house Rauser had renovated, the dining room with an open kitchen behind it. My body let me know I'd reached that leaping-off point. No turning back. That's when the rest of the world retracts. I heard my own breathing and the *pat-pat, pat-pat* of my pulse. Everything else shrank away. That's what pure, blind fear does. It pulls you through the keyhole.

I swung into the dining room, saw Miki and Jacobs. Something struck a window, was whirled away by the wind. There was blood spatter under the officer's chair. He was struggling against his restraints. The birthday candles on the cake flickered. The gun was gone. My eyes swept the kitchen. The light changed. I'd been in Rauser's house enough to know something had just moved in front of the living-room windows. I hit the floor and heard the quick pops of the 9mm. I scrambled on my elbows to get out of the way.

'We've been waiting for you, Keye. You're the missing party guest.' It was the first time I'd heard his voice undisguised. It was weirdly high pitched and deeply southern. I was at the far end of the table, pressed against the floor. I needed to get into the kitchen and away from Miki and Jacobs before they got in the way of a bullet. I heard footsteps approaching and Richards called my name again, tauntingly. 'Keye . . .'

That's when I felt it – pressure, like coming up from the ocean floor too fast. I felt it in my head and in my ears a split second before it sounded like we were on a tarmac. The air smelled like sulfur and natural gas. The entire house trembled. The windows shattered, popped out. A filthy, black cloud slammed into the front of the house like a transfer truck. Richards was thrown forward. His gun went off again. I saw him hit the floor on his stomach. I aimed. He raised his head, looked at me through the table legs.

'Jesse, freeze. *Now.*'

And then a bomb went off. The ceiling split. Drywall and insulation and everything stored in the unfinished attic rained down. Tree limbs punched through the roof, punctured windows, whipped out across the house like they'd been rubber-banded, sweeping away anything loose, scraping against my body like huge wire brushes. Dirt and water poured into the house. I looked up and saw the swirling sky and the wide trunk of a pine tree, thousands of pounds balanced on brick and wood.

Richards had disappeared. Miki and Jacobs had both been knocked over in their chairs. The table had tipped. Cake splattered on the floor.

I climbed over a tangle of broken branches to get to them. The house shuddered, the pine tree broke through. It seemed to split the place in two. The noise was unearthly. The roof groaned, then began to cave. Long branches that had punctured the house shifted, whipped up, lashed out. I lost my balance, fell on my stomach. My Glock spun out of my hand. Something hit my back, hard. A hand grabbed my ankle, jerked me backward. He was dragging me. He wrenched me up and over the big limbs that had stabbed through drywall and stone and brick. I fought to yank myself free, flailing and kicking at him. He grabbed the front of my shirt and jerked me up. A closed fist slammed into my face. The world turned a gold-speckled navy blue. It registered somewhere in my brain that water was splashing my face. Gasping, I felt his knee on my chest, hands squeezing my nose shut, the bottle shoved between my lips, the searing pain in my eyes. My throat was on fire. I was choking on it, trying not to swallow, strangling on the bottle of bourbon that always sits on Rauser's counter. He was pouring it down me as I choked, as I fought to keep from drowning on the thing that had almost killed me already. I tried to open my stinging eyes. His gun. Where was his gun? I saw him leaning over me wearing the cone-shaped party hat, now soaked and drooping crazily. Blood ran down his face and neck. His temple and cheek had been sliced by glass or brick. His dark eyes were fixed on me. He took the bottle away. I saw movement in the background. Miki was on her side, still bound to the chair, pushing herself toward us.

Richards followed my eyes, turned for just a second. I didn't wait. I jerked the 9mm out of his waistband and shot the sonofabitch. Right through the forehead as soon as he turned his bloody, frosting-splattered face back to me.

A symphony of sirens played in the background – car alarms, security systems, ambulances, cop cars. No rain or wind. Just an eerie stillness. I pushed his body off me, flopped over on my side, retching. I heard Rauser's voice.

39

Enormous trees had been yanked up by the roots out of the soaked red-clay ground and toppled over on houses, blocked streets. Parts of the city were still without power. Cops at intersections tried to control traffic under blacked-out traffic lights. It was my first chance to see in daylight what the super-cell had unleashed on us yesterday when a tornado twisted out of it and roared down Atlanta's streets. I saw a telephone pole with the top half sheared off. A section of Dekalb Avenue had been closed because of the tangle of cables and wires in the street. You really don't get a sense of how huge a telephone pole is until you see one lying across the road. Some businesses had boarded-up windows. Others were dotted with black punctures where windows had been.

Atlanta was shaken, but it had survived another storm. And so had I. Still, my dreams and sleep had been tainted by the alcohol Jesse Owen Richards had poured down my throat. I had my first hangover in years. I had stood in the shower last night feeling the water stinging the cuts on my body, letting myself cry, too softly, I hoped, for Rauser to hear. Later, he had propped up behind me in my bed with his arms tight around me and a towel-wrapped ice pack pressed against my face as I drifted off.

I pulled up to Miki's old Victorian and saw a Mercedes in the driveway. My mother and father had driven her home, then gone to the pharmacy and gotten the sedatives she'd been prescribed. She was sobbing as they walked her out of Rauser's torn-up house. Officer Jacobs had been rushed to the hospital. Richards had shot him in the stomach when he'd opened the door.

I tapped on Miki's door. No answer. I tried the knob. Locked. I sent a text message to tell her I was here. The door opened a minute later and I looked up at Cash Tilison.

'That's quite a shiner you got there, Keye. I hoped we'd meet again under better circumstances.' He stepped aside for me. 'Miki's in the sunroom.'

I found my cousin on her love seat, leg propped up. 'It's my hero,' she said. 'Hey, we match.' She pointed at the bruise on her face. There was a vodka bottle on the table, a bottle of pills, a hand mirror, a razor blade, lines divided out on the mirror. Cocaine, I assumed. She smiled at me. 'Help yourself.'

'Miki, what are you doing?'

Tilison came in and relaxed in one of the chairs. I ignored him. 'Are you okay?' I asked my cousin.

'She's wondering if you're safe here with me,' Tilison told Miki. 'She really thought I was your stalker, can you believe that?'

I kept my eyes on Miki. 'Do you seriously want to go back to that place with him? With drugs and alcohol, with him calling you names, following you? Haven't you had enough?'

'I want him here,' Miki told me.

'Because he brings you that shit?' I pointed at the mirror. 'Is that the hold he has over you?'

Miki unrolled a *Time* magazine, tossed it at me. I looked down at it – acres of green land with a swirling black tornado bearing down on a farmhouse. It was a stunning photograph. 'You should see the spread inside. I'm not just going to be a finalist this time. I'll get that award and more awards. You're always on your high horse, Keye. I'm going to be a star. How's *your* career going?'

'You're drunk,' I said.

'Oh Christ, relax. Pour yourself a drink. What does it matter anyway, after yesterday?' She laughed. Cash laughed with her.

I had wanted to protect her so badly, but I couldn't save her. Not from herself. I wanted to cry again. I didn't. I turned and walked out.

Epilogue

auser and I were sitting at Southern Sweets. He always knew how to cheer me up. We each had an enormous wedge of old-fashioned chocolate cake on our plates, the best cake in the city, in my opinion. The café had that old-time ice-cream-parlor feel, with heart-shaped wrought-iron chairs and little round tables and a black-and-white tiled floor. Rauser always looks funny to me sitting in a small chair. He was turned sideways because his legs wouldn't fit under the table. An overdeveloped sweet tooth was just one thing we had in common, and another reason I loved this man.

'Man, this is good. I didn't think I'd ever eat cake again after seeing the remnants of the creepy birthday party,' he said.

'Tell me about it.'

He checked his watch. 'We have to be there in an hour. Then I'm taking the rest of the day off. How about we order in tonight, find some chick flick, and process our feelings?'

'Sweet talker.' I smiled and glanced at Hank the poodle.

Just outside the glass doors, he was licking a cup of doggie ice cream. His new leash was wrapped around a bicycle rack. Rauser had thrown away his old leash and collar and bandanna and hit the pet store for a new look for Hank. 'I really can't believe you adopted a serial killer's dog,' I mumbled, my mouth full of cake.

'Oh come on, Street. Poor dog didn't know the guy was a freak.'

'You held him up like a toddler this morning and baby-talked him, Rauser. I don't know if it was endearing or just . . . alarming.' I took another bite of cake so moist and dark it was almost black. 'Also, White Trash is *not* happy.'

'It's gonna take three months to rebuild my house. They'll get used to one another.'

'He was dry humping my foot in bed last night.'

Rauser took a greedy bite of chocolate cake. 'That was me,' he admitted. We both laughed. Life was back to normal. Our normal, anyway. 'Listen, Keye, I been thinking. You and me, we get along pretty good. And I love you and all. Why don't you marry me and make it official. I promise to love you and make sure you get to shoot somebody now and then. We could get old in rocking chairs.'

I set my fork down. 'We could talk about all our aches and pains.'

Rauser nodded. 'And how all our friends have died off.'

'I could help you to the bathroom, 'cause you know you're a *lot* older than I am.'

Rauser smiled. We were quiet for a minute.

'That sound like fun to you?' I asked.

Rauser frowned. 'Not so much. Forget I asked.'

I leaned over and kissed him. 'I love you, Aaron Rauser.'

We left Avondale Estates and drove through Decatur toward Midtown. We were quiet. Hank was lying across Rauser's lap. Rauser parked in front of a little redbrick building near the power station off Monroe Drive.

'We'll be waiting,' Rauser told me. 'I think Hank misses the freak. We need to talk it over. He's kinda mopey.' He squeezed my fingers. 'Hey, it'll be okay, Street. It's like riding a bike.'

I pulled open the glass door and saw a table with foam cups, a commercial coffee dispenser, a couple of boxes of doughnuts. Jon stood at the front of the small room. I hadn't seen my sponsor in two years. He smiled, held out his hand for me.

I walked past rows of gray folding chairs, turned and looked at twelve complete strangers. 'My name is Keye. I'm an alcoholic.'